CORONA

Also by Millicent Eidson

MayaVerse Series Titles

Microbial Mysteries: A Story Collection (Book 0)
Anthracis: A Microbial Mystery (Book 1)
Borrelia: A Microbial Mystery (Book 2)
Dengue: A Microbial Mystery (Book 4)

Short Works

Monuments: A Ten-Minute Play
Red Thread
Pariah

CORONA

A MICROBIAL MYSTERY

Millicent Eidson

Maya Maguire Media - Vermont

DEDICATION

For healthcare and public health staff, who gave their all

Praise for Millicent Eidson

"Millicent Eidson's unparalleled talent shines through in this remarkable work, ensuring a thrilling reading experience. I confidently predict that this offering will be warmly embraced by the literary world, solidifying Millicent Eidson's place among the most esteemed authors of our time."—Midwest Book Review, ***Anthracis: A Microbial Mystery***

"Dr. Eidson's medical thriller serves up unique and carefully drawn characters, fascinating and chillingly realistic threats, and enough Happily For Now resolutions to satisfy any women's fiction or romantic suspense fan. You won't want to miss this new entrant into the genre. I hope the author is busy writing the next book in this engaging series."—Reviewer, ***Anthracis: A Microbial Mystery***

"This 2nd book in the Maya Maguire series follows the intrepid CDC veterinary detective as she tries to track down the mysterious tick microbes causing Borrelia infections. Her travels lead her from her home in New Mexico to the European sites of other outbreaks. Meanwhile, Maya is dealing with her own professional and romantic issues. This is a fascinating insider's look at the increasingly menacing diseases arising from animal microbes worldwide."—Reviewer, ***Borrelia: A Microbial Mystery***

"The author's background as a scientist working for the CDC gives you an insider's view of this public-health agency at a time of crisis. I recommend Corona to all fans of medical mysteries."—Reviewer, **Corona: A Microbial Mystery**

"The mystery, the characters, the setting, and the uncanny timing of this book make it a compelling read. I would recommend it to anyone who loves medical thrillers, mysteries set in Hawaii, mysteries with diverse characters, books with a strong female protagonist, and fictional tales related to climate change."—A.M. Reade, USA Today Bestselling Author, **Dengue: A Microbial Mystery**

Author Note

"Corona: A Microbial Mystery" may be the most challenging novel in the alphabetical MayaVerse series because readers experienced the pandemic along with Maya Maguire. This story is unique with its emphasis on the mystifying and exciting coronavirus animal connections.

Authenticity requires that Maya's timeline coincides with our own. The scientific information about zoonotic diseases (those from animals) is accurate, and most settings and organizations are real.

However, the characters and specific plot incidents are fictional. Anything a MayaVerse character does when working for a real agency represents an alternate world. Character actions are scientifically based but do not necessarily reflect what an agency did do or would do in specific situations. The MayaVerse is a world of imagination, but still provides insights into the science and practice of public health related to zoonoses.

Two stories about the previous SARS and MERS coronavirus outbreaks are included in the shorter works of "Microbial Mysteries: A Story Collection."

To keep updated, join the MayaVerse Reader List at https://drmayamaguire.com/. For a universal link to all MayaVerse formats and distributors, see https://books2read.com/millicenteidson/.

Readers who would like to consult on future stories or provide feedback are encouraged to email: drmayamaguire@gmail.com. **Ratings and reviews are critically important to help others discover the MayaVerse.** Share impressions of "Corona" at your favorite bookseller and at https://www.bookbub.com/.

ZOMBIES

Reanimated corpses, once dead, now alive. Moving automatically, without thought. Thrashing through the environment, destroying all in their wake.

But at least you can see them coming, unlike their tinier cousins. Viruses are almost invisible, a threat revealed only by the destruction wrought by their invasion.

ONE

Tongling, People's Republic of China—Saturday, November 30, 2019

Li Huiping, wheezing and fighting for every breath, boosted herself out of bed to peer through the open whorls of the carved wooden panel. Neither Māma nor Bàba stirred in the central courtyard of their hundred-year-old home. With her own parents massacred in the Chinese Cultural Revolution, Li Huiping revered her husband's relatives, especially after his death in the copper mine.

By this time of day, the elderly couple typically brewed Qimen, Anhui Province's popular black tea, to counteract the brisk winter wind off the Yangtze tributary. Hearing another series of raps on the main door, Li Huiping realized what had awoken her. Normally fit and energetic at fifty-six, she was shocked by legs that suddenly felt like rice noodles, barely supporting her weight. She grabbed her surgical mask and stumbled through the unroofed courtyard to answer the incessant pounding. After opening the door a crack, she had a brief, terse exchange. She apologized for having none of the aromatic ginger to sell.

The corpulent man shuffled his feet in the dirt, raising a small brown cloud. He'd driven five hundred kilometers to purchase one of the esteemed eight treasures of Tongling. Li Huiping turned away for an uncontrolled spasm of coughing. Then she bowed again and pointed to a neighbor farm, which might have more of the root crop. After displacing millions to cities like Wuhan, the Three Gorges Dam did not protect their downstream farms from flood damage as promised.

Li Huiping shut the door and kept the mask on, wobbling through the courtyard between the ground floor rooms like a

Yangtze giant softshell turtle. The unaccustomed frailty made her wonder if she should contact her beloved twenty-two-year-old son, Mu Jian. He had completed university and started a job managing Yangtze aquatic life, including programs to rescue rare river dolphins and alligators. Last week when she became too infirm to work her shift at the Wuhan hospital where she had cleaned the intensive care unit for twenty years, she advised Mu Jian to keep himself safe in the small flat he rented in Hefei, the provincial capital. After all, she had seen him not long ago as they celebrated the National Day Golden Week holiday in early October.

This respiratory infection had her spooked. Her mind filled with images of dying patients in 2003 from the SARS coronavirus. Her supervisor joked it was the one that wears a crown, and would kill you just like the ancient emperors. Similar to other pneumonia cases hospitalized in the past couple of weeks, Li Huiping tested negative for bacteria. The boss insisted that Li Huiping not stay alone in her studio apartment close to the hospital. So it was back to Tongling, always wearing a mask outside her room.

She called out one more time to her elders and received no answer, then collapsed back into her bed, pulling the blanket tighter to smother the chills. Were they deathly ill upstairs, incapable of responding to a daughter-in-law too weak to check on their health? She couldn't bear the shame if she'd brought this sickness home.

But they couldn't be far. When shifting to her side after another coughing fit, her fingers contacted a cool wet cloth in the basin next to the bed. She draped it over her eyes and focused on the sweltering day last summer when Mu Jian was awarded his diploma. Then the happy image of the graduates was shoved aside by wails more distant in time. In Shaoyang, her first māma was raped and buried alive with her bàba while Li Huiping hovered in the shadows, too young at four to help them. Why did her self-control suddenly fail, allowing these ancient phantoms to creep back in?

Clearly her trouble breathing and mental fog meant she should be hospitalized. As soon as someone appeared, she'd ask them to drive her.

Drifting in and out of sleep, or perhaps brain function, she jerked awake with the warm touch of strong fingers on her arm.

"The past is horror; the present, joy," she whispered. "My son, how did you know I needed help?"

In the background, her in-laws honked at each other like a pair of old knob geese. "You forgot to charge the mobile."

"We should not have left Li Huiping alone."

"But I used Neighbor Hwang's phone before you found Neighbor Deng."

Mu Jian shoved them into the courtyard. "Please give my mother peace. You did well to reach me in time. I'm taking her to the hospital."

Her son, her greatest blessing. The only child she was allowed to keep, after her husband vanished both her daughters within minutes of their births. As she had forced them out between her legs, the pain of delivery was pushed aside. Mewling cries triggered a wave of warmth and her arms clawed for their small bodies. But they were whisked away, never to be cuddled or kissed. 1993 and 1995—the years were seared in her memory. Mu Jian came in 1997 in a final reward for her prayers, and her husband forced her to be surgically sterilized, all in accordance with the One-Child Policy. Unfathomably cruel, cruel, cruel.

The old ones tossed the blanket over her and held the door. Mu Jian cradled her like a baby. The motion focused her mind back on reality and the dark, dank confines of the old bedroom. Then her eyelids drooped, stitched shut to all of life's unbearable burdens as she slipped into final unconsciousness.

TWO

Santa Fe, New Mexico—Monday, December 2, 2019

Psy's warm tongue slobbered her left hand before his nose sniffed her upper thigh. As a veterinarian, Maya appreciated the emotional comfort the Irish Setter could bring. But nestled on the psychiatrist's couch, she flinched away from the therapy dog. Less than a month since the November 8 flash-bang grenade exploded during the Atlanta Lyme disease demonstration, both the leg burn and the suture area closing the gap for her missing baby finger radiated hot like an electric stove. At least the skull wound on her forehead at hairline was superficial, and she had discarded the white mummy head wrap.

"Psy, get back here." Dr. Kim's imperious tone directed the dog to his crate but she left the door ajar as he curled up, head on his paws, mournful eyes drooping. "Sorry, Maya, he was just trying to help." The psychiatrist clicked through her computer records to open the file titled **Maya Maguire, DVM, MPH**. "Catch me up on what we discussed on the phone."

Maya broke out in a body-wide shiver, feet wet from forgetting snow boots on the first slushy day back to work at the New Mexico Department of Health. Or were the shudders related to the mind-blowing subject she needed to discuss?

When Maya twisted on the couch to tug her down jacket over her shoulders, Dr. Kim pulled open a drawer from the credenza and handed her a purple blanket emblazoned with pink dahlias. As Maya's discarded loafers created a puddle on the Saltillo tile, she wiggled her toes and draped the fleece over them. The vibrant fabric cocooned her in comfort.

Dr. Kim's severe face creased with a rare toothy smile. "Isn't it spectacular? I shipped it home when I visited my omma in Seoul during the Korean New Year."

Maya had joked with her friend Erika that Dr. Kim was a clone of Morticia, matriarch of the Addams family. When Maya noted the dearth of others who shared her Asian heritage in northern New Mexico, Erika had recommended Dr. Kim so the therapist could address Maya's fish-out-of-water isolation.

"Feeling warmed up?" Dr. Kim asked. "More people come to me with depression in November than any other month. Some dread the upcoming holidays but others love them. Which camp are you in?"

"I have good memories with my family, and now Manolo." The ground-hugging wood smoke from neighborhood kiva fireplaces clung to Maya's hair and tickled her nose. Last Christmas, the odor of ponderosa pines in the Chaco campfire had sweetened her first overnight with him.

"How's Dr. Miranda doing? That's a gorgeous diamond."

"Thank you. We got engaged." On her right hand, Maya twirled the small square jewel embedded in a platinum band. "Manolo's back to work as an infectious disease specialist for the Indian Health Service in Arizona. His recovery from anthrax has been remarkable."

Maya recalled the times she'd gotten crosswise with Dr. Kim about her anxiety meds since Manolo became ill. Friends suggested she seek a more soothing counselor. But they'd achieved a sufficient level of familiarity that Maya could broach the primary purpose of her visit. There were others she should have discussed it with, but the phone call to Dr. Kim had confirmed her decision to wait.

The psychiatrist tapped her computer screen. "When we talked a couple weeks ago, you asked about the definition of sexual assault. 'He said, she said,' and not an on-going threat."

With her right hand, Maya fingered the good luck silver-and-turquoise bear claw earrings Manolo had gifted a year earlier when they started dating. She needed the bravado of a bear to talk about this. Once she said what happened out loud, there was no going back.

"Everything we talk about is confidential, right?"

Dr. Kim dipped her chin. "I would never discuss or share your records."

The reassurance didn't fully quell the stabs of anxiety. No longer on meds, Maya focused on deep breathing techniques and purposeful positive thinking to slow her heart rate. The room turning gauzy didn't mean imminent death, only a panic attack programmed into her nervous system by a childhood car accident.

Sweat beading on her forehead, she pushed aside the blanket. At the bottom rung of the Centers for Disease Control and Prevention shock troops in the Epidemic Intelligence Service, she was still feeling her way on CDC and EIS protocols.

"My work's complicated by multiple bosses." She wasn't sure which one would be most accepting and effective in handling her complaint. Dr. Jaworski provided CDC oversight from Atlanta. Dr. Grinwold as the New Mexico State Epidemiologist was her local supervisor. And Dr. Bingham directed her temporary assignments in Arizona.

Dr. Kim leaned forward, arms on the desk reaching closer to Maya. "You said the sexual assault was work-related. Does this supervisory arrangement confuse reporting the incident?"

Maya got up from the couch and bent down to rub Psy's ears, then turned to stare out the double-hung window to the street illuminated with a ghostlike glow. "Nancy Bingham asked me to mentor her new Arizona EIS Officer, Enzo Russo."

Maya moved back to the couch and wrapped herself in the fleece again, chilled by the cold air filtering through the single panes. "Nancy's hinted at health problems and retirement. Smaller states have a shortage of public health physicians, so designating Enzo as her successor is reasonable."

She raked the fingers on her good hand through her hair and turned away, unable to meet Dr. Kim's piercing dark gaze.

"Is he the one associated with the sexual assault?"

Maya paused a full minute before answering. First step on the path of upending both their lives. The only sounds were a snuffle from Psy as he curled back into the crate and the quiet tick-tock of an intricately carved grandfather clock in the corner. "He's an internal med doc from Harvard, very personable and confident. Too confident."

"And what exactly did he do?"

Maya's chest rose and fell with a deep sigh. It was almost too much to remember and yet so little, depending on how one looked at it. "I didn't like him right off. He asked me a difficult question at a conference. Then on his Phoenix apartment hunt, his appearance and movements reminded me of an actor in a horror movie, Bill Skarsgård in *It*."

A frown formed on the psychiatrist's face and Maya winced. "I know, those reactions are stupid and unfair."

Dr. Kim shook her head, clearly impatient. "But what did he do?"

Maya waved a hand in exasperation. "I'm getting there—it's just that my interpretation of him started out unreasonably prejudiced." With apprehension, she gripped her jiggling right leg.

"During the July training in Atlanta, he rubbed my arms after dinner. The next week, he removed bee stingers when I disturbed a swarm, and his touch made me uncomfortable. Then on a scheduled FaceTime call, he answered from the shower and dropped the phone for a full frontal private view."

"Not likely to be accidental."

"I gave him the benefit of the doubt, but no, I think it was deliberate. Then in September, they assigned us to investigate a new *Borrelia* strain in the Grand Canyon. The second night camping, not sharing a tent, he pinned me in my sleeping bag for a kiss."

Dr. Kim typed on her keyboard. "I can see why you're upset. Any chance of miscommunication and misreading of interpersonal signals?"

Dr. Kim's cool reserve once again triggered Maya's defenses. Why were some psychiatrists better at analysis and drug dispensation than counseling? "That's his story—I hope you're not accepting it. Enzo guessed my relationship with Manolo was at a rocky point when he picked me up for the trip." Her shoulders cramped with the memories of Enzo's weight.

She grabbed one of the water bottles on the lampstand and cracked it open. With several swigs, she soothed the strictures in her throat. "His pursuit escalated last month in Atlanta. A few days before my injuries at the protest against CDC, Enzo forced me down on my hotel room bed. He reached under my skirt and touched me." Her muscles tightened with the memory and her knees crossed tighter. Why had she opened the door to him?

Dr. Kim stretched her sweatered arm to close the drapes against the burgeoning storm and shifted her chair forward. "Was there penetration? I'm sorry, Maya, but I have to ask."

"His hand went beneath my underwear and he groped me, clearly hoping to turn me on." The words unrolled the scene like a movie, except more immersive with Enzo's strong cologne, his lips on her neck, his Boston accent and overweening tone. *My need for you has grown.*

"I persuaded him to stop before any penetration, fingers or otherwise. It wasn't easy; I had to threaten to yell or call the police. But he gave up and left."

"On the phone, you told me the threat was no longer imminent. So he hasn't contacted you after that incident?"

Maya's shoulders shrugged forward in a slow arch, then relaxed. "He visited me in the Atlanta hospital when I was unconscious from the flash-bang. Since then, he called on the phone to check on me and sent a couple of emails on the *Borrelia* outbreak."

"Maya, it's good you're considering how to handle this before it goes any further."

"You can't imagine how relieved I am to talk about this. Am I making too much of his advances?"

Dr. Kim closed her laptop and stood up. "No, I'm glad you discussed it with me. I'll help you determine the future steps that are best for you. Let's keep up our sessions, although I need to finish for today." Then she turned for her scheduling book. "Group therapy on Wednesday. It's your decision whether to share this, but you might find you're not alone. Also, you were insistent this summer about getting off the anxiety meds. Do you want to reconsider?"

When Maya shook her head, Dr. Kim checked her watch and guided her to the door. "You haven't reported this to anyone else?"

"In Atlanta, I was on my way to talk with my CDC supervisor when the bomb went off. Since then, I've focused on recovery and decided to sound you out first."

"All right, you should consult our Solace Crisis Treatment Center which has a specialized team. They're wonderful, including a support group of other women in similar situations."

The idea of broaching this with strangers threatened to knock Maya off the tiny step of confidence she'd gained by revealing it to Dr. Kim. How would they react to a whiny government employee who was groped and not raped? Compared to what other women went through, this was nothing. "Uh, thanks, I'll consider it. But I'm mostly focused on the next legal steps, if any."

"No problem. We're required to report assaults on anyone who's young or impaired, which isn't you. At our next appointment, let's talk more about how you're coping and your plans to handle this issue."

At the door, the storm outside whistled and shrieked like La Llorona, the vengeful mother of southwestern ghost stories. Dr. Kim wiped the glaze from the window and warned, "Please consult your attorney. Your administrative situation is complex and we need to talk through how I can support you if you decide on a workplace complaint."

Sleet pummeled Maya's face as she pulled the down coat and hood tighter when exiting the adobe strip mall. Her feet turned to blocks of ice when she stepped into a puddle at the Prius door. With the heater cranked to high once safely inside the car, she rested her hands on the steering wheel. Exposing Enzo's actions would open legal floodgates at the CDC and two state health departments. The process ahead loomed long and fraught with hazard.

For one more time as she weighed the pros and cons of outing Enzo, she cursed her hesitant, over-thinking nature. Should she blame her cautious personality on her unknown biological parents in China or her bureaucratic by-the-book adoptive family?

Beads of sweat broke out on her forehead and she turned down the heater. In earlier decades, women sometimes waited years to report sexual assault, even rape. But in the #MeToo era, other young women would carpet bomb Enzo. Despite her fear, she should too.

THREE

Phoenix, Arizona—Tuesday, December 31, 2019

Maya used her engagement ring, still on the right hand, to trace Manolo's spine. A perennial late sleeper, he didn't respond. She stroked his soft dark hair and slipped her fingers to his chin, missing the goatee shaved off when he went back to work. When she feathered his full lips with her fingertips, his breathing accelerated but he still didn't open his eyes. She pulled back the sheet and took a more intimate approach.

That worked—he rotated to face her, flashing his Lin-Manuel Miranda grin. "I remember doing this a year ago right here in my bed."

"Sorry, señor, your anthrax brain is clouded." She was ecstatic he had recovered enough for her to tease him. "Last year we were at the Livestock Show press conference about new infections."

"Okay, querida, I stand corrected, we made love on New Year's Day." He traced the arch of her waist from ribs to hip. "How about this time we go for both days?"

"Cállate." She leaned over to capture his lips with her own and forced his roaming hands lower. "Show me you mean it."

. . .

"I wish we were spending the holiday canoodling instead of going to a work party," Manolo grumbled as he donned a pale-yellow shirt, navy suit, and blue-striped tie.

Maya tugged on a full-length silk slip, then a sleeveless flowy aqua dress. "We never talked about your New Year's traditions."

"Sometimes my family would go back to Puerto Rico. At midnight we said goodbye to Año Viejo by sprinkling sugar outside the house and eating twelve grapes for good luck. And lots of fireworks."

"I hope you don't mind Nancy's invitation to celebrate our recoveries. Dr. Grinwold's flying in from Albuquerque. My first time to see them as a couple—might be weird."

"Maintaining office relations is important." From the back of a chair, he lifted her high-collared red silk jacket embroidered with peacocks. "This is gorgeous, where did you get it?"

Maya's fingers traced the intricate pattern. "My parents bought it on our China orphanage visit when I was twelve. Fits perfectly now. I could wait until Chinese New Year's at the end of January, but I'm impatient to show it off."

Manolo unlocked the red Corvette parked on the street and opened her door. "Your chariot awaits, mi amor. With this warm weather, I'm tempted to put the top down." Then he lowered into the driver's seat and reached out to caress her hair, skimming her shoulders. "But we'll stay neat and presentable for your big bosses."

"I'm sorry to cancel our plans for Chaco camping. Missing three weeks of work for my injuries, I couldn't ask for more time off. Thank God the tinnitus stopped—it was unbearable." As she leaned over to peck his cheek, her lips lingered and she breathed softly into his ear. "And now I can hear your passionate whispers."

He pulled away from the curb with its palm trees encircled by white lights, and she tugged the decorative jacket out from under the lap belt to avoid it wrinkling. "Work's been hectic. Dr. Grinwold assigned me to a diarrheal outbreak. The family left the Thanksgiving turkey out too long and *Clostridium perfringens* spores formed that were resistant to reheating."

He wrinkled his nose, then turned at the red light. "I hope you're not going to swap foodborne outbreak stories at the New Year's Eve party."

"First of all, it's not really a party. Nancy only mentioned Dr. Grinwold. And you've shared some pretty scary work stories too, like violence against Native American women."

"Let's make a deal," he said while entering the highway. "Just happy talk unrelated to our jobs as we welcome in 2020. After all, we've got a June wedding."

. . .

Maya struggled to pick out Nancy's home from the other fake adobe single-stories. But as she searched the numbered tiles embedded next to front doors, Nancy stepped out in a white satin pantsuit with a braided gold necklace replacing the reading glasses hanging from a chain.

When Maya and Manolo joined Nancy on the porch, their host's brown eyes popped with blue eyeshadow, azure sea glass dangled from her ears, and her mousy hair was puffed and curled. If Maya had passed her on the street, she might not have recognized the plump, reserved Arizona State Epidemiologist.

"Welcome, Maya." Nancy vibrated like a wind-up toy. "I'm so excited to have you here on a happier occasion." She swung her head from side to side and grimaced. "What a horrible memory— FBI parked out here monitoring you as a suspect for spreading anthrax." Then she pumped Manolo's arm. "Dr. Miranda, you still look like a Broadway star, or so your fiancée tells me."

Maya blushed at Nancy's comment but Manolo bowed over Nancy's hand and gave it a kiss. "You were so generous with your visits to my rehab facility, and Dad appreciated your guidance on the medical decisions."

Nancy appeared almost giddy over Manolo's smoldering Latin charm. "Well, my clinical training was in family medicine, not neurology. But it can help to have a doctor in your corner when you're sick and can't fend for yourself."

She stepped aside to let them enter, and Dr. Grinwold's bulk filled the frame. Unlike Nancy, he looked exactly like he did in the office, plaid jacket and all. No dressing special for the occasion. Same wisps of brown hair stretched over a balding head with eyes of a similar nondescript brown, made more prominent by thick lenses in his wire rim glasses. But his unusual broad smile might have been influenced by the empty martini glass he sported in his left hand, as he reached out his right hand in greeting.

Tinkling birdsong of an unfamiliar female voice floated from a distance behind him. Maya gasped at the male voice responding, "You're right, doll, I need another drink."

It was Enzo. Like a robot, Maya pivoted for the door. "Nancy, I got the impression it would be the four of us."

The older woman's thinning eyebrows arched. "I'm sorry dear, I've been distracted, must have slipped my mind."

Dr. Grinwold's meaty hand held Nancy's arm. "Not to worry, chérie. Maya and Enzo worked together before, and I only recall one disagreement about rodent collection." He smiled and turned for the crystal pitcher on the table.

Maya had never seen Nancy and Dr. Grinwold in the same room, let alone touching. Perhaps that was the reason for her legs frozen in place. But Dr. Grinwold's shift for a drink exposed Enzo, the real source of her discomfort.

Like an invading fungus with its mycelia extending into every orifice, he'd dominated her focus in the past few weeks. Dr. Kim said sexual battery in Georgia was defined as physical contact with intimate parts without consent. Seemed like a case, but only a misdemeanor.

Allegations of assault against a doctor could ruin a professional reputation even if they didn't lead to conviction or medical license revocation. And she had no proof. At the time it happened, she recounted the incident to no one, until Dr. Kim several weeks later. Her attorney would be next when he returned from a Hawaii vacation.

Disciplinary actions might be in process if she hadn't been injured walking across the street to sound out her CDC supervisor within a few days of the hotel groping.

Maya stood straighter and locked on Enzo's amber eyes. Her muscles tensed with rigid courage. Soon enough, she'd have it out with him. And it wouldn't entirely be his word against hers. Although she bottled up the canyon and hotel assaults, she'd discussed some earlier concerns with others, which might support a pattern of behavior.

He looked surprised by her assertive stance and turned for the martini pitcher. On his other side, the source of the female cooing came into view. Almost as tall as him, at least six feet, she had the body of an athlete. Her hair was California blonde cascading to her waist, framing a fine-boned face and blue-gray eyes.

Nancy tugged Maya's right hand. "Let me see that rock—it's a beauty."

With his arm around Maya's shoulders, Manolo guided them in two more steps from the door. "Thank you, it was my mother's."

"Where are my manners?" Nancy gushed. "Let me introduce you to Astrid Buckingham. I don't think you've met. She's been our vector control specialist for three years."

Based on the tiny lines around Astrid's eyes, Maya guessed she was a bit older, closer to Enzo's age of thirty.

"It's nice to meet you, Dr. Maguire," she said. "Enzo told me about your September expedition to Havasupai. We got down there before Thanksgiving on a rodent sampling trip and the waterfalls were spectacular." She beamed at him and smoothed his jacket.

Enzo reached a hand out to Manolo. "Dr. Miranda, we meet again." His eyes went to Maya's ring. "Looks like you two have mended fences. Does that mean what I think it does?"

You're a prick flashed in Maya's mind at Enzo's reminder about her estrangement from Manolo. But Manolo answered first, expression cautious as he glanced between them. "We've set the date, June 20, 2020, when Maya finishes her EIS training."

A spoon clinking a glass interrupted the awkward greetings as Dr. Grinwold invited them to join him for dinner. When all were seated, Maya faced Enzo across the rectangular wooden table. Their hosts at either end, Dr. Grinwold made a toast. "To new beginnings, including the engagement of our M and M couple, Maya Maguire and Manolo Miranda."

Enzo's arm jerked as he swigged his martini in one gulp and Nancy continued. "We're so happy Enzo and Astrid have hit it off." She winked to their side of the table. "I'm even more confident he'll stay in Arizona."

"Yes, the Grand Canyon State will have to do without Nancy soon," Dr. Grinwold said. "She's retiring in April to join me in the City Different."

"Santa Fe," Maya blurted. "You're moving to Santa Fe?"

Nancy nodded. "My replacement is up to the health department director, but if I have any influence, Enzo will receive my vote."

Maya wasn't the only one in shock as Enzo's complexion darkened and he downed another drink. He had alluded to an eventual career with the World Health Organization, but he was only a few months into his two-year CDC training program. It was too soon to become a big fish in a small pond. However, with Astrid on the side, it might be too tempting to pass up.

Maya's toes curled and she poured another glass of water. She should have warned Nancy earlier. All her dithering over the right steps allowed the succession planning to go too far. The sudden advancement of Nancy's retirement by over a year was unexpected when Enzo was still so green.

Then she remembered Manolo, munching his salad and taking the news in silence. Did he sense her extreme unease related to Enzo? In Sedona, he'd expressed relief not to know of all the men who came onto her. And if she'd told him about Enzo, Manolo would have flattened him to the floor, despite Enzo's advantage in height and fitness. Manolo was still frail—she couldn't chance his getting hurt.

Nancy and Dr. Grinwold donned matching green aprons imprinted with Canyon De Chelly, and he opened the oven to remove the baked ham. With a flourish, she deposited an apple pie, cinnamon and nutmeg wafting, on a cactus-themed trivet. As he provided slices of the main dish to each plate, she chatted with their guests.

"Do you follow ProMED, the online alerts from the International Society for Infectious Diseases? Last night's notice described hospitals in Wuhan, China with an increase in acute respiratory distress syndrome. We see ARDS here with hantavirus. This latest outbreak is linked to a market selling live animals for food."

Maya recalled that wild flavor was a new fad in the US but a long cultural tradition in China.

"There was an update today," Enzo said. "They isolated the market to prevent any zoonotic spread from the critters." His chest enlarged as he leaned back with a smug smile. "It's rumored to be the Severe Acute Respiratory Syndrome from 2003."

Maya ducked her eyes. While Enzo was on top of outbreaks worldwide, she'd been lolling in bed with Manolo.

Enzo bent forward as if to continue, but Dr. Grinwold's gruff voice interrupted. "You young'uns may not be aware that Nancy was in charge of controlling the previous SARS outbreak here in Arizona."

Nancy passed Maya the sweet potatoes mixed with marshmallows and honey. "You didn't want me to do it."

"And I was right. You wore yourself out handling it—had me scared there for a while."

Maya ate quickly and begged for the dessert to go. Enzo's pale penetrating eyes, too similar to the Arizona anthrax bioterrorist, were doing her in. He no longer acted afraid of her outing him— his posture dared her to do it. His final insult was rubbing his foot against hers under the table, then studying her to see how she'd react.

As she jerked her leg back and stiffened, her foot and arm bumped Manolo. He placed his hand on her sleeve. "Are you okay?"

"Sorry everyone, some residual vertigo from the flash-bang. I really should head out." From the other side of the table, Enzo grinned.

. . .

Finally home, safe in Manolo's bed, they lay entwined under the covers. "Are you sure you're all right?" he asked with the TV turned to the New York City celebration.

"The party was just more than I expected. I want to share this night with you."

But he was right, she wasn't okay. The first time seeing Enzo in two months had a stronger impact than she anticipated. Relief that she wasn't his sole focus warred with his continued arrogance about crossing boundaries. She couldn't stay on the fence—she had to figure out her next steps. The choices weighted her eyelids and shut down her brain.

A foot nudged hers and crowds screamed as the NYC Waterford Crystal ball descended. For a moment, the stroking leg transported Enzo's image to the bed and she twisted away, repelled. With eyes half open, she realized her mistake with Manolo's gentle smile and whispered words. "Feliz Año Nuevo, mi corazon."

My heart. In answer, she created her own fireworks by sliding on top and grinding until he was aroused and entered her. She directed their sexual intercourse with force and speed, stamping out all visions of a looming, leering predator stealing her sense of control.

FOUR

Phoenix, Arizona—Wednesday, January 1, 2020

Manolo's fingers stroked the two scars on Maya's brow, from the Atlanta flash-bang and a bad fall during an unusual reaction to stopping anti-anxiety meds. His lips followed, then brushed her eyes until she opened them.

"Am I damaged goods?" she whispered.

"Not hardly. These make you a relatable woman who's suffered, not some beautiful biological computer who's only good with numbers."

She nestled into his chest and wrapped her legs around his. "I'm not the same person you were hot for more than a year ago."

"Same here, still struggling to get back my strength, but you never abandoned me."

She shivered and pulled the blanket higher. "There will never be anyone else for me."

He massaged the small of her back, then lower. "This sexually assertive Maya is a wonderful new wrinkle, first in Sedona after Thanksgiving and then last night."

"Coming into my power. You like it?"

"Feel free to continue the surprises."

Her hand slipped over her eyes. "Microbes invade my worklife, and I never know when we can be together." She refocused back to Manolo and moved her fingers to his chin. "I need to make the most of our sporadic moments."

"Your bosses seem supportive of a work-life balance, but you sure were tense at their party."

"I'm surprised that Nancy wants to move Enzo up in

responsibility so quickly. As you might have noticed, he's rather obnoxious." She uncurled from Manolo's embrace and rolled out of bed. "Can I lure you into a sexy shower? I need to swing by Nancy's to find out more what she's thinking."

He acquiesced to her tugging him into the bathroom. Kneeling in front of him as the warm rainshower sprinkled, she tried to concentrate on his pleasure but found herself rushing. She didn't allow him to do the same for her, and they dressed quickly.

When Manolo parked at the curb opposite Nancy's home, Maya asked him to wait in the Corvette. "Nancy might be more open about her plans if it's just me."

Nancy greeted her soon after the bell rang. "Back again, my dear? You didn't call—is Manolo coming in?"

"He's waiting to take me to the airport. I'm sorry to interrupt your New Year's." Maya settled next to her host on the fading velour couch and fingered the long sleeve of Nancy's satin robe painted with red candy canes. "This is gorgeous—I'm happy you're still celebrating. Is Dr. Grinwold here?"

"No, he's driving home by way of the Very Large Array Radio telescope west of Socorro. He's an astronomy buff."

He probably spent the night, but their personal relationship was none of Maya's business, and not the boundary crossing she stopped by to discuss.

Familiar with Nancy's kitchen, Maya offered to heat water for tea, then brought two green teabags back to the coffee table. "Your retirement announcement caught me off guard. What's going on?"

Nancy sighed as she mussed her gray-streaked hair. "At a meeting in Nogales, Mexico twenty-five years ago, I was bitten by a triatomine, one of those psychedelic kissing bugs."

Maya searched her memory banks. "Chagas disease."

"Yes, the *Trypanosoma cruzi* parasite nailed me. With some residual side effects, I've really slowed down. Can't do field work like I used to." She smiled and patted Maya's hand. "I've got you and Enzo to back me up."

So Nancy might be ill enough to retire a decade early. Her

decision wasn't fun-in-the-sun while still in her fifties. That needed consideration when deciding what to confess about Enzo. The original game plan was best—work out the options with Dr. Kim and her attorney before increasing Nancy's burdens.

But Maya had Nancy's rapt attention, no interruptions from a busy office. Perhaps with tentative toes in the pond, she could feel out Nancy's openness to disturbing news about her protégé.

"You're so dedicated to Arizona." Maya stirred the hot water and her tea bag. "Bad timing for a transition when Enzo's so early in his training. And now SARS-like illness has poked up in China."

"No one remembers our local SARS cases. If it hits again, I can rely on my experience and Enzo's extraordinary talent. When you're in Phoenix, you can focus on your fiancé."

"All we've figured out is the June date for the wedding. Nothing about where to live, our future jobs, or starting a family."

"You have time. Thank you for mentoring Enzo since July. He seems to have settled in personally and professionally."

Maya studied Nancy's benevolent round face, summer tan faded with the shorter days of winter. She didn't seem to have a clue that Enzo could be problematic. And that was all Maya's fault for sitting on her concerns.

"I hope he's getting along with the vector program in Fort Collins and their new EIS officer, Keegan Williams," Maya said. "Is CDC involved in Enzo and Astrid's rodent study in Hualapai Canyon?"

Hand shaking, Nancy wiped her forehead with a paper napkin. "No, but they're processing the specimens Enzo collected."

How much could Nancy handle? Maya resolved to keep going. Baby steps toward transparency. "Enzo got crosswise with Keegan in Atlanta. They were teammates on the *Salmonella* survey, with some differences of opinion."

"He doesn't hesitate to express himself." Nancy ambled to the kitchen and brought back a tray of red- and green-sprinkled Christmas cookies "Just like me in my younger days, full of energy and confidence."

"As long as he's sensitive to others." Maya chewed the cookie, sugar high zapping her brain. "I thought he'd get more seasoning before becoming top dog."

Nancy set down her cup, missing the coaster on the wooden table. Her face was wide open in shock. "You're looking for a new job in July and Manolo is here. Do you want to be Arizona State Epidemiologist?"

The pressure of that level of responsibility sent hot blood coursing. Slow breaths—the question should flatter, not scare. "Well . . . Lila Becker, the California EIS officer . . . she said that in her state, no recent EIS Officer would be considered."

Maya's iPhone tweeted with an unwelcome text. "It's Manolo reminding me of my flight. Again, thank you for the party to celebrate our engagement, and I'm sorry I left so abruptly. I've got a lot on my mind."

. . .

Santa Fe, New Mexico—Friday, January 10, 2020

Maya checked the clock one more time as she washed her breakfast bowl. She was haunted by her decision not to tell Nancy about Enzo, justified by compassion for Nancy's health. But it might have been a lack of courage, she wasn't sure. She wouldn't make the same mistake with her lawyer.

She took the bus to avoid finding a place to park in the narrow warrens of downtown Santa Fe. The attorney's adobe building, like most in the area, was unprepossessing from the outside. As snowflakes swirled, she ducked under the protective portal of hand-scraped pine vigas, connected by a diagonal grid of thin unpeeled latillas. The sky-blue door matched the hue of a small sign hung by two strands of barbwire. *Mark Zielinski, Attorney at Law*. No clues that he headed a multi-attorney firm covering two states.

In the lobby, she waited only a few minutes, swallowed up by the deep leather couch. Mr. Zielinski wheeled out of his office.

"Maya, one of my favorite clients. When did we last touch base, the end of August? That's right, I let you know that the Jicarillas had dropped any plans for civil charges after your car accident."

The Jicarilla war veteran died from alcohol and exposure, so the memory of sideswiping his body was unwelcome. But she peeled herself away from the leather and stooped to shake Mr. Zielinski's gloved hand. "On more than one occasion, you've been my savior. I'm sorry to see you had a setback."

Like the nimble cowboy he used to be, he easily pivoted the wheelchair on the red Saltillo clay tiles and led the way into the cave-like setting, walls lined with bookshelves and western paintings. "That fuckin' rattler not only killed my horse but is taking me down too. Should lose weight if I want to switch to crutches again." His eyes sank to her hands. "Like my damaged spine, your fingers tell quite the story."

"Yeah, good news . . ." She rotated the diamond on her right hand. "And bad." She cradled to her chest the left one, missing a digit.

"Your mother gave me a heads up about the Atlanta explosion, in case your family needs to pursue civil litigation to cover any long-term medical expenses."

Maya grimaced at the reminder of her mom's helicopter parenting. "We still don't know who tossed the flash-bang and my body has healed, with adjustments for typing and piano. No one gets through life unscathed."

"Well, I'm lucky this wheelchair didn't keep me from two weeks on Maui."

After lowering to another couch that shouted cost and comfort, Maya pulled out a water bottle from her cloth bag imprinted with kokopellis, the traveling salesmen of Native American lore, bringing genetic diversity to distant villages through seeds and semen. Was Enzo's impulse to mate hardwired into male DNA?

She took a slow drink, uncertain where to start. Despite limited discussions with multiple female friends and the full story with Dr. Kim, she couldn't recall even hinting at the Enzo problem with a man. But like a well-trained captive grizzly, Mr. Zielinski always made her feel warm and protected—threatening when necessary, but on her side at all times.

With his wheelchair pulled close, she lost herself in the dark pools of his eyes. "Should I call in Maria with her laptop?" he asked.

Talking about it with a stranger recording her every word could be uncomfortable, and make it more official. "I, ah, I'm not sure this is anything formal yet."

"All right, but I'll jot down a few reminders for myself." He turned to grab a notebook from the top of his carved pine desk.

"I've been discussing a workplace problem with my psychiatrist. She's helping me sort out my feelings on what to do. The consequences have me scared as a bobcat in a leghold trap."

He responded to her attempt at humor with a wary smile. "Whoa, that's alarming. Lay it on me."

Leap right in—he charged by the minute, no matter how kindly. "An Arizona co-worker inflicted some unwelcome physical contact in Arizona and Georgia, off-hours but during work-related trips. He claimed to be expressing sexual attraction, encouraged by me."

"Often sexual attraction is a component, but it's really about power. Is that how you see it?"

Maya's mouth dropped open. "That's it, exactly. It started when I tried to direct his work at a July training conference. He constantly shifted from flirting to challenging."

She tried to be charitable. He probably was nervous being new on the job, and given his personality, unable to admit it.

Mr. Zielinski tapped his pen and dropped his eyes to the notebook. "What are your legal concerns?" Maybe he guessed it would be easier for her to talk if he wasn't staring at her.

"In September, he pinned me in my sleeping bag on a field investigation, and forced a kiss. Then in November, he swung by my Atlanta hotel room to discuss our workshop, and I didn't stop him coming in."

She squirmed on the squeaky leather and crossed one boot over the other. "He shoved me to the bed, reached under my skirt, and . . . touched me beneath my underwear, skin to skin. But he left when I threatened him."

"Criminal sexual contact in New Mexico. A misdemeanor when

perpetrated with force or coercion means a year in county jail, a fine of a thousand dollars, or both. I'd have to check with a Georgia colleague, but it might be similar. You should consider talking to the police who will determine next steps with the district attorney."

The couch seemed to swallow her body into its depths as her limbs lost all feeling. "I can't imagine what it would do to my career, my organization—him going to jail. We're supposed to be the good guys . . . and there's no evidence, my word against his."

Mr. Zielinski took a sip of coffee and ran one hand through his thick dark hair. "I understand why so many women wait years to file 'me too' cases, and they sometimes lose in court. But Bill Cosby was finally sentenced and jailed. Justice still rules."

Maya vigorously shook her head. "There were no drugs, no rape." Resolute on her direction, she leapt to her feet with legs like California redwoods. "I can't bring this into the criminal system, and I don't want a civil lawsuit either. If I take any action, it should be through my workplace. I need to decide how to inform his supervisors."

He looked up, wrinkles crevassing his leathered skin. "I understand—the whole thing is daunting. And I'm guessing he would fight back, possibly bringing your mental health into question. Is he aware you see a psychiatrist?"

Reaching down for her bag, she steadied a hand on the couch cushion as the room began to swirl. "Oh God, I don't know. I can't remember if I ever said anything."

"Take your time, we can talk again if you need to. By the way, how's your job going? Still saving the world, one animal disease at a time?"

She reached deep to paste a confident smile. "I'm handling the workload, but there's a new respiratory problem in China similar to the 2003 coronavirus outbreak. Dr. Grinwold says we're prepared and the impact might be minimal."

Grateful to have more closure, she leaned over to give Mr. Zielinski a quick hug. "Whatever I decide, it gives me peace of mind to have you in my corner."

FIVE

Santa Fe, New Mexico—Wednesday, February 5, 2020

The note from Lila, Maya's California counterpart, shared that CDC Atlanta staff were hosting a big fiftieth birthday celebration for their mutual boss. Maya hadn't checked in with Dr. Jaworski in a month. She'd been too preoccupied by teens hospitalized from vaping with E-cigarettes. Worried if she was doing enough to prevent more lung-damaged kids, Maya composed a quick email to Dr. Grinwold and the public information officer with the link for a youth-centered documentary.

One task crossed off her checklist, Maya picked up the phone. The excuse to call Atlanta might renew goodwill and restart the Enzo discussion.

"Dr. Jaworski, Happy Birthday! Anything fun planned today? I still remember that shindig at your beautiful home in July. Such a gracious introduction to Atlanta, one of my favorite memories there."

"Thank you, Maya. Yes, Roseline has a surprise for me after dinner. I'm guessing she has tickets to a show at the Fox Theatre."

Maya hesitated, triple-guessing herself on how to begin. "Today may not be the best day, but I need to talk over some issues with Arizona's new officer, Enzo Russo."

"Speaking of Enzo, Nancy asked to borrow you one more time to assist him." The gravelly Long Island accent sounded more clipped than ever as Dr. Jaworski seemed to miss Maya's too-tentative signal of an Enzo problem. "Arizona is announcing their first coronavirus case, a college student who didn't go overseas, unlike most of the other eleven US cases with travel to Wuhan.

That makes everything a hell of a lot more complicated because transmission's at the local level."

Maya gulped, dismayed she hadn't found the gumption to talk sooner to Dr. Jaworski. "Dr. Grinwold complains I've assisted Arizona too much. How about Lila? She's close by."

"California has its own cases from China travel. Lila is working with Quarantine staff to screen incoming flights. How this spreads isn't clear, but probably respiratory droplets like SARS. Tell Fred he should let you assist Arizona for a few days to trace exposures."

Not the moment to report Enzo. Perhaps she was just a major coward, unwilling to hold him accountable, or the world was conspiring against her disrupting their public health work with her allegations. But in Phoenix, she could finally confront him alone, then make a decision about telling Nancy. He deserved a heads up on what she was planning, even if he was the one crossing boundaries.

A few hours later, Dr. Grinwold poked his head in her office. "I briefed the Governor on our E-cigarette efforts, and he was pleased. I appreciate your epi and stats skills for the summary reports."

Maya picked up her notes. "CDC asked me to help Arizona with its first 2019-nCoV case."

His eyes wandered to the bleak snow-covered landscape out the window. "If I find your dedication, energy, and brains invaluable, I can't fault Nancy for doing the same. Plus, the President declared this a national emergency."

"Dr. Jaworski wants me in Phoenix early tomorrow. With the latest CDC update about more than twenty thousand cases in China, everyone's fairly freaked out."

He rose to peer out at the traffic slipping slowly by on St. Francis Drive. "Storm's projected to get worse. Ask Stephanie to bring you to the Sunport shuttle and fly from Albuquerque to Phoenix. Don't drive with these bad roads. I worry about you."

The rare solicitous comment floored Maya. He'd been compassionate a few times in the past year and a half, letting her have time off when Manolo was hospitalized and when she suffered her own injuries in November. But mostly he seemed on edge. He'd admitted a diagnosis of Type 2 diabetes, so it wasn't surprising he occasionally felt out-of-sorts. Nancy had mentioned his interest in astronomy, but he might not enjoy any other hobbies to take his mind off the job.

She didn't have time to figure out the minds or lives of her bosses, no matter how big a role they played in her life. She twirled the diamond on her right hand. Getting assigned to the Arizona health department wasn't all bad when she could sleep in the same bed as an inventive fiancé.

. . .

Phoenix, Arizona—Thursday, February 6, 2020

With high temperatures anticipated in the seventies, Maya left her puffy jacket in the rental car. Recalling the Albuquerque airport van almost skidding out on the ice, she relished the threaded clouds losing a battle with the bright morning sun. Manolo was back to work full-time at the Indian Health Service and she'd see him for dinner. First time in a month. When he was ill, she managed to fly to Phoenix more often. Now that he recovered, were they getting complacent about their long-distance relationship?

As she maneuvered the corridors inside the Arizona Department of Health Services, some of the staff greeted her. She continued on toward Dr. Bingham's office, until Enzo's voice startled her.

"Maya, going to walk by and not say hello?"

White shirt stretched tight over his tall, muscled frame, he stepped into the hall, blocking the way forward.

"I'm sorry, Enzo, I didn't realize this was your office." To avoid his piercing amber eyes, she glanced to the right. His walls were decorated with tasteful masterpieces of female figures. *Girl with a Pearl Earring* by Vermeer, *Las Dos Fridas* by Frida Kahlo, and the shimmering golden *Portrait of Adele Bloch-Bauer I* by Klimt. With two semesters of art history as a distraction from pre-vet classes at the University of Colorado, she recognized high-quality, expensive copies.

He tugged her inside. "I saw a glimpse of this beautiful ring at Nancy's party but didn't get to check out your flash-bang injury."

He cradled her left hand. "Scar healed nicely. Someone might not notice you're missing that finger. Any residual pain?"

She ignored his question and turned back toward the hall, but he was quicker, closing the door and revealing on its back the *Chinese Girl*. She remembered the spooky green-faced painting from *Frenzy*, the movie about a London serial killer. Her admiration for Hitchcock's skill had overshadowed her squeamishness with horror movies.

"I thought of you when I purchased her. That beautiful floral pattern below her neck reminds me of the flashy jacket you wore New Year's Eve."

Maya never painted bright red lips or curled her hair in deep waves like the portrait. But the dour expression likely reflected her own at the moment. "Enzo, how long have you had this?"

His charming tone edged with defensiveness. "These reproductions are very popular. If things aren't going to work out with you, you can't fault me for a small reminder."

"I'm sure your new girlfriend is thrilled with it."

He shrugged. "Astrid is my Vermeer, front and center."

Maya turned to look out his window at the small picnic table next to the parking lot. "Your interactions with me need to be addressed."

A rare look of doubt crossed his tanned sculptured face and his voice lowered. "Maya, you don't intend to talk to Nancy about us?" He reached out a hand to her upper arm and she knocked it away.

"I haven't decided on what I'll say, but we can discuss it."

His eyes flitted around the room, then out the window. "Not appropriate for here."

Maya's stomach flip-flopped. She cringed at the thought of being alone with him, out of earshot from other people. He was unpredictable, particularly if cornered. At the picnic table, they'd be in visual range of staffers in their offices, while keeping others from listening in.

She jerked her thumb in the direction of the window, and he consented. After following him out the closest exit, she sat on the bench with her back to the building. It wouldn't hurt for Enzo to see the offices and be reminded of what he had to lose.

In the shade of the building, a light breeze ruffled Maya's loose hair and she rebuttoned her blazer. Enzo's long legs snaked under the table, once again bumping her foot. "Look, I'm with Astrid now, so we have no relationship and nothing to talk about."

Maya took a deep breath. "Enzo, you attacked me twice in work situations and you keep coming up with ways to touch me, like today. According to my attorney, you could be convicted of misdemeanor sexual assault, with a fine and jail time."

His fist slammed the wooden table. "Fuck, Maya, you talked to a lawyer? What the hell are you thinking?"

She shivered and leaned back, pulling her legs tighter under the seat. "You crossed the line, Enzo, and your conduct was unprofessional, if not criminal. How can men and women work together if you're going to take advantage of us?"

After a glance to the building, he answered. "We talked about this and I apologized. I thought you were fed up with Dr. Miranda, and interested in me. This didn't happen on the job—it was the evening, both times. Bottom line, I stopped when you asked me."

Maya shook her head. Was there any way to get through to him? "You should have asked before you started."

He twisted up from the bench, the height difference reinforcing his dominant tone. "You've got to be kidding. A guy can't make a move anymore if he's attracted to a girl? Some women love men taking the lead, including rough sex. Just ask Astrid."

Uncomfortable with him looming over her, she also leapt up. But their height difference still gave him an advantage. Tempted to jump on the bench to meet him eye-to-eye, she didn't want to draw attention from staff behind the windows. So she fired back with an icy glare and words popping like a BB gun. "I've been on the knife's edge of warning other women about you."

His hand swept through his short brown hair. "Oh my God, this keeps getting worse. Do you want the whole world thinking you're a histrionic bitch?"

Lightning flashed through her muscles, and it took all her willpower not to strike the cavalier expression from his face. Then he lowered himself to the seat, his face transformed into a little boy's. An emotional reaction or a deliberate act?

"I'm sorry, Maya. You stimulate strong feelings and I get carried away. But I would never hurt you, or anybody. Please don't take this any further. This job, in a new part of the country, is intense. Let me get my feet under me." His eyes were red and moist.

"Enzo, you were very convincing before you started calling me names. But you have a point, it's your word against mine. A fatal problem for women with 'me too' cases."

"Throwing me in the pool with Jeffrey Epstein? You're not an underage victim."

"No, I'm not. But do you have the maturity to be Nancy's replacement as State Epi? That's what I'm struggling with. She asked me to mentor you, with my whole extra year of training." Her sarcasm dripped as her left hand twinged with phantom pain.

The confident, winning smile flashed back on his face. "And you did that, you suckered me into this assignment. I apologize again for misinterpreting your thorough job. Can we let it drop? You're an excellent teacher, about women as well as epidemiology."

Need to meet about coronavirus. Maya angled the text message from Nancy toward Enzo. "We're overdue meeting with your boss."

"Before we go, tell me what you're going to do next." His tone was imperious—a major trigger.

She spun in anger at the building's back door. "I have a lot to sort through, and I'm not making any promises."

SIX

Phoenix, Arizona—Thursday, February 6, 2020

Perched next to each other across from Nancy as she held court behind her desk, Maya and Enzo opened their laptops to take notes. Maya struggled to leave the picnic table fight with Enzo behind. Her head echoed with *tell Nancy, tell Nancy* as she tried to concentrate.

"CDC has a couple hundred persons under investigation for 2019-nCoV," Nancy said, "including our Phoenix community college student. Their health center reported his fever and shortness of breath when they heard about a relative recently back from Hong Kong. But our student went home to Tucson before the lab confirmation, so that complicates isolation and contact tracing."

"If you want me to handle the family, I'll stay with my grandmother," Maya said. A surge of adrenaline reinforced her cleverness at separating their duties, but Enzo scowled.

"I'm the Arizona EIS Officer so I should be in charge of the patient."

Nancy pointed her finger at Enzo. "You're in charge of coordination from here, including follow-up with the community college."

His expression transformed to a brown-nosing student. "Of course, I'll get out there today."

Nancy continued her instructions. "You won't be in contact with severely ill patients in a hospital setting. But if this is anything like SARS, you should wear a mask when interviewing suspect cases."

Maya rose to leave. "My attention will be on this one hundred percent."

She hoped Enzo would pick up on her emphasis. As much as

he discombobulated her, she wanted them both laser-focused on coronavirus, not distracted by her next decision about his behavior.

. . .

Maya texted Manolo. **Hot time at your place?** She tingled when he texted a smiley emoji. After meeting in front of his apartment with a passionate kiss and hug, she explained her need to get on the road, so they ate lunch quickly and jumped into bed. "Sorry to throw a wrench in our plans to stay here together."

His fingernails triggered erotic pulses as they traced lightly from her mouth down to the soles of her feet, ending with a foot massage. "Your abuela will be thrilled to see you."

She traced the same parts of his body with her lips, then relaxed back on his arm, which had regained its muscle mass after months of physical therapy. "I still haven't put time into my job search."

He shifted out from under her and rested on one elbow, fingers toying with her hair. "Did you ask Nancy about working here? We need to live in the same house if we have kids." His hand dropped to her belly.

She stopped his stroking and turned away, attempting to get her thoughts together. "Not yet, please be patient."

"Nancy values your anthrax and *Borrelia* work. Now you're helping with coronavirus, and Arizona doesn't have a public health veterinarian."

But Enzo was the reason she avoided a permanent job with the Arizona health department. The only times she got crosswise with Manolo was when one of them withheld something from the other, always with good justification, but to damaging effect. He took months to reveal he was separated but still married while courting her. Then during his anthrax recovery, she shrank from the story about hitting a dead man in the road when returning from a field trip.

The rough verbal confrontation with Enzo crowded her brain. If she revealed his sexual aggression, she couldn't trust what Manolo might do in her absence.

She peeled herself out of bed, unable to meet Manolo's eyes

when giving a half-truth. "Nancy wants Enzo as her successor but working for him would be awkward—he has less training."

"Might be worth it if we can be together." He followed her to the bathroom, wrapping his arms around her waist. "You can spare a few minutes for slippery sex. We'll sort everything out when you're back." In the shower, his soapy hands brought her to a rapid climax, obliterating all other obstacles.

. . .

Hypatia yowled when Maya knocked on her grandmother's door, but no one responded except for the cat. Maya's nerves amped up. She was uncomfortable with a ninety-one-year-old beloved relative living alone. When she called on her iPhone, a groggy voice answered. "Hello, hello, who's there?"

"Grandma, remember I'm staying the night? I'm at your front door."

"Oh, sorry dear, give me a minute." Five minutes later, the door opened to the tiny woman with a thick robe pulled around her body. The sable Persian bumped their legs. "I fell asleep after Meals on Wheels dropped off my lunch."

Maya stooped for a long hug, then guided her grandmother to the couch. She grabbed a hairbrush from the end table to corral the white hair into a neat, low bun. "You still look ready to put the fear of God into high school students. I almost wish you hadn't retired so you'd have other people around."

"Don't worry about me, sweetie. Your folks are driving down from Flagstaff for a Sunday matinee. The play's called *The Wolves* about a women's soccer team. Why it's called that, I have no idea."

Maya kicked herself for not keeping in closer touch with her parents. Although they talked by phone weekly, she hadn't seen them since Thanksgiving dinner at Manolo's. They probably planned to sleep on the pullout couch.

"Grandma, when Mom and Dad come, I'll move to a motel." Maya checked the time. "I'll be back at five to cook dinner for us." Then she turned on the public radio station and lifted the cat into her grandmother's lap.

After leaving a message for the local health department, she drove along straight streets lined with midcentury ranches. At the student's home address, a college-age young man with a blond buzz cut was shooting hoops in the driveway with younger boys. A chunky older man lounged on a rusting metal chair in the front yard, drinking a beer and cheering them on. Two girls drew chalk pictures on the sidewalk.

Maya tossed an N-95 mask into her daypack and crossed her fingers that she had the wrong address. Maybe Nicky was isolated in his bedroom. "Mr. Clark?" she asked the man on the chair.

He lowered the can and turned in her direction. "Who's asking?"

She kept several feet back and didn't offer her hand. "Dr. Maguire from the Centers for Disease Control and Prevention. I'm helping the health department on this respiratory illness that might be related to China. How's your son doing?"

He waved to the driveway. "Ask him yourself. Nicky, get your butt over here."

With a twist in her stomach, Maya watched the taller youth detach himself from the group and stroll in her direction. "Hi Nicky, I'm thrilled to see you're feeling so well. I need to slip on this mask while we talk."

Mr. Clark shook his head and laughed. "Doc, do what you gotta do."

To compensate for the mask, Maya raised her voice. "The health department ordered you to stay isolated from other people. Didn't you get that message?"

Nicky tossed the ball from one hand to the other. "I'm okay. No more fever or cough. I'm driving back up to school on Sunday."

"This new virus is worse than the common cold. The number of infected people here is low, but cases are exploding overseas. Did you travel outside the country?"

Mr. Clark stood up and squared his shoulders. "My sister got back to California from a foreign trip a couple weeks ago. Her son visited Nicky for a campus tour—that's the only way Nicky could catch something from China. But nobody in that family is sick."

He turned toward the front door. "Dr. Maguire, we need to get inside. The neighbors will think we're a threat, you standing there in a mask."

Maya checked her phone—no messages from Janey Johnson, the Pima County epidemiologist. But she couldn't pass up the invitation to find out more. "That's fine, Mr. Clark, but let's send the other kids home."

"Well, one of the girls is ours, and one of the younger boys."

Once the neighbor kids left and Maya was inside, sinking into the flowered sofa with failing springs, Mr. Clark ushered the younger siblings out. "You guys do homework while we talk. Nicky, you stay here." He poured Maya a glass of lemonade which she set on the coffee table.

"Nicky's the first in our family to go to college—we're proud of him."

Trying to build a connection, Maya said, "My mom and dad graduated from the University of Arizona and my grandmother taught for decades at Regis High School."

When Nicky coughed from the chair in the living room corner, Maya flinched, but Mr. Clark stayed focused on their conversation. "Small world, Nicky graduated there last May. Great school, good Catholic and academic values. Not sure why he couldn't go to community college here."

Nicky answered with an exasperated tone. "Dad, we've been over this. Camelback has my computer game design program."

"Well, we got him to Mass and Confession this week, so at least when he's here, we keep him on the straight and narrow. How about you, Dr. Maguire?"

Shit, the story kept getting worse. Why hadn't Nicky stayed home during his recovery? She could hardly focus on answering Mr. Clark's question, but deflected it with humor. "Mom's Irish Catholic so I was raised right, despite Dad being Protestant. I value Catholic social teachings about human rights and dignity."

Enough greasing the wheels to enhance cooperation. Hopefully, he didn't notice her dodge about whether she was a practicing

Catholic. It was time to get back on track. "Let me check in with my county counterpart. We need to talk about how to keep everyone safe."

Maya left Nicky and his father in the living room and pushed through the front screen door. In the yard, she FaceTimed Janey Johnson and breathed a sigh of thanks when the image appeared of the energetic face, brown eyes, and ponytail the color of tumbleweeds.

"I tried to reach you earlier. Sorry we didn't connect." Maya was chagrined to have started the interview before connecting with Janey.

"I had the afternoon off to help Óscar get ready for a fancy fundraiser. His restaurant is doing well with his perfectionist tendencies and political savvy."

"Is he nervous about his President's re-election in November?"

Janey's face broke into a grin. "Nah, he's MAGA-confident. But you work for CDC, so Trump's your boss too."

"I'm pretty insulated from political pressures with my placement in New Mexico."

Anxious about the Clark family, Maya refocused their discussion. "The address for our Tucson patient is close to my grandma's and I swung by to see if it might be a higher-risk apartment building like those in Hong Kong. I didn't expect to find family and friends playing basketball in the driveway, so I started an interview without you."

"Are you still there? I can join you in twenty minutes."

"Sounds good, but I need to keep going. I'm not sure how long Mr. Clark's hospitality will hold out."

SEVEN

Tucson, Arizona—Thursday, February 6, 2020

When Maya knocked and stepped through the screen door with her mask back on, Nicky jerked his Xbox controller. "Give me a second," he said. "The T and G-virus outbreak is exploding in Raccoon City."

"Which game is that?"

"Resident Evil 2. Ya know it?"

"One of my coworkers is a fan. Let's talk more about this coronavirus." She glanced around the combined living and dining room. "Your dad still around?"

Footsteps in the hall indicated Mr. Clark approaching. He wiped his hands on weathered jeans, picked up her lemonade, and cleaned the pooled liquid on the glass countertop. "You didn't take a sip."

In a potentially germy household, she paused, then tugged down her mask to soothe her tight throat and maintain his hospitality. Mr. Clark pushed past Nicky's outstretched legs and grabbed a package of hamburger from the refrigerator. "I'm happy to answer more questions, but I need to start my lasagna."

As he turned on the stovetop's gas flame, he yanked a frying pan from a lower cabinet drawer. He dropped the ground meat into the pan and began to stir as Maya pulled out her pocket notebook.

"You said Nicky went to church this week. Which one, and what times?"

"St. Agnes, on Campbell Avenue. Sunday mass, ten o'clock. He's at college without close adult supervision, so I made him go to Confession on Saturday at three-thirty. Sorry, I know the church now calls it Reconciliation—reuniting your soul with the Lord."

What a disaster—how many people could that be? But if St. Agnes had individuals confess their sins in private to the priest in a tiny booth, that would limit the contacts.

She flicked her heavy hair off her shoulders as sweat beaded, then glanced at the mocking inactive swamp cooler in the wall.

"I'll check in with the church," she said, "and make sure they don't have any illnesses."

"Maguire. Strange name for an Oriental, but explains why you're interested in this nasty Chinese disease." He turned off the burner under the hamburger. "I'm not crazy about St. Agnes knowing our business."

Maya ignored his initial remark, unsure if it reflected prejudice or curiosity. It wasn't the moment to explain her adoption or the origins of the virus in China. "We won't provide Nicky's name to the priest. The other kids playing here, what are their names and addresses?"

He filled a pot with water and started the flame. "Look, I believe you about the church, but how can you ask questions of our neighbors without them figuring out something's going on?"

Before she could answer, the front screen door vibrated with a rapid knock. "Nicky, go get that," Mr. Clark yelled.

"It might be my county colleague," Maya said. She stepped over Nicky and recognized Janey through the wire mesh of the screen, even with her mask on. "You must have flown a jet to get here so quick."

Janey pushed in with a curt greeting, eyes laser-focused on Nicky. Was she miffed at the interview starting without her? Maya felt a few tingles of anxiety. She'd never been at cross-purposes with Janey before and all her careful efforts to improve interpersonal skills might have been in vain. She leaned against the door jamb to counter a brief wave of dizziness.

The epidemiologist sat down next to the patient and took over. "Nicky, my name is Janey and here's how to reach me."

He scowled with the interruption but stopped the videogame and studied the card. Janey's voice dropped to the resonance of a gentle brook. "You can call me anytime, day or night. No questions off-limits. If you've got a special girlfriend or boyfriend, let's talk about that soon. I want to make sure everyone you know is safe."

Maya handed over her notes written in clear cursive. "We have these church events to check on. Mr. Clark is concerned about confidentiality if we reach out to families with kids visiting this week." She looked up as he rejoined them.

"Don't worry, Mr. Clark." Janey handed him her business card. "But the virus and our need to talk with people expand if Nicky moves around and generates more contacts. You must make sure there are no guests or time outside the home for Nicky during the next week."

"So you won't let him go back to school in Phoenix like he planned."

Maya opened her mouth to answer but got distracted by a Siamese cat who'd snuck up and started clawing and biting at her ankle. If only she'd worn socks and shoes instead of sandals, she'd have some protection. But brushing it away might be bad form when trying to negotiate Nicky's plans.

Janey swiped her phone and looked at the calendar. "When did your symptoms start, Nicky?"

"Uh, I started feeling lousy last Thursday. That's when the student health center took my blood specimen. Then on Saturday morning, I drove home."

Maya tried to ignore the teeth piercing her flesh but shifted her foot slightly. "Amazing that they were suspicious enough of the Chinese coronavirus to notify the health department."

"Well, my cousin was still visiting from California, checking out the campus. The nurse overheard us talking about his mom getting back from Hong Kong in late January, after they had cases."

As the cat roared off into the kitchen, Maya opened up her calendar as well. "CDC is concerned about the two-week period after symptoms start. So you should stay home one more week. If you feel well enough, email your teachers about work you can do from here."

He snorted. "My college doesn't have anything online for my classes. We're still in the dark ages where everyone learns from books."

At the entrance to the kitchen, Mr. Clark said, "Ladies, I need dinner on the table by the time the wife comes home. Can we finish this tomorrow?"

Janey stood and turned for the screen door. "If you send me tonight the names and contact info for the kids who visited, I'll follow-up and keep you fully informed of our progress."

Maya added, "For your own safety, it would be better if Nicky can wait out this period in his own room."

Mr. Clark shook his head. "Impossible. He shares a bedroom with his brother, and there's no TV for his gaming."

Feeling out of options, especially with Nicky acting healthy except for the occasional cough, she gave in. "Keep Janey informed if any of you get symptoms."

"I'll contact you tomorrow about repeat testing," Janey said.

Outside in the yard, they pulled off their masks. Maya grabbed hand sanitizer from her purse and offered a squirt to Janey, then flinched as she wiped it over the drops of blood pooling on her ankle.

"How did that happen?" Janey asked.

"Sneaky feline." Maya took a deep abdominal breath. "Listen, I apologize for jumping in with both feet, not waiting for you."

"People respect your leadership for multiple diseases. That's your job—CDC values EIS Officers who leap into the fray."

If that was true, it might partly explain Enzo's aggression. Was he chosen by CDC and Nancy for his boldness? She pulled a tissue from her pack and dabbed the still welling cat wounds. Enzo had to stop creeping into her thoughts.

She offered another sanitizer squirt to Janey. "CDC only mentioned transmission through respiratory droplets like SARS, but better to be careful."

Janey's face had a bemused expression, probably in response to Maya's dogged handwashing. "I'll follow up on the neighbor contacts tomorrow," Janey said. "Want to join me and Óscar at his restaurant for dinner?"

Maya shook her head. "No thanks, I promised to cook for Grandma, plus playtime with her kitty who gets stir-crazy never going outdoors." She glanced one more time at the punctures below, finally clotted. "At least hers is friendlier."

Maya walked Janey to her car. "Let's touch base in the morning and work out the plan for the day. If we get everything handled, we could have our weekend off."

. . .

Tucson, Arizona—Friday, February 7, 2020

Coronavirus came from bats or possibly pangolins amid 'acceleration' of new zoonotic infections. Maya scanned the title and content of a *Washington Post* article on her laptop while eating cereal as her grandmother slept late.

She opened email replies from Nancy and Enzo, thanking her for the Tucson investigation. By early afternoon, Nancy planned to announce a single Arizona infection, anticipating considerable attention as one of the few without China travel or contact with a known case.

The *Post* linked to an October article about pangolin viruses, including coronavirus. While waiting for the press release, Maya took advantage of the time difference and called Faye Simpson, her public health veterinary mentor from the New York City internship. More than any other epidemiologist, Faye was privy to Maya's deepest desires and fears. Her guidance was wise and welcome.

"Maya, good to hear from you." Faye's throaty voice conjured Broadway actor Harvey Fierstein, perhaps because she and Maya were both musical fans. "Are you fully recovered from that awful explosion in Atlanta?"

With a twinge of pain in her left hand at the memory, Maya pushed past it. She appreciated friends worrying about her, but had tried to move on. "I'm great. Did I tell you Manolo's family wants a June wedding in NYC?"

"Hey, kiddo, I'll be there with bells on, no matter where you hold it." Faye's voice faded. "I'm at JFK helping CDC Quarantine staff screen travelers from Wuhan."

"Then I shouldn't bother you. I'm not sure how to interpret genetic sequencing results in pangolins."

Faye chuckled. "Aren't those the strangest looking creatures? Like an armadillo mated with an anteater. I just don't have a picture of the phylogenetic tree in my head."

On the laptop screen, Maya studied the diagrammed branches with tiny species names. "Pangolin coronavirus is nestled between humans and birds, so perhaps pangolins are an intermediate host. Arizona has our first human case and I want to be prepared for animal origin questions."

"Well, most new diseases are zoonotic. People forget that HIV-AIDS came from chimpanzees. Then there are swine and avian flus. Did your Arizona patient have animal contact or travel to China?"

"He has a relative who returned from there."

"Your thermometer's not working, I'm fine," filtered through the phone.

"Sorry," Faye said. "An arriving passenger needs a comprehensive assessment. I'll call when we can talk longer about animals and coronaviruses."

Maya's hair fell forward as she hung up and dropped her head to her hand. Too dependent on Faye's experience and judgment, she'd have an unfortunate delay in gaining a veterinary perspective in preparation for the media spotlight. Nothing worse than feeling stupid.

EIGHT

Tucson, Arizona—Friday, February 7, 2020

Below a phalanx of curved red tiles on the roof and two towering palm trees on each side, the pink-orange adobe walls glowed in the sunlight. After texting the parish priest of her arrival, Maya entered the carved double entrance doors of St. Agnes under an immense steel cross.

Her sneakers squeaked on the polished tile floor of the center aisle as she strode past rows of ancient wooden pews. The thinly-padded kneelers reminded her of painful hours at lengthy services as a child with her mother. The church retained its Hispanic heritage with a two-story golden cross behind the altar and brightly painted statues of Mary and Jesus to either side.

"Dr. Maguire? I'm Father Cassidy." Tousled hair in the style of Prime Minister Boris Johnson capped a rotund pale body. "Your lovely name brings me back to Annascaul, County Kerry. My cousin runs the famous South Pole Inn started by an Irish Antarctic explorer. Have you heard of it?"

Maya shook her head, overpowered by his strong handshake and bonhomie.

He continued. "The Maguires were the leading Gaelic family in County Fermanagh in Northern Ireland. We're all so relieved the Troubles are behind us."

"Dad's family was Protestant, so that fits with the Northern Ireland connection."

"Maguire means son of the dark one. With your hair and eyes, you fit right in." The first time anyone ever said that her Chinese heritage meshed with her Irish one. She liked him already.

He seemed casual by nature, dressed in open leather sandals, khaki cargo shorts, and a striped polo shirt barely covering his ample midsection. Maya decided to reinforce the positive start to their discussion before it might turn hostile.

"You probably know my grandmother, Martha Robinson. She speaks very highly of you, Father, and is thrilled you still have High Masses in Latin for holidays."

"Yes, our dear Martha. We treasure our members in their ninth decade. She was here last weekend for Reconciliation and Sunday Mass."

"She may stop in tomorrow for her weekly confession, as she still calls it. What she has to confess at her age, I have no idea. My parents will be visiting and I'm not sure of their plans."

He pressed his hands together, as if in a prayer of gratitude. "Wonderful, you should all come to Mass on Sunday. Even your apostate dad." He winked. "But what's our meeting about?"

She motioned to a front wooden pew and pulled one of the cushions under her tailbone, heading off any future back pain associated with her childhood accident. Glancing quickly around the nave, she didn't see anyone else.

"The Chinese coronavirus has hit this area. We just confirmed a case in a college student. He attended both the Reconciliation and Sunday Mass last weekend before the lab results, when he was potentially contagious."

Saying it out loud cemented a freakout fear. Could her grandmother have been exposed? But it was a big open church, and little person-to-person spread was suspected outside China.

The priest's blue eyes rounded up, pupils dilated. "That's terrible. Who's the student? The family will need pastoral care."

"I apologize, Father Cassidy, but confidentiality keeps me from providing his name. I'll share with them your interest in helping."

"A guest minister assisted with the Sacrament of Penance on Saturday, so I'm not sure which of our flock participated." He pulled out his smart phone and checked the calendar. "February first was one of our rare cold snaps with a nasty icy drizzle."

Maya wished her grandmother had avoided the bad weather. But there was still the Mass. "Did you conduct the Sunday service? Any guess on the number in the pews?"

"There's been a decrease—we're failing at engaging younger people. Last Sunday, maybe a hundred."

"A colleague is talking to the patient's contacts. Anyone they report who sat close by in church will be interviewed." Maya thought creatively for another option to spread the word. "Could you include an educational message about respiratory infections in your sermon? Mention that they're more common in the enclosed spaces of winter, people should seek medical attention promptly if they're ill, and isolate to avoid spreading microbes to others. That may reinforce more protective behavior."

He smiled and took her hand. "I'm happy to help, but I won't mention that we have a patient among our congregants."

Maya hesitated, recalling her instructions for other respiratory outbreaks. "I agree—we want to avoid panic."

"Jesus was always looking out for the welfare of his flock. I'm sure I can tie the message in."

"Thank you so much." Maya rose and grabbed her notebook. "I'll email additional information about clinical signs and appropriate follow-up."

An older woman with permed gray hair burst in. "Father, can we touch base on the religious education classes for Sunday? I'm short a few instructors."

"Dr. Maguire, I need to switch gears. I hope to see you for services this weekend."

She drew in a deep breath, suddenly wanting to keep her family nestled safely together at her grandmother's apartment. "You've been very kind, Father Cassidy. With my parents visiting, we might just hunker at home for meals and card games."

Back in her rental car, she reclined the driver's seat and called Atlanta. As the phone rang multiple times, she tapped the steering wheel with impatience. Dr. Kim's cognitive therapy reduced her lifelong panic disorder, but it could flare up suddenly with potential threats. Why had she chosen a career with so many risks and uncertainties?

Just as Maya was about to disconnect, the phone was answered and she plunged ahead.

"Dr. Jaworski, I need to make sure I'm triaging this coronavirus case correctly. I visited his church where he participated in events both days last weekend. They're short-staffed on religious ed teachers—that might be a signal of community transmission."

"I've been in touch with Nancy. The news outlets will promote her press release," Dr. Jaworski said. "She's got things well in hand— keep following her instructions."

Maya repressed her resentment of the government line that the agencies were on top of things. Being a worrywart about what could go wrong wasn't fun, but it allowed her to prepare for the inevitable hiccups. "Father Cassidy is including a general winter respiratory disease warning in his homily this Sunday."

Dr. Jaworski was a 'just the facts' supervisor, not typically loquacious, but her Long Island accent turned upbeat. "Maya, how creative. I'm sure that will reinforce the press message."

"If I give the church Nicky's name, we could be more thorough in follow-up. If I describe what Nicky looks like to the priest who took his confession, perhaps we can determine who was in the same tiny confessional booth before and after him." She didn't add that it might be her grandmother.

"Maya, if we name places where someone could have been exposed, those people will look out for symptoms and others will feel off the hook. We want everyone on alert. Double-check with Nancy on how to handle it."

As the sun heated the car interior, Maya pushed her thick hair out of her eyes and sighed. "I understand. I'm hyperalert after the anthrax outbreak."

"Uncomfortable for you, but not a bad quality for an EIS Officer. Keep up the excellent work."

Next, Maya called Janey. "I'm done with the church and getting hungry. Should we meet and update each other?"

"Let's do fast food in Reid Park; it's not far away."

Maya tried to counter any simmering tension over starting the family interview alone. "I'll pick up the lunch. Do you have a preference?"

"Tico Taco is a mile south of you on Campbell Avenue. Get me a diet coke and a carne asada taco bowl with extra sour cream."

Within ten minutes of purchasing the food, Maya found Janey at a concrete picnic table next to a small lake and central fountain. White and red oleanders splashed brilliant colors on one side, and palm trees, some as tall as those at St. Agnes, pierced the partly cloudy sky.

A little boy cowered in a group of teenagers. He'd been chased by a goose begging for food or chastising him with a territorial warning. Two of the older boys hollered and whooped, herding the birds back to the water. When one threw a rock, Maya yelled out. "Hey guys, that's not necessary."

Janey chortled. "Look at shy Maya, where'd you get your cojones?"

"My veterinary instinct kicked in. He probably wouldn't hit one, but I want them to know we're watching."

"We shouldn't antagonize the gangs," Janey joked, "and I'll keep my phone handy in case we need help after your posse pose." On a quiet Friday with families strolling and playing in the park, Janey appeared untroubled. She dug into her taco bowl, the fragrance of beef and spices wafting in the warm air.

Maya swallowed two bites of her guacamole-infused soft taco, then updated her friend. "The priest at St. Agnes was a trip—I appreciate why the Diocese keeps his church going. He's amazingly friendly, and willing to insert a public health message in his Sunday sermon."

"Nicky's contacts are primarily limited to the one group of kids, but other family members have continued their regular lives. So if they're incubating, we could be in trouble soon. Plus Nicky and his dad stopped by a shoe store in Alvernon Mall to pick up a pair ordered online."

Maya felt like they were dueling to top each other with tales of greater risk. "For St. Agnes, we have Confession on Saturday in a small booth, and Mass on Sunday in the open nave. I called Atlanta to find out if we should announce locations where someone with a contagious disease has been, to get those people on higher alert. Dr. Jaworski said it's a local decision."

Janey nodded. "Pima County has done it rarely, but I'll check with my boss. We could include both the mall and the church."

In a habitual displacement of nerves, Maya reached back to tighten the scrunchie on her ponytail. If they went public with two named places, reporters might want a local official interview. She had no experience with the media beyond a prepared statement at a press conference announcing anthrax letters, and she'd stumbled over a reporter's question about CDC competence.

"If we release locations," Maya said, "I'll need to notify Father Cassidy."

Janey's cell phone rang and she put it on speaker. "Mr. Clark, I'm here with Dr. Maguire, what's up?"

"My wife called from our vet's office. Our old Siamese named Suri threw up and pooped all over the carpet. Then Suri got a hacking cough, but no hairballs. When Irene mentioned Nicky's illness with the China virus, the vet collected samples. Any chance Nicky gave it to the cat?"

NINE

Tucson, Arizona—Friday, February 7, 2020

After Janey hung up the speaker phone call with Mr. Clark, Maya buried her head in her hands and scrubbed her cheeks. The roar of a lion drifted over from the Reid Park Zoo, reminding her that she always needed to consider animals even when her epi skills were applied to human illnesses. The bucolic scene of kids feeding ducks in the pond couldn't counteract the spinning in her brain.

"Shit, their vet's considering this novel coronavirus for their cat. I didn't even think to ask about the cat's health. Pretty embarrassing, especially because I was thinking about animal origins when I talked to Faye in NYC this morning."

Janey touched Maya's arm. "Don't beat yourself up. Nothing's been reported yet about this virus in cats or dogs."

Zooanthroponosis, or reverse zoonosis, was a disease that people gave to animals. But this new Chinese virus was spreading person-to-person. No evidence was available of people getting infected by animals, let alone the other way around. Maya scratched her fingers through her hair, then slapped the table.

"The Clarks are confused. The vet probably means feline coronavirus, FeCV. Sometimes it mutates to cause feline infectious peritonitis or FIP, which can be fatal. But the virus doesn't infect people."

"Sounds like you have some cat follow-up to do. I should get back to my office to work out which of Danny's locations can be included in a press release."

Maya stood to collect their trash. "We need to touch base with Nancy." Maya's phone rang and 'Dave' flashed on the screen. She dropped the waste into the garbage can and hurried to answer the call from her US Department of Agriculture colleague.

"How are you doing after the flash-bang? Feels like you've been MIA."

Dave's Texas drawl still reminded her of a sleepy rattler on a cold day. Not looking for any fights, but best not to step on.

"I'm recovered and catching up on work. Sorry to be out of touch."

"Well, you have no more excuses. Your office said you're in Tucson and I am too."

"I'd love to see you and hear how Braxton enjoyed the holidays." The Schwartz family was sheltering Dave's young half-brother, booted out from a polygamist sect, and she felt a pang of guilt for not having checked in with them sooner. "Why are you in the Old Pueblo?"

"The new University of Arizona vet school. Ben's here too for a meeting with the Dean, then dinner and a tour of their Oro Valley campus tomorrow morning. You should join us."

Maya wasn't surprised that Dave and Ben Smith, the Arizona Department of Agriculture's State Veterinarian, would be consulted about the momentous occasion of a new veterinary school in the Southwest. Other than a private college in the Phoenix area, Arizona students for generations had no local options.

"I still have some work on my latest outbreak investigation, and my parents are driving down from Flagstaff for a family dinner."

"Meet us at eight if your relatives sleep late on a Saturday morning. Ben and I want to make sure the new school emphasizes public practice careers as well as clinical practice."

He was right. So many vet students had bucolic James Herriot *All Creatures Great and Small* stars in their eyes about caring for individual animals, but never considered how much they could accomplish through academia, laboratories, drug companies, or government agencies.

"Let me touch base when I figure out my work and personal obligations."

After Dave said goodbye, Maya fanned her face with her cap. "That glistening pool with the geese is tempting in this intense sun."

"I wish we had time to explore all the improvements they've made here since I was a kid." When the lion roared again, Janey added, "That's Zuba, he's eight years old."

The animal sounds and pungent odors made a zoo visit hard to pass up for a veterinarian, but the detour would have to wait. "We'd better touch base with Nancy," Maya said.

The Arizona State Epidemiologist picked up on the first ring. "About time you checked in." Her voice was caustic, a tone Maya had never heard from her. "Enzo's here with me to prepare a TV press conference scheduled in the next half-hour. At least we won't be the first one, with multiple California cases and local spread in Chicago."

Would Enzo be on camera? He didn't hide his fondness for the limelight and Maya had been disconcerted lately about Nancy's decision-making.

"Nancy, the Clarks have a sick cat being tested for coronavirus, but I don't think it's related to Nicky's infection. A long list of problems can cause vomiting and coughing—"

Enzo's brusque voice interrupted. "Paranoid hysteria—the nuts are bound to come out of the woodwork. No need to add pets to the panic when we name multiple places."

Maya glanced over at Janey. "Do you mean the church and the shopping mall? I need time to warn them, and Janey has to alert her supervisor at the county."

Enzo continued to answer. "You should have told them about that possibility, like I did with the community college."

Nancy allowing him to control the discussion was a surprise, but Maya had wondered about the same issues. "We can call key people here right away. I planned to stay in Tucson for the weekend, so I can help with the fallout."

Janey jumped in. "You've got to give me an hour to reach my office and have my boss review your draft remarks before you're in front of the cameras."

Enzo's tone conveyed his dissatisfaction. "But our press officer has scheduled the announcement for—"

He was interrupted by Nancy. "We can hold them off until three."

"They'll be pissed and it could affect our coverage." Enzo clearly wasn't intimidated by his boss.

"Enzo, settle down." Nancy sounded more tired than impatient. "Ronnie's been doing her job for decades and she has the reporters in the palm of her hand. No need to worry about a slight delay."

"We appreciate the time to prepare," Maya said. "I'll notify the church and mall while Janey coordinates with you and the county. But first I'll let the family know that you won't name them or their neighborhood, even though there have been some neighbor contacts."

"We should list the neighborhood," Enzo said. "Help those people get on special alert."

Maya didn't wait for Nancy's response. "Naming the church will accomplish the goal without identifying or ostracizing the family."

Janey jumped in. "Our staff can call the neighbors so they'll be in the loop, without putting them in the public crosshairs."

Maya read one-thirty on her phone. They finished the call and raced to their cars.

. . .

Using an empty office in the modern medical complex on the south side of town, Maya conducted her notifications. The only cheerful phone call was to Mr. Clark, ecstatic that no details would be released allowing Nicky's identification.

The mall owner negotiated that the specific shoe store where Danny shopped wouldn't be divulged, and Maya assured him there were no plans to close the businesses down. Father Cassidy's Irish lilt became abruptly harsh when she informed him St. Agnes would be named, but he was relieved that the government wouldn't restrict access or services. Maya phoned those agreements into Nancy's office in Phoenix, and prayed they'd be honored.

Despite the physical distance from the livid parish priest, Maya was shaking with stress and anticipation when she joined Janey and other Tucson staff in front of a small TV. Maya was stunned that Nancy remained seated as she introduced Enzo and let him read the press release. He mentioned no closures for the community college, the mall, or the church, and Maya stretched out leg muscle cramps, taking in deep breaths.

Nancy concluded, "This is a single case of the new coronavirus, possibly related to an asymptomatic relative in another state who returned from China. It is not a local emergency. Unlike Chicago, we have no evidence of ill family members, and the young man's clinical course was mild. He was never hospitalized."

A grizzled reporter hobbled with a cane to the closest microphone. "The first CDC weekly report about this huge China problem was only two days ago on February fifth, and I wonder if our health agencies are on top of this."

On the screen, Maya could see Enzo's squirming body, clearly indicating he wanted to handle the response. To Maya's relief, Nancy took the lead. "CDC's Emergency Operations Center was activated two weeks ago and ours at the state level has been opened today."

Enzo's discomfort flashed Maya back to the New Year's Eve party when Nancy expressed hope he'd be her replacement. Whether her expectation coincided with his ambition, his eagerness to control the press conference was palpable.

But the reporter wasn't done. "Dr. Bingham, is there anything from SARS in 2003 that you'll use for this case?"

Nancy stood as if to respond, her face contorted. Instead, she dropped back to the chair. Her head swayed and her eyes dropped to the table, then over to Enzo. "Uh, we need to look closely at that past outbreak."

Janey and her health director frowned. Perhaps the Arizona SARS outbreak details were too distant in time for Nancy to remember. Maya wanted to reach through the television screen to comfort the supervisor who had nurtured her. A gentle hand to wipe the brow of confusion.

TEN

Tucson, Arizona—Friday, February 7, 2020

Maya FaceTimed Nancy in Phoenix. Despite Nancy's weak performance, Maya put a positive spin on the event. "Other than the aggressive reporter, the press conference went fine."

Enzo's voice flared off-screen. "I can't believe the old codger's slamming us."

"Eddie's status should be respected." Nancy's response was soft and Maya turned up her volume. "Enzo, I'm catching that nap before we work out weekend plans. Can you finish talking to Maya?"

"Is there anything you did with SARS that we should consider for Nicky's case?" Maya tried to keep Nancy focused.

"In 2003? I advised contact isolation for ten days, but we couldn't enforce it."

"Nicky's feeling better," Maya said, "and eager to get back to school."

Enzo howled. "You can't let him do that. I'll have a huge problem on my hands if he spreads it to the other college students."

Maya kneaded the chronic pain in her lower back and spun in the chair. "I didn't say we approved it. Janey and I both asked him to stay home, and the family agreed. But we don't have a way to enforce it. Nancy, you sound exhausted, are you doing okay?"

"Working on SARS gave me a heart attack, but I was never infected—probably the long hours plus the residual damage from Chagas. I need to pace myself."

"Now you've got me." Enzo's voice became his most charming. "Instead of an office nap, why don't you go home and rest? I'll ask CDC for their recommendations."

"I agree with Enzo." Maya glanced around the local office for Janey who had disappeared with her health director. "We'll manage things here in Tucson, then I'll join you in Phoenix Monday morning."

"Make sure everything's covered before you rush back," Enzo warned. "Nancy knows I've got things in hand here."

Maya's muscles clenched when she recalled her confrontation at the picnic table. No wonder Enzo wanted to keep her away from Nancy. He likely assumed she wouldn't reveal his transgressions over the phone, but in the past two days, there hadn't been a moment to process any decisions. Now Nancy appeared under the weather, and Maya didn't want to add to her difficulties.

"I'll follow your advice and head home." Nancy's voice dropped to a whisper. "I have every confidence the two of you can work it all out."

. . .

After checking with Father Cassidy and the mall owner, Maya squeezed in a personal call. "Manolo, did you catch Nancy on TV? How do you think it went?"

"I was surprised to see an EIS Officer reading the press release." But as usual, his tone was diplomatic and optimistic. "Hopefully this new coronavirus will have no more impact in Arizona than the last one. Still stuck in Tucson?"

Maya answered with a sigh. "Yes, but there's some benefits. My folks are driving in from Flagstaff, plus I'll see Dave and Ben tomorrow to talk about animal risks."

"Will you stay at your grandmother's?"

"Mom and Dad plan to do that, so I'll find a hotel."

"I just finished a workshop on Native American diabetes but my weekend is free. Our lunchtime rendezvous yesterday was too quick. Let me book the Tucson hotel and we can sleep in the same bed."

At the speed of a hummingbird's wings, Maya's pulse accelerated with anticipation. "Text me. I'm headed to Grandma's for an early dinner with the family."

At the small apartment, Maya's dad raced around pulling a string with feathers as Hypatia stalked and pounced to catch it, then let it go to prolong the game.

Her mother tossed spinach noodles in a colander under hot water while Maya scraped the fry pan with a metal spatula and called out to the cat, splotching a dab of the sautéed chicken onto the cat bowl at her feet. Hypatia skidded to a stop and devoured the treat in one bite. Her grandmother clapped her hands in enthusiasm over her pet's antics.

"Grandma, Manolo and I would love to join you at the play on Sunday."

"It's about women's soccer. I had a friend in the Bobby Soccers, a St. Louis team in 1950."

"Did you ever play?"

"No dear, my parents wouldn't approve. Doctors back then said such activities could make a woman's uterus fall out."

Maya twisted off the burners and dumped the chicken into the noodles. "And did they think going to college would make your brain explode?"

Her grandmother tittered. "No, sweetie. It was challenging to compete for admission against all the men returned from the War, but I guess a female wanting to study math intrigued them."

Maya's mom served the casserole as other family members banged their forks on the glass table.

"Bring it on," her father shouted.

"That's my recipe," her grandmother bragged.

"You guys are too much," Maya teased them.

Her mom struggled with a pocket hidden in the geometric patterns of her African dashiki dress, her face glowing as brightly as the dyed red hair piled on top of her head. She finally dropped on the table a piece of paper covered front and back with black squiggles. "With your wedding only four months away, you need to get your butt in gear."

The pressure flashed Maya back to age sixteen when her mother chided her for delays in choosing a college major. In contrast, her father had been an energetic rock of support when Maya was tempted by illegal dorm parties with alcohol. "Just because you have the brains of an older girl doesn't force you to take on those burdens," he advised, and paid for a private career counselor to review degree options.

Her grandmother came to the rescue and grabbed the paper from the tabletop with spidery wrinkled fingers. Her voice turned stern, like the no-nonsense high school teacher she used to be. "I've got local contacts with my former students. You tell me what kind of flowers and food you want—I'll make it happen."

As they completed their meal, her dad let out a belch followed by a chorus of chortles and jabs. Then Maya cleared the table and hugged her family goodnight. "I have a morning meeting, but Manolo and I would love to take you out to lunch."

"Can't wait to see your handsome beau again," her grandmother said with a wink. "Remember, if you don't get a wedding band on your finger soon, I'll try to seduce him myself. And don't worry if you're too busy to join us at *The Wolves* on Sunday. The playwright said it's like a Greek tragedy—might be a downer."

. . .

Hurrying along the hotel room corridor, Maya pushed aside all thoughts racing around her brain—an emerging coronavirus, Nancy possibly ill, Enzo taking over, and family pressures about the wedding and new job. She wouldn't allow any of it to overcome her excitement for the reunion with Manolo. His text message provided the room number and she knocked on the door.

When it inched open, he emerged in skintight trousers and a matching short jacket embroidered in blue and gold.

"What on earth are you wearing?" she asked.

"Traje de luces or suit of lights." He pulled her hand up to caress the fur on his black hat. "This is my matador's montera. These bulbs on the sides represent horns of a bull, and perhaps something else you can fondle."

He grabbed a red cape from the bedspread and draped it in front of him. "Want to be my bull and come after me?"

She took a step closer. "You've gone to a lot of trouble for our first night together in weeks."

His twinkling black eyes complemented the brilliant flash of his grin. "I got inspired by your initiative after Thanksgiving in Sedona. Don't worry, I didn't spend any wedding money. A buddy had this costume and loaned it."

Maya fingered the silk of the cape. "Señor, why is this cape red? Cattle are red/green color blind."

"The muleta is intended to hide my sword, although I hope you find it. The color is to mask the bloodstains, but this matador promises to be gentle."

"Bueno, mi amor. If you don't mind my change in gender role, I'm thrilled to service mi toreador as tu toro. Let me get into my own costume."

She Googled 'bullfight music' on her phone and found an album of corrido and mariachi tunes. As brass instruments pulsed and guitars strummed, she stripped off all her clothes while Manolo preened and waved his cape. She put two fingers above her head and charged. When he wrapped the red cloth around her body, she reached her hands through the folds to stroke his metaphorical weapon and began to remove his costume. Its fabric was rough against her skin as he tugged her in for a passionate kiss, tongue signaling his intention for other body parts when she completed her task.

After setting his elaborate clothing on a chair, she yanked back the bedcovers and lured him in to join her. They continued role playing as he brought her to multiple climaxes, each one la petite mort.

ELEVEN

Tucson, Arizona—Saturday, February 8, 2020

An old Palomino nipped at Maya's ear and Manolo jerked her back.

"Our horses here at the Campus Agricultural Center are donated." The new vet school dean lowered her red cap with the Wildcat logo over her freckled, wrinkled forehead. "They're animal teachers for our ag and vet students."

She shook Dave and Ben's hands with her sunspotted ones. "We're thrilled to have our federal and state ag vets visit. We want students to learn about ag agencies as a potential career and how to report diseases."

"If I'm still in the Southwest this fall," Maya said, "I'd love to do a guest lecture on One Health. Just like ag agencies, our public health ones want to work with students."

"We pride ourselves on being innovative." The dean's tone turned mildly irritated. "Look at our website. One Health is explicitly integrated within four semesters of training."

"Maya's been flat-out on multiple outbreaks." Manolo sounded like he was jumping to her defense. "She hasn't had time to focus on anything else."

Maya was unsure if he picked up on her tense posture, but he shifted back to professional mode. "Your new school has a great holistic approach. I've been encouraging Native American and Hispanic youth to consider medical careers."

"Same with me for African American students, especially here in the Southwest," Ben added.

"Maya and I will have a tough choice." Dave adjusted his

cowboy hat and grinned. "I've always pushed pre-vet students to Texas, and I'm sure she's done the same for Colorado. But we're happy to support this new opportunity within Arizona."

The dean stepped away from the corrals and headed for the white-washed buildings, red tile roofs baking in the sun. "Let's do a quick tour of our facilities including the surgical simulation room and our mobile unit. Then we'll swing up to our Oro Valley campus."

On the ride north along the western edge of the Catalina Mountains, Maya tried to distract herself with views of the Tohono Chul botanical garden, golf courses, and fancy homes. She wanted to chew Manolo out for his paternalism, protecting her from frisky equines and proud deans. She never resented his protective attitude before—what had changed? Squeezing the irritation into a small Silly Putty ball, she put it back in its plastic egg. She'd bring it up when he wasn't distracted by driving.

At buildings clustered near Pusch Ridge, dotted with saguaros and low-growing trees beneath more distant ridges of ponderosas, the dean continued her tour. "This is where our students will focus two years of preclinical work. We have a fitness center to counteract pressures of our extreme demands."

"This area is its own stress reliever," Maya said. "If I was going to school here, I'd run up to Catalina State Park for lunch. But it looks like you're not offering a teaching hospital like we have at Colorado State."

"Our students will do their final clinical rotations with a number of partners. Some are local, like Reid Park Zoo." The dean looked at her cell phone. "Even on a Saturday, we're slammed with admissions work. If you have more questions, grab any of the staff."

Maya spotted a bench and invited the three men to sit down while she paced in front of them. Too warm in the intense sunlight, she tugged off her outer jacket and draped it over one arm.

"Have you heard anything about cats and coronaviruses? Our first patient has one that bit or scratched me on the ankle. Turns out it's been sick and the vet submitted samples for corona testing."

Manolo leapt to his feet and began to kneel with his hands reaching for her pants leg. "Don't even think about it." Maya's annoyance cracked like a lightning bolt.

"Sorry." Looking chagrined, he slipped back to the bench between Ben's bulk and Dave's height. "Guess I'm not much of a fiancé if I didn't notice that." He poked elbows toward the men on each side.

"Manolo, cut it out." Her words popped before she regretted her short temper.

Dave fingered the brim of his hat and glanced between them. "I haven't heard anything about cats and this new virus, but *P. multocida* causes bone infection. Also *Capnocytophaga* can cause heart attacks, kidney failure, and limb amputations. You need to monitor for redness, swelling, or pain."

"After tangling with the cat last summer in Portugal, I think I'm up on those risks." A high-pitched kee-eee-ar scream distracted Maya. A red-tailed hawk dove toward the ground, then clutched something small in its talons and swooped back to a platform of sticks on top of a saguaro. With the men's attitudes, implying she mismanaged the cat bite, she felt trapped like the rodent in the hawk's grasp.

"Let's stay on coronavirus. Ben, were there any infected livestock for SARS patients in 2003?"

His arms were crossed over his broad chest, perhaps to ward off the fray. "We didn't find anything. I haven't heard about the risk to domestic animals from this new virus. Based on previous experience, transmission between animals and people shouldn't be a major factor."

"But it started in China," Maya said, "presumably from an animal source."

Dave rubbed his eyes. "The *Washington Times* blamed China's biowarfare program and the Wuhan lab. If that theory is true, we can't lay it at the feet of animal transmission."

"Maya, I need to get back to Phoenix." Ben rose to shake her hand. "I'd be happy to check with our vet diagnostic lab to monitor the cat samples, and follow up if they need to go to the USDA lab in Iowa."

She pumped his arm in gratitude—he was always a monument of calm support. "I appreciate your help. Nicky's dad heard about the Chinese doctor who died after sounding the alarm from Wuhan. The family's concern is ramping up."

"Ben, be right with you," Dave called after his retreating form. "Hit me up if you two need any wedding words of wisdom. Emilia's family wanted a huge Catholic one and planning was a nightmare."

Manolo laughed. "Maya's mom is leveling the heavy guns at our lack of preparation. Can't wait until she aims those beady blue eyes at me this afternoon."

Maya rapidly turned the attention back to Dave. "Things okay with Braxton?"

"You can't break a wild kid overnight. He had a couple months in the halfway house rebelling from all those family religious prohibitions, so sometimes he sneaks a cigarette or a drink. Hopefully those yearnings aren't from being related to me."

"Does he talk about your mom?"

"Occasionally, when we're in the barn working on chores. Not ever knowing her, I appreciate his stories."

"Any idea why she still refuses contact?"

Dave shuffled his feet and waved at Ben, waiting by the state truck. "As I suspected, she blames me for Sam getting killed by the bull, because we identified and then chased him."

Maya put a hand on his arm. "It's hardly your fault he became a bioterrorist hunted by law enforcement. Sure, the three of us spotted him in the barn, but it was the FBI who led the pursuit."

The honk of a horn interrupted and Dave reached out a hand to say goodbye. Maya leaned up and pulled him into a hug, then he shook Manolo's hand and joined Ben at the truck.

"You're a bit on edge," Manolo said. "I'm worried you're coming down with Nicky's virus."

"Part of the problem is you. Let's find some shade." She remembered a spot at the botanical garden.

After he pulled into the Tohono Chul parking lot, she led him to a wooden bench within a dense cove of overhanging trees, spindly ocotillo, and prickly pear cacti. She inched up her pants leg and thrust her ankle into Manolo's lap. "Look over my tiny scabs. Do you see signs of infection?"

"No." His fingers gently palpated as his dark eyes studied her skin. "Any pain?"

"None. I think these are claw scratches, not bites." She pulled her leg back and perched stiffly on the bench, facing Manolo. "I appreciate your concern, but you must realize what it looks like in front of my colleagues when you treat me like a child."

His faint wrinkles deepened into chasms and temple veins became cliffs with his shock at her confrontation. But she plunged ahead, still unnerved by her mother's criticism and recent work dilemmas. "In the year and a half since we met, our relationship has changed multiple times."

"I realize that. You had to take charge when I was ill, and I appreciate the new stronger you." Then he squinted. "Mostly."

"My decisions have to be my own. I love you, but you can't protect me from myself or anyone else." She removed her scrunchie to shake out her hair. "Our success or failure is our own responsibility."

He rested one arm around her shoulders. "This is a shift I didn't see coming. Well, I take that back. I have been appreciating your new assertiveness in the bedroom."

She held his other hand, tight. "I can be a tigress in private as long as I'm a lady in public?"

"Maya, I'm not that much of a hypocrite. Just be lenient while I figure out the boundaries."

She gulped. "Unfortunately, I don't know them either. Maybe we can be flexible enough to find them together."

His face relaxed in agreement.

"One more thing. You're marrying into this family and need to work out the dynamics of your relationship with them. However, I'll keep their wedding plan meddling in check, not you."

His fingers slipped up from her shoulders to the back of her neck under her hair. "I'd love a hug like Dave, or even a better one."

Relief that he took her demands with equanimity flooded her skin along with a gentle winter shower. She'd been so preoccupied by one of their few fights that she hadn't noticed the skies clouding over. The water, penetrating the plant cells, released that exquisite desert-in-the-rain smell that never failed to soothe. Maya ignored museum visitors and draped her legs over his. Nestled into a tight embrace, her lips met his with grateful thanks.

"I suppose we should head to the car to avoid getting soaked." Her practical side won over the passion. "We can put off wedding planning only so long. If we wait until the restaurant, perhaps Mom won't be so demanding in public."

Then her phone chirped and she dug it out from her waist pack.

Her mom's sharp voice was modulated with gasping sobs. "Grandma collapsed and we called the ambulance. Meet us at Tucson Medical Center."

Fingers clutching like a *Walking Dead* skeleton, Maya groped for Manolo's arm. She fought against heart palpitations, hyperventilation, and spine locked in tight.

TWELVE

Tucson, Arizona—Saturday, February 8, 2020

At six-feet tall with her bright hair and thrashing arms, Maya's mom dominated the open lanes between the emergency room chairs. In one corner, an elderly woman mopped the brow of an equally ancient man stooped over with his head in his hands. In the opposite, a child scratched frantically at a rash on his face as a woman applied a wet washcloth to his swollen eyes. At the intake counter, a squalling infant was clutched in the arms of a young man as the odor of diarrhea mixed with an aura of fear.

Guiding her mom to a molded chair, Maya tugged on one arm and her dad the other. The anxiety level of the room reduced just a fraction. "Dad, what's happening?" Maya asked.

Her mom's face froze into a death mask. "Total silence. Silence unending."

"Let me get some answers." Manolo rushed over to a gowned staff member guiding the man with the infant to the back and asked for permission to check on Martha Robinson.

Maya's rapid breathing eased when he disappeared. Manolo could be counted on to take care of it. Maya held her mom's clenched hand and stretched the other across to her dad. "Bringing a physician into the family, not my worst decision."

Her dad returned her gentle squeeze. "Manolo's a blessing."

With the crying infant gone, the room devolved into a charged hush, other than an occasional low moan from the elderly man swaying over his knees. One minute morphed into five, then fifteen, as Maya repeatedly tugged out her phone to check the time. At twenty minutes, she leapt to her feet, determined to do anything to assuage her mom's locked-in zombie stiffness. The automatic door to the back sighed open as Manolo emerged.

Maya studied his face and posture as he approached. Could she guess his news by his expression? He remained impassive, professional, but he ducked her eye contact.

"Barbara and Tom, don't get up." He laced his fingers through Maya's. "They tried everything but couldn't bring Martha back. She passed away. I'm very sorry, this must be devastating."

Maya knelt before her parents as her dad wrapped both arms around his wife. Only her mom's mouth moved.

"I need to see her."

"Of course." Manolo helped Maya to her feet, then both men guided her mom's robotic steps.

A nurse held open the curtain. "Take all the time you need."

A technician moved away equipment they had used to try and revive her. They had readjusted her paisley shirt, navy sweater, and tan slacks. Her face and posture were relaxed, as if napping. Only the straggling hair from her loosened white bun betrayed the struggle to bring her back to life.

From the piercing blue eyes of Maya's mom, a lone tear slipped, the trigger for a gush from Maya's dark ones. Last night, her grandmother had been so on top of things, keeping their family sane. She'd been tired, not unusual for her age.

"I realize she's ninety-one," Maya whispered, "but it's still hard to accept."

Maya's dad put a hand on Manolo's shoulder. "Do you know what happened?"

Manolo's eyes darted between the three Maguires. "Yes, it was a malignant ventricular arrhythmia. Her heart muscle couldn't maintain a regular beat."

"Why?" Barbara asked the question without removing her gaze from her mother's face, as she reached long fingers to stroke it.

"I don't know." Manolo handed Maya a handkerchief as her tears flowed. "She hasn't been ill, right? An autopsy usually isn't done at Martha's age."

Barbara's tone became firm. "I want a proper Catholic mass and open casket wake." She shuddered. "No dissection."

"Then that's what we'll do." Maya's dad turned to Manolo. "Can you tell them that?"

Manolo nodded and Maya knelt to kiss her grandmother goodbye, memorizing her peaceful face. She hugged her parents and said, "Let me take care of things. Just focus on Grandma, how much she loved all of us."

The end table drawer in the apartment had a will and final instructions. Her mother was clearly not in a state to write an obituary, so Maya would pull herself together and get it started.

She never spent much time writing until the anthrax and *Borrelia* scientific papers. With only a few months in a Chinese orphanage, English should have been wired into her brain as a native language. But something blocked an easy flow between a busy brain and her hand on paper or computer keyboard. Perhaps it was an obsession for getting it right that paralyzed her.

. . .

"You're handling this better than I might have expected," Manolo said to Maya as they raced for his Corvette in the torrential downpour.

"Gee, thanks, I appreciate your faith in me." She hopped into the front passenger seat. "Counting dead people in my work has left me numb. Do you think it's inevitable for anyone working in medicine?"

He paused before turning the key. "I don't think you'll become immune to suffering—that's one thing I love about you."

Leaning over, she gave herself totally to his healing embrace. "Thanks, Manolo, for helping us through it."

"There's no place I'd rather be. Let's get back and kickstart the administrative burdens. In high school, I gave my dad a hand when my mom died, so I know the steps."

Once inside the apartment, they slipped off soggy footwear and fed a restless Hypatia. Did the cat know her owner was never coming home? One more issue to solve. Maya's work schedule was too unpredictable for a pet. Maybe her mom and dad would bring the Persian to Flagstaff.

Maya tugged open the drawer of the old oak table. Her grandmother's neat penmanship covered several sheets of creamy, floral-flocked notepaper. To her dad, Maya texted the name of the funeral home where her grandmother had prepaid a cremation and burial plan. Then she called the business to give them a heads up, and they promised to contact the hospital.

"We offer grief counseling and help with the obituary, if you would like those services." The woman's voice was kind over the speakerphone.

"We're squared away on those fronts, but coordinate with St. Agnes and Father Cassidy. My mother wants a full Catholic mass, with the wake at your building."

"That's not a problem. Can you stop by to work out the details?"

Manolo gave a thumbs up and Maya continued. "Yes, as soon as we've made those decisions." She sank to the couch after ending the call. "St. Agnes. That's where Grandma went for Confession a week ago, then Mass on Sunday, along with Nicky Clark."

Manolo joined her, holding her restless hands. "You're worried about Nicky giving her coronavirus? But she didn't have respiratory signs."

"I'm just paranoid, turning coincidences into causes. I'll call Father Cassidy and get the funeral mass in motion."

Reaching for his daypack, Manolo pulled out his laptop. "If it eases your mind, I can see if heart failure is associated with 2019-nCoV."

"Thanks." Maya paused for a deep breath. The last time she spoke to Father Cassidy, he emitted a few cross words about the church being named in the press announcement. With his Catholic faith, perhaps he'd be generous and not hold that against her.

The church secretary put her through to the priest, on a short break from the Saturday reconciliations. "Such sad news for our dear Martha Robinson and your family," he said. "We don't have any Requiem Masses scheduled for Tuesday. Would that work?"

"I think so," Maya answered, stomach knotted with the finality of the schedule. "That would allow us to have the wake Monday evening." She wished she could slam a pause button on time and spend a day wallowing in her grief.

Her tears started to flow again as she studied her grandmother's notes. "She would like *Danny Boy* sung at the service. She listed a name and phone number—I'll call him to see if he can do it."

"That's fine, Dr. Maguire. It's a common request among our Irish parishioners."

"Father, you haven't had any reports of unusual illness, including the visiting priest who took care of the confessions?"

"No, and the student's family never reached out for assistance."

While Maya talked to the funeral home again to request the wake for Monday evening, her parents eased through the front door, as quiet as the winter mist. Maya confirmed with them the service timeline before they retreated to her grandmother's bedroom. The closed door muffled her mom's weak sobs and her dad's soft consoling voice.

"How are you holding up, Maya?" Manolo handed her a cup of peppermint tea.

"Muddling through, thanks." She reached down to calm the roaming cat. "I'd love it if you could go through Grandma's address book and notify people about the services."

"Sure. How about your friends?"

"I'll tell Janey and Nancy when I check in about our coronavirus investigation, but first I want to draft this obituary."

She flipped to the next page in her grandmother's notes.

Barbara, Tom and Maya, If you're looking at this closely, my time to move on has come. Please remember all the wonderful years we shared, and don't fret about the future. When you write me up, avoid flowery language like the plague (a little joke for Maya) because no one will recognize me. Say that Martha Robinson was a kickass math teacher, always working for the best for her students. After years of separation from her beloved Liam, she's gone to join him in a better place.

Maya followed instructions and handwrote a simple death announcement. As Manolo typed it into his laptop, she called Phoenix, almost ready to hang up before Nancy came on the line. "Uh, hi. I was just dozing. What's up?"

"I'm sorry to disturb you." Maya couldn't recall Nancy taking naps before, except for yesterday afternoon after the press conference. "How are you feeling? I can imagine it was stressful announcing one of the first corona cases in the country."

"Hopefully it will have no more long-term impact than SARS. Nicky's family physician in Tucson will submit another lab test on Monday. If negative, Nicky can come back here for school."

"Father Cassidy's unaware of other ill parishioners, which is good news considering Nicky was at St. Agnes twice last weekend." Maya took a deep breath. "But there's another reason I called Father Cassidy. He's arranging the funeral mass and wake for my grandma. She died of a heart attack around noon."

"Oh my God, Maya. What a shock. How's your family doing?"

"My parents were down for the weekend, so she wasn't alone." Maya had a flick of guilt over whether her grandma could have survived if she and Manolo had been with her when it happened. Maybe Manolo would have picked up an early sign.

"Grandma was at St. Agnes around the same time as Nicky, and in the tiny confessional booth minutes after him, from what we can piece together."

"Hmm, we think of coronaviruses as causing respiratory illness, although we also had gastrointestinal signs with SARS. I'm not sure it could cause a heart attack, with no prodrome."

"Manolo is doing a PubMed search on his laptop."

"I'm happy he's there to support you." Nancy's voice kicked into gear, back to its old assertive tone. "Without fever or symptoms of lower respiratory tract illness, your grandmother doesn't meet the criteria for testing. But I'll authorize samples and work with CDC to arrange it, just in case."

"Sounds good. It was Tucson Medical Center."

"It's a long shot but may provide you closure."

When Maya said goodbye, Manolo asked, "Is Nancy following up with the hospital?"

"She'll see if they have specimens that can be tested." Maya swallowed hard—it was difficult thinking of her grandma as only tissues for testing.

"I found an article about the first forty-one cases in Wuhan," Manolo said. "Five had acute cardiac injury, but they also had viral pneumonia."

Maya lowered to the chair next to him. "I don't remember anything about cardiac arrest in either of the two reports CDC released this week."

Manolo shook his head. "The case fatality rate for SARS was much higher than what they're finding with this current outbreak."

At the sound of an opening door, Maya turned her head, wishing she had insisted on a medical checkup for her grandmother after learning of the St. Agnes connection.

Maya's mom, a head taller than her husband, rested her arm around his shoulders but strode with strong steps into the kitchen. "Enough time giving into grief. What needs doing?"

"We've got it covered." Maya angled the laptop toward her parents as they sat down at the table. "Can you look over this draft obituary?"

Computer keys clicked as her mom made a few edits, then turned the screen back to Maya. "You did a good job—Grandma would be proud."

Buoyed by the unexpected compliment, Maya rose to check the cheerless refrigerator. "You all relax and I'll cook dinner. Tomorrow should be a better day." Maybe not better, but a different day, a fresh day. Even as nature wept.

THIRTEEN

Tucson, Arizona—Monday, February 10, 2020

"My God, what have you done to her?" Maya's mom prostrated herself over the open casket in a desolate keen.

The funeral home director swung between Maya and her mother. "I'm sorry, I don't know what you mean."

"You've made her skin a different shade—I don't recognize her."

The director cleared his throat. "I apologize. When Dr. Maguire stopped by yesterday, I assumed a biological connection like a mixed marriage at some point. I used her coloring as a guide."

Maya encircled her mother's waist. "Mom, I didn't even think about them using makeup—the subject never came up."

Holding open the door to the front lobby, the director adopted his most grave and obsequious facial expression. "I can see her skin tone should have been closer to yours, Mrs. Maguire. Let me take care of it."

Maya's grip on her mother tightened. "Please, Mom, it will be fine. Some of your friends might have arrived early. Let's say hello."

After dropping her mom off to her dad and one of their UofA classmates, she spotted her Santa Fe colleagues and joined them. She hugged Stephanie and Erika, then shook Dr. Grinwold's hand.

"Thank you for driving so far, especially since you never met Grandma."

"I've made the drive to Arizona many times over the years. It's no problem with these two chatty ladies to keep me awake. We picked up Nancy in Phoenix—she's around somewhere."

"You were so close to your grandma." Stephanie smiled and

held Maya's hand. "All those work trips to Tucson when I didn't have to bill the state for your hotel."

Erika squeezed Maya's arm. "Rolf sends his regards and regrets. These winter months are the busiest at Tax and Rev, plus he's managing Kyle."

"Of course," Maya said, "this would be too much for a six-year-old. He still has all four grandparents, right?"

"Eight." Erika laughed. "Our parents are divorced with remarriages. So Kyle gets an overwhelming number of birthday and Christmas gifts."

Maya's spirits picked up with her friend's joke. Was it sacrilegious to find any joy under the circumstances? But the clamp around her heart eased.

Dave and Ben strolled over to join the group. Beneath the funeral home's fluorescents, Ben doffed his Panama hat to expose his bald pate polished to a sheen. "Maya, we're so sorry to hear of your loss."

"I appreciate the two of you joining us."

"Nowhere else we'd want to be," Dave said. "This gave me a good reason to follow-up with Ben on a *Clostridium* outbreak in an unvaccinated cattle herd. By the way, Emilia sends her good wishes to your family."

"Thanks, Dave. I can't wait to see your wife and kids again. There's no better place to relax than your home."

Ben shifted his weight. "We have an update for you. The family's cat tested negative for feline coronavirus at the commercial lab."

"I made sure samples went to our lab in Ames for 2019-nCoV testing," Dave added. "In China, panicked people are throwing cats and dogs from apartment blocks while volunteers care for Wuhan pets abandoned by fleeing owners."

Ben nodded. "People in Beijing and Shanghai are rushing to find face masks for their dogs, and in a pinch, making them out of paper cups."

Everyone was panicked about pets, and Maya glanced again at her ankle.

The funeral home director poked his head through the door and waved down Maya. She excused herself and joined him inside.

"Could you check our redo of your grandmother's makeup? I don't want to bother your mother."

Maya stepped tentatively toward the dark green casket with a gold band near the bottom. Green was her grandmother's favorite color, harkening back to her Irish heritage. The top half of the lid was draped in white fabric. She steeled herself for another look at her grandmother's lifeless form in the simple emerald dress. But this time was better—Grandma looked like herself, just sleeping, hair in the neat white bun. Maya gripped the coffin's edge, then wiped away tears. "This will make Mom happy," she assured the man. "Thank you."

His lips turned up in a slight smile. "I'm so relieved. All we had was her black and white photo from the obituary. We should have asked for a color one or consulted you more closely."

When he indicated they were ready, Maya opened the doors to welcome guests. Her mom approached first and leaned into the casket for a kiss, holding the still hands with the rosary for a long minute. After her dad did the same, he invited others to join them.

Once the line thinned, he stood in front of the mourners assembled on folding chairs. "We'd appreciate hearing anything you'd like to share about our wonderful Martha Robinson. I can kick us off. I first met Martha when Barbara and I were UofA seniors. She scrutinized me like a germ under a microscope. Was I too short or too quiet, unable to keep up with their religious arguments?"

"You know what it was, Tom," Maya's mom inserted. "His hair was longer than mine."

The group chuckled, gloom dissipated.

"So I wised up and cut it off—joining this family of strong women was worth it."

Maya, seated next to Manolo, rose to her feet, one hand steadied on his shoulder. "I loved hearing her play Irish jigs on her fiddle, until her arthritis got too bad. Music and math, some people say they go together."

"Speaking of which . . ." Maya's dad headed to a side table and an iPod hooked up to speakers. "Martha ordered us to play her favorite tunes. Despite being a traditionalist, she enjoyed younger fiddlers like Eileen Ivers."

The solo somber notes of *Caoine Ui Domhnaill* filled the room, in synch with the pensive mood. "Maya, she wanted you to have her violin," her mom added. "I know you're devoted to piano, but perhaps you can take lessons."

A dark-haired woman in her fifties stood to take her turn. "Mrs. Robinson could be tough. She chewed me out for making a paper fan to cool down during a sweltering class. According to her, I was generating more heat from my body movement than it was doing me any good." Smiles broke with nods of agreement. "But when I struggled with calculus, she stayed late every night until I got it."

Manolo spoke from his seat, holding Maya's hand. "I got lucky, meeting her in the more relaxed retirement phase. If I greeted her cat Hypatia right after entering the front door, I was a 'fine thing,' as she used to call me."

The stories continued for an hour. Maya was amazed by the number of former students, in addition to St. Agnes parishioners and her parents' friends from Flagstaff. Martha Robinson had a wide reach.

Maya finally hugged Nancy hello after the gathering, as both of them stood close to Dr. Grinwold. "Thank you so much for coming," Maya said. "I know you're not Catholic so no need to stay overnight for the Mass tomorrow."

Dr. Grinwold reached out an arm to hug Nancy's shoulders. His voice was graveled, filled with emotion. "It was a lovely event to honor her, a good reminder of how we impact others, however long we have." His brown eyes dropped to meet Nancy's.

She pinched his arm. "Don't go soft on me, you old coot."

He ignored her jibe. "Maya, our carload is staying the night. We'll see you at St. Agnes tomorrow."

Dave approached from behind and touched Maya's elbow. "Ben and I are taking off; unfortunately we can't join you at the Mass."

"We need to be at Wickenburg on the clostridial problem by noon," Ben added. "The dead cattle have reddish-black leg muscles which crackle when pressing on the skin. Initial lab tests identified *C. chauvoei*. Like with anthrax, the risk increases with extreme weather stirring up spores in the soil, but it's unusual to have winter cases."

"No problem, I appreciate your coming tonight. I'm just happy blackleg isn't zoonotic."

Manolo's expression was hesitant. "I treated a guy who ran into an iron pipe at a construction site. Despite a minor chest wound with that organism, he suffered cardiopulmonary arrest. We brought him back, but he only lived two hours. The chest scan showed destruction of muscle tissue and gas contamination in arteries and veins."

"Wow, we're a fun crowd," Dave said. "Maya, don't get your brain going on its hamster wheel. You concentrate on family while Ben and I attack the animal diseases."

Maya hugged her colleagues goodbye, then rounded on Manolo. "Why did you bring up that case and get me panicked about another potential outbreak?"

He shrugged, sheepish. "They should know that human cases are possible."

She wiped her hand across her eyes. "Sorry, I don't know why I'm snapping at you again. Reminds me of my months on Klonopin, which reduced my anxiety so much I constantly ran off at the mouth, offending everyone."

"But you stopped those meds in August. Besides the coronavirus and your grandmother's death, is anything else bothering you?"

She lowered to one of the chairs. "The wedding, new jobs, and my mother's pressure." Don't forget Enzo, a little gremlin on her shoulder whispered.

"Let me do more planning. Maybe your mom will be nicer to me about it than she is to you—sometimes it works out that way."

"I'll consider it, once the Mass and burial are over."

She cornered the funeral director who had closed the casket and reminded him of the next day's schedule. Stooped over the guest book, her parents reviewed the entries with hushed voices. Maya joined them in a family circle.

. . .

Tucson, Arizona—Tuesday, February 11, 2020

The soaring tenor voice of the large-chested man swelled the vast spaces beneath the vaulted ceiling of St. Agnes. Unused to crying at all, let alone in public, Maya dabbed at her tears with Manolo's handkerchief. Maya's mom took Communion as the remaining practicing Catholic in the family, and Maya's soul filled with solace from the ancient rituals and prayers said in Latin.

By noon in All Faiths Memorial Park, sparkling blue skies belied the serious mood. Father Cassidy said another prayer as the coffin containing Martha's cremains was guided into the interior vault. Maya helped her mother adjust the silk flowers on the outer door, a mixture of pink, purple, and white lilies. Her parents drove back to the apartment for a rest, after Maya promised to pick them up later for dinner.

Maya's carload of colleagues waited for her in the parking lot. "We're heading out to Phoenix," Dr. Grinwold said.

Nancy slipped her arm in Maya's and pulled her aside, out of earshot from the others. "Antibodies were found in your grandmother's serum sample, but cross-reactions can occur between coronaviruses. We're following up with CDC, so we don't know what this means at the moment."

Maya's muscles turned mushy and she braced her hands behind her waist to support her back. "You're right, we shouldn't get ahead of ourselves. But I'm glad you checked on it. Any chance I can convince you not to retire? I can't imagine public health without you."

Shoulders shrugged, head tilted, expression pensive—nothing in Nancy's body language gave Maya reason to hope.

FOURTEEN

Tucson, Arizona—Friday, February 14, 2020

"Happy twenty-seventh birthday, Maya!" Her dad dropped a plate overfull with blueberry pancakes in front of her, followed by a second one for Manolo. The steamy aroma was a warm balm, especially after she dribbled maple syrup on top. She lowered her face and took a deep inhale, then carved off the first bite with her fork.

"It's no cake but I love this, Dad."

"Do you think we should add a candle?" Manolo asked with a grin.

Maya held her hands over the plate. "Don't even dare to interrupt this beauty. In fact, let me take a photo." She grabbed her phone to snap the picture and send it to Facebook. Between the Yuca frita con chicharron and Marquesote cake at Óscar's restaurant the night before, Maya's stomach still felt full.

Words caught in her throat as her eyes moistened. "Grandma would have loved all this. Where's Mom and Hypatia, by the way?"

"After our celebration yesterday on Chinese time, she stayed up late sorting Martha's things. She and Hypatia are sleeping in."

"Sorry I haven't been more help. Contact tracing to make sure Nicky hasn't spread his infection has taken all my time. We dodged a bullet—no cases related to his home, neighborhood, church, or mall visit."

Her dad dug into his own pancakes. "Luckily Martha was her thorough self with all these notes on who's getting what. Manolo, I appreciate your help in moving furniture to friends or the donation center."

"Are you keeping the rental truck to bring any of it up to Flagstaff?" Manolo asked.

"Our apartment's full, but I'm sure we'll keep something."

"Dad, I'm relieved you can take Hypatia," Maya said. "But I'm not sure how she'll greet the cold weather."

Her dad laughed. "When we left a week ago, we had a foot of snow in our tiny backyard. Can't wait to see the cat's expression when she spots it from her post next to the window."

"I'm glad Mom let Hypatia sleep with her. Poor kitty's been disoriented with Grandma gone."

"Do you really have to head up to Phoenix after breakfast?" her dad asked.

Maya glanced over to Manolo. "Yeah, Enzo might need help with community college contacts and Manolo has work commitments."

"There's an epidemic of battered, missing, and murdered Native American women." Manolo rubbed the back of his neck. "We have a big task force meeting today."

"We're grateful you both could be here. Let me rouse Barbara so you can say goodbye."

. . .

Maya had returned her rental car to the Tucson airport days earlier. When they headed back to Phoenix, she dozed as Manolo drove. Her sleep had been disturbed all week. The death of her grandmother generated too many horror nightmares. Tuesday night, she was taking a photo at the Grand Canyon when Grandma stepped back too far and fell over the rim. Thursday morning, a mountain lion leapt out between palo verdes and dragged Grandma from a picnic table at Saguaro National Park. Once Maya awakened, the visions were too ludicrous to share.

Recognizing the state health building, she scrubbed her eyes and reached for her bag. "You know, I never asked how you managed to get this."

"The Corvette or the back seat?"

"Either, both." She dug in her purse for a scrunchie to pull her hair into some semblance of put-together.

"I bought it from a guy in Scottsdale. He loved his 'Vette too much to put it through Minnesota's winters and salty roads when he moved. He paid for the back seat remodel at purchase."

"It sure came in handy when you were using the wheelchair."

"An awkward fit, but we made it work. What time should I pick you up?"

"I'll let you know." She leaned over for a quick kiss. "See you later."

Inside on the second floor, she located Nancy in her office. "Thanks again for coming to my grandmother's services. Our whole family feels so close to you since Manolo's hospitalization. They said to make sure you know how much your support means to us."

Nancy crossed her hands over her heart and smiled, then waved Maya to a chair facing her desk. "The feeling's mutual, Maya. I've been thinking about what you said after the burial on Tuesday."

"Are you reconsidering retirement?" Maya's body pulsed with hope.

"Even though we got through SARS, I have an uneasy feeling about this new virus. I've never seen China in such a panic, and cases are slowly ramping up here. CDC's still developing their serologic test so we don't have anything definitive on your grandmother."

"Are they working on any other samples?"

"Wires got crossed with my instructions and no additional tissues were taken. It's too late now that she's been cremated."

Maya's buzz turned into a jolt. "We'll never know."

"Without any symptoms, I doubt she was contagious. Your family is all well, I assume?"

Maya nodded. "So what about retirement?"

"I'm meeting Fred at our favorite Pinetop resort to work it out. Arizona doesn't have anyone with sufficient experience to take over. Enzo's drive and confidence are impressive, but he's new to the job, and sometimes rubs people the wrong way. I already gave him a heads up."

Without Maya revealing the sexual assaults, Nancy was picking up on Enzo's issues. If she wasn't supporting Enzo as her successor, maybe Maya wouldn't need to stir the pot. She'd be thrilled if Nancy stayed on as State Epi. Perhaps working with Enzo would be tolerable if Nancy was still the boss.

But she shouldn't be selfish. "You've been exhausted lately—is your health up to continuing?"

"This new virus could be a game changer, requiring all hands on deck."

Maya shifted on the chair, conflicted feelings raging. "Dr. Grinwold will literally murder me if he thinks I influenced your decision. He's been so excited at the prospect of your moving to Santa Fe."

"He'll get over it. At our age, we're not rushing off to start a family, like you and Manolo."

"Yeah, we never made any progress this week in our planning. Forgive the gallows humor, but Grandma dying was the only thing to get Mom off my back."

"We should talk about establishing a State Public Health Veterinarian position here. I got the sense moving to Phoenix wasn't high on your list, but Manolo staying on with the Indian Health Service would be a huge advantage."

Nancy's first explicit mention of an Arizona job—Maya needed to consider it seriously, and not let Enzo factor into the decision.

"This is Enzo's report on the community college contact tracing." Nancy lifted the reading glasses hanging from the chain over her chest. "It looks like he's on top of it, but stop by his office to make sure he doesn't need your help. When I see Fred tonight, I'll tell him to expect you back in Santa Fe on Monday. Maybe that will put a blanket on his blowup when I drop on him my change of plans."

Maya stood to leave. "I'm thrilled you might stay on, and that would influence my decision to take a job here." But she remembered all those times recently when Nancy was spacy or weak. Nancy could be seriously slipping. Maya gulped before potentially derailing her option to work for Nancy full-time. "See how things go before making a final decision. If anyone deserves time off, it's you."

Nancy also rose and rounded the desk to give Maya a hug. "You're so sweet to worry about me with everything on your plate." She walked to the window and raised the blinds to admit the streaming sunlight. "Check in with Enzo, then enjoy this weekend with your handsome fiancé. I think he's even more attractive than Lin-Manuel Miranda. Manolo doesn't sing or rap, does he?"

. . .

Maya plodded down the hall to Enzo's office, reluctant to see him or the *Chinese Girl* on the back of his door. During their fight a week ago at the picnic table, she told him she was undecided about her next decisions. He might be expecting an answer, but she was no closer to sorting it out. The only relief was Nancy maybe, possibly, staying in her job.

His door was closed, and she knocked. It flew open, bringing her face-to-face with his glowering expression. "Nancy comes back from Tucson and dumps on me that she's not retiring. Did you have something to do with that?"

At the entrance without going in, Maya put her hands on her hips. "Your condolences on the death of my grandmother are much appreciated, Enzo."

"Oh, so you got my flowers, that's good." His face went from annoyed to livid. "With that extra time together, you lobbied for her job. She's waiting until you're available in July, right?"

Maya formed both hands into fists, then relaxed the left one with the residual pain from the missing finger. "Enzo, you couldn't be more off base. I'm here to assist with college contacts."

"I knew she didn't trust me. But I have it all under control and Astrid's helping."

Raising an eyebrow, Maya couldn't restrain her snark. "And what does vector control have to do with coronavirus?"

"Nancy values people with multiple skills and Astrid wants to prove her worth, too."

His stubborn need to be on top played into Maya's own intentions. "Good, then Nancy said I can go home to Santa Fe."

He kicked at the door jamb, clearly aware he'd been

outmaneuvered. "What kind of cunt would leave me hanging? Tell me what you said to her."

Maya wished she had the foresight to record him on her iPhone. She flashed a sardonic smile. "I can't imagine what you're talking about."

After glancing both ways down the hall, he dropped his tone to a whisper. "Don't play coy with me."

"I'll get back to you on that." Maya pivoted for the building's front door, stopping only long enough in the lobby to text Manolo. Then she burst into the sunshine, a powerful antiseptic for her haunt and dread.

FIFTEEN

Phoenix, Arizona—Saturday, February 15, 2020

But she wasn't dead—Grandma only needed assistance on the crisp December day, telephone poles entwined with Christmas strands and wreaths dangling beneath the street lights. Maya waved at Manolo as he parked his Corvette by the curb and she wheeled her grandmother to the passenger side door. Grandma smiled and said, "Thanks, dear." She lowered into the seat, adjusted her winter wool coat, and fastened her seat belt. Maya closed the car door and took one step back with the wheelchair, careful not to slip on the icy sidewalk. The loud throttle of an engine ahead triggered her attention. She raised her eyes as a Hummer hurtled on the wrong side of the road straight toward Manolo's car. Just before the vehicles collided, she spotted Enzo's pale eyes and leering grin through the windshield. She jerked violently out of the way and fell out of bed, screaming.

"Maya, what's wrong?" Strong hands reached over to pull her up. She kept thrashing, struggling to unglue her eyelids. Manolo tugged her into a tight embrace, naked skin to naked skin, the warmth insisting the vision wasn't real.

Her fingers caressed his back, then lowered. "Oh, God," she muttered, "just another nightmare. I'm losing track of how many I've had this week. Take me now—wipe everything else from my mind."

He didn't need a second invitation, and for a short time, the sensations drove away all the demons. Panting after their coordinated climax, she brushed the curl back from his forehead, "Boy, do I love your dark eyes."

"You'd kick me out of bed if I wasn't Puerto Rican?"

She tongued each of his ear lobes. "With your creative role-playing, don't ever wear lighter contact lenses."

He drew back to study her expression. "Got it—no white boys."

Grimacing, she dragged her engagement ring on the left hand across his muscled belly. "Now you're making me sound prejudiced."

"No, I'm just thrilled to meet your specifications."

Her feet hit the floor and she located the cat slippers under the bedframe. Grabbing the red silk gown he gave her after the flash-bang injury, she wrapped it around her body and dropped to the rocking chair. "Sure glad you have a rocker; it's so comforting. Were you thinking of babies when you bought it?"

"Angela chewed me out royally. She accused me of pressuring her to get pregnant." He slapped his open hand against his cheek. "Shit, not sure why I said that."

Maya tugged him down to her lap. "You shouldn't be afraid to talk about your ex. I don't even know what she looks like—guess I should have Googled. Do you have a type?"

"I never thought about it. Angela's dad, a surgeon like her, is Black, and her mom's a nurse who emigrated from the Philippines."

Maya shifted his weight to a more comfortable position. "Does it bother you that she never came to visit when you were near death, or during those long months of rehab? You were married for eight years."

He placed a kiss between her scrunched eyebrows. "Angela checked up on me through Ramona."

"Your sister should have said something."

"Cariña, Ramona's your biggest fan. I'm sure she didn't intend to hurt you. Tell me about your nightmare."

Maya pushed on his chest with her fists, urging him to get up. "I'm forgetting details already." She had no interest in wasting their weekend on Enzo. At some point, she'd probably have to reveal what he had done, but if Manolo's family kept secrets, she could too.

He reached for his robe on the closet door hook, then lifted her from the rocking chair. "If we're moving away from Phoenix when your EIS training is done, we've got to fit in the Heard Museum."

"I'd love to do something fun." Diversion, distraction, anything to deflect.

. . .

Inside the white-washed, tile-roofed complex, they started first with a special exhibition of Yosemite iPad drawings by a British artist. "You've lived longer in the Southwest than me. Have you ever been there?" Manolo asked.

"We made it to the national park once. I prefer your wonderful black-and-white landscape photos. Other than the Grand Canyon, I haven't seen you taking pictures."

"Too preoccupied, but I can start again on our honeymoon in Africa."

Maya shifted over to the basketry made by Miwok and Mono Lake Paiute women. "Aren't these incredible? I wish my hands had that talent."

Manolo's lips caressed her fingers. "You're plenty good with them to satisfy me."

She led him over to a Hopi katsina. "I've never seen one like this, yucca and galleta grass, whatever that is. If you buy me a wedding gift, a carved animal would be spectacular." Like an eager child, she dashed over to the Zuni silver and turquoise jewelry. "Or a concho belt, not museum quality of course."

He laughed at her enthusiasm. "You can get me a bolo tie." He lingered at one with three silver kokopellis above a rectangular turquoise stone.

Maya's stomach grumbled loud enough for her to twist in embarrassment. "My body says it's time for lunch."

Manolo led her out to the courtyard café and chose one of the umbrella-shaded tables.

Maya fingered the menu. "I'm tempted by this Dreamcatcher salad. I wonder if the gift shop has a dreamcatcher for sale. I could hang it over my bed to ward off nightmares. Can we check after lunch?"

He nodded. "Your salad's wheat berries come from the Gila River Indian Reservation." He patted his white shirt in the stomach area. "This growing guy needs something more filling. Grilled cheese packed with roasted red bell pepper, fresh spinach, five cheeses, and bomba hot sauce."

The waiter brought them tall glasses of prickly pear lemonade, and Maya savored the watermelon-bubble gum flavor. "I hate that Grandma's passing was the cause of it, but you avoided Mom pinning you to an insect spreading board about our plans."

He laughed. "I think she holds me in higher regard than that. But have you thought any more about it?"

"Yesterday, Nancy mentioned creating a public health vet position. There's a national goal of a veterinarian in every state health department, like they have with the state ag agencies."

"I can imagine Dr. Grinwold might be thinking along the same lines. Has he said anything?"

Maya shook her head.

"Don't take that as a negative. Maybe he's overly confident the allure of New Mexico will keep you there."

"Have you looked at jobs with the Albuquerque Indian Health Center?"

"Fred said he can put in a good word for me." His skin flushed darker. "Sorry, that's awkward."

Maya swallowed her irritation that they'd had the discussion without her, then chatted amiably during the meal about what it might be like to live in New Mexico permanently. When the waiter asked about dessert, she eyed the menu listing fry bread.

"I haven't had this since my *Borrelia* investigation at Havasu Falls."

"We can share one if you're too full."

Everything about her first joint study with Enzo flooded back. Surely Manolo wouldn't pop off and do something rash if she finally confided in him. "That trip was incredibly tough, physically and mentally. Plus we were estranged—I worried about our relationship the whole time."

He placed the order. "Havasu Falls is such an iconic place—I always thought it would be me and you. Instead, your first time was for work, with that asshole Enzo."

"Manolo, I told you he's my hesitation about moving here. Working for Nancy would be wonderful but her health may not allow her to continue." She took a deep breath as the fry bread and honey was delivered. "Enzo's an issue even if Nancy's still the boss. He's overstepped—"

She was about to say "boundaries" when her phone rang with a call from Janey.

"Remember Zuba, the lion we heard roaring at the Tucson zoo? He's got a cough, sneezing, lethargy and nasal discharge. I need to return a call to a local TV station."

Maya surveyed the crowded tables and excused herself for a quieter spot. "Seems a stretch, but I'll check into whether zoo animals have tested positive for the virus."

She eyed the mammoth palm trees along the perimeter of the museum grounds and took slow breaths of the gentle cool breeze to counter her anxiety. Things were getting more complicated, and maybe she needed to stay in Arizona. Was there any chance Nicky had visited the zoo without telling her or Janey? She clicked through her contact list and pressed her thumb on Faye Simpson's name.

"Howdy, Maya, I'm plumb done in by gloomy sleet out my window." The voice retained a down-home Colorado rancher tone despite decades in NYC. "So don't tell me about your sunny, warm weather. How're you holding up; did you get my flowers?"

"Thanks, Faye, they were beautiful. Mom and Dad are cleaning out Grandma's place, and I'm flying back to Albuquerque tomorrow. You know I've been working on a case of this disease they're now calling COVID-19."

"Sure, we have one too, someone who flew here from Wuhan."

"One of the zoo lions has a respiratory illness and they're including COVID in the differential diagnoses. Ever since vet school, I think of you as my topline expert on zoonotic diseases."

Maya heard slurping which immediately conjured up an image

of the NYC public health veterinarian kicking back with a Big Gulp in her hand. Memories crowded in of intense but exciting summer days at her internship, with Faye the nurturing and humorous core.

As a winter gust prickled her skin, Maya pulled her sweater tighter. "Can you remind me of all the animals implicated in earlier coronavirus outbreaks?"

"China banned exotic species sales after SARS, then allowed them again when the disease vanished, like we did here after prairie dogs and monkeypox. We let down our guard when threats aren't killing people right and left. Now China has eight times the number of infections as SARS and sixty million people under lockdown, but they still haven't permanently banned the sale of wildlife."

Maya rounded the corner of the gift shop and headed back to the calmer climate of the café courtyard. If she chose her words of response, she could avoid letting slip anything confidential.

Manolo offered a piece of fry bread with honey-sticky fingers, and invited her to sit down. "Better eat your half or there'll be nothing left."

Maya mouthed "go ahead" and settled into the chair as Faye alternated Slurpee swallows and zoonotic syllables. Scary syllables.

SIXTEEN

Phoenix, Arizona—Saturday, February 15, 2020

Maya welcomed the light windbreaker Manolo draped around her shoulders when she shivered in the brisk breeze. As he cleared away their lunch dishes, he left her alone in the Heard Museum courtyard to finish her call to NYC.

"SARS happened when I was only ten so it didn't register," she told Faye. "Helping you with Middle Eastern Respiratory Syndrome in London during vet school was amazing."

"Too bad you couldn't join me working with those camels in Saudi Arabia."

Maya glanced around to verify no one sitting close. "Anything come out of your study there?"

"Thirteen percent of camel semen samples were positive. In breeding season, human infections also increase." Faye snickered. "I wonder what accounts for that?"

The cooler air and tension over her first emerging viral disease frosted Maya's attitude. "Everything from SARS or MERS might not apply to this new coronavirus."

Faye's deep voice croaked like a bullfrog. "You're right, I took a side road and your patience. Respiratory transmission is more likely than sexual."

A sudden gust swooshed a museum handout into the air, then under Maya's table. She retrieved it and weighed postponing the conversation. "Faye, I need to get out of this bad weather. Can I call back later?"

"Sure, hun, I'll be home, doing my rare housecleaning."

. . .

Nestled into Manolo's rocking chair, Maya rolled her feet from ball to heel, creating a gentle soothing motion. She glanced at the time, unsure how long he'd be gone to the grocery store.

"That was quick," Faye said when answering the phone.

To counter her anxiety, Maya pulled an afghan blanket around her shoulders, the crocheted worsted conferring her grandmother's warmth and fortitude through her skin. "I want to finish our discussion."

A half-truth. She had more on her mind than the microbe. "We were talking about MERS transmission."

"Yes, the virus was detected in camel nasal swabs and breath samples. Evidence was mixed on risks from camel urine, milk, and meat. But with 2019-nCoV, we don't have direct links to animals. Sorry, I mean SARS-CoV-2. The World Health Organization renamed the virus this week."

"Tucson has a lion with respiratory signs." Not many had that information but the zoo staff were freaking out because of the public alarm about the human case.

"I've got connections with the Bronx Zoo, which uses its animals as surveillance sentinels. Also, Cornell University has animal testing."

"Great resources, thanks." Maya relaxed tight muscles with an image of her happy place, floating in the ocean, then ventured a high dive. "Remember last summer when I mentioned problems with the Arizona EIS Officer, Enzo Russo?"

"He dropped trou when answering your FaceTime call, and he's a bully. Did something else happen?"

Six weeks had passed since Maya detailed Enzo's transgressions to Dr. Kim, and a month since informing her attorney, but only a week since confronting Enzo. His focus had shifted to another more willing workplace conquest, yet he seemed to deliberately bump her feet under the table on New Year's Eve. And he clearly hadn't grasped how his actions impacted Maya.

"Faye, please promise not to mention this to anyone."

"Sounds serious. What did he do?"

The back door banged. "Give me a sec." Maya checked it, phone in hand. But no one was there. Manolo probably forgot to close it tight when he left. She locked it, then sank into a kitchen chair to keep an eye out for his return. What was that Sandburg poem about fog coming in on little cat feet? Perhaps the gloomy mist was alive and pawing at Manolo's door.

She took a deep breath and screwed up her courage. "When we were together for work, but not in the office, Enzo forced a kiss and later groped me."

Faye's voice deepened further. "I know how you mull things over before sharing. Are you sure nothing else happened?"

Maya shivered. "If you mean rape, no. He claims he's attracted to me and it was an aggressive come-on. He thought Manolo and I were broken up, which we were."

"There's not much tolerance for such behavior in the workplace these days. Did you blow the whistle on him?"

"Not officially. I was embarrassed talking about it to a counseling center support group. My situation's mild compared to other women, but my lawyer said a police report could result in misdemeanor sexual assault charges."

"You're in a tough spot. I mentioned once that our female EIS Officer was transferred after something inappropriate happened to her. Then Dr. Moskowitz established a zero tolerance policy." Faye chuckled. "Guess he didn't want to lose another trainee."

Seconds ticked by, then Faye continued. "I won't squeal on you, but if I were your supervisor, I'd want you to tell me."

Maya leapt up from the chair and paced the tiles of Manolo's kitchen floor. "I'm paralyzed by all the consequences. My job, Enzo's. Manolo's overprotectiveness. Whether anyone would believe me with my panic disorder. I couldn't bear any public scrutiny. After all, Enzo stopped before things got worse; not immediately, but quickly enough. Maybe I should chalk it up to foreplay, like he said."

"W-e-l-l." Faye prolonged the word before plunging ahead. "I realize this could get messy with dueling stories, but I still think you should tell someone. Which supervisor are you closest to?"

"Nancy Bingham. But I've tried before, and she's so happy with Enzo. She's got a lot going on—I'm not sure how much more she can handle without jeopardizing her health."

"Maya, if it was one and done for the kiss or the groping, perhaps you could set it aside. But only if he was truly apologetic and you believed it wouldn't happen again. This is clearly getting you down and distracting you, when you should be proud of your well-earned confidence gained during EIS training. And Manolo—how can you marry him if you're hiding something like this?"

The wind blew pebbles from his patio against the kitchen windows. Maya startled with the noise but refocused on ending the call before Manolo returned. "I think it's too late. Twice we've had major blowups over secrets. This might be third strike and I'm out."

"I can't advise you about that. I let everything get in the way of committing to a long-term relationship. But I'm old and terribly set in my ways—you're not. Rip the bandage off soon."

The characteristic growl of the Corvette penetrated the glass panes, and Maya promised to use Faye as a sounding board in her decision-making.

. . .

Santa Fe, New Mexico—Tuesday, February 25, 2020

Every day, Maya checked her messages for lab results on the Tucson lion. An agonizing wait to find out if the virus was spreading invisibly through the city. Should they close the zoo with one symptomatic animal? She was thankful Nicky's human contacts yielded no new illnesses. Finally, Faye apologized on a FaceTime call. "Cornell's Animal Health Diagnostic Center didn't find anything on your zoo cat."

Maya thought Faye looked more disappointed than relieved. Like many epidemiologists, Faye tended to be energized by new disease outbreaks.

"So the patient's only possible spread was to Grandma."

With the back of her hand, Maya wiped away tears, still prone to spill ten days after the death. Work distracted from pain, yet pain imbued work with poignancy.

"I still can't believe she's gone, from a disease I'm supposed to control."

Faye's wrinkles cratered in concern. "I'm so sorry for your loss, but she didn't meet the criteria for a case."

"No typical clinical signs or proven close contact with another infected person. But her antibody levels are presumptive evidence."

The camera view jerked to the ceiling with the sound of Faye's fingers tapping on the keyboard. "We have fifty-three cases in the US and older adults are at greater risk for severe illness. How would the patient have spread the virus to your grandmother?"

Faye reoriented her phone and Maya answered. "The visiting priest remembered she was in the confessional booth after a college-age man. But the priest stayed healthy, so that little barrier likely protected him."

The view temporarily tilted again as Faye leaned back in her chair and Maya heard shoes thump the desk. "Your grandmother had a heart attack, unrelated to COVID. It may sound callous, but we all get old."

Maya closed her office door and glanced out at the dirty snow almost obscuring the light through her high window. "I have a tendency to catastrophize."

"You're a spider, spinning her web to catch clues. Being hyperalert in epidemiology can be an asset, as well as a curse."

Maya's tears transformed into a giggle. "Not the most flattering image."

"I didn't say a black widow."

Maya tried to redirect the focus away from her. "Are you still tied up with screening at the NYC airports?"

"I'm headed to LaGuardia with our EIS Officer. Have you done anything about Enzo Russo?"

Maya groaned. "I'm overwhelmed helping with New Mexico's COVID surveillance. But I'll be in Arizona for a friend's birthday on Saturday, and will try to sort it out there."

Faye's complexion became an overripe strawberry, too reminiscent of Maya's mother when upset. "Don't weigh your decision about Enzo too long or the decision may permanently weigh on you."

. . .

Santa Fe, New Mexico—Wednesday, February 26, 2020

Maya looked up from her desk when Stephanie entered her office. She quickly grabbed a tissue for her eyes, embarrassed by the wet streaks on her cheeks. If distance didn't distract from the loss of her grandmother, perhaps time eventually would.

"Everyone else has gone home," the secretary said. "Erika left to pick up Kyle from his afterschool program. It closed early for the storm. She called in and warned that the roads are hard to see in the sleet and slippery as hell."

"I'm wrapping up this *Campylobacter* situation so I can get the weekend off."

"Have you been crying?" Stephanie asked.

Maya scrubbed her face again. "Sorry, I know it's unprofessional." She cursed Dr. Grinwold for assigning her the investigation. An elderly couple became infected from a contaminated cutting board when preparing a romantic fiftieth wedding anniversary supper at home on Valentine's Day.

Stephanie handed over another tissue. "Don't be so hard on yourself. Who wouldn't be moved by the husband dying and the wife paralyzed with Guillain-Barré?"

"Dave will call if USDA testing matches the uncooked chicken in their refrigerator to the *Campy* from their stool samples."

"Want a ride home with me?" Stephanie reached a hand to Maya's shoulder. "Quetzy will be happy for someone else to shriek at, and I'll cook you dinner."

Maya grabbed her purse from the file cabinet and followed Stephanie out the door, both bundled like polar bears against the weather. Stephanie's snow tires made quick work of the drive to her adobe, tucked in west of the railyard.

As Maya relaxed with a glass of red wine, the hyacinth macaw perched on the end of the couch to keep an eye on her. Stephanie warmed tortillas in the wok and slipped them onto plates.

"I usually make my fajitas with chicken but you probably are spooked to eat it right now."

Maya looked up and smiled, grateful that her older friend knew her paranoia so well.

"Tonight I'm using flank steak." Stephanie sautéed marinated meat strips and added multicolored peppers and onions into the hot oil. "Secret to this recipe, have all the hard work of slicing done the night before."

Holding the half-peeled banana that Stephanie had given her, Maya entertained Quetzy as he nibbled. After washing her hands, she set the table, familiar with the home from staying there before.

"Anything else going on?" Stephanie refilled Maya's wine glass.

"Grandma's death hit me hard. My brain accepted her age and the probabilities, but my emotions weren't ready. This couple with the *Campy* is a reminder of life's fragility. We're all a microbe away from doom."

Stephanie took a fajita and ladled it with sour cream. "You sure are in the dumps. But invisible germs aren't responsible for all bad things. My Tony's lung cancer, for example."

"You lost someone you loved, then learned to regroup. You're a great role model." Maya recalled bile duct cancer from eating undercooked fish infected with flatworms, but quibbling about infectious links to cancer wasn't good guest behavior. She moved back to the couch and the macaw who screeched "Hello."

Stephanie covered her uneaten portion with plastic wrap and set it on a refrigerator shelf. "Sure there isn't more on your mind?"

When both women were seated next to each other, Maya continued. "Something Faye Simpson said this week has been festering. She's the NYC vet."

"Yeah, you're always eager to pick her brain about zoonotic risks."

"This time it was about sexual harassment in the workplace."

Stephanie's face scrunched in confusion. "You should talk to Erika—she got that guy locked up."

"My situation wasn't here in New Mexico."

"Thank goodness, I'd hate to think we have another pervert in our midst. Want to tell me more?"

"Not yet. I'm trying to sort it out."

As Maya shivered, Stephanie handed over a knitted throw. "There's so many ways things can go wrong between the sexes. Discrimination, insults, inappropriate language and behavior. When I started working, it was 'go along to get along.' But now, each organization has rules and offices for reporting."

"This situation is unusually complicated." Maya set her glass of wine on the coffee table. "I'm exhausted and should tackle the roads before I'm too sleepy. Can you run me back to the office?"

Stephanie rose to peer through the window. "Snow has stopped. If you're not feeling better by the time we get to your car, I'll drive you all the way home and pick you up tomorrow morning."

"Thanks again for dinner, even though I didn't finish it. I never cook like this for myself."

"I got in the habit with Tony and am happy to share the results with someone." She lifted Quetzy into his floor-to-ceiling cage. "Besides this crotchety one."

"Watch out," the bird croaked.

Stephanie laughed as she grabbed Maya's plate. "Don't mind him, he's always on guard."

Maya prayed that he wasn't prescient, as well. There were no restrictions yet on air travel in the US but the increasing COVID cases worldwide had her wondering. Fortunately her flight between Albuquerque and Phoenix was only a bit more than an hour—nothing to worry about.

SEVENTEEN

Tucson, Arizona—Saturday, February 29, 2020

Maya bent over to wipe up a dust bunny from the corner of the empty bedroom. To keep her hair out of her eyes, she pulled it into a short ponytail. "I'm glad Mom and Dad moved out the furniture and Grandma's stuff. We only have to worry about cleaning."

"Why did they leave the sofa bed in the living room?" Manolo asked.

"It's a bitch to move and the landlord liked it," Maya answered. "I don't mind one more night on it, to remember all the good visits."

Manolo knelt down with a damp rag in his hand. "I'll take care of the dust on these floor moldings if you tackle the sinks. Leave all the lower stuff to me—I don't want you aggravating your back."

She snapped a wet towel toward him but failed to connect. Her words dripped with sarcasm. "You weren't around last summer to keep me from crawling in the dirt with Portuguese pigs. But I'll take advantage of you being a gentleman. Have at it."

An hour later, they perched side-by-side on the sofa, chowing down on croissants picked up during the drive down from Phoenix.

"CDC's predicting COVID to get worse." Maya handed a paper towel to Manolo so he wouldn't drop crumbs.

He nodded, frowning. "Strong chance of an extremely serious outbreak."

"Flu measures might be enough."

As Maya arched her back, Manolo reached over to rub her shoulders. "If we need home quarantines or cancelling public gatherings, how will you pull that off?"

"I'm only a lowly EIS Officer and don't have to figure it out.

Faye mentioned NYC imposed limited school closures in the past for flu."

"Can you imagine if you never immigrated to the US and were caught in those forcible Chinese quarantines? Door-to-door searches, very draconian."

Maya stood up, frustrated by the escaped croissant crumbs on the floor. "I'm going to wet mop before Janey's party. According to the President, everything's well under control here."

Manolo set his water glass on the counter and winked. "Just the expert we should trust."

. . .

Maya swept into Óscar's restaurant in a flowing black dress embroidered with colorful flowers. She was determined to enjoy Janey's 32nd birthday party despite her mourning period, disease outbreaks, and Enzo angst. Manolo followed close behind in his best blue suit, hand on her back.

The opposite wall was filled floor-to-ceiling with a painted mural of a rural Salvadoran village, adobe walls and red tile roofs. The corner featured a glowing two-towered church surrounded by waterfalls and mountain peaks with the words 'Mi Tierra' splashed in red letters across the blue sky. All the round tables were draped with white lace tablecloths, anchored by fresh flowers and candles.

Janey, sparkling in an iridescent golden dress and heels, turned from Óscar's arms and ran squealing to her new guests. Her light-brown hair brushed her bare shoulders as she drew Maya into a hug.

"Thanks so much for being here, after coming so recently for such a sad occasion." She shook Manolo's hand. "But I imagine I wasn't the only influence to make you travel."

"Good timing," Maya assured her. Óscar strolled up, chest high and arms spread wide for a hug embracing Maya and Manolo together. Like a true Tucson business leader, his resentment of Maya was put aside. Or perhaps he cleverly hid any remaining ill will for Janey's broken leg in the mine when she and Maya searched for ticks.

"Buenas noches, amigos. We have Ceviche Chapin, if you

like shrimp. And tamales, of course." He lifted each buffet lid in turn. "Garnachas are tortillas with beef and cabbage. Yuca Con Chicharron is fried cassava with pork. And Pollo de Pepian—chicken. If you are vegetarian, our chiles rellenos son maravillosos."

"Don't worry, just wave me down if you have questions about the menu." Janey turned away to greet new arrivals.

Manolo ingratiated himself and Maya with the party patrons. His Puerto Rican Spanish was different than other guests but he energetically translated when Maya's school learning couldn't keep up. For a couple of hours, eating and drinking and conversing drove the coronavirus from her busy brain. Until a text pinged from Nancy. **First confirmed US COVID death in Seattle. Nursing home.**

Maya pushed her plate to the middle of her table and texted back, **Community acquired?**

Nancy answered. **No travel, but widespread transmission not occurring, they say.**

Screams of excited children interrupted Maya's train of thought as the kids slugged the piñata. Janey was front and center, tying the blindfolds and handing them the bat.

"What's up?" Manolo asked.

She tilted her phone his way.

"Thank God it wasn't here," he said, "even though we're still wondering about your grandmother."

Waiters brought out the tres leches cake covered with thirty-two candles. Janey waved them out with a paper plate as *Happy Birthday* was sung in Spanish, then English. Maya and Manolo followed the crowd out the back door to a ten-minute barrage of fireworks.

As everyone strolled back in, Maya caught Janey by the door. "We're going to take off. I'm dog-tired from cleaning Grandma's apartment."

Janey beamed. "I made Óscar promise he can only go all out on my real Leap Year birthdays. So you're spared from all this crazy for another four years."

Maya gave her a long celebratory embrace. "Thanks for a wonderful reminder of all the joyful things in life."

She and Manolo headed to his Corvette. Temperatures had dropped sharply through the evening and she rezipped her jacket. Still, she was grateful to be out of the dismal gray days of snow in northern New Mexico. She appreciated the fluffy white stuff when she had time to cross-country ski, growing up in Flagstaff. But lately climate change seemed to make everything more intense, including the long-standing drought and summer heat waves. "May you live in interesting times"—a traditional Chinese curse.

. . .

"I forgot you're a fan of classic movies." Manolo held her close under the extra covers as the surprise winter storm pelted the windows with hail. She clicked the TV remote to select *Charade* on demand. When the tour boat went under a bridge on the Seine and the characters kissed, she hit pause and wriggled on top of him, their skin contact burning warmth into the chill room. "Our turn."

Manolo's lips responded eagerly to hers. Breaking for a breath, she teased, "Are you as debonair as Cary Grant?"

He shifted his hand to her breasts. "I'm not capable of his accent, but you're as appealing as Audrey Hepburn, and I'm happy."

"Me too." The phrase's double meaning reminded her of Faye's warning and took her out of the lovemaking mood. The longer she waited . . .

The film ended with the revelation of Cary Grant's deception and marriage proposal. "They both came close to blowing it," she whispered.

Manolo pulled her back on top. "Lucky we learned our lessons. Let's get back to our coitus interruptus. Want to ride this bronco?"

She twisted off the sofabed, then slipped on her robe and perched in the sole remaining folding chair. "I've waited way too long to tell you this. But I'm always just about to fly home and I don't want to leave you alone to process it."

His dark eyebrows pinched together as he lowered his feet to the cold floor. She looked away from his taut muscles highlighted by a streetlight glowing through rare desert snowflakes on the window above the curtain rod. "Please put something on," she commanded.

He grabbed his own robe from his suitcase and returned to stand in front of her.

"That won't work either." Her voice snapped with tension. "You need to sit down."

His expression morphed from puzzled to alarmed. "Why don't you join me in bed? We'll be warmer, not so far apart."

A throbbing pain started in the area of her missing finger, and she twirled her engagement ring, hoping to interrupt it. With no luck, she slipped the band off to rest on the blanket.

Manolo grabbed the ring. "What the fuck's going on?"

She tugged at his hand, trying to open his clenched fingers. "I'm sorry, I didn't mean to take it off—just a reflex response to some hand pain. Please don't misinterpret it."

"Then how did we go from cuddling during a romantic movie to fighting at midnight?"

"I couldn't be handling this any worse." She moved to sit beside him on the bed and forced his arms around her. She stroked the frozen planes of his face and fingered the dark curl over his forehead. "This is my problem—I shouldn't take it out on you."

His body stiffened. "How many times will we re-enact having secrets? It started with my omission of my ex, but we can't keep doing this to each other."

She closed her hands over his. "That's why I'm biting the bullet. There's never been a good time. It's only two weeks since Grandma's heart attack here in this apartment, so this isn't a great time either."

His face softened and his right hand gently massaged the tense muscles in her neck until she rested her head on his shoulder. She tried to time her breaths to the slow rise and fall of his chest, without success.

Then his lips feathered her ear. "You're like a terrified Hypatia, primed to explode. How about we get into bed?"

She kept her robe on under the covers, not ready to be intimate. Staring out out the foggy upper window was easier than seeing any judgment in the deep pools of his eyes. "You mentioned once that you didn't like Enzo," she said. "Me too, for good reasons."

"Fuck, I never trusted that guy."

"During the summer course, he was occasionally flirtatious, but not just with me. Then on the Grand Canyon trip, when you and I were at odds, he forced a kiss when I was trapped in my sleeping bag. After that, I thought he understood I wasn't available. I didn't see him again until the November meeting in Atlanta."

Her voice caught as her heart hammered. She should be overjoyed that she finally found the courage, but instead was scared shitless.

"And then?"

Her hands covered her face but she continued. "He cornered me in my hotel room, and reached under my dress to touch me." She opened her eyes to see his contorted face. "Nothing else happened, I swear. He stopped when I threatened him and later claimed it was nothing but foreplay. Now he's with Astrid."

His words were low and bitter. "So why's he still haunting you? Why did you cover it up?"

"He's rude and argumentative, like a cornered animal. If I report him, he'll fight back. But I can't let him replace Nancy without her knowing about it."

"Puñeta, el cabrón es sato." The phrase seethed like a curse.

"I know cabrón is a swear word for a bad guy, but I don't recognize the others."

"He's a dirty dog, a promiscuous bastard, taking advantage of women. I'm not going to let him get away with it."

Maya shoved away in anger. "This is exactly why I didn't tell you sooner. You think you need to take care of it."

He was silent, appearing to struggle with various options. "One thing's for sure. I'm not going to let him have the satisfaction of breaking us up."

Her lips turned up in a tentative smile. They wouldn't fall into old patterns of separating after fights. They were engaged to be married, committed.

"We're sleeping in this sofa bed, no matter how pissed I am right now at Enzo, and you."

He tossed his robe on the floor, soon to be followed by hers. His hands were rough, then tender. She couldn't tell if they were having revenge or makeup sex. He'd never come into her so forcefully, as if wiping out all memories of anyone else ever touching her. But it worked—whatever his reasons, she was turned on and satiated.

EIGHTEEN

Santa Fe, New Mexico—Wednesday, March 11, 2020

Maya had a hard time getting in touch with Manolo when back at home. He finally responded to a text and blamed COVID workload. She sympathized but needed connection. He answered her FaceTime call after eight rings, wiped spaghetti sauce from his face with a napkin, and said, "Sorry."

"My New Mexico duties ramped up, too." Maya tried to keep recriminations from her voice about his lack of response. "We announced our first cases but no evidence of spread, thank goodness. The Governor issued warnings about large gatherings and non-essential travel."

"And WHO declared a pandemic today."

"Yeah, that too." She ran her fingers through her hair. "We still haven't talked about the wedding or honeymoon trip to Africa at the end of June. Do you think we'll get this under control by then?"

He frowned. "I can't focus on anything else. The Navajo Nation declared a state of emergency."

"You're right. The way things are exploding, both of us may still be working on COVID."

His phone jerked as he walked to the sink, giving her time to consider her next words.

"Manolo, is it just the coronavirus, or are you still upset about my not mentioning the incidents with Enzo?"

The silence was painful as he avoided answering the question. Then he finally settled on the rocking chair in his bedroom. The black-and-white photo of Camelback Mountain on the wall flashed in and out of view as he rocked and rocked.

Maya's hair trigger was set. "Manolo, can you hear me?"

His expression was stamped with fury and frustration. "I think you put a comforting gloss on what he did. And why haven't you told Nancy, so she can boot the guy out of here?"

Her trigger went off. "First of all, it happened to me, not you, so don't act otherwise. Nancy's health has been dicey and now she really needs Enzo. It's not for you to decide how he's handled."

Like one spark igniting another, he answered in kind. "Fine, you let me know if and when you get around to taking care of it." Then he hung up.

. . .

Santa Fe, New Mexico—Tuesday, March 17, 2020

"Happy Saint Paddy's Day!" Maya's parents squeezed together to fill her FaceTime screen, olive-green sweaters and emerald hats contrasting with their flushed faces.

"You're going all out this year," Maya observed wryly.

"Well, Arizona's not limiting public gatherings, but Flagstaff kicked us out of the bar at eight o'clock. So we decided to bring the celebration to you." Their expressions morphed from intoxicated joy to concern. "How are you doing?"

Maya put on a happy face. "I'm coping. We're allowed to do contact tracing from home. After our initial cases last week, we're up to thirty-five." She paused with her big news. "We finally confirmed community spread."

She was uncertain what to say next. As a daughter, she wasn't used to telling her parents what to do. But as a public health professional, she felt obliged. "I'm surprised you went to the bar. Ours were ordered closed yesterday."

Her muscles weakened with fear. With the stress of heavy work demands, she'd forgotten about their annual St. Patrick's Day celebration. A chance to warn them was missed, but she could correct it now. "Pick up those disinfectant wipes and clean your purchases. SARS-CoV-2 hangs around the air for three hours and several days on surfaces like plastic and stainless steel."

"Yes, dear, we'll take care of it." Her mother's words were

slurred. Maya couldn't recall ever seeing her so inebriated. Perhaps they were dulling their fears. She couldn't blame them for one last fling, given the uncertainties of when they'd get another one.

"How is Hypatia adjusting to Flagstaff?"

Her parents' phone rotated to the cat post where the Persian slept, kneading her front paws in her dreams. If her family was spending more time at home, at least they had a cuddly animal for companionship.

"Thanks again to you and Manolo for handling Martha's apartment." Her dad's voice sounded more in control. "Make any progress on the wedding?"

"Our work's too hectic, but Nancy says the earlier SARS outbreak was controlled without much disruption. When this settles down, we'll restart our planning process."

Her dad nodded. "All right. You be careful out there."

Maya smirked, recognizing *Hill Street Blues*, his favorite old TV show. "You know I will, Dad. You do the same."

. . .

Santa Fe, New Mexico—Tuesday, March 24, 2020

Maya awoke with the sun peeking over the crest of the Sangre de Cristo mountains. She wolfed down a banana, then hopped on her old bike to pedal the Santa Fe Rail Trail. The path was clear of snow or ice, and the brilliant blue skies and crisp air invigorated her. It was impossible to imagine invisible viruses wafting whenever she passed another cyclist. Within an hour, she was showered and driving to the Runnels building, streets deserted with the Governor's order yesterday to shut down nonessential businesses.

She was startled to find Erika at her computer, processing the week's reportable diseases. "Schools are closed for three weeks. How are you managing Kyle?"

"Tax & Rev is allowing time working from home so Rolf and I are trading off. And somebody's gotta keep the regular work going—it doesn't go away 'cause we're overwhelmed with COVID."

Dr. Grinwold advanced on Maya from the hall. "I need to talk to you."

They settled into opposite chairs at his conference table. "There's a meeting in Gallup tomorrow. Our governors haven't aligned their public health orders, yet the Navajo Nation spans both states and Utah. Some agencies are looking to achieve consensus."

She hadn't kept updated on Arizona, other than limited information from her parents and Manolo. "Can I handle anything while you head there?"

He rubbed his wide forehead, expanding as his hairline receded during the two years she'd known him. "The Governor needs me at the Roundhouse on a moment's notice. I'd like you to attend. Nothing official will be decided; it's only sharing strategies."

He was asking her to represent the health department at a multistate pandemic planning meeting, less than two years after her public health degree. She could handle this—she was a ridgetop ponderosa, strengthened by fierce winds and fertilized by the contributions of others.

NINETEEN

Gallup, New Mexico—Wednesday, March 25, 2020

Maya tried to relax while still focused on I-40. She'd left a message for Manolo, excited by the possibility of seeing him at the meeting. But he didn't return her call. Nancy texted that she'd like Maya to provide a CDC update.

Soon after Maya exited the highway on Gallup's eastern edge for historic Hwy 66, a billboard sported a buxom dark-haired waitress balancing a tray of burgers and fries in one hand. Maya used their drive-through service to grab a cheese enchilada and a coke.

On the southwestern end of town, she located the sprawling school complex surrounded by low dusty hills barely visible on the dark night, absent a moon. In the gymnasium, she whispered hello to Manolo as she grabbed a folding chair behind him and the cluster of Commissioned Corps officers. Nancy picked up the microphone.

"In these trying times, we appreciate your taking some hours to offer ideas on combating this pandemic. We all have different constituencies to serve, yet we share this beautiful Southwest with its wide-open spaces. Perhaps our geography will aid us in the distancing needed to reduce viral transmission."

Nancy called Maya up and handed her the mic. Maya adjusted her navy blazer over her navy pants, distracted by a few wrinkles. To refocus and combat her nerves, she pretended it was their office Grand Rounds.

She summarized from her printout of CDC's *Morbidity and Mortality Weekly Report.* "Global estimates are 170,000 cases, with 7,000 deaths in 150 countries. For the US, case reports are exploding with more than 500 new ones per day in the past week."

She paused when catching Manolo's eyes, but his expression was placid, impossible to interpret.

"The highest percentage of severe outcomes are among those at least eighty-five years old. In China, more than eighty percent of their deaths occurred in those sixty and older."

A white-haired man whom she recognized from Aging & Long-Term Services raised his hand. "Could you summarize the situation in Washington State?"

"Of course. Washington has a long-term care facility with 129 cases among residents, staff, and visitors, and 23 deaths. CDC recommends identifying and excluding symptomatic staff, restricting visitation except for compassionate care, and strengthening infection control."

The man continued. "What about PPE?"

Maya scrutinized the audience and saw a few face masks. "Personal protective equipment is not readily available in many areas, so CDC continues to prioritize it for health care workers when handling infected patients."

A masked uniformed officer next to Manolo raised his hand. "The Surgeon General says masks are ineffective in preventing the public from catching the virus. I realize he's my boss, but I question that information."

He added with a chuckle, "No one's recording this, right? I respect prioritizing PPE for those of us in primary care, but I wonder if there's anything to back up his assertion."

Hoping Nancy would help her out, Maya hesitated. Then she froze. Enzo was in the shadows next to Nancy. As her eyes met his, he leapt up and rushed to grab the mic.

"I'm Enzo Russo, EIS Officer for Arizona. We're recommending social distancing, washing hands, and getting flu shots. I support the Surgeon General's message to stop buying face masks."

Maya had to restrain herself from shaking her head. Masks were a standard component of infection control, and their ability to prevent viral inhalation depended on the virus and mask quality. Enzo hadn't answered the question, but she didn't have anything to add. Perhaps saying they were ineffective was the only way to curtail public hoarding.

When she and Enzo sat back down, she pulled on her own mask and glanced around at the cavernous high-ceiling gym, comforted by cool air moving through open doors.

Other groups took turns sharing plans to handle limited supplies. The Navajo Nation President announced the closure of all casinos, parks, and tourism sites. Maya was grateful she wasn't required to make commitments on behalf of the state health department. She'd report to Dr. Grinwold, for his tough decisions.

As the meeting ended, Maya reached forward to tap Manolo on the shoulder, but he ignored her and rushed for the sidelines. Nancy stepped in Maya's direction and her brown eyes narrowed in concern above the mask covering most of her apple cheeks. "I haven't seen you since your grandmother's funeral. I hope you're doing okay."

"Yes, thank you. I need to—"

The young officer who disagreed with the Surgeon General brushed by and Maya stopped him. "Did you see where Manolo went?"

"Outside. We're leaving soon to make it back to Phoenix for our early morning shifts."

Maya ran for the door. In the parking lot lit by towering fluorescents, she spotted two figures, one on the ground moaning. The hovering one straightened and she recognized Manolo, his complexion bright even in the dim light. Below him, Enzo held his hand to his face and screamed, "You mother fucker, I'm going to be scarred!" Blood oozed from a gash on his cheek. Maya dropped her pack and searched for anything clean to stop it, then bent to apply pressure with an extra cloth mask. "Ow, that hurts," Enzo yelled again.

"What's going on?" Nancy's voice filtered from behind.

"Enzo tripped and fell on his face." Manolo's voice was an angry accusation.

"No way," Enzo snarled. "I was sucker punched."

"Let me see it," Nancy ordered, adjusting her reading glasses from her neck and bending to push aside Maya's hand. "Ugh, these old bones don't get down too easy. Enzo, stand up and let's get inside so I can get a closer look."

He followed her command and rolled to his knees, fingers clutching their car keys. "I'm going to Urgent Care and the police station to file assault charges."

Nancy glanced from Maya to Manolo. "I want to hear what happened, but Enzo's right—he should get this cleaned and possibly sutured."

As their state sedan pulled away, Maya pinched Manolo's arm. "Tell me you didn't slug him."

His voice was bitter. "Of course not. I confronted him about what he did to you, he swore at me and pivoted, then tripped and fell."

A few more vehicles filled with passengers and drove off. "I hope there are witnesses to back up your version." She tried to soften her tone, but the words came out exasperated.

"Miranda, get your butt in gear." The carload of PHS officers halted next to them and the backdoor opened.

Manolo ducked to pick up his hat from the dirt and brushed it off. When he leaned in for a kiss, she pushed him away. His cheek muscles flexed, then he joined his team and they sped off.

Maya collapsed in the front seat of her Prius, sobbing. All her fears for telling Manolo about Enzo had come to pass. She knew enough about the men to trust her fiancé's version of the story, but others might not. Finally engaging the engine, she drove to the drive-in for a coke. Caffeine was bad for her nerves but essential to focus her scrambled brain on the three-hour drive home.

But first, she had to check on Enzo and Nancy, so she detoured to the hospital. Nancy leaned on their car in the parking lot. "They kicked me out while they stitch him up—COVID protocols. Why were those two fighting?"

Maya sighed, then sat with Nancy in the front seat of her state car and unloaded the details of Enzo's transgressions.

"You should have told me sooner," Nancy said. Jowls sagging, her expression reflected disappointment. She ran her fingers through thinning hair. "I recognized he was cocky, but this is beyond the pale. I'll have to follow-up with human resources in the morning."

"I know how much you've come to rely on Enzo, especially with your retirement planning. He's not a hundred percent evil—I don't want to represent him that way."

Nancy rubbed a wrinkled hand over her face. "Maya, I'm too invested in public health to quit when we're most needed. Sure, this body's getting worn out, but it'll hang on a while longer."

Maya twisted in her seat. "I don't know my next steps, through CDC or your department. My attorney said Enzo could be get jail time. I can't imagine taking it that far. We're all overwhelmed with COVID—we need more public health workers, not fewer."

Nancy pulled Maya's blazer closed. "You're shivering. This is a lot coming to a head right now. Leave Enzo to me; focus on repairing whatever's going on with Manolo. Are you capable of driving home tonight?"

Maya nodded, taking another sip of her cola. "I'm worried about Enzo's threat to file charges. Can you get him to delay until tempers settle down? But with his ego, he could hold a grudge forever, especially if there's a scar to remind him."

"I have a long drive to straighten him out."

Back in her Prius, Maya called Manolo's phone—no answer. Perhaps he had taken over driving and couldn't pick up. Then she texted. **We need to talk. Call me tomorrow.**

The long, dark highway loomed ahead. She could obsess over prevention—somehow stopping Manolo from going after Enzo. Or she could hit play for *Hamilton* on her iPhone and listen to *The World Was Wide Enough* on repeat. Apparently not wide enough for Manolo and Enzo, especially with both of them in Phoenix and Maya stuck in New Mexico, unable to referee. With any luck, unlike the duel between Hamilton and Burr, neither of them would end up dead.

. . .

Santa Fe, New Mexico—Thursday, March 26, 2020

Maya found Dr. Grinwold pacing the hall when she arrived at seven o'clock. His chest heaved as if a gremlin was bursting to be born. "What time did you get back to Santa Fe?"

"Just after midnight."

He lumbered to his office, grunting over his shoulder. "Nancy called me from the road. Enzo was bitching about the fight, but in good enough shape to drive after several stitches."

Maya hovered near the edge of his desk, not wanting to sit down. "I'm guessing she told you why it happened."

He pushed his glasses higher and Maya rushed on. "I never wanted to tarnish my EIS years with something like this. What Enzo did was serious, but I'm uncertain if he deserves to lose his job or go to jail over it."

"There's more than one person at danger of jail. Someone texted Enzo a distant video clip that captured angry voices and Manolo raising his hands before Enzo went down. With that evidence, he told Nancy he'll go to the authorities if she disciplines him."

Maya finally collapsed on the guest chair. "Oh my God. I didn't think this could get worse."

Dr. Grinwold slammed the desk with his fist and shouted. "It was bad enough she changed her plans to move here next month. Now she's got this goddamned stress. I told her to do what she has to do—to hell with any threat to Manolo. If you had reported this when you should have, we wouldn't be in this situation."

Maya stammered an apology. "You're right, of course. I regret all of it. I'll support what you told her. Do you need my resignation?" The image of her grandmother in the coffin, dead from a heart attack, morphed into Nancy's beneficent face in rigor mortis, her cardiac condition from Chagas exacerbated by Maya's stupid choices.

Dr. Grinwold's voice dropped in volume and severity. "Don't be ridiculous. It's the fault of that entitled millennial, not yours. You need to spend more time with Nancy to learn how to maneuver the workplace as a woman."

"What do you want me to do now?"

"Set this aside until you hear from Nancy, and type up notes from last night's meeting."

Maya headed for the door but he continued. "We're about to do a press release on twenty-four new cases including our first death. Check with Erika and see what she needs for surveillance. The local offices are handling most of it, but they're reporting to her."

By noon, Dr. Grinwold sent Maya home to handle her assigned contact tracing calls while social distancing. She zapped a frozen dinner in the microwave and looked over her list. Then she clicked open FaceTime to reach Manolo, bleary-eyed and not in uniform.

"At least you answered my call." Her voice snapped with irritation. She hadn't planned how to greet him, and starting out with sarcasm wasn't the best choice.

"My supervisor told me to stay home. Confronting a guy while we were both in uniform—not my finest move."

Manolo getting in trouble with the IHS or Public Health Service—the consequences of her decisions kept expanding.

"Enzo's considering formal charges," she said. "Someone sent him a video that appears to show you raising your arms to hit or push him. He's using the threat to bargain for a better outcome from Nancy."

"I intended to stop him when he turned his back on my concerns, but he fell before I touched him." His tone was combative, then his features transformed into a little boy's. "I'm sorry, Maya, I fucked up. That guy's arrogance got to me. When I saw him in person, I couldn't get him assaulting you out of my mind."

Despite his contrition and abject expression, Maya lost her temper. "I warned you about being overprotective. A bad situation escalated because you thought I needed defending. This is not the Middle Ages where I'm the damsel in distress relying on a knight in shining armor. This isn't a romance novel."

"Maya, I swore not to let what happened with Enzo derail us. You did the same, right?"

"I'm not making any promises. There's too many moving parts

and I'm not sure I can cope. Maybe Nancy can placate Enzo, but you need to sort things out with your job. Anything personal will have to wait."

She threw herself into contact tracing calls after she hung up. Things would work out as they would work out—there was little she could do to influence the track of fate. The only good thing about COVID—no time to think about anything else.

TWENTY

Gallup, New Mexico—Monday, April 20, 2020

Excited to see Manolo again, Maya sang Donna Summer's *I Feel Love* as she drove to Gallup. When the highway sign said twenty miles, she remembered her last time at the Gallup Indian Medical Center. A little girl had a painful, ulcerated hand from anthrax exposure at a petting zoo. But Maya's brain was also imprinted with the blackened lesions on the face of a terrified Flagstaff boy who died the next day. This time there were no animals implicated, just human coronavirus transmission overwhelming the Indian Health Service.

Native peoples took pride in managing their own affairs, with assistance from the federal government. But COVID hammered the northwestern corner of the state, and Dr. Grinwold assigned Maya to assess what the Navajo Nation needed.

At GIMC, she paused for an ambulance pulling up to one of the gray tents, then saw them unload a patient as she parked. Manolo waited near the front entrance to the multistory building.

"It shouldn't take work to bring us together," he groused as he enveloped her in a too-tight hug.

"Trying to pick another fight, señor?" But she relaxed into his embrace and pressed her lips to his.

"I hope our kiss will answer your question." He stepped back as a staff member exited.

Maya waved at the parking lot. "How are these tents being used?"

"For overload. When the ER or ICU are full, we do rapid resuscitation of patients crashing, plus separate out those with milder symptoms." He took her hand and led her to one of the tarps shading a group socializing and downing bottled water. "I'm finishing an orientation for dietitians and diabetes care workers doing triage. Put on your mask and listen in."

Maya picked a folding chair in the corner as Manolo restarted the staff training. "Welcome back from your break. You now have procedures for patient evaluations. If you become involved in critical care, we'll have additional protective gear. The National Guard has been flying in supplies on Blackhawk helicopters, so we're not short of PPE for the moment."

A large man with a black shirt and turquoise bolo tie raised his hand. "I'm Edward Newton with the Jicarilla Apache Environmental Services. Dr. Maguire and I worked together on *Borrelia*. Could she comment on CDC's response to COVID?"

Was it her imagination, or did tension sweep through the group like a swarm of hornets? Besides Mr. Newton, others were unlikely to have heard about her association with a Jicarilla elder's death on a deserted highway. But she stood in a proactive, non-defensive posture.

"I'm meeting with Dr. Miranda and the IHS today. CDC and our state health department have expressed strong support to Washington for your federal funding."

Digging into her pocket, she took out a handful of business cards. "You're welcome to call me with any specific ideas and requests." She stepped forward to place one in Edward Newton's outstretched hand. Noticing his black cowboy hat on the seat, she wondered if he ran cattle or sheep on the side of his regular job. He might be a rancher like Dave, with concern about his herds.

"We don't have much information about spillover to animals, and it's probably not a major issue. But as a veterinarian, I'll meet soon with our regional USDA vet Dr. Dave Schwartz, so feel free to let me know about those questions, too."

She nodded toward Manolo and sat down, tugging slightly on her mask to allow more circulation. He reviewed their procedures for managing Navajo residents sheltering at hotels.

Rigid expressions, shifting postures, and challenging contentions reflected everyone being on edge. Maya admired their bravery to work in public health and clinical roles bringing them into close contact with contagious people. Her mother gave daily thanks for her daughter's less-dangerous role as an epidemiologist.

Stepping away from the group into the sun with Manolo, she tugged off her mask and inhaled a deep breath of fresh high-altitude air. "You're good at this, handling complex tasks and stressed-out people. At least most of the time." She couldn't avoid the slight dig about his short temper with Enzo. "I couldn't handle the pressure."

He put an arm around her shoulder and drew her closer. "Whatever influence you have on Nancy is working. She's keeping Enzo so busy, he's had no time to complain about me."

"Dr. Jaworski was less than pleased to hear about all of it." Her Atlanta supervisor had reminded Maya of procedures in place for a reason. But no one could spare time or resources to go down that path. "Nancy's alert to any pattern with sexual aggression, but she's seen only a level of confidence out of proportion to his experience."

"My DC headquarters is being generous with my behavior," Manolo said. "Just a letter to the file. Remember when you, Dave, and Ben all got them after the unapproved anthrax sampling in the wildlife refuge? Now we're all equal with a black mark."

Maya laughed, surprised she could find any humor in the situation. "Dave might have an edge on us. He implied he already had some disciplinary actions before that one."

Manolo guided her to his Corvette. "Can you join me on my drive to Shiprock? I don't want to be on the road after dark. We'll find a place for takeout lunch."

Near the same drive-in she visited a few weeks earlier, they passed one of Manolo's teams strolling through a motel parking lot, easily spotted by their gowns, face masks, face shields, and clipboards. After wolfing down a cheeseburger, she offered to drive so Manolo could eat too. She thrilled at the power in her hands, calmed by the sense of control. Soon they passed a gigantic billboard with the sign **Navajo Nation Curfew 8 PM – 5 AM.**

"Is that why you want to reach Gallup by dark?" She loosened her ponytail and relished the temps in the sixties.

"But I don't want to be delayed with a speeding ticket," he warned.

She tilted her head with a sly smile. "This barren landscape, only a few hills on the horizon, fertilizes my speed freak." With the top down, she imagined fresh air filtering out the COVID risk.

He reached over to stroke her neck. "Yeah, I'd like to stay west when we resume our future plans." Then he checked an incoming text on his phone. "Mr. Newton just arrived at one of the rural homes off a Navajo Service Route. The nurse with him is concerned about a resident."

Guided by Manolo's instructions, Maya followed graveled roads until they turned to dirt, where Mr. Newton was pulled over in his four-wheel drive vehicle, waiting for them. He ran a hand over the Corvette hood. "You have a beautiful car, but it can't handle where we're going."

Maya jammed into the middle between the two men. Mr. Newton focused on the truck as it shimmied and bounced through sand made slippery by the previous night's storm. He gave a quick glance to Manolo. "Glad I remembered your trip to Shiprock. The nurse wanted to call for an ambulance, but the patient's refusing to leave her home. Maybe you can persuade her."

Within twenty minutes, he pulled up to a traditional Navajo hogan, wooden door facing east to greet the day, rounded earth roof above a lattice of log walls. "Thank goodness your cell service works out here," Maya observed.

"There's been a push for rural broadband," Mr. Newton answered. "We're doing checks of local needs, then found this elderly woman in a bad way."

The nurse greeted them at the door in full PPE. "Thanks for coming. Mrs. Begay's oxygen saturation is only eighty-two percent, with fast, shallow breathing. She has chest pain and trouble speaking. Comorbidities are hypertension and diabetes. But she won't go to the hospital—no one to care for her sheep."

Manolo opened a pack on his back seat and donned his own PPE, then accompanied the nurse inside. Maya and Mr. Newton huddled in the shade of a piñon pine.

"You're not Navajo—it's good of you to help." Maya hoped the compliment would demonstrate she had no hard feelings after he put her on the spot during the training. "I can call my USDA colleague about the animals." Maya pulled out her phone.

Mr. Newton nodded. "When we're done here, I'll check with the neighbors—maybe they can lend a hand."

No animals were in sight, likely grazing at a distance. She reached Dave by the second ring. "I need your recommendations for a Navajo COVID patient who can't care for her livestock. And I don't know what to say about its zoonotic potential. There's been two asymptomatic but seropositive dogs in Hong Kong, a sick cat in Belgium, and positive big cats at the Bronx Zoo."

"USDA's got food distribution and loan programs which you can let them know about," Dave said, "but nothing like what you need. For the bigger question of spread between people and animals, a lot of people are working on it."

The young nurse came back out the hogan door and lowered her mask to smile. "Dr. Miranda has the magic touch—Mrs. Begay agreed to an air ambulance. I'm calling them now."

After making the arrangements, she joined them under the tree cover and motioned toward a portable tank of water on a table next to the north wall. "She has no running water, not even from rain catchment 'cause of our twenty-year drought cycle. Edward set up that tank while I evaluated her. She thinks a lack of handwashing led her to infection with the Big Cough, Dikos Ntsaaígíí-19."

She hurried back inside and Manolo came out, shaking his head. "Too many Diné deaths already, way higher than off the rez. At Shiprock, we'll start supplemental oxygen and glucocorticoids to reduce inflammation. We may have to consider a ventilator."

The thump-thump-thump of helicopter blades pierced the silence, and PPE-protected staff loaded up the elderly woman. After the chopper departed, Maya crawled into the truck's jump seat. When they reached the Corvette, Manolo took over driving but his mind remained focused on his patient.

"I'm not sure we have enough resources at Shiprock. In Phoenix, we've started studies on interferon and remdesivir, but it's too early to determine benefits."

The remaining drive went quickly with Manolo crafting plans to identify more nurses and handwashing stations. As they got closer to the town of Shiprock, its namesake volcanic rock with wings rose sharply out of the high desert. With only occasional tiny green bushes dotting the variegated tan rocks and dirt, nothing distracted from the monolith's majesty.

"Have you explored there?" Maya asked.

"Access is restricted, even before the pandemic. But you can snap some quick photos with your phone."

They lingered for a drink of water, leaning on the hood of the sports car. A few minutes of silence enveloped them, roads empty from the stay-at-home orders. Maya took off her jacket and tossed it in his back seat. "I love this high altitude. I don't want the NYC humidity again."

He rubbed her bare arms. "Well, now you've got lovely youthful skin. But our older patients complain about the Colorado River basin drying up. They need humidifiers for breathing and to reduce itchiness."

She arched one hip and fluffed her thick hair with a hand. "Three more years until I even turn thirty. Do you think I'm concerned about such things?"

His moist lips met hers. "I'll adore you even if you get wrinkles."

"Well, I'll head that off by getting out of this intense sun." She turned for the passenger seat. Within half an hour, they pulled up to the Shiprock Northern Navajo Medical Center, brown walls fading to tan wings piercing the blue sky, echoing the natural monolith.

"I'll check on Mrs. Begay and ICU infection control. You can't come in. Can you gas up and occupy yourself for a while?"

She headed back to the bridge over the San Juan River, then located a small park to pull over and enjoy the benefits of snowmelt.

As much as she had professed joy in the stark spaces south of town, the taller green trees clustering the river bottom provided welcome shade and the wafting scent of weeds and wildflowers. She kicked off her shoes and socks before wading in mud at the water's edge.

Then she perched in the Corvette front seat and opened her laptop to edit an educational campaign about handwashing, until Manolo texted to meet back at NNMC. She reinstalled the fabric roof of the car as the bank of dark western clouds marched in from Kayenta, sharing their immense sorrow from the COVID hotspot.

Braced against the wall near the hospital front door, gown off one shoulder and mask pulled down to his chin, Manolo was fighting back tears when she picked him up. "Their staff couldn't stabilize her; she crashed too quickly. We didn't have time to consider relocation to Phoenix."

As they had loaded the woman from the hogan to the helicopter, Maya got a brief glimpse of her wrinkled face and gray ponytail. Now the death flashed her back to the hospital with her grandmother. But her grandmother had the privilege of health care closer at hand, even though it didn't save her.

"I'm so sorry." She wrapped her arms around his heaving shoulders. "I wish there was more I could do."

She'd seen him upset when a Hopi sheepherder died from anthrax, but otherwise, he always held it together. Maybe the unceasing, relentless number of deaths and Native Americans struggling to breathe was becoming too much. She adjusted the position of her feet to hold him up. When he put on his hat, she stood back, and he lowered into the passenger seat.

From the driver's side, she tried to console him before starting the engine. "The Governor met with universities and nonprofits delivering water and food. Those can keep people stronger, able to fight off the virus."

He sank lower, failing to fasten his seatbelt. "I need more critical care training. My infectious disease expertise isn't enough."

With the back of his hand, he wiped away moisture from his eyes. "Patients as young as fifty fighting for a final breath. Low moans and coughs from the corridors. Staffers staggering from cubicle to cubicle. Too much virus, not enough of us."

Maya reached over to embrace him, pushing aside thoughts of an invisible menace he could have brought with him. "What's next?"

"Head to Gallup. I won't yell at you for speeding."

The engine roared to life. "You got it."

"One more thing. They want me back in Phoenix tonight—they need workers for the early shift."

"No problem," she answered. "I should get home this evening, too. Maybe tomorrow night, FaceTime sex?" Her half-humorous, half-seductive words eased her sense of inadequacy. From their first night together during Chaco camping, they'd always connected physically.

She glanced at him as the Shiprock monolith loomed in the distance on his right. His hand rested on his forehead, face in a mournful droop.

"Tse Bit' a'i," he said. "The remains of a giant bird that brought ancestors here from up north. Climbing was forbidden after lightning destroyed the path to the top, stranding women and children who starved to death. Wouldn't want to disturb the ghosts."

Maya sighed, anxious about his mental health. She always counted on Manolo being the more mature and stable one. She never anticipated he could have his own demons.

TWENTY-ONE

Bernalillo, New Mexico—Wednesday, April 29, 2020

"Can I top off your ice tea, or offer something stronger?" Emilia handed Maya a cushion to soften the seat of the wooden bench on Dave's back porch.

Maya savored the two girls chasing each other around the corral on their ponies as Dave and Braxton tossed a baseball under skies pinkening through tree branches bursting with new life. "A glass of white wine would hit the spot. This is one of my favorite times of year."

The greens were a Monet palette and the temperature around seventy was perfect. After roughhousing with Bo, their black Lab, Maya brushed specks of soil from her bare arm. The sensation reminded her how much she missed Manolo's touch. Intimate moments on FaceTime warmed the frost on their engagement, but phone sex took precedence over sorting out future plans.

Contented clucks emerged from a coop inside of the barn. "I assume your delicious dinner was locally sourced."

Emilia's gaze shifted from her daughters to Dave's half-brother. "The chickens are Braxton's contribution. I can't say anything good about religious groups that kick out their teenage boys, but at least the kids know how to care for animals." She reached up to touch the porch overhang. "And construction. He repaired our leaks."

After pouring two glasses from a bottle of Riesling labeled with the name of a nearby Corrales vineyard, Emilia rejoined Maya on the bench. "You okay with staying the night? We're not social distancing."

Maya smiled her thanks. "Our jobs don't allow hibernation."

Emilia tossed her two dark braids over her shoulders. "I'm blessed my restaurant is open with curbside pickups."

"Does Braxton help out with the school closure?"

"He's good at caring for younger children. Summer break's coming soon anyway."

"Manolo and I considered starting a family right after the wedding." Maya shook her head—COVID closures were hard on working families. "But everything's on hold. I'm unsure how to achieve your work-life balance."

"We won't have to do this much longer. The President says you've got this all under control, right?"

Maya took another sip, the alcohol relaxing her limbs, inch by inch. "COVID's predicted to wane during the summer like flu, and I can get back to wedding plans."

"How are your parents doing in Flagstaff?"

"They've embraced isolation with a vengeance. Thank God Hypatia gives them company." Essentials like groceries were delivered, and they washed every package. They abhorred help and refused to let her or Manolo visit with their chances of infection on the job.

Braxton threw a wild pitch which ended up in the corral, and both girls raced to be the first to throw it back.

"Some Hispanic families are fatalistic," Emilia said. "My parents aren't too concerned, so they help with babysitting. Speaking of children, I'm going to get ours ready for bed."

Maya joined her heading to the corral fence. "Dave and I can put away the ponies. We have some work stuff to sort out."

When the two women caught up with the girls, Emilia told them, "All kids have the night off from barn chores, thanks to our generous guest. But I'll be enforcing baths and showers."

To a chorus of whoops and yippees, the girls and Braxton raced each other inside, Emilia trailing.

Maya used a rubber curry comb and her pony leaned against her as if falling asleep. Dave slapped the back of the gelding, who shifted his weight. "If you're not in charge, he's the boss."

"Is that your advice for how I should manage males of all species?"

He flashed his laconic cowboy grin. "Is it working for your guy?"

Switching to a hard brush, she knocked off the loosened dirt and hair. "Let's focus on our job tomorrow. The Bronx Zoo had four sick tigers and three lions, apparently infected by a staff person. Do you think that's what happened at the Albuquerque wildlife park?"

Dave finished off his pony with a rub rag for extra shine. "They're pissed at having to close under the Governor's order, so we won't be welcomed."

They hastily completed the chores as bugs accumulated around the barn lights, until Dave flipped most of the switches off. "Let's get some rest. We're expected at ten."

. . .

Albuquerque, New Mexico—Thursday, April 30, 2020

Maya, Dave, and Braxton started out along the Mesa Point trail in Boca Negra Canyon at eight-fifteen. Spotting the public health warning next to the small bridge spanning the arroyo, they donned their face masks.

Still wet from the early morning rain, the desert plants exuded pungent odors, and mourning doves cooed contentment. With each step along the rocky path as the sun rose higher, Maya considered tossing her jacket into her day pack.

The first petroglyph was the traveling salesman of southwestern peoples, the kokopelli. The lighter-colored hunched figure stood out from the dark volcanic boulder, representing Puebloan artists scraping away black desert varnish hundreds of years earlier. Maya didn't comment that it was anatomically correct, but pointed instead to the animal on its left. "Looks like a coyote, doesn't it?"

Braxton agreed, then took off to lead the treasure hunt, light hair blowing in the morning wind. "Thanks for suggesting this," Dave said to Maya as they struggled to keep up with Braxton's thirteen-year-old energy.

"The petroglyphs are close to the wildlife park, and I thought a quick outing with your family might be great for morale."

Maya climbed carefully around boulders littering the trail. Some steps were so steep that she braced with a hand on a rock, careful to avoid any with carvings. "Braxton, what do you think this one is?"

"A mouse-lizard king holding a lollipop."

She laughed. "That's my guess too."

They paused to catch their breath at the **One Mile above Sea Level** sign. Albuquerque's suburbs spread out below, towered over in the distance by the Sandia Mountains. Maya's gaze was diverted by a collared lizard darting across a basalt boulder.

Braxton's lips turned up in a slight smile. "I sure hate being slowed down by a couple of old farts."

Dave cuffed his ear but beamed his approval.

"Braxton, this is more fun than I've had in a long time," Maya said. "Thanks for coming along." She hadn't thought about the pandemic or fraught relationships with the opposite sex in almost an hour. Braxton's enthusiasm and humor reflected his kinship with Dave, a cantankerous but loving compadre, and an eager parent.

Birds with peacock feathers and a masked human figure with a headdress greeted them from a rock face. Braxton slowed and offered Maya a hand over some of the larger trail obstacles. When they paused for a final view at the hillside summit, Braxton looked shyly toward her, then away. "Can I call you Auntie Maya?"

As an only child, Maya never expected to have that role. Dave jumped in. "Kinda miss all those relatives, buddy?"

With a moment to gather her thoughts, Maya answered, "I'd be honored. Thanks for thinking of me in that way."

Braxton hopped an outcropping, leading the way down. "Well, you guys are so close, I thought you wouldn't mind."

Her family had shrunk with her grandmother's death. She probably had relatives in China, but rarely gave them a thought. She'd never learn who they were.

Headed down, sandwiched between Dave and his new son, she was encouraged by their protective glances to make sure she didn't take a tumble.

At the parking lot, Emilia played tag with her girls around their car. "Just in time. I was having trouble keeping them from climbing the rocks."

"I wouldn't recommend this trail." Maya shaded her eyes against the sun as she glanced back up it. "It's too steep in a few spots. Rinconada Canyon has three hundred petroglyphs so I'd head over to that one. You'll find some strange creatures pecked out on the boulders."

"Can I come with you to see the wild animals?" Braxton begged.

"Sorry, son, this is a work inspection, and Emilia needs your help. Make sure the girls don't vanish into the wilderness chasing the next pretty rock."

Emilia gave her husband a kiss and stroked his cheek. "Have a safe day."

Maya tamped down a twinge of jealousy. Had she ever seen them fight? Emilia got angry last year when he drank too much after his mother refused to see him. Since then, they seemed an inseparable team during the stresses of a pandemic, three kids, and two jobs.

As Dave's family drove away, Maya waved goodbye. "Braxton surprised me with the 'Auntie Maya' request, but I'm flattered."

"It's been seven months since I found him at that St. George halfway house. His life is so changed, it's like being on a different planet. What kid doesn't like television, video games, school science projects, and his own bedroom?"

"I can't imagine what it was like for him, surrounded by siblings and sister-wives. He'd never have time to feel lonely."

Dave drove north past suburban cul-de-sacs encroaching on the volcanic cliffs. "With all the plural marriages, I could have countless relatives. Braxton tried to explain it, but he doesn't know who slept with whom. Or which young girls were raped by which pillars of the church."

Maya glanced over to him, his feedstore cap pulled low over his eyes. Her laconic cowboy turning emotional—the only time that happened was related to his mother and the LDS sect. "Sorry, I shouldn't bring up something like this while you're driving."

"It's not a new subject, just a painful one."

He parked close to the huge billboard announcing ADAM'S ANIMAL ARK, a painted cowboy hat in one corner and Noah's Ark on the other. "You know, I never hear you talk about China."

"I have less information than you." When she visited at age twelve, the orphanage director verified she'd been found on their doorstep. Families wanted boys, so the number of girls her mother might have birthed was unknown. It wasn't worth thinking about.

The park founder met them at the gate. He looked like his website photo—a westernized Mark Twain or Albert Einstein. His shock of white hair was partially hidden under the rim of a beaver fur cap. Sixty years earlier, he had started the sanctuary as a religiously-inspired college student, wanting to rescue God's creatures. Decades later, he continued his dedication on top of leading an ecumenical church south of town.

"Dr. Schwartz and Dr. Maguire." He reached out a black-gloved hand to shake theirs. "I guess you're here to find out what's going on with our felines."

"Pastor Heaton, is it still just the lions and tigers with respiratory illness?" Dave asked.

The owner unlocked the wooden gate, topped with a spiral pattern of thin branches that Maya recognized as ocotillo. They all put on their masks.

"Please call me Pastor Adam." His reedy voice was harder to make out with the mask in place. "Yes, only our cat species are affected."

In separate cages near the entrance, a porcupine snoozed and a raccoon washed a corn cob in a bowl. In a tall flight cage, a great horned owl cranked its head around to shoot them a baleful golden gaze. The tufts on either side of its head flattened in apparent annoyance.

"That's Ollie. Since we've been closed, the animals aren't used to strangers. Our dedicated staff still come in for animal care, but it's hard to keep going without the visitor income. Thank God we have a strong donor base."

As they strolled an arching path past a pen with elk, deer, and antelope, the herbivores grazed contentedly on the desert scrub. "In nature, these species might not be found in such close proximity," Maya said.

"They come as rescues, orphaned or injured. Perhaps they're grateful to live out their lives here in peace." Pastor Adam laughed. "No animal altercations, just a rare human one. Does that say who's really in God's favor?"

In the next chain link enclosure, an overweight black bear lay on his back under a juniper. "Bruce is a favorite—way too many snacks. He was shot raiding a fishing cabin, desperately thin and searching for food. Since we healed him, he's food-obsessive, but content."

At the farthest end of the oval track in a huge metal cage, four coyote pups annoyed their mother as she snoozed under palo verde branches drooping from outside the enclosure. "Cora was a HBC— hit by car—four months ago. Our volunteer vet repaired her broken leg and discovered she was pregnant."

Maya wondered at efforts exerted on behalf of species that weren't endangered, but the rolling balls of fur and snapping teeth were undeniably adorable. "Is this enclosure spacious enough when they grow up?"

Pastor Adam's tone became defensive. "We're working on it. Anyone who donates to an expansion fund can suggest a name for a pup. Hopefully you'll let us reopen soon so people can see them and get motivated to help."

Separated by picnic tables from the coyotes, additional large cages housed a grizzled male lion and a sleek young tiger. The lion's ruff was matted and he opened only one eye to plead with Maya, *I'm dying, can you help me?*

"Your other wildlife is native to this area," Maya said. "How did you end up with these exotic animals?"

"Crazy breeders. Did you catch that TV series *Tiger King?* I'm glad the aftershow exposed the bad side of the industry."

Dave had been silent on their walk, taking notes and comparing them to his copy of the USDA Animal Care permit. "Pastor Adam, the lab test is called polymerase chain reaction. When I called yesterday with PCR confirmation on these two, I mentioned infection control. Disposable gloves and surgical masks for staff; eliminating volunteers from animal access. Did you get that in place?"

A young girl, barely a teenager, rounded the corner with a mask slipped to her neck and a hose in her bare hand. She took her thumb off the nozzle and began spraying down the cages. Dave waved in frustration toward her. "And this is how you follow my orders?" His shout was loud enough to startle the girl into turning off the water.

Maya remembered his short fuse at the petting zoo infected with anthrax near Flagstaff. The biblical flood was unleashed for Pastor Adam and his Ark.

TWENTY-TWO

Albuquerque, New Mexico—Thursday, April 30, 2020

The girl outside the lion cage visibly trembled, wet streaks on her cheeks below her cornflower blue eyes.

"Grandpa, did I do something wrong?" The tenor of the child's voice was as shaky as her limbs.

Pastor Adam's expression was intimidating. "Look, Dr. Schwartz, there's no need to scare this little one. My extended family is heavily involved in our Ark. I can't maintain humane treatment of the animals without their help."

Dave was good with kids and Maya was surprised he yelled. But she'd seen him get stern with Braxton when he acted up, so he was no pushover.

She glanced at Dave's copy of the permit. "Scout's twenty-five years old, about the maximum lifespan for a lion in captivity."

"He was here before I was born," the girl offered.

"Thanks, sweetheart," Maya said. "Why don't you let us grownups talk? Take a break from your chores."

At the faint screech from the park entrance, they all turned their heads. Pastor Adam still appeared upset, but put his hand on the girl's shoulder. "That's Ollie, he's hungry and wants a mouse. Can you take care of it?"

He turned back to Maya. "Scout lost his appetite, then coughing and diarrhea. With the fecal sample positive, what do we do now?"

"Antibiotics won't help with viral diseases," Maya said, "but make sure your vet monitors for secondary bacterial infections." She remembered the tiger's name from Dave's list. "And Ariel, what's her story?"

"Similar to Scout, a day or two later. As you can see, she bounced right back, no signs of illness."

The sleek Bengal tiger paced the next cage, pausing to rub her cheek against the front bars. She emitted a low chuff, a hybrid purr and growl.

"That's her happy sound," Pastor Adam said.

Dave interrupted Maya's attempt to ease the tension. "There's nothing to keep your granddaughter from sticking her hand through cage bars and getting it ripped off. Do you smell that liquid feces pooling in the corner? And paint's peeling from these metal bars— it may have lead."

Pastor Adam matched Dave's combative tone. "I'm used to dealing with your state vet. What happened to him?"

"He retired." Dave glanced over to Maya. "Want to switch your focus more to animals? You could apply for the position."

Although she'd welcome working closely with Dave, she didn't have the political skills to manage ranchers on contentious animal agriculture issues.

"I'll stick to epi, thank you." She didn't add that crunching numbers was soothing, at arm's length from the illnesses and deaths the data represented.

In a calmer voice, Dave turned back to Pastor Adam. "Continue once-a-day fecal specimens on both animals for testing. I won't lift restrictions until negative. Our Animal Care team will be back for these bigger structural and maintenance issues."

Maya also refocused on easier deliverables. "I'll create a form for your staff to log their own health each day. That will help you keep on top of any changes."

She dug into her pocket for a business card. "I need a list of anyone having contact with Scout and Ariel in the two weeks before they became sick."

Pastor Adam's eyebrows drew together. "They're all fine."

"A person without symptoms can be contagious," Maya said. "The animals must have been been exposed by someone with SARS CoV-2 infection, unless you added new animals lately."

"Only the mama coyote. But one of our coons died a week ago, and our cougar refused a chicken bone this morning, one of his favorites."

A quiet "shit" slipped out from Dave; Maya hoped it wasn't loud enough for Pastor Adam to pick up. But no luck—he swung around to Dave and raised his voice. "Dr. Schwartz, we're doing the best we can. Everyone's hit hard by this virus—kids out of school, governor closing us down."

Dave stepped forward and his expression telegraphed a harsh response. Maya put a hand on his arm and jumped in. "If you have the raccoon carcass, we'll take it for testing. Can you show us the mountain lion?"

"Calah's over here." He led them to a third cage behind the other two, and the tawny cougar's rounded ears pricked forward above steely hazel eyes that matched Dave's. The chicken bone rested between her front paws, gathering flies. She lowered her head to smell it, then raised it again haughtily in disgust. *This ain't what I want, get rid of it.*

"Are these animals trained for taking clinical specimens without sedation?" Dave's tone implied he knew the answer.

Pastor Adam was again defensive. "We don't use vet care often enough to work on it."

"All right," Dave answered. "We won't try for a nasal swab or blood today. I'll call your vet, but we can take Calah's feces. And get rid of that bone."

Maya assessed the wide expanse of scarcely-vegetated dirt beyond the perimeter fence. Hard to believe anyone could maintain animals in the increasingly parched conditions of the Southwest.

"How about I get that information on staff and volunteers?" she asked. "I can manage the interviews, but will touch base with my boss about human specimens."

In the cluttered office, Pastor Adam sent Dave off with a keeper to collect fecal specimens. "Our payroll is computerized."

"Give me a printout," Maya ordered. "What about the volunteers?"

He tugged a lined yellow sheet from the bulletin board. "Here's the list with names and phone numbers."

"Make a copy. And you've got to reduce the number of people having close contact with the animals, particularly the sick ones. Can you triage your volunteers into more support functions, away from animal enclosures?"

He sighed. "We can try." His fingers reached for his mask. "It's just the two of us; can I take this off?"

"CDC's recommending them now."

"My wife made this one. How do you like these horses?"

Maya had been so nervous and focused on their investigation, she hadn't noted the mask design. "That might be a moneymaker for your refuge."

He made a polite bow. "Excellent suggestion, Dr. Maguire. Maybe we'll keep this place going, despite your Nazi colleague."

She was pleased to get on the owner's good side but had to defend Dave. "He's trying to do the right thing."

Dave pushed open the office door with his shoulder. He held a box of samples in one hand and a black trash bag in the other. "Thank you for preserving dead animals like this coon. We better pray this is negative so we don't have any spread to free-ranging wildlife."

Maya waved her lists. "I got what we need. Pastor Adam, we'll be in touch for those interviews and human lab testing."

As they approached Dave's truck, he asked, "Do you think they're taking this seriously?"

"He's concerned about the health of his animals."

Inside the vehicle, Dave turned on the engine. "I'm dropping these at the vet lab, then we can swing home. Want to stay the night, or at least for another home-cooked meal?"

"Only for dinner. I have a lot to discuss with Dr. Grinwold about these employees and volunteers."

. . .

"I got the best petroglyph picture." Braxton aimed his cell phone toward Maya.

"We don't allow those at the dinner table," Dave warned.

Emilia took his hand. "Amor, we're done eating. Braxton can help clean up after he shows Maya his photos."

Teresa grabbed toward the phone. "Papa, I'm almost seven, can I have one too?"

Dave stood to clear the plates. "You'll get a cell phone when you're able to take over Braxton's level of responsibility in this family."

Braxton moved closer to Maya. "Look at the weird shields these guys are carrying. This one has eyes, and the other one has footprints."

"It's pretty dramatic. I wonder what it means."

"They're looking out for danger, to run away if they see it. I learned in school about cliff dwellers pulling up ladders when bad guys come. What do you think, Dad?"

Dave gulped, then slowly answered. "We all need to learn the times to stand and fight versus an intelligent retreat."

"I like your photo composition," Maya complimented. "I'll introduce you to my fiancé. He's a photographer in his spare time, especially in beautiful natural areas like this one."

"I'm walking Maya to her car," Dave said. He reached down to tickle Teresa. "Impress me how you manage the cleanup by yourselves."

After Maya hugged Emilia and the two girls, Braxton stepped forward with his arms out. First time. She wasn't sure how affection was expressed in a polygamous sect. For a moment, she allowed herself to imagine having a teenage son. But she felt barely out of her teen years—way too soon to think in that direction.

"That was a new one," Dave remarked as they moved around the side of the house to her Prius.

"Braxton giving a hug?"

"And he called me Dad."

Maya took his weathered hands. "I'm so happy for you, Dave. Did you consider making it official?"

"The pandemic hit, and I've no clue if it's possible with his mother, our mother, still alive. She'd probably block me and Emilia trying to make Braxton legally our son. I don't even know who his father is. He doesn't talk about him."

"When we get back to normal, you'll resolve this family mystery. You keep serving as an example of domestic bliss, and I'll follow."

As she drove north on the highway, her skin glowed with the golden light flowing from the western horizon through her car windows all the way to the Sandia slopes. Tomorrow she'd start on solving coronavirus spread within Adam's Animal Ark. Tonight, she'd phone her fiancé to share a glass of wine and toast the small miracles of family life.

TWENTY-THREE

Santa Fe, New Mexico—Wednesday, May 13, 2020

Maya obsessed over her computer spreadsheet, making sure it was clear and accurate, before clicking **Send** to Dr. Grinwold. Fifty-two rows on the file, representing individual interviews she'd conducted from home with an Adam's Animal Ark staffer or volunteer.

She shuddered over her memory of the picture on Pastor Adam's office wall. A bear cub on a bench was hugged on each side by two children. He assured her it was taken pre-COVID and no one was bitten or scratched. But she'd posed for a similar photo with a panda cub in China when she was twelve, and the animal gnawed her hand.

Pastor Adam didn't have thorough notes about when the three big cats first appeared sick, and early clinical signs were non-specific. Although he guessed they'd only been ill since mid-April, he couldn't rule out the beginning of the month as the outside window.

The state ban on mass gatherings didn't include religious services. Little old church ladies who baked treats for weekly worship dropped off leftovers to those handling animal care. At the wildlife center, Pastor Adam tried to comply with the order to reduce the in-person workforce. He asked them to stay six feet apart when feasible.

With schools closed, youth volunteers had free time to take over grounds cleanup. Maya worried about their handling potentially contaminated waste without masks and gloves—something to check on at her next unannounced inspection with Dave.

She finally settled on March 23 as the cutoff date of concern for potential exposure. Some always did the same things and they had no recall problems. Others helped out wherever they were needed, so their recollections of animal contact were more sketchy.

Maya concluded each interview by asking about illness. For anyone reporting fever, cough, chills, muscle pain, or fatigue, she tried to persuade them to meet with the Bernalillo County health office for nasopharyngeal samples and blood draws. Knowing that people shed virus without showing symptoms, Dr. Grinwold considered ordering lab tests on anyone working closely with infected animals. But he was overruled—no one wanted TV cameras filming the sheriff dragging someone to the health clinic.

Eleven cooperated with NP swabs and four were PCR-positive, including the pastor. A volunteer had antibodies but was negative for virus, perhaps their index case. All five had close contact with the big cats. Maya planned the notification process for those who were positive, with the county taking care of the negatives.

As she opened her office door, Dr. Grinwold surprised her at the entrance.

"We solved the mystery," she said with a bright smile and confident pose. "Human cases and the big cats—we know how the wildlife center outbreak happened."

He nodded his head. "In your report, make sure to note when the symptoms started for everyone, human and otherwise. Even with inexact data, it may clarify that the people infected the animals, not the other way around. What about the raccoon?"

"It's negative."

"Thank God. We don't need Albuquerque slaughtering raccoons, afraid they'll spread the virus to pets, livestock, or humans."

Maya's stomach tightened, imagining that level of fear. "CDC still has no evidence of any person catching COVID from an animal."

"What are the results on the dead lion?"

Her mind snapped back to the emaciated animal's carcass spread-eagled on the stainless table. "Nothing remarkable on gross pathology but tissue samples are pending."

"Ask Dave if USDA can share the animal genome sequences. If they don't match human samples, then the human and animal infections might be coincidental rather than causal. Also find out when they'll be ready to issue a joint press release."

She sank to her computer chair. Were there ever any clear wins in public health? But she had her marching orders and would keep going. "Pastor Adam doesn't require masking except inside his office. With these results, I can insist on it for those working around susceptible animals."

"Make sure he accepts the change voluntarily so we don't have to force the issue."

Maya nodded, energized that her efforts might reduce disease transmission. "USDA has the permit for animal welfare, so Dave can lean on them too."

Dr. Grinwold's eyes wandered up to the greening grass outside Maya's window. "I'm sorry the EIS Conference was cancelled. Your last chance to present and connect to possible job opportunities."

"Me too. Lila, the California EIS Officer, had promised we could spend a few hours at Callaway Gardens enjoying the azaleas."

But then she flushed. "It's awful for you too. You were going to recruit my replacement."

His face was surprisingly complacent. "We'll work it out. Maybe CDC could give you a Preventive Medicine Residency assigned here."

Maya was heartened by his first overture for her staying in Santa Fe. She'd heard of the PMR program allowing another year of CDC training, but knew that veterinarians were rarely chosen, even though vets had board certification eligibility for preventive medicine like physicians.

"We've been so busy with COVID, my job search took a back seat. Let me talk to Dr. Jaworski and find out if Atlanta would support my PMR application."

He turned for the hallway, face again in a frown. "At least for the length of the pandemic, both of us may be condemned to limited time with our loved ones."

The reminder of Manolo brightened her mood. He was investigating COVID clusters at the San Felipe and Zia Pueblos between Albuquerque and Santa Fe, and had promised to sleep over. Every moment together would be treasured.

. . .

Manolo had texted he'd be at her place by eight for a late dinner, and by nine she began to pace the floor, pausing only for sips of water to calm down. Being late didn't mean something was wrong, unless he had an accident like she did last spring on the dark New Mexico roads.

If he had irregular hours in Phoenix, she'd never know and couldn't worry about it. Would this be the downside of being married? With her anxiety disorder, even partly managed with psychiatric care and group therapy, she might be a constant bundle of nerves. When he was in Arizona, it was easier to go with 'out of sight, out of mind.'

Confused by jumbled emotions, she glued herself to his body when he unlocked her front door at eleven. "I wish you'd kept me updated on your arrival time." Her tone chastised while she maintained the embrace.

He tossed his white uniform cap to her couch. The navy coat followed. "The meeting at San Felipe ran long, then an older man showed up late to the Zia Health Center. I was concerned enough about his respiratory function that I drove him to the Albuquerque Indian Health Center—no other transport was available in time."

She led him to the kitchen table. "I understand."

He dropped into one of the wooden chairs. "I've never done that before—driven a patient in my car who might nosedive any second. Not the best choice, but we're all operating at a new normal."

She massaged his shoulders, thumbs moving up to his neck. "I made you lasagna with spinach and hamburger. I got the idea from Mr. Clark, the dad of our first Arizona COVID patient."

He turned in the chair and took her hands. "I might be swimming in viruses. Let me put my uniform on your patio to air out, and take a quick shower."

She dropped his jacket and hat onto the table outside. He stood watching her, braced on the sliding door frame. "And give me those pants," she added.

Glancing over the fence, he hesitated.

"Come on, chicken, nobody will see you this time of night." She unbuckled his belt and pulled the pants down as he cooperated, half-asleep. Then she put an arm around his shoulders and guided him to the bathroom before she finished undressing him.

Her clothes were piled on top of his on the floor. "I'm joining you, to make sure you don't collapse midscrub. And if you contaminated me with your cooties, I'll get clean too."

No matter how many times they shared a shower, she never tired of it. What would it be like when they could do it every day, year after year? Maybe it would be their way to briefly bond, if too busy to share anything else. But if they had kids, she'd make sure he connected more than just under a spray of water. Another reason to postpone wedding and family planning until COVID settled down.

He was passive, barely moving as she washed him down with the soap bar and washcloth. She prayed the stress of long hours wouldn't cause a neurologic setback from his anthrax infection. As he sat on her bed with eyes closed, she searched the single black bag he'd dropped on the floor. Nothing to wear during dinner. But when she glanced up, he'd fallen back to the pillows, snoring. After shifting his legs, she crawled in next to him, pulled the covers over, and turned out the light.

TWENTY-FOUR

Santa Fe, New Mexico—Thursday, May 14, 2020

Using the spatula, Maya slipped the bigger omelet half onto Manolo's plate. When he opened up the back door to retrieve his uniform from the patio furniture, the sky was a tranquil yellow-blue-gray just before the sun peeked above the mountains.

"Guess I got lucky it didn't rain last night," he said with a grin. "Sorry to conk out on you."

She grabbed chopped green chiles from the refrigerator. "I should have brought your clothes in, but I was too concerned about you. You were like a zombie. All I could think about was anthrax."

"Don't let yourself go down that road. I'm back to complete health." He lifted the plate to his nose and sniffed. "This looks great, what did you put in it?"

"Two kinds of cheese, ham, tomatoes, and chiles. I figured you'd be hungry after missing dinner."

He smoothed a spoonful of extra chiles on top. "Nothing like a big meal to trigger wonderful brain tranquilizers, but I need to check on my patient."

After he completed the call, she asked, "Everything okay?" She poured him a cup of black coffee.

He smiled. "He's in the ICU but avoiding a ventilator. Glad I made that detour to Albuquerque."

"You go the extra mile for everyone, that's why I love you." She inhaled steam from her green tea, hoping it would kick in a caffeine boost even quicker than just drinking it.

"Are your parents mad? I haven't focused on our plans for July, after you finish your EIS training."

Maya took another bite of the omelet, the Gruyère and cheddar cheeses melted perfectly into a creamy delight. With COVID requiring her to stay closer to home, an unexpected benefit was improved cooking skills.

"Dr. Grinwold can keep me on another year if CDC approves me for a PMR."

"How many vets are board certified in preventive medicine?"

"Not that many; it would be a career boost."

He carried his plate and utensils to the kitchen sink. "Let's talk about it when I'm not so rushed. I promised to stop by Acoma Pueblo on my way back to Phoenix."

One or both of them in a hurry—she was getting used to it.

. . .

Midmorning, she finished her allotment of contact tracing phone calls and placed one to Erika. "How's working at home with Rolf and Kyle this week?"

As usual, her friend's tone was bright and assertive. "With this good weather, we don't feel like cave captives. I'm on my laptop, supervising Kyle using the slide."

"Does he miss his friends?"

"Our neighbors are allowing kids to play together in the backyards." Erika paused, then sounded sheepish. "Don't chew me out—he'd go nuts without other kid contact. We're creating our own neighborhood bubble to keep each other safe."

"The state's doing so well that the Governor might allow summer camps to open."

"Probably limited capacity and masked, but that would be a godsend for us."

"My fingers are crossed," Maya said. "Could you follow up on some genome testing for cases? Dr. Grinwold wants to see if the animal and human ones match at Adam's Animal Ark."

"Of course. Rolf just came out to throw a ball with Kyle, so I'll head inside and get started."

"Thanks, I'm trying to wrap up this outbreak report." As soon as Maya ended the call with Erika, another one came in from Manolo.

"I'm at the Acoma-Canoncito-Laguna Indian Health Center. A COVID patient has respiratory illness in her pets and I'm wondering about a connection."

"There might not be veterinary services in that area. I'll pull together my notes and join you."

After the two-hour drive, Maya pulled off I-40 at the closed Sky City Casino. The ACL hospital, blending with the browns of the surrounding soil, was distinctive with multiple triangular peaks. She texted Manolo and waited under the portal of adobe-colored and lighter swirls.

He pushed through the front door and pressed his body full-length into hers for a lingering kiss.

She finally broke away. "You make me tingle. But you're in uniform—I don't want anyone complaining about protocol."

He smiled. "All right, let's focus on work. Catch a ride with me to Sky City."

They provided their identifications at the security checkpoint and ascended the road, then he pulled the Corvette over to park next to the San Esteban del Rey Mission Church.

"This has got to be one of New Mexico's most beautiful old churches," Maya said.

"The mesa's been occupied for a thousand years but the Spanish built this in the early 1600's. Look at those massive adobe walls supporting the ponderosa vigas up top."

Maya glanced around at the dusty open plaza and narrow dirt lanes crowded with one- or two-story adobe homes. "It's pretty quiet. I don't see any animals or people."

"No tour buses during the pandemic." He consulted his notes. "Let's find Mrs. Chino's daughter to ask about her pet issues."

Near a lonely green tree, a huge woodpile clustered both sides of a white-framed door. Manolo knocked and they put on their masks.

"Dr. Miranda, please come in." The door was opened by a masked young woman with dark hair falling to her waist. Maya immediately focused on an orange-and-black pottery lizard in the window, next to a vase with a black deer and an orange arrow from his mouth to his heart.

"That's my mom's work. I had a table outside selling it before the pandemic."

"Incredible pieces," Maya said. "I love animals in art."

"Becca, Dr. Maguire is a public health veterinarian with the CDC. She may be able to answer your questions about COVID in animals."

"Do you have any sick pets?" Maya asked.

"I have two draggy dogs and my mother has a sneezing cat."

Maya brushed her hair out of her eyes. "Cats have been infected experimentally, plus a couple of dogs and one cat in Hong Kong tested positive without symptoms. Then two cats in separate New York households last month became ill and were confirmed with COVID. One owner had COVID before the cat got sick."

"How do we know if my dogs have it?" Becca opened the front door and peered anxiously out. "Could they give it to me?"

"Were they around your mother at the time of her illness?" Maya asked.

Becca nodded and Maya's pulse quickened. Based on the incredibly small number of cases, the odds were long, but the possibility of adding to COVID science excited her. "We have no evidence that pets can spread it to people, but I can take samples for testing."

While calling for the dogs, Becca led them down a hard-packed dirt street to the edge of the ancient village. They paused when she spotted movement in the jumbled boulders, but it was only a rock squirrel. "This is the oldest community in the country, yet we still don't have running water or electricity." She pointed toward a higher butte in the distance. "That's Enchanted Mesa, our first home. No one can climb it because it's haunted."

Becca tried a different alley. "We didn't always live here. The Spaniards sold us into slavery and chopped the right foot off our men of fighting age. That's why we hate the statues of Don Juan De Oñate." She glanced at Manolo and looked sheepish. "Sorry."

He adjusted his cap. "Not my fault—my people are from Puerto Rico."

Maya hoped his joking tone was clear, despite his mask. She didn't want their pet search halted before she got her eyes and hands on them.

Becca called again as they gazed out toward the modern village of Acomita and its greening grasslands below. Two mutts emerged, both a dun color matching the landscape and the homes. They leapt through a natural water hole, then wriggled in excitement around their owner, spraying everyone down.

"This is Lucy, the bigger one, and Jessie. I named them after two of our Four Matriarchs who revived Acoma pottery."

Maya pulled out her notebook. "Tell me what you're worried about."

"Today, they're looking lively, but both have stayed close to home the last week."

Maya knelt down to perform a physical exam on Lucy. When she palpated the dog's throat, Lucy coughed. "Are they up-to-date on all vaccinations, including kennel cough?"

Becca shrugged. "They have special clinics for rabies—I can't remember if they did others too."

Maya pulled out her stethoscope to listen to Lucy's lungs and Becca held her still. Manolo kept the other dog's attention by throwing a stick.

"I'm hearing crackles, particularly as I move toward the bottom of the lungs. I wish we could get an X-ray, but vet clinics may be reluctant to bring her in as a COVID-suspect. I can take lab specimens here."

Lucy cooperated with nasal and throat swabs, although she coughed with the second one. Maya was relieved they had kept on their masks and she'd added gloves, even though outdoors. For a moment, she wondered if she should have been gowned with a face shield, but it was hardly a high-risk setting.

"Any diarrhea?" she asked.

"Yes, with Jessie."

"Okay, I'll take rectal swabs too." Becca held the dog's hind end while Maya collected the specimen. "All done, now it's Jessie's turn."

The tiny dog required both Becca and Manolo to help with restraint. When Jessie tried to bite after the throat swab, Maya tied gauze around her nose while collecting the remaining specimens.

"You can let her go. I got everything without anyone getting hurt, so you're a good dog, Jessie." She reached down to pet her, and Becca offered a treat. Jessie's ears perked up and she responded with a doggie grin, all invasions forgiven.

Maya stood with her hands on her hips. She'd never evaluated COVID in pets and her clinical skills were rusty. Was there anything she was leaving out? She dug through her supplies for sterile wipes.

"Let me rub this over their fur. It won't diagnose infection but could pick up viral particles in the area." Specimens in her day pack, Maya followed Becca to Manolo's Corvette.

"If you want an adventure, Dr. Maguire, you can walk down a four-hundred-foot drop on a hand-cut staircase carved into the sandstone." She squinted and grinned. "Forgive me, I miss being in tour guide mode."

Maya shook her head. "Tempting, but another time. Can we can check out your mom's cat?"

"Sure, just follow my car."

When they reached a cluster of adobe homes at the base of a small mesa in Acomita, they parked their cars in the shade of a cottonwood. Becca located the black and white cat on her mother's empty bed. "What's this one's name?" Maya asked.

"Tuxedo. She's been sleeping a lot and sneezing."

The pet was lethargic and Maya made quick work with the specimens. "I wish I could recommend something to help Tuxedo recover, but there's no specific treatment for COVID. Is she still eating and drinking?"

Becca held a plate of canned food close to Tuxedo's nose. The cat sneezed once, gazed forlornly around at all of them, then began to nibble. "That's a good sign," Maya said. "If she stops eating and drinking, get a vet clinic to take her in for evaluation and fluids."

"Dr. Miranda," Becca said. "I want to check at the health center to see how Mom is doing."

He frowned. "You may not be able to visit her, but I'll meet you there. If necessary, I'll transfer her to Gallup or Albuquerque, whichever hospital has more room."

Becca picked up her keys and pivoted for the door. "See you in a few minutes."

Once parked again at the clinic, Manolo walked Maya to her car. "I don't know how long I'll be."

"Don't worry about it. I'll drive these specimens to the lab in Albuquerque. What's it like in Gallup? I heard the governor invoked the Riot Control Act to lock it down."

"It felt like a ghost town with all the roads closed, but barriers were removed Sunday. Unfortunately, McKinley County continues to have more COVID cases than anywhere else in the state."

Maya's entire body suddenly shook with a deep dread. "Manolo, your job takes you to all the COVID hotspots, and you're helping with patient care. I'm worried."

He flashed his widest smile, whether in confidence or to reassure her, she couldn't tell. "You can rest easy that I'm taking appropriate precautions. I'm not at risk like staff working the ICU full-time."

"All right, you know what you're doing." A nursing group had estimated that more than ninety thousand health care workers were infected worldwide, but he wouldn't appreciate a reminder of the danger, as if she didn't trust his ability to stay safe. "I wish we had a vaccine."

"The President promised one by the end of the year."

Maya hugged him tight. "It's such a nightmare." More than a million cases in the US and more than eighty thousand deaths. She could restrain herself from freaking him out, but couldn't stop her own brain.

"But the vaccine director just filed a whistleblower complaint," he said, "after arguing against the President's push for hydroxychloroquine."

Fear flooded her body from her head to her toes. Finding the time to untangle the logistics of their lives would never come, unless they prioritized it. She stroked her favorite curl on his forehead and locked eyes, feeling more determined than she had in months. "Even though we don't get weekends off work, I'm going to call you Saturday morning."

"Okay, anytime we FaceTime is wonderful."

She shook her head. "This won't be a routine call. I want to finalize a decision about this PMR with Dr. Grinwold, and our marriage. Everyone's postponing wedding ceremonies, but I don't want to wait on ours."

His embrace was like a weighted blanket and all her tension melted.

"That's music to my ears," he whispered.

TWENTY-FIVE

Santa Fe, New Mexico—Saturday, May 16, 2020

Maya stopped her bicycle before the Santa Fe Rail Trail intersected Rodeo Road. Pulling out her phone from the daypack, she checked the time. Manolo had promised to call from Phoenix after his morning hospital rounds, and she prayed he had managed a night's sleep at home.

After hooking her bike helmet and facemask on a handlebar, she sipped from her water bottle and poured some over a pocket handkerchief to wipe her face. The intense sun burned her bare arms and legs—she regretted not taking time for sunscreen. Traffic was light as she put away the bottle, then a loud male voice startled her into looking up.

"No Chink virus here!"

A beer can flew out a car window and slammed her in the cheek, spilling the pungent alcohol down her neck and chest. In a too-late reflexive action, she jerked away and tumbled to the asphalt path. Her bicycle gloves protected her hands, but her left forearm and calf scraped the pavement before her head hit.

"Woo-hee, got one," the guy screamed as the vehicle roared away.

Head spinning, she slowly raised to her knees and fingered the sore spot above her left ear. No blood colored her fingers, but it oozed from the arm and leg scrapes. She reached for her helmet and mask as FaceTime chimed.

She answered Manolo's call, sitting next to the bike path. "Good morning, Maya." His expression and voice were surprisingly cheerful considering his recent long work hours. "Are you outside?"

For a moment, she hesitated about sharing the incident, but keeping things to herself had caused rifts between them. She tilted her phone toward the bicycle, half on and off the path. "I had a tumble."

His eyes grew larger as he held his phone closer to his face. "Did you ride without a helmet?"

Irritated by his implication and overheating, she took another drink from her bottle. "I'm not an idiot, Manolo. I removed it during a rest break. Someone in a car threw a beer can and I shifted to avoid it."

"Shit, I never was comfortable with your being out alone. Is anyone still threatening you?"

"No, he's gone, just give me a sec." She poured water over the scrapes, flushing away dirt and small pieces of gravel. Then she tilted her phone to show them. "Nothing deep, just need to clean them up."

"Did you hit your head?"

She reversed the camera to see herself. "No visible head wounds." She paused at the tiny red welt on her cheek from the can, then felt above her ear again. "My head hit the pavement right here, but it wasn't hard. I'm just hot and anxious to get home."

His dark eyes narrowed. "You could have a concussion. Call 9-1-1 and get to Christus St. Vincent."

"Manolo, we don't need to interrupt their COVID care. Erika's a nurse—I'll ask her to meet me at home, then we'll call you."

"Can she pick you up? I don't want you on the bike again."

Getting out of the sun was her top priority. "I'm only a few minutes from the apartment. If I reach her now, she can be there by the time I walk back."

He removed his cap and scraped his hand through his hair. Maya finally noticed the wide expanse of green grass around him. "Are you out, too?"

"Madison Park. If I don't get a break from the chaos, I'll flip out." He put his cap back on and started walking. "Check in when Erika gets there. If I don't answer, leave a message."

His exhaustion and despair as he ended the call refocused Maya from her pain. She'd intended to ask for an update on Becca Chino's mom and pets, but forgot. Becca's worry tugged at Maya, reminded of the death of her grandmother.

The asphalt under her right calf seared like a frying pan and Maya shifted onto the grass. "Hi, Erika, do you have time to give me a hand? I took a spill off my bike."

Multiple kid voices filtered from the background. "Rolf can supervise these hellions. Where are you?"

"Can you meet me at my apartment?"

Maya tried putting her helmet back on to shield the sun but the moment it touched her aching head, she changed her mind and slipped it into her pack. The dizzy walk wearing her claustrophobic mask took twenty minutes, longer than she expected. More than once, she considered taking the mask off, but others were on the trail, walking and biking, some pausing to ask if she was okay.

The jeering driver and his words looped through her brain like a movie trailer. Attacks on Asians were increasing but she never anticipated being one of them. With only a few Asians around when growing up in the Southwest, she was used to stares and questions. A darker complexion and hair were common, so she didn't stand out until someone got close.

But she still didn't understand why this happened on an otherwise cheerful morning. Did he have reason to blame Chinese people for a slow response to keep COVID from spreading worldwide? Or their cultural practices of eating wildlife? Conspiracy theorists were already fingering arrogant scientists for letting the virus escape from a Wuhan viral research lab.

Erika pulled into the parking lot as Maya leaned the bike against the wall outside the apartment.

"I'll clean up those scrapes," Erika said. They kept their masks on as Maya unlocked the front door and lowered to the couch. "I assume you were wearing your helmet?"

"I fell over after I took it off during a rest break. I bumped my head, right here."

Erika's long fingers parted Maya's hair. "It's red and swollen already. Let me get an ice pack." She sniffed the air and adopted her stern mom tone. "Did you fall because you're drunk?"

Maya shook her head but the action increased the room's spin. "Someone threw a beer can and yelled a racial slur."

"Jesus." Erika turned for the freezer. "Any confusion, headache?"

Erika applied the ice and shifted Maya's hand up to hold it. Maya flinched at the pressure. "My head's hurting a bit and I got overheated and dizzy on the walk back."

Erika began to clean the wounds. "My clinical skills are rusty. I thought about helping at the hospital but we're too busy with our own jobs."

"Your bedside manner is still excellent."

"You won't sue me if you drop dead?" Erika's joke made Maya smile. "Get checked out by someone with an active license. And report it to the police—this kind of attack can't go unpunished."

"It happened so fast, I have nothing to tell them. Dark car, didn't see the driver, threw the can away. Listen, I can't stand another minute of this odor. Let me take a shower."

"Okay, but I'll wait right here."

Maya gave Erika her phone. "Can you call Manolo? He wants an objective report."

Erika's voice from the hall was barely audible over the warm shower spray. Maya made the cleanup short so Erika wouldn't worry. She fingered the bump above her ear while using the shampoo, then toweled quickly and dug out a clean mask from the cabinet.

When she opened the door a crack, Erika handed over her bathrobe. "Your fiancé ain't happy. I mentioned the size of your swelling and he almost came through the phone."

"I hate to get him sidetracked."

Erika led Maya to the couch and spread a thin layer of antibiotic ointment over the scrapes. "I thought you two were focused on transparency."

"We are. I don't want him abandoning his patients in Phoenix just because of this."

"Don't take aspirin because it increases the chance of a brain bleed. Any double vision, nausea, or tinnitus? Manolo wants you evaluated."

"Hospitals are overwhelmed—my slight injuries don't rise to the level of importance."

Erika rose and grabbed her purse. "I'd better get home. Rolf's the best dad but he doesn't supervise play dates as often as me. The kid workload isn't equally distributed."

Maya walked her to the door. "Thanks again, you're always available in a clutch. I take way too much advantage of your friendship."

Shaking her head, Erika reached out to hug Maya. "I know we're not supposed to do this anymore, but what the heck. You give back as much as you take, especially with that creep at work last year."

Back in the living room, Maya FaceTimed Manolo.

"Are you going to the hospital?" he asked, in full gown, mask, and face shield.

"I'm fine, no slurring of speech, nothing to indicate a concussion."

Even through his PPE, Maya could see his anger. "Too many people are dying from other causes, afraid to see the doctor because of COVID. I'll be damned if I let that happen to you."

"Manolo, it won't." His fear was unnerving, but he was working with patients who were distant from medical care and struggling to get by with fewer services. "I'm blessed with a nurse as a best friend and physicians as a boss and a fiancé. No way will I slip through the cracks."

"If we lived together, you wouldn't bike alone."

Maya carried the phone to the kitchen for a glass of water, hoping to counteract a rush of resentment. "If we get married, I can't go anywhere without you? Like that would be reasonable with the hours you're keeping."

She regretted her short temper but seemed unable to corral it. "Can you harangue me some more when you're off duty? They can't work you 24/7."

He appeared about to argue when a faint voice filtered from the ceiling above his head. "Dr. Miranda, room C13."

"If anything changes, call immediately," he ordered. "I'll check in with you later."

Maya was dying to put harsh words behind them. "Please do that, no matter how late. We have a lot to talk over."

TWENTY-SIX

Santa Fe, New Mexico—Sunday, May 17, 2020

FaceTime chirping at one AM woke Maya up. She opened her eyes to see it was Manolo.

"I'm sorry, this was the first time I've been able to get away from the hospital. How are you doing?"

Maya sat up higher in bed, trying to stimulate her brain cells. She felt like she'd been hit by a beer keg instead of a can of Coors. It wasn't a concussion—she'd Googled all the symptoms and had none of them. Her fingers went to the area of her head where she fell, and it was a bit less sore. No ugly red streaks on her arms or legs indicating infection beyond the gauze bandages.

"I'm fine, really. Just a few more scrapes among many." She was freaked out about him, the hours he was keeping, his exposure to COVID. She had tried to nap while waiting for his call, but woke every few minutes to check the time.

"Any chance Dr. Grinwold can look you over in your office tomorrow? Sometimes symptoms get worse."

"We work from home to minimize the number of people having contact. But he's often there, with a much smaller in-person staff. I'll talk to him about my accident, if it makes you feel better."

He set his phone on his nightstand and unbuttoned his white shirt. "Yes, it would." Maya admired his well-defined muscles, a reward from endless physical therapy during anthrax recovery. He was even more attractive to her than when they first met.

"Two months since we slept together," Maya said. They had tried, first in Gallup and then Acoma. But each time they intended to spend quality time alone, he was off to another COVID emergency.

After seeing the work-life balance of her European colleagues, she'd planned for the same. Instead, the SARS-CoV-2 virus stole their lives.

She flushed with embarrassment about any resentment of their sacrifices. Only a few months into the pandemic, millions of people had it worse. Businesses bankrupt, employment disappeared. Families in jeopardy when they couldn't afford rent or mortgages, and lost learning at critical stages of kids' development. Hundreds of thousands of deaths worldwide. Maybe even her grandmother.

But for a few minutes, she'd focus on their relationship. "We haven't made love since I told you about Enzo, and both of you almost blew up your jobs."

He continued undressing in full view of the iPhone camera. "You have to admit, this phone sex has been kinda nice."

Maya followed his cue and slipped out of her silk negligee. "I'm sure I look appealing with these new wounds."

Jumping naked into his bed, he crooked his finger as if to draw her closer. "It's the underlying structure that counts. You're built beautifully, in body, intellect, and soul."

Maya had insisted he call her for a discussion of work and marriage. But neither of them was fully coherent at one in the morning. She opened her drawer and pulled out her vibrator. "Mind if I use this?"

. . .

Manolo's videochat pinged again at five PM. "I finally have a night off. Not enough time to drive there, but we can have the talk you wanted."

She appreciated his making the effort, although not talking in the wee hours had been nice, too, even if mimicking his touch didn't match the real thing.

Plunging ahead, she decided to lay her cards on the table. "Everyone's cancelling weddings right and left, but I want to schedule ours. Let's do it as soon as possible after I'm done with EIS on June 30. We can honeymoon by holing up in whatever city we have the ceremony."

"My family can't come in from NYC—they'd have to quarantine for fourteen days after flying."

"We'll have another ceremony or party when travel's more feasible. I don't want anyone to risk their lives by being together in a group. Ultimately this is about us."

He nodded, a surprised but joyful expression on his face. "Most women want the big, fancy wedding. I don't want you to regret giving up yours."

"I'm not most women, if you haven't figured that out by now."

He laughed. "Too true. Okay, what's the setting for this great occasion?"

"The county clerks here in New Mexico are issuing marriage licenses again by appointment."

"Sí, mi amor, you got a date."

Maya loved the adrenaline rush from their enthusiastic planning. It was almost too easy settling the wedding. Now the more challenging issue.

"I'm going to take the PMR position. Dr. Grinwold worked it out with CDC."

His face fell. "I hoped you'd do something similar here in Phoenix."

The last thing she wanted was another argument, but she pushed on. "I have to change job titles because my program is done, so it's logical I'd move. But I'm not comfortable working closely with Enzo."

"It's not my first choice either, but we'd be together. He couldn't use the excuse of us being broken up."

Maya's steely determination started to waiver. Why should the fear of Enzo derail what she and Manolo wanted? Maybe she wasn't as courageous as she had hoped. Faye said that working with difficult people was part of the territory in all jobs, but Enzo was a particular stress she preferred to avoid.

"According to Nancy, Enzo's reformed, afraid of others blackballing him. But I'd much prefer to work with Erika and Stephanie every day than see Enzo."

Manolo stayed silent and didn't look convinced. She tried humor. "Come on now—northern New Mexico has fewer people, a comfortable four-season climate, hiking and skiing and history out the back door. It's no contest."

His lips inched up into a smile. "I feel about my Phoenix colleagues the same as you do—I'd hate to leave them. But IHS needs staff everywhere. I'll request a transfer to Albuquerque."

She danced around in a circle, twirling the phone. "Why did we ever think this wedding and job planning would be so difficult?"

He laughed along with her ebullience, then warned, "Your mom won't be happy that she's not part of the wedding team."

Her mood turned somber. "COVID has them spooked—they're convinced it killed Grandma. They can throw us a blowout reception when the pandemic is over. I'll call them with the good news."

"Cariña, I'm counting the weeks, just six to go. I hope we don't have to wait that long to see each other, but even if we do, it will be worth it. I'll keep you posted on my discussions with IHS."

Maya hung up, happier than she could ever recall, even more than on their first days of intimacy in the Chaco Canyon tent. Then she laughed at herself. A plan and commitment for lifetime love was more important to her than sex. Fortunately, they'd work out a way to have both.

TWENTY-SEVEN

Santa Fe, New Mexico—Monday, July 6, 2020

Their fingers entwined as they walked down the sidewalk toward the central fountain of Harvey Cornell Rose Park. The bushes burst with luminescent color. As the temperature threatened to reach eighty degrees, the rose fragrance was potent enough to inspire.

Maya had chosen a sleeveless white silk dress with a bow at the waist. The hem skimmed her knees above bare legs, black sandals, and rare red-painted toenails. She knew white was the color of death for the Chinese, but she was fully American and wearing white was her one nod to tradition. No veil or makeup, just a single red rose Stephanie had pinned behind her ear. Her only jewelry besides the engagement ring was a new pair of turquoise pendant earrings, a gift from Manolo.

He looked dashing in black pants topped by a white guayabera, the traditional short-sleeved Puerto Rican men's shirt with embroidered vertical stripes. Approved for a few days off work, he'd allowed his facial hair to grow into her favorite goatee.

Erika, ahead on the grass, waved at them. "Maya, your mom asked you to stop for a minute so she can talk to you." She was Zooming on her iPad with both families from Flagstaff and New York City.

Manolo tightened his hand and brought Maya to a halt. "Is it bad luck to kiss before the ceremony? I can't wait."

His fingers tugged down their masks and his lips moved over hers with tender care. She responded passionately until hoots and hollers from Erika's iPad reminded her of the audience. Maya pulled Manolo closer to the screen.

"Mom, do you have some final advice?"

Her mom nudged her dad and winked. "Be your own woman, but let him think he's in charge."

Maya didn't answer but hugged Manolo tight. Stephanie opened her phone, showing them the screen with Linda Ronstadt's *Tú Sólo Tú*. "Are you sure you want this song? Desperation, crying, mourning—it's kind of dark."

"We know," Maya assured her, "but the passion is over the top. We just love how it sounds."

The throbbing notes accompanied them as they continued their approach to the low stone wall surrounding the brilliant blue of the pool and the ornate black central fountain.

The lines around the middle-aged minister's eyes deepened as she smiled above her own mask. She'd supported Maya's use of the Unitarian Universalist piano on occasional weeknights while Manolo healed from anthrax. Maya had stopped that practice during the pandemic, but the minister was excited to officiate the wedding service.

"Do you have the marriage license?"

Maya nodded. "We picked it up Friday from the county clerk."

"And your witnesses?"

Maya introduced Stephanie, resplendent in a wide-skirted red dress that complemented her graying dark hair, and Dave, towering over her in a sky-blue chambray shirt with blue jeans and a black cowboy hat.

Manolo squeezed Maya's hand and glanced at Reverend Tricia. "Should we get started?"

As Erika drew closer with her iPad, the minister began. "This ceremony is the personal statement of Maya and Manolo. It was adapted from previous ceremonies dating as far back as 1855. This man and this woman stand in our midst today to celebrate what has already become a reality within and between themselves."

Maya projected her voice through the mask, realizing that her family and friends on the Zoom call were hanging on every word. "We both have goals and ambitions of our own as well as shared ones. We will give to each other comfort in our failures and encouragement in our successes."

Manolo did the same, his confident voice projecting even louder. "Our relationship is inspired by our belief that we are equal human beings. We've also learned the hard way to be totally honest as a demonstration of our commitment."

Maya took her turn again, still holding his hands and gazing into his eyes. She pushed aside the thought of the Zoom spectators and focused only on Manolo. "I love your enthusiasm for life. You treat everyone with respect. You're passionate for your work as a physician helping Native Americans, and equally passionate for your family and for me."

Manolo's dark eyes moistened. "Maya, nobody is more scrupulous about figuring out the right thing to do than you. It's almost a fault, really." Laughter erupted from their small audience.

"Ain't that the truth," Dave interjected.

"But it's your courage," Manolo continued, "to persist no matter what's in your way, either personal demons or outside obstacles. That's what I love."

Reverend Tricia raised both her hands. "With these words, Maya and Manolo dedicate themselves to the strength and fragility of the marriage relationship. They're saying no to the world's cynicism and skepticism. Recognizing all the challenges ahead, especially in a pandemic, do you, Manolo, take Maya to be your wife, to love her and to cherish her?"

Manolo nodded. "I do."

"And do you, Maya, take Manolo to be your husband, to love him and to cherish him?"

Maya bounced up and down on her toes in excitement. She'd never been one of those girls who dreamed of the perfect husband, yet somehow she'd found him. "Without a single doubt, I do."

The group laughed again, and Stephanie whispered just loud enough for Maya to hear, "Dios mío qué hermosa boda."

"And how will you demonstrate your commitment?"

"Through our rings," they answered in unison.

Stephanie handed Maya a simple platinum band carved on the edges with a black lightning pattern, which Maya slipped on Manolo's finger. To the single diamond of the engagement ring on Maya's left ring finger, Manolo added his mother's antique platinum band crowned by five small diamonds.

Maya blushed as she gazed at it. When he showed it to her a few days earlier, he said the stones represented their children. She'd poked him in his arm. "Are you planning to give birth to some of them? Let's take it one kid at a time."

Reverend Tricia stepped forward and joined their hands together, raising them above her head. "With much joy, I now pronounce you husband and wife. You may make it official with a kiss."

Both whipped off their masks and embraced to the cheering of the others present and the Zoom audience. Stephanie handed Reverend Tricia the marriage license, then she and Dave signed as the witnesses.

"Thanks again for performing our ceremony," Maya said, "even though we don't belong to your congregation."

"It's no problem. Erika and Rolf are great supporters, especially of the kids' religious education program. And we appreciate your donation."

Manolo looked around the empty park. "Your suggestion of a weekday to reduce crowds was a good one."

"I stroll over here often from our church, so I knew this would work for social distancing."

A horn blasted as someone hollered from a passing car. Maya jumped in a reflexive response to the memory of the beer can. Manolo rubbed her bare arms.

"Are you thinking of your bike accident?"

"Which one?" she asked in a wry tone. But a thrown beer can and a racial slur didn't have the same lifelong impact as the teenager in the pickup mowing her down on her bike when she was five.

She glanced down at her left arm and leg. Abrasions healed, just a slight discoloration as a souvenir of the man's attack, nothing like the hate crimes others were facing. In March, a man stabbed three members of a Texas family including children because he thought they were Chinese and spreading coronavirus.

At a picnic table, Stephanie broke open a bottle of Gruet sparkling wine bottled in New Mexico and poured glasses for the small wedding party. When the minister waved goodbye, walking north through the rose bushes, Erika redirected her iPad.

Maya studied the thumbnails on the screen. Hypatia's tail zoombombed the one with her parents' ecstatic expressions. "As you can see," her dad said, "your favorite kitty is right here, one of the celebrants."

"You left me nothing to do," her mom complained, ruddy cheeks glowing as bright as her dyed hair. "But I couldn't be happier. As soon as it's safe, we're meeting in person to plan the reception."

"Make that two receptions," Sebastian Miranda added, to the nods of Ramona, Abdi, and Johnny crowded in. "NYC is waiting to PAR-T-Y!"

"Mi esposo, did you get some pictures?" Emilia asked, surrounded by Braxton, Teresa, and Lydia. Bo jumped up and barked before Dave could answer.

"You guys are reaching a vet's heart with all your animals sharing our joy," Maya said.

"Then you should see what we've got here." Janey shifted her laptop to show Óscar on the couch with her three cats and the terrier. A camera-ready grin, hinting that Maya's previous transgressions have been forgiven since Janey's birthday.

"I wish I could have performed the ceremony," Ben said from the thumbnail with Nancy. "But with our travel reductions, I'm glad you worked it out. It was beautiful."

Nancy's smile was as broad as Maya had ever seen it. "Our whole crew in Phoenix sends their congratulations. You made a lot of friends here, Maya, when you helped us out with anthrax and *Borrelia*."

Maya said hello to the Santa Fe Zoom contingent anchored by Dr. Grinwold. Dave took a few more posed photos, then everyone took off. Maya and Manolo lingered in the park, awash in color. In one corner, velvety purple irises. Along another path, brilliant tulips, almost as red as Stephanie's dress. And the roses. Pink roses blending to a pale center emanating luscious lavender. A vibrant yellow rose wafting lemons. And orange roses floating fruity fragrance.

"Look at this." Maya fingered an unopened bud with a ladybug. "Some people believe they're good luck."

"Beneficial for fighting off nasty invaders, like your job."

She blushed. "You give me too much credit. I'm one of thousands working in public health, you included." She glanced around—the park was theirs alone. "I hope no one minded that we skipped a celebratory lunch." She twirled her arms around Manolo's neck and stole another kiss.

"None of us can afford to be sick, and I'd like a quiet couple of days before I start work in Albuquerque on Wednesday."

He had the tougher job—she should have pushed harder for that little adobe they spotted for sale near the university. But his wanting to ease her driving stress won out, and they stayed put in her Santa Fe apartment. "Maybe we can ride together on the days I help teach one of the UNM public health courses," she offered.

As they approached the Corvette, a golden low-rider, striped with green, bumped on by. The teenage driver exclaimed "Congratulations" out his window. Then Maya spotted the *Just Married* sign on the Corvette's back bumper.

"Now I know why we got so many shout-outs," Manolo said.

"I'll have to use my medical detective skills to figure out who did that. I bet it was Dave, but I wouldn't put it past Stephanie and Erika, either."

He opened the car door. "Right now, I just want to get home to the privacy of your, I mean our, apartment."

. . .

She was reminded again of her friends' help when they entered the living room. Over the July fourth weekend, Dave had used his pickup to haul some of Manolo's furniture to Santa Fe, with the rest going into Phoenix storage. Gone was her couch with the failing springs and the Formica-topped dining table with uneven legs.

"You must hate moving from your modern two-bedroom to this tiny dump."

He gestured to the walls, covered with his black-and-white landscape photos. "As long as I have these and my kitchen utensils, I'm doing great. We'll buy a house when you're in a permanent position."

Maya tugged him down to the comfortable sofa. "Dave can help us find an old adobe in the Bernalillo bosque. Or Mr. Zielinski raves about his Pecos ranch. I'd love to nest near nature."

"Has Dr. Grinwold said more about the State Public Health Veterinarian position? I guess he might have to wait until next summer when your residency is complete."

"Yeah, I don't think I can have a named state position while still a CDC employee."

He smoothed the wave of dark hair away from her left eye and kissed the small mole next to it. "Have I told you lately how I love this beauty mark? Your skin would be too perfect without it."

Her lips brushed the hairs growing over his upper lip, then she drew apart. "I'm having trouble relaxing. COVID's spiking in our age-group."

His expression became serious. "And we're running out of remdesivir to treat it. But the world won't end if we take this small break from work."

The doorbell rang and Maya went to answer it. She carried a FedEx box from Nancy.

"Wedding present?" Manolo asked.

Maya sliced open the tape with a knife, then pulled out a small pottery figure. The handpainted Native American girl wore a bright red dress and cape and towed a yellow kite. "A DeGrazia windchime—so precious." She read the note out loud.

Maya, I hope you treasure this small keepsake from Tucson's famous artist. May it remind you of your beloved grandmother and your Southwestern heritage. With Manolo joining you in New Mexico, I won't get to see you as often, but keep in touch. As soon as this pandemic is over, I still plan to retire and join

Fred in Santa Fe. So I look forward to becoming your New Mexico neighbor.

Manolo cradled the figure in his hands. "This is too fragile to hang outside. Maybe here, by the front window?"

Maya nodded, then spotted a padded envelope at the bottom of the box with a large sticky note and Nancy's handwriting.

Enzo asked me to include this as a wedding present. I'm not sure what it is, but I hope you can accept it in good faith. He seems genuinely remorseful about his missteps and has been a godsend here.

"Remorseful, huh." Maya handed Manolo the note. "He hasn't expressed that to me recently."

Manolo answered with a sly smile. "I haven't told him I'm sorry for scaring him into a fall."

Maya opened the envelope to reveal a small framed print of the *Chinese Girl*. "Yikes, this is way too personal. A larger version's in his office."

Tugging her back to the couch, he took the print from her hands. "It's trash, just like him. Throw it away."

"I probably will. The picture is beautiful but eerie. I don't think he's recovered from his obsession over me."

Manolo stroked her eyebrows. "Relax this frown. We're living in New Mexico now. He's out of our lives."

"Your wish is my command, mi esposo." Both hands slipped to the front of his pants, one to unzip them and the other to remove his cell phone. She turned it off and did the same with her own.

When they entered the bedroom, she smiled at the rose petals garnishing Manolo's king-sized bed. "That's why Stephanie wanted my keys. We're spoiled by the quality of our friends."

"You're the one who inspires such loyalty." He tugged the white dress over her head to reveal she was naked beneath.

"Quite scandalous for wedding attire. Good thing the wind didn't blow your skirt up." His grin indicated his approval and he quickly removed his own clothing, dumped on the chair.

"I remember one occasion with this bed and silk scarves

as restraints." Maya pulled back the sheets. "But not today." She withdrew a peacock feather from the drawer. "A new prop for entertainment."

She pushed him down and danced the plume over his belly, causing his flesh to flinch. He moaned and pulled at her arm to join him.

"Not yet, it's my turn to make my husband totally thrilled to marry me. When I get the desired reaction, you can return the favor."

He accepted the passive bliss for only five minutes, then moved her under him to officially consummate the marriage, no going back.

TWENTY-EIGHT

Albuquerque, New Mexico—Tuesday, August 11, 2020

Under the shade of a UNM honey locust tree, Maya sipped her cola from the vending machine as the meeting to update vaping guidelines finished up. She was grateful the meeting was outdoors for COVID safety. The picnic tables were close to the duck pond, where spray from the fountains drifted over with a light breeze to cool her bare arms.

Anytime she came down to Albuquerque, she tried to touch base with Dave, so she gave him a call. "Manolo's tied up at the hospital here. Can we can arrange a last-minute lunch?"

"Sounds good, I've been meaning to show you the pictures I took at your wedding. Emilia packed a lunchbag with fried chicken— we can share. Where should we meet?"

"I'm between the UNM library and the duck pond."

Ten minutes later, he strolled up, black cowboy hat cocked and rattlesnake boots dusty.

"You must have broken the speed limit."

"Ma'am, you sayin' I'm a lawbreaker?" He set the Halloween-themed lunch bag on the table.

Maya studied the arched black cat, skeleton tree, and flapping bat on the bag. "I like your style."

"I borrowed this from Lydia. The girls are at a horse training camp this week." He split up the chicken on napkins.

Maya took one bite and swooned. "Never in my life will I cook like Emilia."

"Yeah, Dr. Maguire, it comes with being a well-trained traditional wife."

Maya kicked him under the table. "Is that a dig because I didn't change my last name like she did?"

He chortled. "So easy to get you going."

After wiping her fingers, Maya took a swig from her cola. "And what's Braxton up to?"

"We adopted a Bureau of Land Management wild mustang. He's helping Emilia around the house and breaking the mare."

"Anything new with your extended family?"

He shook his head, expression turned to disgust. "Utah decriminalized polygamy so they probably shifted across the border. Let's change to a happier subject." He skimmed the wedding photos on his phone. "This one of Manolo holding the rose up for you to smell is my favorite. Your face is the picture of bliss, and you're mighty purty, just like the flower."

Maya smiled—his banter always cheered her up. "Why thank you, kind sir. You've got a good compositional eye. Email them to Manolo. He's got photo editing software and can generate some beautiful prints."

Dave put the phone away and waved a drumstick. "How's married life treating you?"

The question was casual but felt loaded. "A month is hardly long enough to tell." She hesitated. "You and Emilia didn't live together before marriage, right?"

"Nope, mortal sin, according to her Catholic faith."

With the sun creeping onto the table, Maya poked her ponytail through the strap on her Yankees ballcap. "Well, we're getting gritchy with each other. He forgets to put the seat down on the toilet, that kind of thing."

Dave snorted. "Yeah, and I suppose you don't do anything to annoy him."

"I hate washing dishes right after a meal, which is a major pet peeve for him. We actually raised our voices about it, then decided to let whoever is bothered more by something take care of it."

"Fighting already—an ominous sign."

Maya's heart clutched and her hand with the cola trembled.

"You're teasing me."

"Kid, if you haven't figured that out by now, you don't know me well." Sweat beading his neck, he helped her up and shifted the table into the shade. "So is this lunch date just for the pleasure of my company?"

Maya dug out her water bottle from her daypack and relaxed. "I heard about COVID outbreaks in farmed European mink."

Dave laughed. "Those animals sure are nasty little buggers. One guy here trains them for pest control."

"How the heck does that work?"

"They can nail nuisance rats or muskrats under structures where dogs can't reach."

"Does USDA have any details on the European outbreaks?"

His laconic face turned serious. "At least one person was likely infected by a mink in the Netherlands, which is contrary to the trend of people giving it to animals. And they're blaming cats for spreading it between farms."

"They're culling mink—any idea how many?"

He shook his head. "Spain and Denmark, too."

That much animal euthanasia made her nauseous. "Reminds me of the 2001 outbreak of foot and mouth disease in the UK." Gruesome photos from vet school flashed—millions of cattle and sheep with legs rigid in rigor mortis dumped into the smoke of a funeral pyre. "The impact on farming families is devastating."

Maya was comforted by the limited animal transmission with COVID. Becca Chino's cat and two dogs were confirmed, but her mother got off a ventilator in Gallup. Based on viral sequencing, CDC concluded human-to-animal transmission. Somehow Becca got lucky and hadn't shown any clinical signs.

But Dave counteracted her relief. "I got an internal USDA alert about increased mink mortality in Utah and Arizona. Sometimes it's linked to contagious diseases or predation on each other, if the cages aren't far enough apart."

"CDC and state health will want to evaluate staff if COVID is confirmed."

"That's why the heads up, but this better not leak out. Mink farmers are sensitive to damaging press, with so many people opposed to the industry."

"I don't know the health department staff in Utah."

"It's a different district and not my responsibility. Hopefully Arizona animal deaths aren't COVID. The farmers are part of my mother's, and Braxton's, polygamist group. I'd rather not get tangled up with them in a regulatory capacity."

Maya checked her phone. "Can you drop me at the southside water reclamation plant? I'm meeting someone from the environmental health department to consider sewage testing. Coronavirus can be shed in the feces."

He packed up the remnants of their lunch. "How would you use that info?"

"Italy thinks they've had SARS-CoV-2 in their wastewater since December, even though their first human case didn't pop up until February. Same with France and Australia. The virus might have been spreading out from China before we heard about it on New Year's Eve. Monitoring sewage could give an early warning."

He unlocked his truck and held the door. "Huge task, filtering all that wastewater for tiny virus particles."

Within fifteen minutes, he dropped her off to the facility wedged between the Rio Grande River on the west and clusters of trailers and older ranch homes on the east. Staff gave her a quick tour on the catwalks between the huge aeration basins. With a slight breeze, the odor triggered involuntary nausea. She and Manolo had decided to discontinue birth control, but she couldn't already be pregnant.

The meeting at the outdoor table was brief, and skepticism high. A city environmental health staffer asked, "Why would this assessment go any faster than human testing?"

A water specialist from New Mexico Environment Department agreed. "We have no idea on cost or feasibility."

The lack of enthusiasm was contagious but Dr. Grinwold had tasked her with the initial exploration, so she kept pressing, proud that she felt confident to argue against the tide. "We're struggling to manage COVID in high-risk facilities, like nursing homes and prisons. Maybe there are grants for testing there. Could Albuquerque try a pilot project?"

When the debate broke up, she strolled to the perimeter close to the river and removed her mask to inhale oxygen emitted by the dense band of trees. Anything to counter the wastewater odor. Then she pulled out her phone and called Manolo.

. . .

Maya drove the Corvette home to Santa Fe so he could decompress. He leaned back in the passenger seat and exhaled a sigh, deep from his core.

"Another COVID death—thirty-year-old Zuni woman with hypertension. She delivered her baby by C-section in the ICU last week, but never got off the ventilator. Her husband asked us to reduce the sedation so she could be aware of their new son, but she became too distressed and we had to reinstate it. I'm not sure if she ever realized she gave birth before she died."

"Oh, God, Manolo, I'm so sorry." She reached over to steady his trembling hand for a moment, then merged into rush hour traffic.

He brushed her hair behind her ear. "We're both at risk of COVID and I couldn't bear losing a baby, too. We have to postpone your getting pregnant until all this settles down."

"But the husband has his son." Her consoling words sounded wrong, like the loss of his wife didn't count.

"Other hospitals have increased stillbirths." He twisted in the seat. "They keep talking about a vaccination, but it's months away."

Her cheeks and forehead heated up with exasperation. She had to get him off the doomed pregnancy talk that hit too close to home. "Let me focus on the road so I can get us there safely." When the traffic eased, she provided quick updates on her vaping and wastewater meetings.

He hadn't eaten all day, so she let him shower alone while she focused on a new chicken pot pie recipe from the Barefoot Contessa. She'd used any spare time cocooning at home in learning to cook. Doing it for herself had never been enough motivation.

When Manolo rejoined her, smelling of her honeysuckle shampoo, they relaxed on the couch with trays of salad and Sauvignon Blanc.

She hesitated about the kid discussion. It had been important to them, a significant contrast to his first wife. Maya wasn't sure they should allow COVID to derail them, like they didn't let it delay the wedding.

"Manolo, I won't go back on the pill, but we can use condoms for a while."

He caressed her ear lobe, expression relieved. "I can't handle anything else."

In the depths of his anthrax recovery, he had struggled to walk and speak again, but she'd never seen him anxious. This was a new ballgame. "Does IHS have counselors on board?"

"They're overloaded. I'll be okay. With my infection control duties, my ICU rotations aren't as heavy as most."

Dave's news about possible SARS-CoV-2 in Arizona mink flashed through her mind. He had warned her to keep it quiet, but secrets had jeopardized her relationship with Manolo too many times. He'd feel obligated to notify the Native American nations in the Four Corners, and she'd be at fault if the announcement leaked. A lose-lose predicament.

Like an ostrich with its head in the sand, she pretended they weren't immersed in an atmosphere of virus. She picked up his hand and led him to bed with no resolution.

TWENTY-NINE

Freedom City, Arizona—Thursday, August 20, 2020

With Dave snoozing under his cowboy hat, Maya pulled out of his ranch at six AM for the Arizona/Utah border. Strong winds heaved monsoon clouds toward the glowing sunrise and danced a few leaves carpeting the bosque with splashes of yellow. Maya's mood was optimistic, despite the first night away from her new husband. On FaceTime, Manolo had pulled out every Spanish endearment he could think of, with translations in loving detail.

Once they exited I-40, Dave took over on the two-lane highway through Hopi country, driving with a lead foot. Around two PM, he climbed out of his truck at the gate to the Fundamentalist Latter-day Saints compound. Hat twisting in his hands, he ambled around to open Maya's door and bent to whisper, "There's more barbed wire since I visited last summer."

He offered his business card to the armed security guard. When he asked for Eden Farnsworth, his and Braxton's mother, the guard's rugged face exploded in rage. The man leapt at Dave, grabbing him from behind with one arm locked around his throat and the other pinning Dave's fist between his shoulder blades.

Maya leaned a shaky hand on the truck hood, the other grasping her phone. But Dave twisted out of the guard's grip like a lithe panther. Leg out—trip—the guy went down. Then popped back up.

"Buddy, do we really want to do this?" Dave cocked his fist—a wallop. Knuckles crunched nose.

A handful of women in floral-print prairie dresses peered around the buildings, and a phalanx of men in dark suits with rifles emerged. Maya stepped between them and Dave. "Please, can we just go?"

A tall, ascetic man raced a four-wheeler through muddy tracks, then helped off a thin middle-aged woman who had clung to his back. He waved aside the patrol and approached Dave without offering his hand.

"I'm Aaron Farnsworth, chief elder of the First Order. This is my second wife, Eden."

Dave blanched under his deep tan and Maya remembered that he'd never met his mother.

"Schwartz." Aaron Farnsworth spit out Dave's name like a poisoned pill. "You have our son."

"Thank God for that."

Maya caught her breath, astonished at Dave's impudence when confronted by so many automatic weapons. In a somber gray dress, Eden Farnsworth stepped forward, hair upswept and the color of yellow corn. Her narrow lips, Roman nose, and deep-set hazel eyes matched Dave's.

"I regret I did not greet you when you came by last summer." The voice was as dull as the high desert sand.

"I wish you had too." Dave straightened his spine, readjusted his surgical mask dislodged in the altercation with the guard, and adopted his professional voice.

"Dr. Maguire and I are here to inspect your mink farm. A Utah mink farm was confirmed this week with coronavirus. We need to look at animal health and speak with the workers."

Eden Farnsworth reached a hand toward Dave, then pulled it back. "How is Braxton?" No curious questions for Dave, the son she abandoned as an infant, about his own health and well-being. To the mass of onlookers, they might have been unrelated.

He grunted. "Smart kid. You did him a favor by tossing him out like the trash."

Maya stood close enough to see moisture dampen the woman's eyes. But Dave's antagonistic attitude wouldn't defuse the tension. She tried to appeal to a mother's values as she handed Eden her business card. "Do the children help with mink farm tasks? We're concerned that the animals could spread COVID to people."

Aaron Farnsworth took Maya's card out of his wife's hands and tore it up, pieces floating like snowflakes to the red soil. Then he pulled out a handgun and shoved it into Maya's side to force her back to Dave's vehicle.

"You're not invading our homes today," he shouted in her ear. He waved at the head guard, who strong-armed Dave as he tried to leap to her defense. The militia remained wide-stanced with fierce expressions and weapons aimed, until Dave's truck skidded out of the dirt to the paved road.

. . .

At the café takeout window, Maya ordered a chicken salad sandwich and Dave a cheeseburger. Then they glowered across the patio table at each other like two alpha wolves circling. No words, just hostile body language and quiet groans as they adjusted for comfortable positions on hard wooden benches. With Dave's stubborn Texas cowboy roots, Maya knew she'd have to make the first move. In her mind, she ducked down and exposed her throat.

"I'm sorry, that was scary as hell. If they were alerted by my telling Manolo about a possible mink problem, I profoundly apologize."

Her legs still shook as she gazed across the highway at the rocky red prominence stamped with a "F" high on its sloping side. No trees in sight, just gray-green bushes dotted the barren mounds of soil mottled from off-white to rust.

Bright midafternoon sunshine couldn't overpower the mile-high elevation and the overnight storm front which frosted the air. End of August in the sparsely populated Four Corners area was always marked by natural signals of the weather change to come. Maya zipped up her jacket to slow her shivers.

Her arms detected earth tremors under the unstable wooden table as trucks roared by at high speed. Like Maya and Dave, they were anxious to get somewhere, anywhere, away from here.

She tried again. "The Utah State Veterinarian put two farms

under quarantine and he announced human infections on the premises. It's probably the reason for a heightened alert."

And Dave's personal connection to the compound—she left that unmentioned. FLDS spies apparently gleaned everything about him, his job, and his taking in Braxton.

He finally responded to her incessant prodding. "We could have been killed, and it's the first fuckin' time I've ever been locked out from an inspection. One more mark on my record." He picked the onion out from his burger and tossed it into the dirt, to the delight of a roaming black-and-tan mongrel.

She tried to get him back on an even keel with humor, their common language. "Dave, you're only thirty-two. Plenty more years to flunk and fail."

He remained silent, teeth ripping out bites from the burger with a vengeance. In the shade of the metal portal, he removed his hat. "Ben should have been the point person as the state authority, but he's tied up with that clostridial outbreak in cattle again."

Maya smiled, relieved to put his implications about Manolo behind her. "CDC-Fort Collins is helping with those human COVID cases. How's USDA involved?"

"Wildlife Services is trapping wild mink."

Maya's stomach clenched. They were worried about mink becoming a new viral host, the first infected free-ranging animals in the US. "Far away from Chinese wildlife, we thought we were safe from the virus being here permanently."

"The wild mink risk is theory, not fact."

The compound confrontation crowded her thoughts. "You haven't said a word about your mother."

He rubbed his forehead. "My made-up images of her merged with Braxton's description."

Aaron Farnsworth hadn't expressed concern about Braxton, not really. Unsurprising, given that he cast his son aside for misbehavior, which was only a masquerade of the fact that there were too many sperm-producers for the number of young available females.

"What will you tell him?"

He shrugged. "The truth—he's getting old enough to hear it, and God knows he's handled a lot already."

Maya gathered their trash for the waste receptacle. "We're done early. Should we keep our motel reservation or head home tonight?"

Dave donned his hat and led the way to the pickup. "No fuckin' way are we staying longer than necessary here—who knows who might be tracking us. If we're lucky, we can be back in Bernalillo by midnight."

Trying to catnap as Dave navigated the long stretch of two-lane highway east, Maya's thoughts were disturbed by sleek furry animals, a million sources for coronavirus mutations. Species like mink had cell receptors that facilitated virus attachment. Confinement farming of densely packed mink could increase the threat of spreading from escaped animals to wild populations or humans.

Her fitful sleep gave her no rest as they cruised through the gloomy darkness after sunset. She took over driving the I-40 miles, occasionally passing a few bright lights from Native American communities. As Dave twisted on the passenger side in a fruitless attempt to snooze, he appeared equally troubled. Perhaps his thoughts of infected mink were overshadowed by images of militant family members strategizing to snatch back his half-brother. Or son, his unofficial son.

THIRTY

Santa Fe, New Mexico—Thursday, August 27, 2020

"Happy Birthday, mi esposo." Maya pressed soft kisses all over Manolo's face and let her hand trail lower. She hated to wake him with his long work hours and lack of sleep, but he had an early meeting in Albuquerque and lovemaking would be a sexier alarm than his phone.

His eyes popped open and he turned to check the time. "I have to get going—can we hold this until tonight?" But his body disagreed with his professed disinterest, and she took advantage of his erection for a quickie.

"I hope you'll get home in time for a healthy dinner," she said. "No more vending machines. There's a surprise recipe I've been working on."

He kissed her nose. "I'll try, but you know how it goes."

She fastened a missed button on his summer dress white uniform shirt and successfully kept any disappointment out of her voice. "Thirty-four isn't a big one but I'm happy to share it with you as your wife." Last year, he was in NYC with his family, so she had sent greetings by FaceTime.

After Manolo left, Maya logged into her Zoom meeting with Dave. She greeted him with a tentative smile. "Hola, amigo, any fallout from our aborted mink investigation?" He might still blame her for the fundamentalists blocking them after Manolo informed IHS of possible human cases.

Dave ruffled his hair. "Ben's upset. He sent a state team and they were met by the same cold shoulder. He doesn't have enough justification to use law enforcement as a backup."

Maya tried to cheer him up. "It makes sense the compound refused our entry. Without confirmed coronavirus, you can't force them to shut down mink farming. Their aggression might not be personal."

"I don't want our home to become an armed camp, on the chance they're after Braxton."

Maya was surprised he hadn't considered security. "Erika installed cameras around her property when that guy targeted her."

He grimaced. "And despite those measures, she was still attacked in her driveway. But I'll look into it this weekend."

"What's happening with the kids?"

"Some days home and some at school, as long as they can keep numbers in the building below fifty percent of capacity."

"Emilia coordinates all that?"

He nodded. "Her restaurant has curbside sales and free meals for the homeless. She's flexible enough to handle the kids' crazy schedules, and I pick up the slack."

"Do her parents still provide backup? Mine refuse to see me in person." Damned pandemic—she hadn't been with her family in months. Zoom was great but didn't dampen the ache after her grandmother's death. Only her marriage kept her sane, even with Manolo's continual traveling between IHS hospitals and clinics.

"Maya, don't hold their caution against them. Emilia's parents are younger and grandkids are a strong motivation. They're careful, so we're not too worried they'll bring the virus home."

She took another sip of her calming chamomile tea. "Thank God for technology keeping us together. Does USDA have any new information on COVID in mink?"

"In the Netherlands, they culled two million, and announced today that their fur farms will permanently close by next March."

She couldn't absorb what two million dead animals looked like, or whether they'd harvest their fur. No doubt animal rights groups would celebrate the end of the industry, but also mourn the animal deaths.

Her contact-tracing database on the laptop flashed with an

updated entry. "I should get back to work. I'm sorry again that our Freedom City visit fell through."

Discussion with Manolo of the failed trip had been tense, as if she were accusing him of causing the problem. Her head echoed with his harsh words: "The cult had automatic weapons—you were idiots to stay and argue" and "Dave's job, not yours, never again." An edict she planned to ignore. She always wanted hands-on experience.

As she signed off with Dave, her abdomen pinched with cramps. Several days late for her period, she welcomed the pain considering Manolo's insistence they wait on getting pregnant. In the bathroom, there was still no flow. Her breasts were sore, but that was common in different stages of her monthly cycle, and Manolo had been vigorous during their morning lovemaking.

When she'd been late a year ago during one of their estrangements, she had freaked. At Emilia's suggestion, she had considered buying a test kit, until her period kicked in. With the cramping, this time she wouldn't need one.

. . .

Completing her phone calls by six PM, she began another Barefoot Contessa easy recipe for an heirloom tomato and blue cheese salad. She had to settle for regular tomatoes, but the red and orange slices contrasted with pops of white Roquefort and freshly torn basil. She imagined her skin getting smoother by inhaling the extra virgin olive oil and spices.

As she put the salad in the refrigerator, Manolo texted. **Short-staffed in ICU, back at midnight.**

Not for the first time, she wondered at the wisdom of keeping her apartment in Santa Fe when he worked primarily in Albuquerque. His driving on the lonely highway late at night twisted her stomach. But the housing market was insane and moving both of them in a pandemic would have been impossible.

She distracted herself with *Homeland* on Showtime. Maya's life wasn't as crazy as Carrie Mathison's but with the armed confrontation in Freedom City, she was struck by similar tensions. She hoped to emulate the CIA spy's courage in the face of mental and emotional challenges.

After only one episode, she turned off the TV and curled on the couch in the dark. Similarities with the fictional character crept in. Nonstop threats that required investigation. Addiction to international travel. Obsessive attention to detail. Unable to turn off her work brain. Loved fiercely, with fraught family relationships.

Another belly cramp, but still no bleeding. Being married to a physician in a pandemic fostered unceasing dread. Like the spy, she could end up giving birth after her partner died. Wrong show to watch when alone, panicked whether Manolo would return healthy.

Arms outstretched to fling away panic, she twirled on the area rug and screamed in frustration. Then she grabbed her purse. A simple pee on a stick would answer her question.

The market's bakery reminded her of Manolo refusing a birthday cake. For him, traditional celebrations were inappropriate when some of his patients died every week from COVID. Maya fretted over his mental health, but he might be grateful if she refreshed the mood with a small raspberry-topped chocolate cake and one candle. The masked clerk stared down Maya when ringing up the pregnancy kit, perhaps uncertain whether to offer condolences or congratulations.

At home, she followed the test instructions. After two minutes, she read a minus sign. With a deep groan of relief, she tossed the kit in the trash. Before COVID, they'd been so eager to start a family, and now she celebrated not being pregnant, on Manolo's birthday, no less. She settled into the couch and turned on the TV again. No more spy thrillers; she opted for *Virgin River*. Another young woman battling demons and striving for a new, stronger life, but a happy ending, at least happy for now.

THIRTY-ONE

Santa Fe, New Mexico—Friday, August 28, 2020

Maya heard stirrings from the bathroom as she vaguely remembered Manolo's return at one AM. Although close in height, his added weight and muscle had allowed him to carry her from the couch to bed despite the exhaustion of his long hours. And now he was up before her, a reversal of their usual pattern.

"What's this?" He emerged through the bathroom door, blue towel around his waist and torso dripping water droplets from his shower. The pregnancy test kit was in his hand.

She propped herself on one elbow. "I wish you'd showered with me. It's one of my favorite things to do together."

"I'm due at the Dulce clinic by nine." He set the kit on the end table and pulled on his underwear, to her regret. But when she noticed the morning light inching through the window and the clock reading six-thirty, she understood his haste to start the three-hour trip.

She crawled out of bed to embrace him, relishing the warmth of his chest against her bare breasts. "Happy Birthday, even if we're overdue on the party."

He stepped into his uniform pants. "Are you gonna tell me about this pregnancy test?" His narrowed eyes and low tone implied concern, not anger.

"I'm only a few days late and it's negative." Her fingers soothed his tight shoulder muscles. "Too much time on my hands last night and I started to worry."

"Good. I want babies, just not now. Timing is lousy."

His statement was too emphatic and it triggered an impulse to re-enact their argument about starting a family during a pandemic. But he faced a long drive. "You got less than five hours sleep—can you handle those two-lane, curvy roads?"

He kissed the palm of her hand. "I'm getting the weekend off 'cause we flattened the curve. We can dine out if restrictions are lifted."

She pulled on her robe. "Please be careful and text when you get there."

After he left, she turned on the radio and ate her breakfast, relieved about the pregnancy verdict. Her only surprise for him would be the small cake in the refrigerator. When she called her office, Stephanie told her Dr. Grinwold was unavailable. "He's finalizing that public health order allowing indoor dining at twenty-five percent capacity."

"I'm not sure how restaurants will pull that off, but Manolo seemed interested."

The virus was in his face every day, so possible spread among healthy restaurant patrons probably felt like nothing. But she couldn't push out of her mind table distances and ventilation. Even if spaced apart, eating indoors around unmasked strangers would spoil any pleasure of a birthday meal. If she and Manolo as public health professionals couldn't agree on risk, how would anyone else? A patio—she'd look for a restaurant that had one.

"Stephanie, I should finish my contact tracing calls by noon. I'll send a note to Dr. Grinwold for my next assignment."

"He's so happy you stayed on after your EIS training finished in June. Erika has pulled her hair out this summer on disease surveillance with some new COVID issue every day."

As soon as Maya hung up, her phone rang and she recognized the number. "Stefan, it's wonderful to hear from you."

The call from her Polish colleague wasn't a surprise—a steady stream of good wishes came in after Maya sent a bulk email announcing her marriage and new position.

Stefan's accented English was high-pitched and excited. "Maya, congratulations. Should I address you as Dr. Miranda now?"

"Sorry, I should have made that clear. My family spent a lot of money on college to create Dr. Maguire, and I'm sticking with it. How are Kondrat and Paula?" Stefan, his partner, and their adopted daughter had created a tableau of love and hospitality during the Oslo *Borrelia* investigation.

"Everyone's healthy and coping. Here in Norway, the lockdowns were strict but they worked."

Maya recalled the hot debate with Sweden choosing greater openness, followed by an unfortunate spike in infections and deaths. "Are you working on COVID?"

"Yes, I want to discuss mink."

"Our only confirmed cases are in Utah."

"Any chance in your new preventive medicine role that you can hop the pond again?"

Maya loved her work with Stefan. Despite some missteps, her confidence had blossomed. As an immigrant from halfway around the planet, she yearned for more international travel. Citizen of the world, Stefan had called himself. That was one of her goals, but his request was coming at a bad time.

"I'm not sure my husband will be thrilled by my flying away."

My husband, a new expression. An unfamiliar, but welcome one. With COVID, she hadn't been on a plane since February, so she couldn't blame her reluctance to travel just on Manolo. But she'd never turned down an assignment and wouldn't start now. "CDC was pleased with our previous studies," she said.

"All right, get back to me. We accomplished a *Borrelia* investigation in three countries last summer, so we can pull off several mink farms."

. . .

Required approvals fell into place. "I'm excited your collaboration paid off with this new opportunity," Dr. Jaworski said on the phone call with Atlanta.

The small part of Maya's brain concerned about the trip tried to find alternatives. "Keegan Williams worked on the Utah mink outbreak. Would he be a better choice?"

"He's still involved in that one, plus you have prior experience with Dr. Duda."

When Maya arrived at the health department, Dr. Grinwold offered his rare support for her travel. "I'm guessing you're a bit tired of contact tracing and eager for different challenges. COVID's more under control—Erika can manage without you for a week."

Maya rushed to the bathroom with renewed mild cramps, but still no blood. She knocked on Erika's door and opened it. Maybe the accomplished mom and nurse could advise her.

"It's great to see you in-person," Maya said as the masked blonde glanced up from her computer screen.

Erika jumped up and gave Maya a hug. "I guess this violates social distancing but I miss social interactions. How's married life?"

Maya dropped to Erika's extra chair. "It's good." She decided not to share the little ups and downs; Erika would be fully aware of them from her own marriage. Maya felt a growing, nesting need to protect the privacy of some aspects of her relationship with Manolo.

"Stefan, my European Union colleague, invited me to collaborate on mink there."

Erika's eyebrows drew closer together. "It could be a challenging trip, newly married, traveling on planes during COVID. You have to recalibrate when your family enlarges—your decisions don't affect only you."

"That's why I need your expertise. I've had cramping but no period, and it was due on Monday. We had unprotected sex, hoping to start a family, until Manolo got cold feet and we went back to condoms." She regretted revealing their intimate choices but needed clinical advice. "A home pregnancy test last night was negative."

"When did your last period start?"

Maya pulled up the calendar on her phone. "July 27."

"Pregnancies are calculated from that date, so you'd be about four and a half weeks along. Some kits aren't sensitive enough to pick up early hormone changes. I recommend testing again with a different brand."

"Or I can wait a few more days."

"If you're pregnant, you'll need a prenatal visit before any trip to Europe. Get it sorted out as soon as possible."

. . .

Maya purchased another test kit in the pharmacy as a summer monsoon invaded. She was drenched from the dashes to and from the car by the time she unlocked her front door and stripped off her wet clothes.

In the hot shower spray, she spread soapy bubbles over her belly, wishing she had asked Erika when she'd start showing if she were pregnant. As she washed her breasts, she noticed that her aureoles had darkened. She looked more closely. Was it her imagination that the veins in her breasts seemed more visible?

Only partially dry, she ripped open the new kit, then slowed down to read the instructions. This one would show results in words, no chance of misreading a tiny plus or minus. Even before the timer was finished on her phone, she glanced at the stick. **Pregnant**. She dropped it to the counter and bounded for the bed, pulling the covers over her head. Jesus. How was she going to tell Manolo?

THIRTY-TWO

Santa Fe, New Mexico—Friday, August 28, 2020

Manolo's tender kiss woke her up. "It's only ten o'clock," he said. "You couldn't wait up for me?"

He turned off the late news and her brain struggled to reengage. She hadn't intended to fall asleep watching TV, but the impending decisions exhausted her. "Sorry, I hoped to have dinner ready."

"Your special salad from last night doesn't require heating." He set his hat on the end table and deepened the kiss with his tongue. She was still groggy and strained to respond.

"I showered at the clinic so I'm not a germ carrier. But let me use the bathroom—long drive."

After he took two steps, Maya finally became alert and called out, "Hang on a second. I need to tell you something important."

Turning his head, he said, "Darling, this won't wait," and kept going. By the time she struggled out from under the covers, he was already washing his hands. As she reached for the pregnancy test on the counter, he beat her to it. "What does this mean? You were negative last night."

Holding the stick with **Pregnant** blaring, he followed her to the side of the bed.

"Erika said some tests don't pick up early hormonal changes, so this is a repeat."

He sighed, then turned the lamp to dim and rubbed his face. "Could be a small chance of a false positive. You should call your doctor."

She began to massage his neck. "First thing Monday morning, I promise. Can I help you get changed?"

Once in their robes, they filled salad bowls and settled in bed. He reached for the TV remote but she grabbed his hand before he pressed the button. "Manolo, shouldn't we discuss this?"

He clicked the news back on. "Let's wait until we know what's real." The weather report warned of flooding and Maya was grateful her apartment was nowhere near a water source. But his disinterest disturbed her. Manolo's attitude was rational—why worry about something ahead of time when there was nothing to do? But it left her feeling alone and bereft of support with the potentially monumental changes.

. . .

Santa Fe, New Mexico—Monday, August 31, 2020

At the stovetop, Maya added ham and cheese to the omelet, Manolo's first home-cooked meal in several days. On Saturday morning, he had left early to consult with the Mescalero Apaches. Their nation in southern New Mexico was a long distance from other tribal lands and the leadership complained about insufficient IHS assistance. While he was gone, Maya had interrupted her nagging concern about pregnancy with a thorough house cleaning to please her neat freak husband. But since his return, he didn't notice.

With force, his fork carved a wedge of omelet from his plate. "I'm going to your medical appointment."

Maya pushed the chopped green chiles toward him. "There's something you should know before I consult with the doctor. Nothing's decided, but Stefan invited me to Europe for their mink farm investigations."

He took another bite, talking with haste as he chewed. "Of course you won't go overseas. Neither of us has flown since the pandemic was declared, and it's not safe, regardless of your pregnancy status."

She expected his reluctance, but not his emphatic denial of the opportunity. "That's not true. Studies show plane ventilation systems can reduce risks, more than buildings with poor HVAC. And I can be tested before and after, wear a mask the whole time."

Shaking his head, he pushed his plate away. "I said I'm not comfortable with it."

This was shaping up to be a bigger battle. "Manolo, you're my husband and I love you. But you're not my ob/gyn, even though I respect your dedication and skills. Whatever she says about my physical status and travel, I'll follow her advice."

His only answer was an abrupt rise from the table. As he washed the dishes, Maya sealed the uneaten omelet in a glass container for the refrigerator. His raspberry-chocolate birthday cake still sat there—no time or mood for a celebration.

. . .

With COVID restrictions, the clinic refused to allow Manolo to remain, even though masked. The visit was long and thorough, including lab tests for Maya's blood type, Rh factor, and anemia. But the doctor texted Manolo to join them for the pregnancy confirmation.

"Everything's looking good for your wife, papa." The doctor's cheerful congratulations didn't change the frozen expression on Manolo's face, and the next words were clinical.

"A few results are pending. We'll get PCR testing for COVID on the nasal swab. Let's start you on a prenatal vitamin and a flu shot. We should see you once a month until the twenty-eighth week, then twice a month."

Manolo took Maya's hand, the first sign of his softening. "What's the expected delivery date?"

"May 3, by calculating forty weeks from the first day of her last period. Of course we'll adjust that based on future ultrasounds."

Maya squeezed Manolo's hand in return. "I've been invited to represent CDC at a European Union investigation of COVID in mink. Timing's not finalized, but probably soon. Do you think I should avoid travel?"

"I understand that your work tasks don't allow hunkering at home full-time, so flights shouldn't be a much greater risk. I assume you're strict about PPE around infected people and animals?"

"You're correct—I wouldn't take chances." She remembered

the safety precautions on her previous European trip and relaxed into the chair. Stefan would take care of her.

Manolo jumped in. "There's no way to eliminate virus exposure even with masks."

Maya ignored his alarmed tone—her pregnancy posed other concerns. "My biological family is unknown. Should I have genetic counseling?"

"I'll give you a referral. Ask the desk to make another appointment a month from now, and your test results will be on your patient portal. I'm happy to be on your team for this joyous journey."

Manolo held Maya's hand as they exited the building for his Corvette, but he grumbled. "She shouldn't make assumptions about what kind of journey this will be."

Maya snapped. "I'm tired of your morose attitude. We used to share a strong desire for a family, one with kids."

He gripped her shoulders. "You're right, I'm not sure what's come over me. Let's get home and talk about it."

. . .

In her parking lot, they rushed for the apartment's front door and narrowly avoided getting wet from the restart of heavy rain. But it pounded the windows as they settled on the couch, its drumming echoing the rapid thumps of Maya's heart.

"I wish you had gone back on the pill instead of us just using condoms."

Maya wanted to slug him. "Can you drop this crap? I'm pregnant, get over it. And the timing means it happened before we started using protection again, so don't blame that."

Her unusually harsh tone startled a change in him. Tears slipped from his eyes and he held her tight. "I'm just scared to death of losing you or the baby in this pandemic. I know too much about the increased risks."

Maya prolonged the argument, voice combative. "I know what it's like to see a pregnant woman die." The memory goosebumped her arms. "That Jicarilla woman last year didn't survive *Borrelia*."

He leaned back and wrenched his hands. "Some of my pregnant patients have had life-threatening lung problems. One's on ECMO, extracorporeal membrane oxygenation. Two others in Gallup had stillbirths. I'd never forgive myself if I allowed something like that to happen to you."

Their role reversal surprised her. Usually she was the one thinking in catastrophic terms, freaked out by the what ifs. Maybe the pregnancy hormones provided a jolt of joy—the nesting instinct kicking in. With every minute after the doctor's confirmation, her excitement to carry Manolo's child ramped up. Nothing in the world could bring her down, except his opposition to the pregnancy. "You're worried about the threat to my health, right?"

"I just said that. Pregnant women with COVID have an increased risk of ICU admission, need for ventilation, and death compared to women who aren't pregnant."

His statement sounded so chilling and official. Her words were barely audible, revealing her worst fears. "You're . . . you're not suggesting I have an abortion."

He clutched her tight to his chest, running his hands through her hair. "Oh, God, where would you get that idea? I'm just overloaded with worry, and not handling it well. I shouldn't be stressing you out at a time like this."

"No joke," she muttered into the soft cotton of his shirt. She lifted her head to gaze into his eyes. "I'm concerned too, but mostly overwhelmed with happiness, and pissed as hell that you're bringing me down."

"You're right. If I push the virus out of my mind, I'm ecstatic about your pregnancy. It's just what we wanted to start our marriage. But we can't wish COVID away—everything's a new normal."

She took his hands again and twirled his ring. "Manolo, we're not the only ones going through this. Women have always faced childbirth risks. At least we're not in the days before modern medical resources."

"They should send somebody else to investigate the mink. I can't let go of my fears."

A clap of thunder made Maya jump and her response was sharp. "Manolo, I never promised to give up my career to have children. My goal is to have both. We know others who have figured it out."

"That was pre-COVID. Families are under a lot of stress now."

Maya got up to pull the drapes, blocking out the storm. "We have shelter, two salaries, and demanding but flexible jobs. Our parents will be thrilled to hear of a new grandchild. I'm guessing someone, maybe your Dad, will move here to help out."

He rose to join her near the window, wind roaring like a freight train. "We can't stay in this apartment long-term, it's not big enough."

She smiled in anticipation of an infant asleep in a crib. "We have a long time to figure all that out. With our income, I'm sure we can come up with a reasonable option. Buying a larger place together would be fun."

He drew her toward the bedroom. "Okay, your pixie dust is transforming my Scroogeness. Let's celebrate this news before you get big as a house and it becomes more challenging."

At the edge of the bed, she sat down and removed his belt. "Mi amor, you know we're creative. There will be no point during this pregnancy that we can't be intimate." She went on to demonstrate they would have plenty of ways to make love that didn't require a flat belly.

THIRTY-THREE

Copenhagen, Denmark—Monday, September 14, 2020

Landing midday in the gleaming Copenhagen airport, Maya was energized by multiple languages bubbling around her. Her fourth trip abroad—she was becoming a seasoned traveler. Fifth, if you counted the first one when her parents brought her home from China as an infant.

Stefan had assured her the airport was one of the best in the world and it lived up to its reputation, with clean lines, glass walls, and bright signage that included English. This time she had a cell phone that worked overseas and she called Stefan. When he pulled up, she recognized his Tesla from the trip last year.

Behind his mask, he still looked like *A Quiet Place* actor John Krasinski, but he'd eliminated his shaggy mane and bushy beard. "This new look suits you," Maya said as she climbed in, "although I'm always a fan of facial hair."

"Many are letting themselves go in the pandemic, so I decided to do the opposite. Masking is challenging with a beard and a sharp appearance makes me sane. There's so much else we can't control."

He took her left hand. "You're blooming—the baby agrees with you. And your rings are beautiful. Any residual pain from losing your finger?"

She shook her head. "Mostly no, just occasional nerve pinches. I try to be positive—it's a reminder that I'm still alive." She tried to lighten the mood with a joke. "You can wear a nice ring too if you tie the knot with a certain handsome stud named Kondrat."

"You sound like my mother." He hit the button to turn on the electric engine and eased into the road. "Let's get going. Other than a quick nap while recharging, I've been driving six hours from Oslo. If you're hungry, I have snacks."

"Thanks." She grabbed a bag of Cheez Doodles from the console and opened it to share. "When do we reach Aarhus?"

"In about three hours. Perhaps you can rest."

Maya closed her eyes as her mind drifted back to New Mexico.

"I'll drive you to the Sunport but I'm still not happy about this," Manolo had said on Saturday as she packed her suitcase. "I know it ticked you off when I wasn't thrilled about your pregnancy. But I'm over the moon now. I don't want you to endanger our baby."

She pulled him in for a hug. "I'm not risking anything. You heard my doctor. And you work a hundred hours a week saving lives from COVID—you could bring the virus home anytime."

"Don't turn this back on me," he snapped. But he looked like a puppy caught in the act of chewing an electrical cord. "You know how careful I am in the clinics and when I come home. If my work ever impacted you, I'd . . ."

"Manolo, if the virus gets out-of-control in our mink like in Europe, we'll be in big trouble. Stefan and I are an experienced team—this is my way to contribute, like you."

On Sunday, his silence and body posture during the drive to the Sunport communicated his continuing concern. She squashed her resentment over his paternalism like a cockroach. Orders from employers usually required compliance; pressure from men like Enzo or Manolo, no matter how different their intentions, didn't require automatic acquiescence.

At the curb, she gave him a quick kiss. "I hate leaving when we're at odds. If we can't agree to disagree this early in our marriage, we're in trouble."

Their final embrace was stiff. "Please be careful," he warned.

During the plane change at JFK, she called his sister. "Ramona, I know your COVID restrictions are lifting now. I wish we could fit in a visit."

"Maya, we can't take that chance with Johnny. You're risking a lot to travel."

So the Mirandas were united in thinking her irresponsible. Once she was pregnant with a family heir, her autonomy to offer her skills to a world in crisis went out the window. Even her own parents were mad at her. She hated upsetting so many family members, but also hated millions of mink sick and dying from COVID. If anything she learned in Europe could head that off in the US, her efforts would be worth it.

In the three-hour layover at London Heathrow, she navigated the huge airport to find her final gate, then nervously removed her mask for a hearty shepherd's pie.

"Great view, huh?" Stefan interrupted her daydreams and she opened her eyes to a spectacular suspension bridge. The route to Aarhus was fairy tale bucolic through forest, farmland, and homes with thatched roofs.

When reaching the port area, he drove by geometric white buildings with striking turquoise balconies. "How would you like to live in that? Isbjerget, modern apartments."

"Trapezoids and rhomboids," Maya joked. "I'm more bonded to the rounded shapes of adobe."

He pulled into a paving stone driveway next to a brick house with a pointed red tile roof. "Part of this home is an Airbnb conversion with a separate entrance." A code unlocked the door and they tossed their luggage into separate small bedrooms.

"It's too late for the mink farm tonight so we can enjoy ourselves. Do you remember the Oslo Folk Museum? *Den Gamle By* down the street is the same. The old houses show off the history of Danish architecture."

Maya patted her stomach. "As long as they serve food. I'm eating for two now." Saying the words lifted her mood.

They strolled on a cobblestone lane of 1800s-era wooden buildings in multiple hues, then ordered open-faced sandwiches at the door of the Gæstgivergården, painted with stripes of red and white. After greeting a wagon driver and his two giant draft horses, they perched to eat on benches along a shaded stream. On the path, a young woman played an elaborately decorated barrel organ. "The period-appropriate entertainment makes me step back in time," Stefan said.

In her lap, careful not to spill on her navy pants, Maya balanced her cheese and artichoke sandwich while Stefan inhaled a croque-monsieur.

"Will this be enough for dinner?" Stefan asked.

"Most definitely. My body clock thinks it's the morning but I'm aching for a mattress. Hey, are you still planning that northern lights tour when Kondrat's done with his biodiversity degree?"

Setting his sandwich on the bench, Stefan grabbed his left shoulder and stretched. A former competitive swimmer, he'd packed on the pounds. "We postponed the trip until the pandemic is over, if it's ever over."

"Manolo and I are in the same boat. We planned an African honeymoon for July but like all pre-pandemic plans, that got derailed. We'll get it in some day, along with our little one."

She put her hand on her belly. "COVID hit us so hard, Manolo's putting in a lot of clinical duty. Management of dying patients is running him down, but he doesn't complain. Those families have it worse than him, he always says."

"Medical care has been managed more easily in northern Europe." Stefan washed down his sandwich with a Carlsberg Pilsner. "So my clinical skills are less in demand. I can focus on surveillance and reporting."

Maya nodded. "New Mexico's state lab switched to a 24/7 work schedule. The increased testing and early mask mandate reduced our morbidity and mortality."

"Germany also emphasized testing, plus they have more ICUs." Stefan gathered up their trash and led her to bins outside the restaurant. "We have lots of different approaches to compare success rates when this is over."

On their way to the exit, they ran into a woman reenacting a Vicar's widow who regaled them with tales of Hans Christian Andersen, the Danish fairy tale author.

"If we have time, I'll show you the Little Mermaid statue in

Copenhagen," Stefan said. "She wanted a human soul so she gave up her life in the sea. All for the love of a man, such a silly girl."

Maya laughed. "You'd do the same for Kondrat or a sweet daughter named Paula."

"Point taken."

In the bookshop, Maya found stationery imprinted with images of older buildings. "These will be great thank you notes for our wedding gifts delayed by the mail. My grandma taught me the importance of handwritten correspondence."

"It's been, what, seven months since her passing?" Stefan said. "But I'm guessing there's still a hole in your heart."

"She's the only relative I remember besides my parents. My grandpa, her husband, died when I was young, and I still have a faint memory of him. My dad's parents passed on before I was born. With a small family, you treasure each person more."

They turned down the street toward their Airbnb. "We haven't visited our families recently, which is hard on Paula. She's very social despite her learning disabilities, so she desperately misses them."

Maya remembered the chatty blonde six-year-old dancing around Oslo's tiger statue. Many of her friends and colleagues had children—the yearning tugged harder. Thank goodness the baby growing in her belly had ignored Manolo's insistence about waiting.

"School has been wonderful for Paula's language and math skills. We got in one trip to Poland last winter before the pandemic. Surrounded by relatives, she blooms."

Inside the small sitting room with modern Scandinavian furniture, Stefan pulled out his laptop. "I'm going to review information on the previous mink outbreaks. Want to join me?"

Maya shook her head, suddenly overwhelmed with fatigue. "I'm sorry to let you down, but the trip is catching up with me."

He stood up as if to embrace her, then stopped. She understood his hesitation—when would she relax enough about COVID to freely enjoy friendly hugs?

"See you at seven for a quick breakfast before the farm inspection," he said.

She studied the mobile phone CDC had provided, longing to use it to call Manolo. But it was for business only. She tugged out her laptop to send a quick email. **Denmark's beautiful and all's well. No sign of a morose Hamlet in sight.**

Beds in new places were always a challenge with her chronic aches from old injuries. She often lay on her stomach to avoid pressure on her pelvis, but her breasts were swollen and painful. At some point she'd get large enough to require side sleeping, so she might as well adapt to it. She cradled the extra pillow in her arms, imagining Manolo before drifting off.

THIRTY-FOUR

Aarhus, Denmark—Tuesday, September 15, 2020

By eight o'clock, they pulled up to a huge complex of metal-roofed buildings, the view jarring against the green mass of fields and trees. The moment Maya got out of the Tesla, she was assaulted by the smell and her stomach turned. She should have anticipated the pregnancy making her extra sensitive.

"Before COVID, there were more than two hundred mink farms in Denmark," Stefan said. "My and your home countries, Poland and China, also have a big industry."

Near the parking area, a woman who appeared to be in her late thirties with close-cropped blonde hair waited in a white gown, gloves, and mask. She greeted them in English. "Hey, Stefan. Good to meet you in person."

He bowed at the waist. "Tilda Knudsen, meet Maya Maguire. With your both being veterinarians, please don't get off into the weeds on animal health and leave this poor species-limited physician behind."

Tilda led them to rubber boots which they pulled on over their shoes. Then they stepped through a liquid foot bath and added PPE to match Tilda. As they entered a wide path between the metal cages, Maya admired the building design. With high roofs and sides open to the outdoors, there was plenty of ventilation to counteract the smell and viral spread that would be fostered in closer confinement.

"I am a contract veterinarian for the fur industry," Tilda said. "We inspect the farms four times a year but come more often for disease outbreaks."

"Before my trip, I reviewed mink farm videos." Maya glanced

at Stefan, hoping he wouldn't be offended if she mentioned his home country. "In Poland, cages are stacked so closely, mink reach through the wire to attack each other. Not to mention the disease risk as the waste from upper cages falls through to lower ones."

"Ja, we are much superior."

An attendant glopped food on top of a cage and two minks pulled it down with agile front paws. The animals' color variations up close were lustrous. "I'm embarrassed that I thought mink coats got that beautiful blue color from dye."

"That's Silver Blue Cross and this one is White Regal."

"Isn't it risky for injury to house two animals together?" Maya asked.

"Staff keep watch for problems. Farmed mink live less than a year on a carefully timed cycle."

Stefan interjected. "Can you explain that?"

"In early spring, we bring a female's nest box next to the male's pen and open the sliding door to allow breeding. We record the mating date, then move the female to a second male a week later, repeating three times to make sure it worked. Females ovulate with intercourse, like cats."

"What is the gestation length?" Stefan asked.

"After about six weeks, we average seven kits. Around mid-June, we move the females first into groups of four and then two like you see here. Males stay with their mothers longer to grow in size and strength."

The mink were lively, entertaining, and beautiful. Maya enjoyed their curious intelligence reflected in their tiny dark eyes. "When are they harvested for fur?"

"December."

The animals had short lives, but Tilda and the staff cleaning and feeding the long rows of cages seemed professional and caring. Maya accepted that farms for animal products would always exist, with veterinarians to improve health and welfare. But they couldn't pay her enough to trade jobs with Tilda—euthanizing healthy animals would be too much.

"How many mink on this farm have you identified with COVID?" Maya asked.

"I will take you to our records office," Tilda said. Within a hundred feet, they entered a small separate building. She offered them chairs after removing her gloves and face shield, keeping on her mask and body suit. Maya and Stefan did the same.

"None of what I am about to share is for public release," Tilda said. "Let it out and I'll have to kill you."

Maya was startled but the others laughed as Tilda continued. "American mob joke, right?" She opened a laptop. "Of our four thousand mink, I have examined thirty confirmed to have COVID. We also did an antibody study on blood samples collected by clipping toenails. The results show sixteen percent of the mink have been exposed."

"I hadn't realized how to get blood from a squirmy animal with sharp teeth," Maya said. "That's good to know. CDC told me I'm on the team for the next mink outbreak in the US."

"Congratulations." Stefan clapped her on the back. "Our collaborations always pay off." He turned to Tilda. "What testing have you done on staff?"

"Nasal swabs identified three positive who are quarantining at home, none seriously ill. People infected the mink, or the mink infected the people, who knows?" Tilda rubbed her hands over her eyes. "Bad news—some mink have a mutation of viral spike proteins, so any human vaccines under development might be ineffective."

Stefan gasped as Maya felt her heart sink. Everyone had been counting the days until people could be vaccinated and life could resume some sense of normal.

Tilda closed her laptop. "I have devoted my career to these animals. My research on optimum housing led to industry improvements. There are preliminary discussions of culling all seventeen million mink in our country's two hundred farms, not just the infected farms like this one." She lowered her head to both hands. "That will kill me."

"But you euthanize millions every year for the fur trade." Stefan's eyes were wide and his voice showed his incredulity. "No insult intended, but how would this be different?"

Tilda raised her head and her eyes locked with Stefan's. Maya could feel lightning crackle.

"I can justify animal death when it serves a purpose." Tilda's accented-English turned harsh. "But this slaughter benefits humans more than mink—our death rate has been low and manageable."

Maya played peacemaker. "The fact that you would consider killing so many asymptomatic, productive animals on behalf of human health—that's admirable. All the farms and people working on them, put out of business. I'm not sure whether my country would be that brave."

Stefan's voice turned sympathetic. "And I assume you can't use the pelts of the culled animals."

"No one wants to wear a fur from an animal possibly infected with COVID."

Maya asked, "Can I see some of the sick animals? It will help me prepare for our farms when I visit."

They resumed full PPE and Tilda led them to the clinic with a dozen animals. Most had watery nasal discharge, looking weak and lethargic. One was on its back, struggling to breathe. The despair on its face reminded her of Scout, the lion that died of COVID after she visited the Albuquerque wildlife park.

"These were collected by the staff this morning. We care for them pending test results, in hope they're ill from a curable disease. But this one in respiratory distress, I will euthanize it for necropsy."

Maya tried to tamp down the acid in her stomach and turned to Stefan. "I'd like to observe, but maybe you should follow up on staff interviews."

Stefan gave her a mock salute, making her laugh with its sloppiness. "I act on your orders, Dr. Maguire. Tilda, I'll pass along my notes when I'm done."

After euthanasia with a portable carbon dioxide machine, Tilda moved the mink to a small cleanroom. She first took throat and rectal swabs. Then she dissected the conchae from the nasal area. After opening the abdomen, she took samples of lung, spleen, liver, and distal large intestines. She was done within a half-hour. Maya respected someone so proficient with pathology, a critically important skill for getting answers to death. But once again, she was happy her skills lay elsewhere.

"Based on earlier results, I expect these will be PCR-positive for coronavirus. But we also submit for other viruses like influenza A and adenovirus, in addition to bacteria such as *Escherichia coli* and *Pseudomonas aeruginosa.*"

Maya took her small notebook from her pocket and jotted down the tissues taken and organism names.

When they came back out into the lines of cages, Stefan caught up with them. "Tilda, two staff today report new symptoms of mild cough. I told them to report to the farm manager and saw them go in that direction. I was surprised they showed up to work since you've had mink mortality for a week. But they were worried about insufficient employees to care for the animals."

Tilda sighed. "We can't bring in unskilled villagers because they are afraid. Culling the entire farm, not just those infected—what a tragedy, an unmitigated disaster."

"But if they're a potential source of human risk?" Maya ventured, trying to remind Tilda of the depopulation benefits. Wrong thing to say—Tilda's expression locked into a demon Kabuki mask.

Stefan intervened. "Science will benefit tremendously from your efforts. I recommend you do air, dust, and feed sampling to determine how far the virus can spread under natural conditions."

Tilda nodded, her face again modeling an impassive professional. "Good idea. On another Danish farm, air samples taken close to the cages of infected mink were positive. However, those outside the mink houses were negative. Still, I expect the government order for depopulation to include neighboring premises."

The three continued to look for illness in the mink cages. Even with her mask, Maya gagged and coughed at the odor emitted by a hump of straw.

"Sorry," Tilda said, her voice strained. "Someone should have spotted this earlier." She got on her mobile and called a staff member who removed the carcass for necropsy.

Maya sank into a corner chair. "I suddenly feel like I've been hit by a car."

Tilda knelt in front of Maya with concern in her eyes. "The smell requires adaptation. Can I get you a drink?"

"Water please. I'm pregnant, early stages, so my body's adjusting."

"Ah, that explains it. Fatigue is a challenge in pregnancy, I know from two of them. You feel like you can't keep your eyes open in the middle of the day. Rest here, I'll be right back."

Tilda returned with a glass of water. "If it's any consolation, our bodies adjust and some problems may reduce in the second trimester."

Maya pulled down her mask for the drink, then used the restroom where she willed herself not to vomit. She drew Stefan aside. "I don't want to impact your work here if you have more to do. I'm sure they have a cot somewhere that I could lie on."

"No, this is enough for today. We didn't even break for lunch. You were such an intrepid soldier last year with *Borrelia*, I forgot about your pregnancy."

As soon as they returned to their Airbnb, Stefan offered Maya the first shower, then she collapsed on the bed with eyes closed, vowing just to take a nap before dinner. Armies of coughing and twitching mink swarmed her brain, beady eyes accusing her of bringing the China virus to their previously happy country.

THIRTY-FIVE

Aarhus, Denmark—Wednesday, September 16, 2020

Banging of plates and cutlery woke Maya up. For a moment, she imagined that Manolo had, for once, beaten her to the kitchen. Funny how after two years of dating and two months of marriage, they had fallen into the patterns of an old married couple. She always seemed to be most alert soon after dawn, while he enjoyed a more leisurely arousal until his morning coffee.

Glancing around the room painted with a cheerful windmill mural, she remembered she was in Denmark and it couldn't be Manolo. She tugged on her clothes and joined Stefan as he opened a bag of pastries.

"God morgen, Maya. I hope my preparations didn't disturb you. But you've been down for twelve hours without eating much yesterday. I picked these up for our breakfast."

On the plate, he arranged a row of eclairs with toppings including raspberries, pistachios, and white chocolate. He handed her a cup of steaming herbal tea, and she inhaled the fragrant fumes, feeling them snuggle from the back of her nose up into her brain.

"Ah, you're spoiling me. Manolo will be grateful." With a shock, she realized she'd forgotten to send him an email update. It was only 10 PM in Santa Fe so she grabbed her laptop.

Successful but harrowing day on the mink farm, she typed before backing over the letters to eliminate **but harrowing.** She finished the note with a promise. **Can't wait to get home and show you how much I love you. Expect surprises.**

She paused in hopes he'd answer immediately, but he didn't— probably working late.

Stefan pulled two slices of warm quiche from the toaster oven, the steaming eggs providing an appetizing ambiance. "You need protein, too." He put the plate in front of her and eased the pastries aside. "Feeling a bit more perky?"

With another sip of the soothing tea, she smiled. "Yes, sir, raring to go. What's on tap?"

"A final check on a farm that closed and culled two weeks ago. It's near yesterday's and may have been the source. They have a worker in common who's in hospital now on a ventilator."

He brought his plate to the sink. "Take your time, we're not due at the new farm until nine. But I'm missing my daily jog and want to stretch my legs at Slotshaven, the Palace Park. When Queen Margrethe is not in residence at Marselisborg Palace, the grounds are open."

"Stefan, you brought breakfast, so I'll clean up."

Once at the park, strolling down the path between swaths of emerald lawn, Maya admired the multistoried boxy palace that glowed white against the soft gray skies. Three playful bronze lion sculptures danced along the walk. "I assume these won't be a source of COVID spread." She stroked the head of the largest one leaping into the sky from his hind limbs. "A researcher infected three cats in a lab with a sample from a human patient. Each of the cats then infected another one housed with it, yet none ever became ill."

"Not definitive proof that cats spread it to humans."

"No, but they can transmit, and even worse, while appearing perfectly healthy."

Maya inhaled the fresh scent of the changing season. Then she spotted a bronze water sculpture and walked over to peer in. She took a rapid step backward, colliding with Stefan, who caught her and kept her from falling.

"My God, that's creepy." She pointed to the green bronzed face of an infant peering out from water splashing in the basin.

"It's called 'A place between dream and reality.'" Stefan said. "Wonderfully dramatic, isn't it?"

"Horribly horrific is what I'd call it." She retreated to a cold bench. "Sorry if I'm insulting the sculptor or Danish culture. My pregnancy must have me on edge."

"Understandable, all those surging hormones. Dr. Miranda okay with this trip?"

"Not really, we had a major fight about it. I think he's the hormonal one. First, he was upset that I got pregnant, despite being so hopeful for it pre-COVID. Then he wanted to lock me up so nothing could harm me or the baby. He'd have been happiest if I quit my job and stayed home cooking and cleaning."

Stefan leaned back and crossed his legs. "Is that a slight exaggeration?"

She smiled. "You're right, we're still working out personal and relationship boundaries. Do Kondrat and Paula worry about you with all your COVID travels? At least for me, this is my first trip."

He adjusted his mask, then moved closer. "Of course they worry. I'm counting the days until there is a vaccination for all of us. But I try to be scrupulous about PPE around infected patients. Like you, my job is epidemiology, not patient care. Of the three of us, your husband's at greatest risk."

She poked his arm. "Thanks, Stefan, for that reminder. Normally he's not full-time in clinics and patient care, but these aren't normal times."

"We all pitch in where we can. After all, who else can say they were on the front lines of the pandemic of the century? Everything we do makes a small difference to conquer this beast."

Maya rubbed her shoulders with a sudden chill, then stood up. "So let's do our duty at this next mink farm."

The clouds released a gentle rain, not drenching, but enough to streak the haunting frozen baby's face with tears. "I'm up for a jog to your car," she told him, pasting on a smile. "Although I can't keep up with you and your athletic physique."

His pace matched hers as they retraced their steps to the vehicle.

. . .

The rain turned torrential within the half hour required to reach the next mink farm. Stefan pulled two umbrellas from the backseat and they headed up to the massive complex of sheds, even larger than the farm from yesterday. As they approached large dirt mounds with the deluge washing away loose soil, Maya spotted thousands of stiffened mink paws rising up toward the sky like the leaping lion statue. She grabbed Stefan's arm and cried out. "They look like zombies."

He pulled her away from the macabre spectacle and they rapidly located the farm manager. "What the hell is going on with those mink bodies?" Stefan's tone was jarring—she'd never seen him so livid. "They're supposed to be buried two meters deep."

In the building's shelter, the manager doffed his drooping hat and his timbre eclipsed Stefan's ten-fold. "That's what we did. But it's been off and on stormy this week. Apparently, gas from decomposition pushed them up from the ground."

"If you can't manage mass burials safely, you should incinerate," Stefan snapped. "And post guards to keep the public away. All you need are photos on the internet."

The rain lifted and bulldozers roared in. Maya and Stefan monitored the effort as some dug deeper trenches while others scooped up mounds of rotting bodies. With odor intensified like a fresh landfill, Maya yanked off her mask and puked into the mud.

"Sure you're up for this?" Stefan asked.

"Yeah, just need to get acclimated. Let's move onto the building inspection." Fortunately, dead animal fragrance was replaced by disinfectant gleaming the empty cages. A tawny, scraggly cat chased a mouse into a corner of the building. "Not what I wanted to see." She turned to the manager. "Capture that one and any others for testing. A Netherlands farm found seven cats with antibodies and one PCR positive."

The manager agreed and assured them that ill workers were quarantined at home or in the hospital.

Inspection completed, they were happy to escape back to their Airbnb in Aarhus. Maya used the bathroom first at Stefan's generous suggestion.

"You up for going out or should I bring something back?" he

asked when both were cleaned up. "You need a good meal with all the food groups."

"I'm re-energized, nothing like a hot shower," she reassured him. They dodged puddles hurrying to the quaint restaurant with a large mock pocket watch hanging above the double wooden doors.

In the foyer with their masks on, they studied the menu. "Can we do takeout?" she asked. "The chicken and asparagus tart looks good."

"All right, I'll order the herring curried salad, and we can share a Danish apple cake for dessert."

Outside, they huddled under the black awnings as the rain finally began to slow. When their order was ready they dashed back to the apartment and consumed their meals with such haste, Maya was reminded she was now eating for two.

Stefan answered a phone call in a language Maya didn't recognize. His expression was sober when he hung up.

"Massive mink mortality on two Polish farms, with multiple workers hospitalized. I need to fly to Warsaw tonight. Want to come along?"

Maya noticed a new email from Manolo, time stamped four AM. **Second wave of cases in Europe. You need to come home.**

She hesitated. She couldn't ever recall refusing an assignment. That's not what disease detectives did. But her pregnancy was a game changer. Nausea and fatigue lobbied for declining Stefan's invitation.

"Manolo wants me back in Santa Fe. How do you say no to a spouse?"

"I do it all the time to Kondrat, and he gets over it. Does Manolo have any specific concerns?"

"The rising case count here."

"Denmark hasn't been hit hard but infections are increasing." He checked his phone. "Still only five deaths reported for the entire country last week."

He continued clicking. "Poland, on the other hand, had a hundred deaths last week. Of course its population is more than six times Denmark's, but that still doesn't account for the difference."

He set his phone on the table. "Perhaps Manolo is right. You're traveling through the UK, correct? Cases are increasing there too, with more in younger people."

Maya ran her hand through her hair. "If I make a decision on the data, my own country is riskier than here."

"No doubt, but you might be staying home more."

"That's not true if we have another mink outbreak in the US and I'm the one trained for it."

Stefan got up to pack his small roller suitcase. "It's your choice, but check with your bosses if you want to join me. I'll call to book my reservation for Poland within a half hour, so let me know if it should be for two."

Maya pulled out the assigned CDC phone. It was six-thirty AM in Atlanta but Dr. Jaworski was an early bird.

"Hello, Maya, I got your email update. How are things going today?"

"Zombie mink erupting from their burial sites, but otherwise Denmark does a remarkable cleanup after a cull. I'll explain more with my next summary."

The Long Island accent thickened with skepticism. "Not sure how to interpret that about zombies, but I'll wait for your report. Why are you calling so early?"

Maya plunged ahead, uncertain how she wanted to skew Dr. Jaworski's decision. "Dr. Duda's flying to Poland for a situation on the mink farms there, much worse than Denmark or the US."

"Could be good information if you want to extend your trip."

"My husband is concerned and would prefer me home. I hate to use my pregnancy as an excuse, but I've been unusually tired."

"Maya, the lessons learned from Denmark are sufficient. As you point out, the conditions in Poland are unlikely to represent what you will see here, plus we have Keegan trained from the Utah outbreak. Come on back."

Dr. Jaworski served as her spotter, snatching her improvident weight load. Dr. Kim advised when feeling indecisive, pretend the decision has been made and assess your reaction. Although a tiny part of her felt like she was compromising too much for her marriage, most of her looked forward to nesting back home. She put a hand on her belly, way too early to feel baby kicks. Life was a new normal in more ways than one, and choosing less travel to protect her little one was the best option.

Dr. Jaworski promised to have CDC arrange her flights. Maya wished she could use the government phone to call Manolo. But on the few occasions she broke the rules, like unapproved sampling for anthrax, a disciplinary letter went into her file. She settled for an email. **On return flight tonight. Will send details when I have them.** After she packed her bag, his reply came in. **Counting the breaths between seconds.**

THIRTY-SIX

Albuquerque, New Mexico—Thursday, September 17, 2020

Maya's nerves ramped up to the level of the jet engines as the plane descended south of the Sandia Mountains, ablaze with midafternoon sun. She had spent the night at the airport hotel after saying goodbye to Stefan, too exhausted to catch a metro ride into Copenhagen for its attractions. It had been seventeen hours since the early morning departure, with stops in Amsterdam and Atlanta.

Albuquerque's infamous East Canyon winds rocked the wing tips close to the ground and the wheels touched the tarmac with a screech. Hunger pangs rivaled anticipation. She'd tried to eat enough for the baby but had been extra cautious about taking off her mask during travel. No way did she want to bring in any European coronavirus strains. Plus, Manolo had promised his traditional spaghetti dinner when back in Santa Fe.

Within the terminal, she passed under the hundred-year-old biplane hanging from the ceiling. A bronze statue of a Native American, tethered to an eagle's tail, launched into the air. In all her previous rushed flights, she'd appreciated the airport's art but now it felt personal, like it was welcoming her home. New Mexico could be the ideal place to settle permanently for her and Manolo.

She didn't spot him in the baggage area, but assumed he was still parking. As she stepped forward to retrieve her suitcase from the carousel, a strong arm circled her shoulders followed by a masked kiss at the back of her neck. "Let me grab it."

With one hand holding hers, Manolo used his other arm to easily yank the bag and drop it at his feet. She threw herself into his arms and clung to him for a solid minute. His seductive tone slipped through his mask with the pressure of his lips on her ear. "We weren't fighting when you left, right?"

She appreciated his irony. "I haven't a clue what we disagreed about."

After exiting the building under the blue-painted portal, he led her across slow-moving traffic to the garage, pulling her suitcase. On the sidewalk, he paused to remove their masks, then invited her into a deep, feverish kiss.

Her muscles refused to relax into his ardor as other travelers bustled around them. "Let's continue this in your car."

Once inside the Corvette, roof raised for privacy, they hesitated no longer. With trembling fingers, she unbuttoned his pants for an unfettered caress. His hand went into her blouse as he prolonged a kiss. Within a few minutes, she pulled back and tried to calm her breathing. "If we don't stop, we'll be giving these other cars some exotic entertainment."

He reached down to fix his clothing, then fastened his seat belt. "You're right, we're feds—don't want to end up in the headlines for indecent behavior."

She laughed. "Can you hold off for an hour?"

"I wish we lived in the same city as the airport."

Head on his shoulder and hands on his leg, she snoozed as he got them to Santa Fe by five o'clock. Yellowing cottonwoods saluted her return during occasional eyelash flutters. She could barely stand without his help when getting out of the Corvette. "Sorry, it's one in the morning by my body clock. But fill me up with your delicious spaghetti, before other things."

He smoothed her hair as he settled her on the couch. She dozed until his basil-lemon tomato sauce lured her to the table. When finally satiated with salad and pasta, she finished her mug of chamomile tea and tugged him toward the shower.

"I cleaned up last night in Copenhagen, but let's do it again to make sure I got rid of all that dead mink smell."

He frowned and kissed her eyes. "No talk of infected animals tonight." He scrubbed every inch of her with tender strokes of the warm washcloth, then accepted the return favor. When she offered to respond to his erection with her mouth, he shook his head. "I've waited too long. I want to be inside you."

With reluctance, she honored his temporary refusal but couldn't refrain from teasing him. "Just five days. You act like it's been an eternity." She turned off the shower and toweled them both dry, then pushed him toward the bed. "I promised a surprise. Would you like me to be the Little Mermaid?"

He enveloped them in the cotton sheets. "From the movie?"

"No." She leaned over for her daypack and pulled out a small bound volume. "This is the Hans Christian Andersen story from the airport bookshop."

She flipped to a page with a folded corner.

If his every thought and his whole heart cleaved to you so that he would let a priest join his right hand to yours and would promise to be faithful here and throughout all eternity, then his soul would dwell in your body, and you would share in the happiness of mankind. He would give you a soul and yet keep his own.

He took the book from her hand and set it on the end table. "Muy romántico, but I always think of us as earthy."

"Why can't we be both?" She kissed the goatee starting to fill in on his chin. "You'll get in trouble with this facial hair, even though I love it."

"I got permission from my Commanding Officer, as a surprise to my new wife."

"Thank him when you see him." She nuzzled below his nose, lips stimulated by the dark hairs.

He propped his head in one hand. "Any other Little Mermaid surprises besides the very poetic reading?"

"I can't talk any more. I traded my voice for these legs so I can be here in bed with you." She pretended to lock up her lips and throw away the key.

His hand stroked from her calves to her thighs. "I've always loved your legs, even this scar." He bent to tongue the keloid on her right thigh from the childhood surgery. His fingers traced a pattern on the skin of her abdomen, a shade lighter with its protection from the sun than her draped arm. "You're sure that you and the baby are doing well?"

She nodded, signaling her affirmation with another kiss, then an enticing feathering of her lips down from his waist. He allowed her to linger, arousing him to the breaking point, then pulled her back up.

His movements as he gently entered her were slow and exquisite. "I know men have been making love with pregnant women for eons, so I shouldn't be nervous. Probably worse once you start showing."

She smiled and reached down to encourage him, asking him with her hands to speed up.

"I'm rather fond of your voice," he whispered as he achieved a rhythm that excited her too. "You don't need to keep up this silent Little Mermaid role."

"Bien, te amo." She never tired of telling him she loved him, even when over-the-top frustrated with his attempts at control. But not tonight. He could do no wrong.

"Me too, el amor de mi vida." He proved his love with hands and lips caressing her breasts.

The 'me-too' phrase would never be innocent again after Enzo. But in her mind, she took on the sea witch's disgusting toad-filled voice and shouted his memory away.

Refocused on Manolo's motion, she relaxed into the glowing sensations spreading rapidly from her pelvis to her fingertips. She climaxed just before him, groaning with satisfaction.

. . .

Santa Fe, New Mexico—Friday, September 18, 2020

Barely making it to the toilet, she vomited spaghetti sauce-tinged fluid. Within seconds, he was beside her, holding her hair off her face. She rocked back on her heels as he pulled a tissue from the counter and wiped her lips. Then his free hand grabbed her toothbrushing cup and filled it with water. Maya rinsed her mouth. "I'm sorry, this is not what I thought of your dinner last night."

"Probably morning sickness. Seven weeks along, so the timing is right."

The nausea eased as she held her belly, then he helped her into bed. "I'll hold off on making breakfast until you feel more stable. Do you have your next checkup scheduled?"

"September twenty-eighth, a month after my first one."

"Are you taking the prenatal vitamins?"

"Of course—you don't need to monitor my every move. I'll move up my appointment if this gets out of control."

He adjusted the pillows. "You look thinner—you need to gain, not lose."

She rested a hand on her eyes to block the brilliant morning rays streaming through the window. "We'll need sun-blocking drapes before the baby comes. Erika mentioned a special recipe for ginger tea—I'll dig through my phone for it."

"For now, ginger ale and crackers." He turned for the kitchen. "Let me get them."

She rubbed the cool washcloth over her forehead, then shouted after him. "Kate, Prince William's wife, throws up nonstop in pregnancy. What's that called?"

Head in the cabinet, he yelled back. "Hyperemesis gravidarum. I'm trusting it won't be you."

As he returned with a tray, Maya slid down further into the bed. "I'm totally wiped out. Are you okay being here? I hate to think of your hospital being short-staffed because of me."

He leaned over to kiss her nose as he checked the time and buttoned his shirt. "No problema. The IHS clinic gave me a few hours off, but I should get going."

"Thanks for taking such good care of me."

She clung to his fingertips as he prepared to leave. "I'm not going anywhere. I'll be here when you get back." With any luck, she'd recover enough to work in the afternoon.

. . .

After a three-hour nap, she FaceTimed her parents. "Mom and Dad, how are you and Hypatia doing?" She angled her phone out the bedroom window. "The aspens on the Sangre de Cristos are swashes of gold. Flagstaff too?"

"It's always beautiful here," her dad said, "no matter how many viruses circulate. Retirement makes it easy to go with the flow."

Her mom jumped in. "We're so relieved you're home safely. Have you heard when the vaccine will be available?"

"Manolo might have the scoop—I'll let you know if I find out."

"Any plans yet for the nursery?" Her mom shook her head and sighed. "I'm not sure how you'll do it in a one-bedroom apartment. You need a bigger place."

"Mom, we've got a year to figure that out. At first, the crib will be with us."

"Good luck with that." Cheeks reddening like her hair, her mom appeared conflicted about arguing but went ahead anyways. "First time you turn over in bed, she'll wake up bawling. That's what you did."

Her dad stroked his chin, then flashed an eager smile, clearly trying to change the subject. "Are you and Manolo accepting name suggestions?"

Their pressure increased her wooziness and gurgling stomach acid. "Let me talk it over with him. Gotta go, just wanted to let you know I'm back, but I need to check in with work."

Chagrined she hadn't contacted her office sooner, Maya texted Dr. Grinwold and other key staff that she needed the day off for recovery.

The next call was to Bernalillo. "Dave, sorry not to say hi on our way through Albuquerque yesterday—the trip slammed me. Has Ben made progress with the Arizona mink farm?"

"No, but your reports about Denmark were intriguing. Did you take any pictures?"

At the reminder of the gassy bodies clawing their way to the soil surface, her gut churned. "I'll forward some phone photos to compare their farms with ours."

An update for CDC was next on her list but her stomach erupted. This time, after rinsing her throat, it was scratchy. Probably from esophageal reflux. The violence of the regurgitation released a few drips from her nose, and she eliminated the rest of last night's dinner with loose stools. She shivered, then hurried back under the warmth of the down comforter.

Manolo's opening of the bedroom door woke her up. "It's five o'clock," he said. "Did you sleep most of the day? I called around three and you didn't answer."

She flushed with embarrassment about giving into the fatigue. "I need a minute to take care of something." She grabbed her iPhone and sent a quick email to CDC, letting Keegan and Dr. Jaworski know they could call her about the mink on the weekend.

On shaky legs, she joined Manolo as he rearranged the refrigerator shelves. "I got lots of groceries, depending on what suits your digestion."

She hugged his waist from behind. "How about some soup? Hopefully that will stay down."

He spun in her arms and kissed both cheeks, then pushed her out of the kitchen. Turning on the TV, she settled back into bed with the national news, her first chance to watch it in a week. When Manolo returned with two bowls on a tray, she patted his side of the bed in invitation. "Pfizer just announced Phase 1 clinic trials for an antiviral."

"Yeah." Manolo turned down the volume. "But when approved, it will be intravenous, so it won't help those with milder illness."

A picture of a mink came on with the word COVID splashed across the screen. As the anchor began to speak, Maya grabbed the remote and turned the sound higher.

"A university study found evidence that cats and dogs can be infected by humans, with some becoming ill. A second study found identical virus from an owner and their cat. Despite no symptoms, the cat had lung abnormalities like humans. Finally, researchers in the Netherlands believe two people on mink farms were infected by the mink."

At the commercial, Manolo clicked off the TV. "The news about animals is getting more attention."

Maya continued to make small dips of her spoon. Manolo's bland chicken noodle soup appeased her stomach, but the steam made her nose run and she wiped it with her napkin. Following a few more bites, she put the tray between them. "All done."

After returning from the kitchen, he joined her naked under the covers. "Would you prefer to shower in the morning?"

She nodded. "Promise me that pregnancy fatigue and nausea will go away."

Wrapping one arm around her, he stroked her forehead. "Symptoms can be worse at the beginning with a sudden surge of hormones. They should disappear in your second trimester."

Fingers crossed, she drifted off into welcome sleep.

THIRTY-SEVEN

Santa Fe, New Mexico—Saturday, September 19, 2020

Maya spent another dawn hunkered over the toilet. Pregnancy was starting out to be no fun. Manolo brought her a cup of tea in bed, joining her with his coffee. "Your cheeks are flushed—let me check your temp."

"But I've been drinking hot tea."

He dug into his bag. "I have a digital one." He pulled the top of her left ear up and back, then gently inserted the tip toward her eardrum. After the beep, he showed Maya the display. "99.9°. Not considered an official fever until 100.4°."

"My normal temp's around 97.7° so it's two degrees higher. No wonder I'm feeling alternately hot and chilled."

He put away the scanner. "About twenty percent of women get a fever during pregnancy, although technically, you don't have one yet. Let me check it twice a day."

Her throat hurt with continued conversation. "I've never caught much more than a seasonal cold."

"You've barely eaten. Can I make you an omelet? No spices, just mild cheese."

She smiled. "Thanks, I'll give it a try."

When he yelled "Breakfast's ready," she managed to join him at the kitchen table and take a few bites, keeping them down. The morning sickness might be manageable, after all.

"Are you feeling any stronger?" he asked, his brow furrowed with concern.

She wiped her nose with a tissue, then nodded. "I've been so cooped up since I got home. Can we take a short walk?"

"Sounds good." He pulled the living room drapes open and she flinched. "Still light sensitive?" he asked.

"Too much time holed up like a hermit. Let's get out there—it's a spectacular day."

After she tugged on jeans and a windbreaker, Maya tapped the seat of her old red bike, sad that she wasn't feeling well enough to use it. "You should get one of your own so we can ride together."

He grinned. "Maybe, although it's been so long, I'll probably fall off. I'd kill for weight-lifting if only the gym was open."

Maya was determined to prioritize walking during her pregnancy. Exercise triggered her endorphin-joy, and she took pride in her lean, muscled look. Like Manolo, she missed the gym, especially the swimming pool.

Despite being outdoors in the cool air, they kept their masks on, encountering the occasional jogger and bicyclist on the path. Maya usually rode south from the apartment toward the freeway, but they turned north through the city neighborhoods. They got only a couple hundred feet before Maya started coughing. She tugged down her mask and took a swig from her water bottle. "The low humidity makes me thirsty."

She adjusted the brim of her cap and relished the colorful mountainside to the northeast. "It's been almost two years since our first official date here on Halloween."

Squeezing her hand, he nodded. "Good and bad memories—it was our first big fight, too. How about this autumn, we make them all good ones?"

She slipped her arm around his waist. "May's good timing for our baby. I'll use saved-up leave, and we can work out long-term plans."

A hazy image filled her vision. She was pushing a green stroller with a five-month-old infant, Manolo jogging next to them on a path carpeted with vibrant leaves. *My son's dark eyes round up when he sees my face. As I stoop to caress his cheek, he giggles.*

She snapped out of the reverie. The baby could be a girl—that would be okay too, even if she wanted a mini-Manolo.

He hugged her tighter. "I love living here. Work's nonstop with COVID, but it's sure more pleasant than Phoenix." He tugged down his mask to flash his wide Lin-Manuel Miranda grin, followed by a quick kiss to her forehead. "Not to mention living with my favorite veterinarian. Have you talked to Dr. Grinwold about the state public health vet job?"

She twisted away with another brief coughing spell, then took additional sips of water. "With usually only one per state, openings don't come up often. I'd be crazy to turn it down if he offers it."

"Ask him about it again. Unless you're worried he won't consider you because you're starting a family?"

Shaking her head, she tugged him in the direction of the apartment. "He's a bit difficult to work with at times, but I don't think he's sexist. I'm sure Nancy wouldn't put up with it."

He placed his hand on her forehead. "Overheated?"

She nodded, then coughed again. "We should get back." She bent to pick up a golden leaf from the path. "But I'm keeping this as a souvenir of getting home to the Land of Enchantment."

When she was inside on the couch, he took her ear temperature. He frowned. "Now it's 100.1° and I'm concerned about your coughing. When did that start?"

"Just now, on our walk." She reclined with her head on a pillow.

He pulled up a kitchen chair beside her. "I assume you didn't have any known exposure overseas to people infected with COVID."

"No, and the number of healthy people I talked to was limited. I looked in the door at some sick mink but I had full PPE and there was good circulation. Perhaps the riskiest activity was watching a mink necropsy, but I was fully protected."

"Have you verified that Stefan is healthy?"

"I'll do that. Of course there's the travel. I rarely took my mask off—didn't eat or drink much."

"No wonder you're run down." He brushed his hand through his hair and frowned. "Guess I shouldn't say 'I told you so,' but you know I advised against travel." He grabbed his phone. "Let me see if I can arrange COVID testing."

She texted Stefan in Poland and he rang within a minute of her message.

"Maya, you should see the facilities here—shocking. I'll send you pictures of the intermink aggression. They don't invest in animal welfare, although I'm not the best judge. I'd love to have you here."

"Any new cases?"

"Many—they're doing colossal culls. I advised burning carcasses. Any method of mass disposal is terribly unpleasant, but at least there won't be mink pushing up from their burial spots like in Denmark."

"I showed Manolo the picture—he thought it was a photo processing trick. Stefan, have you stayed healthy? I have symptoms that may be pregnancy or COVID, particularly a slight cough."

"No issues for me here in Poland. Must be my robust athlete's immune system. Will you get tested?"

She could hear Manolo's raised voice in the bedroom. "Manolo's working on it."

"Thanks for checking in," Stefan said, "and stay safe."

"Will do, and keep up the good work. I could say 'wish I was there,' but that's not true, given what you're finding. Good luck."

She pried herself off the couch and joined Manolo where he sat ramrod stiff on the edge of the bed.

He slammed his phone down and huffed. "The hospital won't test you because your symptoms aren't serious enough, and they require a lab order through a provider. Then I contacted the health office clinic, where they can see you next week, but it will take ten days for the results to come back."

She feathered the curls on his forehead. "I'll call my ob/gyn. She's the only doctor I've seen lately. On Saturday, it might be hard to get through, but it's worth a shot."

With a sudden shock, she dropped her hands away from his face. "Manolo, if we're seriously considering COVID, we shouldn't have contact with each other."

He took her hands back. "I understand, but this is a rule-out. We can't separate every time one of us has something mild, not during your pregnancy. And other than your cough, everything else could be normal with your first trimester."

Her limbs weakened, and she sank onto the bed next to him. "I know, but one of us coming down with COVID scares the shit out of me. Having both of us . . ."

"Let me see if I can arrange it through my IHS system even though you're not Native American. There's always a chance one of my colleagues will do something for a buddy."

She grabbed her phone. "I don't know why I didn't think of this sooner."

Dr. Grinwold picked up. "Maya, sorry to hear you've been under the weather since your return."

"That's why I'm calling. It's probably only my changing hormones, but with a cough starting today, Manolo wants me to get COVID testing. We're having a challenge arranging it on the weekend. Our health office clinic said they can see me next week but it would take more than a week for results."

He grumbled, a familiar sound to anyone who worked with him. "Not sure where that info came from. We're turning around results on average within three days."

She felt relieved—they were making progress on a plan. If she was exposing Manolo, and he refused to stay separate from her, there was a lot at stake.

"I'm not a priority for testing because my fever isn't higher, but my normal resting temp is only 97.7°, a full degree lower than average. So you would think my 100.1° could be interpreted as an even greater rise than 100.4° on a regular person."

"You're right, but we have case definitions and that cutoff value for a reason. Still, my authority counts for something. Let me call the hospital and get back to you." After he hung up, Maya found herself back in the bedroom with Manolo, his eyebrows scrunched, expression grim.

"I can't believe this is happening." He leaned back on the pillow, a hand over his eyes.

She lay down next to him. "Dr. Grinwold's on it. Why don't you take my temp? With all this stress, I'm feeling hot under the collar." When a cough bubbled up from her chest again, she went into her purse for her mask. "No argument, I'm wearing this now."

Manolo pulled himself out of bed and rechecked her ear temperature. "100.2°."

Dr. Grinwold's name flashed on Maya's phone screen and she clicked on Speaker. "You have an 11 AM appointment at the hospital's drive-through clinic."

Manolo jumped on the call. "Thank you, Fred. Her temp's going up and I want this sorted out."

A few dark clouds had slipped in and they grabbed jackets. Maya insisted that Manolo wear his mask in the car, which eased her anxiety as they waited in the long line of vehicles. Even with the windows rolled down, every twinge in her throat conjured the thought of germs wafting between the front seats. Finally she asked him to open the Corvette top and the colder breeze skimming her face above the mask was comforting.

In full PPE, the nurse talked to Manolo in the driver's seat, then moved around to Maya's side and inserted the swab in both nostrils. She'd heard some people complain about the discomfort of the procedure, but all she felt was a rush of happiness—she was one step closer to an answer.

Back at home, she expected Manolo to argue over continued masking, but his infection-control brain had kicked in and he agreed to wearing one when in the same room. "I wish we had two bathrooms," she said as she removed her clothes and crawled into bed.

He dug in the closet and pulled out extra bedding for the couch. "I'm going to hate every minute sleeping apart from you, and it might not even be necessary."

She tried to assuage that little-boy, puppy-dog look that always tugged at her heart. "I promise to text you or holler through the door if I need anything. And this might not last long, depending on when we get the results."

The last thing she expected after a few days apart in Europe was to be separated again. But if extra cautionary steps kept him safe, sleeping alone was worth it. She settled in with her laptop and caught up on emails, until another twinge of nausea drove her to the toilet. The coughing seemed to fuel her restless stomach, and vice versa. Discomfort compounded, with no loving arms for reassurance.

THIRTY-EIGHT

Santa Fe, New Mexico—Monday, September 21, 2020

"I got your weekend message," Maya's ob/gyn said on the phone at noon. "How are you doing?"

"Other than a grumpy spouse, I'm hanging in. Cough's more frequent but nausea and vomiting is still mostly in the morning."

"Any shortness of breath?"

"A bit, when I get up suddenly to go to the bathroom."

"All right. I have your COVID test result, and it's positive."

Maya's skin broke out in prickles. "Oh, shit." Talk about burying the lead—why hadn't the physician started out with that news?

"Your extreme fatigue could be a combination of the pregnancy and the virus. Maya, I want you monitoring with a pulse oximeter. If your husband doesn't already have one, ask him to buy one at the pharmacy. Hopefully they're not sold out."

A tear slipped from Maya's eye. "I'm scared for the baby."

"You're a strong, healthy young woman, and most women have successful pregnancies despite COVID infection. For your appointment next week, enter through the back door to access our separate COVID clinic."

After completing the call, Maya knocked on the bedroom door. "Manolo, can you come in?" Then she scurried back to the bed and pulled out a mask from the end table drawer.

He paused at the entrance, his own mask on, eyes dark pin pricks like the Danish mink. "Good timing, I need to use the bathroom— coffee overdose."

She raised a hand to stop him. "The doctor confirmed I have COVID. Put on full PPE before you come any closer."

He twisted, both hands to his head. "Mierda, my worst nightmare. I pray to God I didn't spread an infection from work."

"More likely it's my fault for the travel," she answered, voice trembling.

"I'll get tested too, but I don't want to leave you alone."

"Do you have a pulse oximeter?"

He headed out the door, then returned in a gown, face shield, and gloves. "I can't believe we have to do this. Now I know why they say you shouldn't be a doctor for your family members. I need to switch out of husband mode."

The pulse oximeter read ninety-four percent. "It's a hair low, but not at a level of concern. I'll leave it here for you to self-monitor." He rechecked her temperature. "No change, 100.2.°"

She finished a bowl of lentil soup he brought in before heading to work, then called her office. "Stephanie, bad news, I've got the 'rona."

"Jeez, Maya, how are you holding up?"

"Reasonably well, considering I have my own personal doctor, although a nervous one. Can you ring me into Dr. Grinwold's office?"

His voice was colored by concern. "I was just about to call—Erika gave me the weekend coronavirus results from the lab. Take sick leave, you should relax instead of trying to work from home."

"I'll see how it goes—I might be able to do both. Is there any genomic testing you can arrange to help figure out where I got this?"

"Yes, we can't do all samples, but when there's a chance it's been imported, we like to follow the variants."

Maya completed phone calls to her family and close friends, chagrined at contacting them so soon with bad news after returning home. The effort wore her out, and she had trouble getting into a comfortable position, her chest feeling heavy. She finally gave into the urge to nap.

. . .

Deep under water, her mind felt split in two. Half gave into the cool sensations of the rocking water between the kelp fronds off her favorite San Diego beach. The other half knew she was drowning. Something snuck up behind her and grabbed her fingers. A shark— she formed the other hand into a fist to punch its nose. Then a new sound drifted into her ears, muffled.

"Maya, Maya, wake up. Can you hear me?"

Her eyes eased open, surprised to find she wasn't in the ocean. Her finger pinched from the pulse oximeter. She barely recognized Manolo in all his gear.

"You were slow to respond, and I checked your oxygen level again." He slipped the painful clamp off her finger.

"Your O_2 is only eighty-nine percent." What did he say? His voice came from a distance, perhaps muffled by the ocean waves. Why did he drag her out on the sand when the water was so relaxing? But then he had her in his arms, like a baby. She gave into the rocking motion and lapsed into blissful quiet.

When she opened her eyes again, she didn't recognize her surroundings. Her nose twitched at the sensation of tubes in her nostrils. Someone squeezed her hand and she turned to her left. Manolo, still all geared up. His expression was fuzzy but seemed to light up as she gazed at his beloved face.

"You're in the hospital COVID ward. Don't worry, it's not the ICU. Your confusion and blue lips when I tried to wake you fit with low oxygen. You're stabilized and will be fine."

Her hand caressed her belly. "The baby?"

"Your ob/gyn conducted a transvaginal ultrasound."

Maya became aware of a slight sensation between her legs. The memories of the procedure came floating back, like through a gauze screen.

"Everything is fine. I even have a picture." He held it in front of her eyes but she couldn't focus. "Our bebé is really tiny, less than an inch, but they detected a heartbeat and leg movement. Our little miracle."

"Boy or girl?"

"At eight weeks, it's too early to tell. But I can't tell you what this means to me." He held the picture up closer to his face and kissed it through his mask.

"How long do I have to stay here?"

"They found patchy lung lesions on your chest CT, so you can't leave."

She had a rapid burst of coughing, and he helped her turn to her side. "How are they treating me?" she whispered.

"Staff are still debating. Pregnancy is a complication because drugs cross the placenta. Many are under study but no definitive results to base a decision."

Her eyelids fluttered and she heard him say, "Get some more sleep. I've got patients so I can't stay, but I'll be back to visit as soon as possible."

She followed his instructions. The few times she had been in a hospital before, the lights and movement and invasive equipment impaired her ability to rest. But not this time.

. . .

Staff came and went. IV fluid bags were replaced. Nurses helped Maya alternate between resting on her side and her stomach, hoping to take pressure off her lungs and relax the fist in her chest. Manolo's voice filtered in and out.

"Methylprednisolone is safer for the baby. Lab said she has the UK Alpha variant, more transmissible and dangerous in pregnancy."

The faint words triggered UK memories. Shoving passengers competing for limited flights at Heathrow. Removing her mask only once to eat.

Her eyes opened to a room fractured like the optical distortions of a kaleidoscope. Manolo held an iPad close to her face. She tried to discern the screen—were those the faces of her parents?

All other voices except Manolo's were distorted. "Baby's fine, you're doing great." Her muscles relaxed at her husband's news—be patient, go with the flow.

No sooner were images of hospital staff formed than they were forgotten. One moment blurred into another. In a few minutes of lucidity, she detected the pinch of a line in her arm and the claustrophobia of an oxygen mask. And the sounds—quiet, but not. Incessant beeping, soft slide of a door. All her senses were on low beam except for smell, notable by its absence. She'd never been fond of that antiseptic odor assaulting her nostrils, but now that was dead. She licked her lips, throat dry. How long since she'd eaten?

Manolo was at her bedside again, strong fingers on her forearm, imagined warmth even through gloves. "Fuck it, you've got to maintain her blood pressure."

Whenever they turned her body, she had brief bouts of awareness. "Maya, eres mi alma. Please fight this virus. I love you—come back to me."

Other voices were less distinct and she made out snippets which she tried to piece together for meaning. Manolo was ill, staying at home to recover. Then something about intubation for a hospitalized doctor.

Consciousness became torture. She clawed at the breathing tube, and they nailed her hands to the bed. Giant space aliens, redwood tall like Enzo, screamed at her. They pawed at her private parts, was he raping her? Where was the sibilant Spanish? Where was her gentle conquistador? Where was Manolo?

THIRTY-NINE

Santa Fe, New Mexico—Wednesday, October 7, 2020

Hip bones dug painfully into the bed. When her elbows pressed to adjust body position, she felt hollowed out, empty, no muscle to direct or cushion movement. Had she lost more weight? Her eyes rose to the wall. No calendar, no way to know how much time had passed.

Her throat felt like it had been reamed by a jackhammer, but it was no longer crammed with the ventilator. Her fingers verified an oxygen mask—breathing was labored but regular, the sensation of a fist in her chest eased.

She held her hand in front of her eyes. No stigmata, so the pounding nails had been an illusion. But her wrists hurt and she spotted bruising. The voice at her side was familiar, although not the doctor she ached for.

"Maya, can you hear me?" His beefy hand went to her hair, pushing it away from her forehead. The stiff and formal Dr. Grinwold. She couldn't recall him being quite so paternal before. "Do you know where you are?"

She turned her head. The room wasn't the one they checked her into. High-tech equipment crammed the walls. "ICU?"

He nodded and she imagined a smile under the face shield, mask, and glasses. Always hard to tell with him, but the lines around his eyes crinkled.

"You're on the mend, kidneys recovering, lungs improving, blood pressure stabilized."

She felt a prick of energy at the news and tried to sit up. "How long?" The question was difficult to create, floating like a bubble.

"Seventeen days." His words slammed her back down and her eyes closed, weeks vanished.

"If things continue to progress, you'll be transferred to a rehab center."

Manolo had stayed at one to regain speech and strength after his ICU hospitalization with anthrax. She needed to get back to full fighting form for him and the baby. Her hand drifted to her belly. Too soon to feel any kicks, despite the passage of time.

"Su . . . supervised . . . exercise." Keep trying, get the ideas out. "Manolo can . . . help me."

Dr. Grinwold glanced toward the ceiling. "Your parents—" He struggled with his words, unusual for a public health physician whose idea of fun was cranking out scientific articles and pontificating at podiums. "They're at your place. Would you like me to get them on Zoom?"

"Manolo first." She paused for another breath. "Where is he?" Likely at an IHS clinic—he couldn't have stayed with her full time when his patients needed him.

When Dr. Grinwold didn't answer, she noticed someone tall as a telephone pole who crept into the corner, hovering over the displays, checking her IV line.

"Are you ready?" Dr. Grinwold asked.

The woman held a syringe in her hand. Gargantuan attacking figures swept across Maya's visual field and she flinched as her flesh broke out in goosebumps. Her eyes dropped to the woman's chest badge stamped with RUTH above a benevolent grandmotherly photo.

Using abdominal breathing to remain calm, Maya remembered Dr. Kim's individual and group therapy, needed all the more with what she'd been through. "Cold." The nurse put down the scary needle and placed a second blanket over Maya's legs, pulling it up to her shoulders.

Maya's weak hand pointed to the threat on the tray. "What's that?" She was way too disoriented to understand her treatments.

The nurse's tone soothed. "Just Ativan, dear, your record

indicates you've had it before." Ruth's eyes redirected from Maya to Dr. Grinwold. "Prophylactically?"

"She has chronic anxiety disorder with panic attacks." Dr. Grinwold took her hand. "Maya, is that okay with you?"

Just reawakened after too many days of forced sleep, she wasn't eager for mood modulation, and she'd had negative reactions to benzos in the past. Weaning off Klonopin last year had been a major accomplishment. But something about Dr. Grinwold's moistened fierce eyes triggered her to trust him. She nodded and the nurse injected.

A familiar wash of comfort, all muscles relaxing and releasing. Fluffy white clouds replaced stormy ones in her mind. Only her dry mouth and throat continued to irritate. "Drink?"

Ruth adjusted Maya's oxygen mask and held a cup to her lips, soothing water coating her membranes like a carpet of fresh snow.

"Thanks," Maya whispered.

Dr. Grinwold clutched her left hand again, a bit too forceful in the area of her missing baby finger. Then his squeeze relaxed as he appeared to grope for words. "Maya, Manolo's not here because he caught COVID. He was hospitalized next door to you, but—"

"He's all right?" Close by—that's why the nightmares weren't worse. All they had to do was bring her over.

Shaking his head, Dr. Grinwold continued. "Maya, he didn't make it. His heart gave out yesterday. There was some residual damage from the anthrax. I'm so sorry."

Yesterday? She would have sensed something from the next room. Why didn't they wake her up sooner? Her body bent forward in a convulsive gasp. Impossible—he was in excellent health. He'd battled COVID in his IHS hospitals for months and never caught it. He knew how to stay safe.

Maybe she was still in a ventilator nightmare, or her overactive, tormenting imagination. She gripped Dr. Grinwold's forearm with both hands. "Not true," she wailed.

He altered his position to hold her shoulders. "Maya, I wish it wasn't so."

Ruth handed him an iPad. "Should I get your parents on Zoom?" he asked.

If this was an illusion, would it extend to a computer screen? "Yes, see them." When he held the device close, their stricken faces popped up immediately, like they'd been expecting the link.

"Mom, Dad." But she couldn't continue. She swiped the hair out of her eyes, trying to read their expressions.

Her dad started. "Maya, our prayers have been answered that we can see and talk to you again. Do you remember Manolo holding the screen when you were first admitted?" His words triggered the faint smoke of a memory, but it swept away into the void.

Her mother's chest heaved. "First Grandma and then Manolo, both from heart attacks. I thought COVID was a lung disease."

This was no delirious hallucination. Maya's sobs synched with her mother's. No longer having Manolo as her partner, raising their children together, impossible to grasp. Her hand slid under the warm blankets. "I still have him." Her baby, the one Manolo dreamed about all his life, except for a few days of pandemic panic when he questioned bringing a child into their out-of-control world.

Her dad's eyes and mouth rounded up. "Dr. Grinwold, you didn't tell her?"

His free hand continued to cup hers. "I'm not good at this."

Ruth cleared her throat and Maya looked in her direction. The woman stroking her forehead elicited sense memories of her grandmother and gave Maya a moment of peace in the desolation of Manolo's death. But Ruth's quiet statement shattered any fragments of solace.

"I'm sorry, dear, miscarriages happen early in pregnancy, although COVID increases them. Your ob/gyn says this will have no impact on your ability to bear children in the future."

A sledgehammer to her head and heart. A future without Manolo and her baby was no future at all.

FORTY

Pecos, New Mexico—Wednesday, November 25, 2020

The guard unlocked the gate just before the Pecos River, then Tom Maguire drove the van across the small bridge and along the snow-covered graveled lane. Like a gentle cup of praying hands, the river ringed the property on three sides. Bare branches of bankside deciduous trees created an artful lattice against the cerulean sky, but the piñon and juniper hugged the ground, evergreen.

Maya was immune to the landscape's drama and beauty. In the back seat, she focused ahead on the palatial cedar log ranch home. White streaks of aspens anchored its north and south ends, palettes of golden leaves at the base.

The van rolled to a stop where Mark Zielinski waited in his wheelchair. Still unable to walk without difficulty after his horseback injury, her former attorney had offered his spacious estate for Maya's recovery once her weeks in the rehab center were over.

At his side stood a buff male attendant and a midsized dog. Blue heeler—she recognized its speckled, blue-gray coat. When Maya's dad hopped out to slide open the side panel, the dog leapt up and barked.

"Chloe, cut that out." Mr. Zielinski's tone was firm but friendly, and the dog sat back down, ears at alert.

The attendant stepped forward to maneuver Maya into her wheelchair and lower her to ground level in the lift.

"Thank you so much, Mr. Zielinski," Maya's mom gushed. "We'd do anything to care for her ourselves. If only our Flagstaff apartment or hers were ADA compliant, but . . ."

He doffed his black cowboy hat with the gleaming silver conchas rimming the crown. "Mrs. Maguire, as well as we know each other, can we get on a first-name basis?" At her nod, he continued.

"With the money I put into making this place wheelchair-accessible, Barbara, someone else should get the benefit. And my rates are cheap." He winked.

Still struggling to assemble words quickly, Maya smiled at his confident humor, contrasting sharply with her mother's squirrelly anxiety.

"Seriously, Mark," Maya's dad said. "We're grateful for your help on multiple occasions over the past several years. We're all happy she's released from long-term care in time for Thanksgiving."

"Good timing, Tom, my chef is preparing a feast. You are joining us tomorrow for it?"

Maya's mom clapped her hands. "Of course, we wouldn't miss it. We're just not used to getting out and about with this second wave of COVID."

Mark stroked his gleaming black hair, skimming the collar of his blue western shirt. "As you can see, I'm not getting out either. I need one of my staff to give me a trim. We have a number of small cabins and everyone's living on the property, mostly masked. So we're in a bubble—less chance for the virus to sneak in."

Her mom tucked a stray red hair back into her bun. "That's such a relief. We're scared to death that Maya might catch this again."

"Barbara, that's unlikely." Her dad's voice snapped but he gently patted his wife's arm. "Her immune system is probably at its max."

"You don't know that, Tom. Corona isn't short of surprises."

Maya couldn't find words to stop them pecking at each other like crows. Mark jumped in. "I have a good internet connection if Maya needs to work from home, like I do."

"She's on a leave of absence from her preventive medicine residency," her dad answered. "So she's got nothing on her plate except healing."

"Cell service is sometimes sketchy, so I have a landline." Mark signaled the attendant who handed over a business card. "If you can't reach Maya on her iPhone, feel free to call us."

After placing Maya's suitcases on the drive, her dad reached for the wheelchair. She shook her head and said, "See you tomorrow."

Mark jumped to her defense. "We'll get Maya settled—I'm sure she's exhausted by the travel. Come at two so we can give you a tour of the house before dinner at three."

Maya's determined expression must have been convincing because her parents left. Mark maneuvered his wheelchair inside as the attendant pushed Maya's.

In the two-story entrance with its gleaming wood floors, Maya glanced up to the wagon wheel lamp covered with antlers. Mark gestured to the carved pine staircase curving up to the second floor.

"That's the guest area. On this floor, we have two master suites at either end. I thought my future wife might like her own cozy enclave, but my career got in the way and I never married."

A woman with curly short dark hair came out of the office straight ahead. With wrinkles around her eyes, she appeared close to Mark's age of fifty. "This is Carmen," he said. "She runs the household. If you need anything, ring the buzzer in your room. You gonna be okay?"

Maya nodded. "Very kind."

Following Carmen, Mark's attendant pushed Maya in her wheelchair down to a large bedroom that maintained the full round log walls of the other rooms. Then he left to retrieve her luggage. Inside the room, the king-sized bed had a huge headboard carved with a water spirit. Lamps on each end table were hammered out of copper with decorative western-themed shades.

"Would you like me to plug in your phone?" Carmen asked, and Maya handed it to her.

Carmen unpacked Maya's clothes into a pine dresser embedded with turquoise Zia symbols. A mirror and makeup table stood against the opposite wall, which amused Maya because she'd never use it.

Maya fingered the soft bedspread with a zigzag pattern of blue and green. All the colors integrated with the sky and trees outside French doors leading to a back patio.

"Western palace," Maya said.

"It's wonderfully comfortable, isn't it?" Carmen's voice was low and friendly. "My room is above yours and I'm always available. Do you need help with the bathroom?"

"Not paralyzed, just weak."

"All right. Mr. Zielinski usually has dinner at six o'clock. Will that work for you?"

Three hours, time for a nap. When Carmen left, Maya tugged back the bedspread and crawled under, fully dressed. Just a brief rest.

. . .

His hands cupped her naked breasts from behind, then maneuvered her hips in tighter to his own. "¿Cómo estás, mi amor?"

"Wonderful when you're here, mi esposo. I wish it was more often. Your absence is torture, and I can't go on without you."

She rotated to face him, thrilled to see his Lin-Manuel goatee. She feathered her fingers over the dark bristles of his upper lip and chin, then followed with a warm and wet kiss, deep and penetrating. "How long can you stay?"

"As long as you want."

He adjusted his position to penetrate her at a comfortable angle, careful to avoid his weight over her growing baby bump. He began with slow and gentle strokes, then increased in speed and excitement. But no matter how he moved or caressed, she couldn't achieve satisfaction. They went on and on, with no crescendo. She twisted away, the sudden movement jerking her awake.

Her hands were inside her unzipped pants, and she groaned in frustration. Were his visits consoling dreams or maddening nightmares?

The soles of her feet tingled with nerve pain when they touched the wide plank floor. She stretched for her daypack at the foot of the bed. Her mother had slipped in Maya's vibrator after her painfully awkward request. She moved it to the drawer of the end table for another time. The alarm clock indicated she had an hour to get ready.

Maya wheeled through the wide doorless opening to the Saltillo-tiled bathroom. Sitting on a chair in the corner, she undressed. The shower with multiple spray heads had grab bars and a built-in tile seat. Using faucets at a lower height, she cleaned up without standing again. Memories flooded of rubbing a washcloth over Manolo's body while he sat on a shower chair.

After his anthrax infection, he'd come back from deeper neurologic trauma than hers, so she could too. Long COVID, they called it, with an unpredictable recovery. But lengthy ventilator use and ICU stays were associated with their own side-effects.

Dried off with a plush white towel, she wheeled herself to the dresser. Pants were more practical when outdoors in the frosty late-autumn weather, but more challenging to put on than a dress. In the closet, she pulled off the hanger a yellow smock with embroidered flowers to layer over a thin creamy turtleneck. Cheerful color to brighten the deep black of the evening—first night alone without the incessant noise of the rehab center. She welcomed the quiet and time to put the visions in their place.

When wheeling herself into the dining room, she focused on the youthful attendant by the door. With a checkerboard mind, she had trouble keeping track of masked faces. Was he the same one who helped at the van?

"Hi, Dr. Maguire, we didn't formally meet earlier. I'm Lukas. I've been with Mr. Zielinski since the pandemic." Everything about his coloring appeared to be Hispanic—all the dark features that Maya loved. Except his hair, an arresting bleached blond.

"Mr. Zielinski's a wonderful employer—all my living expenses are covered here. You're fortunate to have him as a friend."

"Client, first," she managed to eke out.

"Well, he's always looking to help."

"I know." She smiled, then Mark wheeled in from the other entrance. The solid oak table was long with multiple leaves, and he rolled down to the end closest to Maya.

"We've got this set up for our big Thanksgiving dinner tomorrow. But for tonight, let's just share this end together, nothing fancy."

Within minutes, Lukas whisked out two warm ceramic plates with blue corn chicken enchiladas as they removed their masks. Mark moved the tub of sour cream closer to Maya. "A mama bird named Barbara told me this is your favorite."

Maya flushed, ashamed to be hypersensitive about her mother. Barbara Maguire was always thinking about her daughter, sometimes too much. But with Maya's loss of her own baby, long before it was developed enough to be called that, she started to understand. She grabbed the red cloth napkin and dabbed at her eyes.

Mark adjusted his weight in his wheelchair and wiped away a white speck on the sleeve of his black shirt. "I'm sorry, Maya, didn't mean to upset you."

She shook her head. "Don't mind me." Without further conversation, she relaxed into the Vivaldi playing softly through ceiling-mounted speakers. Clearly Mark could tell that talking was challenging, and he didn't press it.

After dinner, he led a wheelchair parade into the library, crammed with antique and modern books. From a shelf filled with poetry authors, he pulled out a leather-bound volume.

"This has one of my favorite poems by Tennyson, *Ulysses*. I've been searching for a first edition, but that's 1842, so might not be possible. Let me read you the final lines."

Tho' much is taken, much abides; and tho'
We are not now that strength which in old days
Moved earth and heaven, that which we are, we are;
One equal temper of heroic hearts,
Made weak by time and fate, but strong in will
To strive, to seek, to find, and not to yield.

Maya accepted the book and retreated to her bed. Still recovering from his own injury, Mark understood what she was going through. A *count your blessings* philosophy, but more beautifully crafted.

Tennyson wrote about a heroic heart. Hard to accept, considering she'd killed her husband and baby with a stubborn choice of duty, or scientific curiosity, or lust for adventure. No one said that she and Manolo were infected with the same variant—he could have been exposed through his work. But in her gut, she knew. Memories of hospital days were few, but included him mentioning the UK alpha variant. She could ask Dr. Grinwold, but wasn't ready for the likely answer.

. . .

Pecos, New Mexico—Thursday, November 26, 2020

Maya's parents joined them for a tour, impressed by the craft and beauty of the hand-hewn log home. Maybe it was her imagination, but in this setting they treated her more like a twenty-seven-year-old adult than an invalid daughter who needed care. Not many attorneys had the wings of an angel to provide help when she was no longer paying for legal advice. She wasn't sure she deserved the recovery retreat, but resolved to follow Tennyson and be strong in will.

Pressure to come up with scarce words for conversation eased when Mark's entire staff joined them at the extended table for Thanksgiving dinner. Most were celebrating a new administration at the federal level, although a few muttered about a stolen election. Mark joshed with them all, keeping the atmosphere convivial. Carmen sat on Maya's left and helped her pick out some slices of turkey and root vegetables grown on the ranch.

"Can you believe we've never done this before?" Carmen marveled. "Mr. Zielinski is usually at his Phoenix home this late in the season. But he decided creating a bubble was easier here on the ranch. I might have to learn cross-country skiing."

Maya almost offered to teach her but remembered she could barely walk. Her dad was an expert and they were only forty-five minutes away at her Santa Fe apartment. Maybe he could help Carmen, if she was serious.

Mark's laugh was audible from the other end of the table. He was formidable but friendly, and like Manolo, had a natural talent for making friends. Carmen's referring to him as Mr. Zielinski was surprising considering the number of years they worked together. But perhaps being similar in age, she felt the need to maintain that boundary with an attractive boss.

During the pause as the staff cleared the main plates, Maya's mother on her other side swiped through cell phone photos of Hypatia snoozing on her cat post, adjusting well to the move from Flagstaff to Santa Fe.

"I guess snow is snow, no matter which state her bird-watching window is in," her mother joked.

Maya held up one of the pastelitos, Carmen's speciality, a slab pie with dried fruit. The plate was warm, but her nose was incapable of picking up any smell. That was probably why she'd eaten so little in the past few weeks—an absence of taste ruined her appetite, and a sometimes shaky will to live.

After dinner, her dad set her up at a table in the library with Manolo's iPad. Before he and her mom headed home, he got the Zoom link to Bernalillo working. The boisterous Schwartz family of five, plus Bo the retriever, vied for center focus.

"Braxton was our turkey wrangler this year," Dave said proudly, and his brother's faint freckles became more visible in his embarrassment.

"Nothing to it," he bragged. "Who processed yours, Auntie Maya?"

She shrugged. "Don't know."

He didn't press her for more conversation. She asked, "What's new?" and Dave caught her up on the world galloping along while she tread like a tortoise.

"Last month, more than a thousand of your current and former Epidemic Intelligence Service Officers publicly criticized the pandemic response, especially on testing."

"Surprised." Shocked would have been a better word—she wasn't sure something like that had ever happened before. EIS Officers were trained to support their agencies, even when pushing internally for more aggressive responses and resources.

"Some airports are using Corona dogs to sniff out infected people."

"Wait 'til peer-reviewed."

Dave chortled. "You can't fool me—your brain is still kicking the tires in there."

Maya wished it were true. She'd probably forget they even talked by tomorrow.

"Mink outbreaks are exploding. They finally depopulated all of them in Denmark and we have new outbreaks here at home."

"Where?"

"Michigan and Wisconsin. I worked with your buddy Keegan Williams from Fort Collins. Wish you were on the team, but your notes from Denmark were valuable. On one Michigan farm, they might have evidence it went from mink to humans."

"Wow." But instead of being awed by coronavirus spread, she felt guilty that she now contributed nothing. An entire world blowing up with a pandemic, and she was relaxing in a life of luxury reading poetry.

With COVID spreading in farmed mink, there was a chance of it spilling over to the wild. If they became a reservoir host animal, no amount of culling would eradicate the risk. "Wild mink?" she asked.

"Yes, our Wildlife Services office has been sampling. But on the good news front, Pfizer released a study showing their vaccine is ninety-five percent effective. Colleagues say it might get emergency use authorization within the next few weeks."

A vaccine. Protection against infection. But too late.

After she hung up, Maya realized that Dave was appealing to her scientific side with the game-changing news. But it only reinforced her despair at traveling for the mink investigation. She should have waited until she was immunized, to save the life of her husband and unborn child. Reckless and negligent—a reckless disregard for the risks and negligent dismissal of her husband's concerns. If she couldn't forgive herself, why would either the Maguire or Miranda families? Someone spiraling into a black hole of misery was of no use to anybody.

FORTY-ONE

Pecos, New Mexico—Monday, April 19, 2021

Lukas pushed Mark in his wheelchair along the hard-packed Pecos National Historical Park trail as Maya kept up, using her cane. "Hiking again," she said. "I can't believe it."

Mark raised his eyebrows and stared pointedly at the cane. "You call that hiking?" he teased.

"You should talk," she teased back.

"If you two old folks are gonna bicker, I'll abandon you right here." Lukas winked and maneuvered Mark's wheelchair up to the low stone walls of the South Pueblo.

"We're celebrating Maya's bickering." Mark grabbed her bare hands with his in the black gloves. "Thank God that aphasia is behind you."

With her leather cowboy boots, a twenty-eighth birthday gift from Mark, she kicked a rock out of the way of his wheelchair. "I'll thank the speech-language therapists, your library, and you, my personal reader."

She tugged out her list of the area's blooming flowers from her jeans back pocket. "I'm grateful the parks are open. I think these yellow discs are Hopi blanketflower."

Lukas grabbed her printed sheet. "The white ones are running fleabane. Have you ever seen so many petals?"

Mark gestured to a cluster of violet flowers. "Storksbill. Chef uses that in some of his dishes—tastes like parsley."

"All right," Lukas said, "if we're done with the horticultural tour, let me tell you about the history of this site. I grew up around here, you know."

"And that makes you an expert." Mark's grin belied his dig.

From the hillside location as they approached the church ruins, Maya slowly pivoted to take in the dark-green peaks of the Sangre de Cristos and the flat-topped Glorieta Mesa, grateful that her body had recovered enough to enjoy the excursion. She stepped carefully to avoid tipping over into the cholla cactus along the trailside, purple buds starting to bloom.

"My ancestors first established relationships with the people living here in Cicuye in the 1600s," Lukas continued.

"Established relationships?" Mark seemed determined to prolong their banter. "That's a polite way to describe invasion."

"Well, the native peoples weren't powerless. They kicked us out at the end of the century and destroyed our churches. This is the fourth one on this site, built in the 1700s."

The harsh high desert wasn't kind to adobe structures. Only a few massive walls still remained and Maya tried to imagine its original state. One couldn't help but feel spiritual in this expansive location. The pale blue sky appeared dotted with a few of Mark's sleeping sheep.

She remained silent, avoiding the friendly fight while sucking in the natural beauty. Mark touched her arm. "I'm lucky to be one of the latecomers to this area." He paused, as if gathering his thoughts. "Rachel Carson in *Silent Spring* wrote about how nature heals us, season reappearing after season. You've come through a tough time, stronger every week. You should be proud of yourself."

He was right—the winter had been interminable, and the first one where she couldn't cross-country ski to burn off her emotion.

Her dad came out to give lessons to Carmen and other staff on the flat areas encircled by the Pecos River and the gentle inclines on its other side. But Maya hadn't started to walk until the end of March, too late to use skiing as a strength and coordination exercise.

She held the back of Mark's wheelchair. "My progress has been incredible. I wish you made as much."

"Your snapping the whip in the weight room helped me lose a few pounds." He patted his belly, slimmer since the holidays.

In the broad open area of collapsed ruins, a cell phone signal got through and he answered it, then pivoted the chair back toward the trail entrance. "Carmen reports some of our lambs are coming. Want to help out?"

. . .

Maya strolled alongside Mark as they headed from the house to the barn. A Komondor guard dog commanded the top of a small hill, white cords of thick hair drooping to the ground. Not far away, a magnificent Dahl ram with his wool coat, like a lion's mane, stood in the pasture surveying his kingdom. His massive set of horns curved almost full-circle.

"That pose—he's inseminated the planet, don't you think?" Mark looked up at Maya and grinned. "This breed was brought into New Mexico by Coronado in the 1500s, and only a couple of ranches still maintain them."

Glancing up to the slowly greening hillside beyond the ram and the riverbed rushing with snowmelt, Maya spotted a herd of white-tailed deer.

"Some ranchers view them as competition for the grazing land," Mark said. "But I don't mind. Getting deer meat during bow hunting season is worth it."

The barn exuded a pleasant hoppy smell of leftover brewery grains used as animal feed. If she hadn't been a beer fan before her extended stay at the ranch, the odor combined with animal feces might have turned her stomach. In multiple pens, pregnant ewes bedded down on thick mats of straw and chewed contentedly. Maybe the grain took the edge off their labor pains. A staff member stayed in the barns 24/7 to monitor each birth.

"Been at it all night?" Mark asked the young woman, who nodded.

"This one's been straining a long time," she said. "I was about to call the vet when Carmen mentioned you were stopping by. Perhaps Dr. Maguire can have a look."

Maya panicked—how much could she remember? But she was here now, and the animal with a smaller set of horns than the ram seemed weak with the effort. She glanced down at her jeans and old shirt, then grabbed a pair of gloves from the table. "I'll give it one try, but if I don't succeed, get more experienced help."

Mild pain and tingling in her hands and feet hadn't dissipated but could be overlooked when concentrating on something else. She prayed her small hands would be coordinated.

With each strain, two tiny feet poked out the sheep's vulva. Lying on her side in the straw, Maya carefully reached her hand inside past the legs and felt for the lamb's neck. As she suspected, it was twisted back. The birth canal kept contracting—her wrist and fingers were numb as she repeatedly tried to guide the head around to align with the legs.

Frustrated about failing Mark and the ewe, she leaned back against a hay bale and asked, "How long have I been doing this?"

"Fifteen minutes. Don't worry, I have faith in you. We'd never get our regular vet in time, anyways."

Somehow with his vote of confidence, her fingers achieved success and the lamb slid out, head and front legs forward. A second one quickly descended on its own, and Maya wiped amniotic membranes from both noses.

The ewe stood and licked off her lambs. Then the staff person picked up one under each arm. Maya followed, guiding the ewe to a new pen. The woman milked off the colostrum and tube-fed it to each lamb.

Maya wandered back to join Mark. "You don't trust the ewe to give enough of the antibodies to her offspring?"

"With multiple sheep giving birth close in time, we can't be certain how well the lambs are suckling. Tube feeding helps us track what they're getting."

Maya's legs felt weak, whether from the historic site walk or the stress of remembering how to birth a lamb, she didn't know. She sank to the straw and leaned her shoulder against Mark's wheelchair.

He stroked her loose hair. Something deep inside stirred at his touch, especially when she looked up into his dark eyes. Larger than Manolo's—everything about Mark was bigger than life.

"Our professional relationship has become a friendship," he said. "That might feel awkward. But it's been more than a year since I provided you legal advice about Dr. Russo and his assault."

With both hands, he helped her stand. Still dizzy from the birthing efforts and his hint of a personal interest, she braced an arm on the back of his wheelchair.

For once, his smile was tentative instead of confident. "I don't want to cross any lines. If you're worried about this wheelchair, all my body parts work."

She nodded. "I assumed." Then laughing, she took one of his hands in her own. "I mean, it crossed my mind."

They'd lived together for months, sharing most meals. Then poetry and Shakespeare, read to each other as part of her speech therapy. Games of cribbage, hours of painful workouts in his home gym. She couldn't help but feel a tug in his direction. But Manolo continued to plague her dreams, inhabiting a burning Zozobra statue accusing her of causing his death. She was unsure if she could ever move on, even with a man as kind and appealing as Mark.

His free hand brushed the jowls under his chin. "Am I too old, too fat?"

She held both of his hands. "No, although you could be my father if you had me in college. But my dad's in his seventies, so that image has never come up when I look at you."

His smile broadened. "Good to know. Do I have a chance?"

"I admire your intellect, your generosity, the way you dominate a room. What girl wouldn't swoon? You're magnetic and loving. I'd be crazy not to lean into this moment."

His fingers stroked her cheek. "But you won't."

She shook her head. "It's been more than six months, but I'm still grieving Manolo and the family we almost had."

"I wish I'd met this paragon."

She flushed, remembering their fights. "Not a paragon—he wasn't perfect, but pretty damned special."

He dropped his gloved hands to his wheels. "Let's get back and clean up."

Her eyes narrowed with an intense flashback of showers with Manolo, one of her favorite turn-ons. She tamped the feeling down. There were no prohibitions against her recreating those sensations with someone else, except that most of her molecules still felt bonded to another.

At her silence, he smirked. "That wasn't a come-on. I'm not a subtle guy—you'll know it when I seduce you. A client wants an in-person meeting in my Santa Fe office now that I'm vaccinated. Would you like to see your folks in town?"

Back to Santa Fe, with all its memories of her wedding and married life. Was she finally ready? She formed a plan as she helped Mark maneuver his wheelchair along the path to the Zia carved double doors. As long as she could reasonably walk and talk, it was time to move home to her Santa Fe apartment and consider restarting her preventive medicine residency.

Her brain was still fuzzier than before COVID, but she'd made progress on that front too. PMRs were a gift of additional expertise from CDC to a few states, so her prolonged recovery didn't leave a major gap in Dr. Grinwold's staff. But every hand was valuable in a pandemic.

Once she turned Mark over to Lukas, she headed to her room for a shower and packing.

. . .

A green planter of sun-kissed daffodils and feathery red tulips brightened her apartment porch. Her mother's work. She leaned over to take Mark's hand again after he parked. "Let me surprise them, then we'll grab my luggage. That won't make you late?"

"No, I'm fine. Come back and visit in June when we move the animals to their summer pasture in the national forest. And a horseback ride—you weren't up for that before."

Her arms stretched around his broad shoulders and she kissed his cheek. "Mark, you're the best host for a sick girl. With that spectacular hot tub, you could advertise your ranch as a health spa."

"No, it's only for certain guests." He tossed his cowboy hat into the back seat and completed the embrace, head against her neck, breathing into her ear for a second until Maya retreated out the passenger door.

She rang the bell, admiring the cheerful Easter wreath on the door, carved white bunnies and colorful eggs glued to the braided base. Her dad answered.

"Maya, what are you doing here? It's been two weeks since that wonderful Easter dinner at Mark's. We were planning to call you and stop by again, but this is great."

"I'm moving back home. Is that okay with you guys?"

Her mother sprang up from the couch. "Are you kidding? We've been counting the days. Where are your things?"

Maya led them to the SUV where Mark rolled down his window. "I hope this is a welcome surprise. I warned her to call you first, but she's stubborn."

Her mom squeezed his hands. "Of course this is okay. How can we thank you? We worried if she'd ever walk again."

"Dad, can you grab my suitcases? Mark's letting me leave the wheelchair at the ranch because this place isn't big enough to store it." With any luck, she wouldn't need it again.

Fluttering in excitement, her mom kept holding Mark's hands. "You should come in for ice tea—we can be the hosts for once."

Maya put an arm around her mother's waist and guided her a step back. "Mark's headed to his office for an appointment and we don't want to make him late."

"Of course," her mom said, and Maya whispered "Thank you" to Mark's smiling but wistful face.

Once inside, Maya draped herself on the couch and Hypatia jumped up to join her. She wasn't certain if the cat remembered her from infrequent visits after doctor's appointments, and she loved embedding her fingers into the thick fur. "How's it going as a cat parent here?"

Her mom pulled a chair close. "Quite enjoyable. We're not sure how anyone survives quarantine without a pet."

Her dad lifted a suitcase. "I'll put this in your bedroom, then shift our stuff out."

"Please don't do that until you head to Flagstaff. I'll manage here on the couch fine."

Then Maya flushed, afraid she sounded like she wanted them to leave. They hadn't lived under the same roof in years, and it felt awkward. Plenty of offspring rejoined the family nest during the pandemic, but it still felt like going backwards.

"You two are the best parents, uprooting yourself from home for seven months. It's been such a comfort with you staying here, coordinating medical care, giving me time and space to heal."

Her mom put an arm around Maya's shoulders. "Where else would we be?"

"We made some money on the deal," her dad said. "Our Tucson friends wanted to ski, so we rented out our place."

Suddenly Maya ran out of energy and voice. Between the Pecos park and the lambing, she'd overexerted herself. "Can we set up the sofa bed now?"

Her dad pulled it open while her mom got the bedding. Maya changed in the bathroom to her gown and robe, then crawled in. "Still no taste or smell—think I'll skip dinner."

Squeezing her arm, her mom said, "Are you sure, sweetie? You're skin and bones."

"Let the kid rest, Barbara." He grabbed his hat and added, "We can drive down the block for takeout."

When the door closed, Maya pulled the massaging vibrator out of her suitcase. All those months in Pecos, she never used it. The ranch at night had been deathly quiet and she'd been sure someone would hear it. She glanced again to the locked front door and turned it on, then arched her arm behind her to rub away lower back pain aggravated by the lambing. But the effort to bring forth new life was worth the discomfort.

She couldn't be sure how long her parents would be gone to pick up dinner so she quickly rotated the vibrator to the front. Months and months without an orgasm, despite weekly dream visits from Manolo. An attractive host at the other end of the ranch home had been tempting. She yearned for someone's touch, maybe anyone's, but she hadn't been willing to corrupt Mark's hospitality even in the changed circumstances of their relationship.

Staying permanently in the isolation of Pecos wasn't an option, and she couldn't let Mark think it was. Better to be alone, strong and independent. A widow at twenty-eight, starting life over. Or perhaps a rewind to the excitement of age twenty-five, beginning her first job placement. New Mexico, the Land of Enchantment. Promising possibility rather than devastating defeat.

FORTY-TWO

Santa Fe, New Mexico—Tuesday, April 20, 2021

The Maguires returned to the apartment for lunch after exploring the Museum of International Folk Art. Maya had hoped for a job in Santa Fe lasting a few years so she could explore its treasures with her husband. She wiped away a tear. One more magical place that she would never share with Manolo and their child.

Her dad tapped the plate holding her unfinished sandwich. "Eat something. Have you thought about work?"

"My mind's been too scattered."

"I hope you can get back to your job." Maya's mom wiped up the crumbs. "We've been so proud of what you accomplished."

"Public health staff are burning out and quitting," her dad said. "They're getting attacked in the press and at their homes."

"You want me to go back to that?" Maya asked. For many of the protracted weeks focusing on speech and physical therapy at the ranch, she couldn't focus on her colleagues, except during check-ins as they sent condolences. Another thing to regret. Relationships not nurtured didn't last, although now that she was home, maybe she could recreate her previous life without Manolo.

Manolo. She didn't have a clue where he or her baby were, other than her dreams. How could her brain be so narrowly focused that she forgot about them? Tears flooded her field of vision. "Their, their bodies, what happened?"

Both parents drew her to the couch and wrapped her in a comforting cuddle. "Right here, waiting for you," her dad said.

"What do you mean?" She glanced frantically around the living room.

"Honey, they were cremated, don't you remember?" her mom asked. Maya shook her head no. Her dad returned with a heavy ceramic urn blending sky and earth colors and set it on the coffee table. "They're together forever."

"Oh God, I can't, it's too real." Maya hid her head under her arms as her chest heaved with deep sobs.

"That's okay, I'll take it away." He hastily picked up the urn and headed to the bedroom.

"You know where it is when you're ready," her mom whispered. "Manolo's family wants a service when everyone can travel safely."

Flits of memory from the hospital and rehab center filtered in. The discussion of cremation had slipped away, until the awful vision of the urn brought it back. She'd stay out of the bedroom and pretend a while longer that her husband and baby were temporarily gone, like in NYC with the Mirandas.

. . .

Santa Fe, New Mexico—Wednesday, April 21, 2021

Bright spring light crept in through the thin kitchen curtains. Hypatia climbed onto Maya's chest and kneaded her paws. "Oh, cat, why are you doing this to me?" Her head rested on a soggy lump of a pillow after she cried all night. What mature adult gave into that much self-pity? She couldn't stand herself and was determined to do something about it.

After a quick shower, she broke out the skillet and made a cheese and tomato frittata. Her parents joined her and she sliced it three ways. Hypatia begged at the foot of the chairs, rotating among them. "So cat food isn't enough," Maya chastised, smiling. She carved off a tiny piece with no spices and dropped it into the cat bowl.

When they finished eating, Maya took one hand from each parent in her own. "I don't want you to feel like I'm kicking you out, but that's what I need to do."

"Are you sure?" her mom asked. "What about your doctor appointments?"

"The most important ones are with Dr. Kim, and I do them

by Zoom." Maya dug in her pack and pulled out a day planner that Mark had picked up for her.

"She's got me fighting long COVID fog . . . I break tasks into components and write them down—marks it in my brain." She showed them her iPhone screen. "Alarms are reminders."

Her dad leaned back in his chair, frowning. "What about driving? You haven't done that in months."

"Reduced executive processing skills—too many stimuli coming at me. Stephanie and Erika always come through in a crunch." In Pecos, wanting to stay COVID-safe, she hadn't seen her friends as much as she would have liked. They'd relish the chance to help, but there were taxis and Ubers, and she lived close to essential services.

"All right," her mom answered. "We'll pack up and drive home, see if Hypatia remembers Flagstaff. Hopefully our renters kept our houseplants going."

Maya was grateful they generated a reason to give her time on her own. She both dreaded and looked forward to being a hundred percent alone with her sorrow.

As they prepared to head off around noon, she hugged them goodbye on her front porch.

"Turn on your Prius a few times to charge the battery," her dad said. "We're here for you whenever you need it."

A wave of vertigo jiggled the parking lot view and she grabbed for the door handle. "I love you. Text me when you're back in Arizona."

Inside, the tumbling clothes dryer emanated a familiar, cheerful sound. She clicked on the television remote, unused to the bright screen and loud voices coming out of Manolo's flat-screen TV. With Mark, they rarely watched it and usually lounged in the library together after dinner.

She missed his company already. Maybe she was premature to reject him out of hand. He was a man of the world with homes in two states. He wouldn't keep her cooped up on the ranch, but they never discussed a relationship. She had no idea if his pass in the barn represented interest in a fling or something deeper. Regardless, she wasn't ready for either. Thinking about it felt like a betrayal, with Manolo's spirit still so close.

Streaming *Sleepless in Seattle* was a good escape, until it was over and she was back to obsessing over the fact that COVID had stolen the loves of her life and her happy ending. She hauled the bedding out of the dryer. First time back in her bedroom, their bedroom, and the colorful urn shouted from the bookshelf. She couldn't touch it, yet putting a book in front to hide it felt like an insult to their memories. Instead, she pulled a pillow over her head and cried herself to sleep for a second night in a row.

. . .

Santa Fe, New Mexico—Monday, April 26, 2021

Determined to put her grief behind her, Maya tried her bike in the parking lot but wobbled, so she went for a sunrise stroll. Her third Santa Fe spring, and she relished the vegetation coming back to life.

Back home by seven, she called Atlanta. "It's wonderful to hear from you," Dr. Jaworski greeted her. "Does this mean you're ready to resume your PMR?"

"Not necessarily," Maya answered. "I'm still figuring out what I can do, maybe out-of-town to escape this haunted house."

"Check in with Fred and Nancy. They miss having you on board."

Dr. Grinwold—they'd talked by Zoom while she was in Pecos. His new physician EIS officer started just before Maya's aborted Arizona mink farm investigation. She never met him; he'd been handling resource parity in the more rural areas of the state the few times she'd been in the office before catching COVID. Dr. Grinwold might not need her after all, but that could be her ego talking. Every public health and healthcare agency was short-staffed.

So she called Nancy in Phoenix, always easier to confide in. "Hi, it's Maya, sorry I've been out of touch."

"Don't worry, dear. Your voice is much stronger—such a relief."

"You too," came Maya's automatic response, but it wasn't entirely true. Nancy sounded exhausted.

"It's been tough," Nancy said. "Fred doesn't realize how lucky he's got it with a governor respecting public health. I don't know how I'd survive without Enzo fighting my battles. He never backs down, but that doesn't guarantee success. Still, he's had a lot of responsibility for a second-year EIS officer, and I've come to depend on him."

Maya was tempted to ask if he'd reined in his aggressive tendencies toward the opposite sex, but didn't want to reopen the wounds. Nancy was in the loop and would monitor as best she could.

"Unfortunately, Enzo's accepted a new job with Health and Human Services in DC. Moving on up, bigger fish to fry. I may decide to take that retirement I've been discussing for a year."

Nancy's heart attack from the long-ago Chagas infection had prompted those retirement plans before the pandemic. Maya couldn't cope with another person close to her dying. "You should relocate to Santa Fe. I think Dr. Grinwold misses you." After two lifetimes dedicated to public health, they deserved to be together for their final years. With the vaccine available, at some point the workload had to become more manageable.

"I won't keep you, Maya. It's hard for us to maintain contact tracing, so let me know if you want to work from home. I'm unsure how effective it is at this point, but the states have federal monies to fund it."

Silence filled the apartment like a formless voice when Maya hung up the call. Did she want to hound sick people about the places they'd been, trying to locate their contacts and convince them to get tested? But it was the type of task she could manage with good computer notes.

FaceTime chimed with the name of someone she'd only talked to once since she caught COVID—Stefan. On behalf of the European Union, he traveled nonstop to each surging city, helping them organize their public health measures. Somehow he avoided getting infected despite his travel, and didn't catch it from Maya. The genomic results indicated she most likely was infected at Heathrow and probably was too early in the average incubation period of five days to be contagious when working with him in Denmark.

His face and posture didn't convey any grudge that she could have affected his health. "Hei min venn, how's your COVID recovery going?"

"I'm fed up with catering to it," she answered. He was polite and nurturing—not his fault she was impatient to make it all vanish.

Fortunately he ignored her grumpy disposition. "Believe it or not, I jumped from the EU to WHO—swimming in a bigger pool."

Maya laughed. Like Dave, Stefan was one of those work colleagues whose sense of humor matched her own. "Well, you were a competitive swimmer. What's your new favorite stroke?"

His eyes and expression lit up like a boy earning his first trophy. "Figuring out where COVID came from, so we can battle it better next time."

She knew he was ambitious, but that was the biggest question of all. "Are you a proponent for the lab leak or zoonotic origin theory?"

"One of our WHO teams visited the Wuhan lab in February. The Chinese government didn't let us inspect everything."

"Any follow-up planned?" The pandemic executing her family was barely bearable if an act of nature. But a mistake by a lab researcher, working either on disease prevention or biowarfare, triggered different levels of anger. Split by a cleaver, she couldn't tolerate prejudice against her birth country but understood the bitterness.

She grew impatient with Stefan's lack of response. "Are you going to tell me what you're up to?"

"If we can't get access to the lab, there's a different investigation to consider." He flashed his engaging movie-actor grin. No wonder no one, including his partner Kondrat, ever turned him down. "I need a bat expert and you worked on them in New Mexico."

"That's true, primarily for rabies and histoplasmosis."

Stefan nodded, looking pleased. "You have another qualification for what I have in mind."

Maya's head swam with the possibilities as she wondered about getting roped into something big. "Dare I ask?"

"You're Chinese and we're expanding our studies in Southeast Asia."

"Stefan, I studied Mandarin for a couple of years in high school with no chance to practice since. Depending on where you're going, that might not be the dominant language."

He brushed his beard, regrown from when she saw him in the fall. "Not a major issue. We just need you to look Chinese."

She enjoyed his cat and mouse game, tantalizing her with tidbits about the trip. "Stefan, this sounds very mysterious but China won't let WHO back in, correct?"

"As the pariah of the world, the PRC is paranoid. Their argument is that you Yanks brought it into Wuhan during the Military World Games in October, 2019."

"Yeah, get to the point. What are you asking me to do?"

He looked off-camera, then leaned back in his chair. "WHO is working with a private foundation. We're going to Thailand to compare human specimens, that's my part, and bat samples from caves—your contribution."

"I assume you have permission from the Thai government."

He flashed a thumbs-up. "This is perfect timing. You're unemployed, I imagine you have medical costs from your recovery period, and you're available for a foundation contract."

He was crazy. She wasn't even driving yet, although that wouldn't be required on such an assignment. Crawling through damp caves—impossible, and traveling to work with Stefan was bad luck. The Denmark trip took away everything she loved. Not his fault, but it made no sense to continue the conversation.

"Stefan, it sounds fascinating but a Thai university could probably help you. Not me."

"It will take several months of planning, so think about it. Talk to you later."

She put the phone in her pocket and wandered into the bedroom, then pulled open the drapes. The shafts of sunshine warmed her brain with ideas on how the project might work while crowding out obsessions on what she had lost, what she couldn't do.

The urn gleamed with the sun's rays. She reached to touch it, the first time. What would Manolo advise her to do? During the pandemic, if she were pregnant, there's no way he'd support such a trip. But now, she wondered if his sense of adventure would encourage her to go.

FORTY-THREE

Photharam, Thailand—Tuesday, June 8, 2021

In the epicenter of Thai bat tourism, Maya peered out the taxi window, amazed by all the bat symbols and signs. The driver consulted her note, stopping first at a large red sculpture, wings penetrated by golden light poles, then at several bat figures mounted above a stick fence similar to the latillas from home.

At a monstrous black bat statue with its wings held aloft by white ceremonial poles, he stopped the cab, opened her door, and removed her luggage. Within fifteen minutes, her flimsy blouse adhered to her skin as she waited in the midmorning heat. Three monks with shaved heads and orange robes squatted on the concrete steps below the statue. No one gave her a second glance, just another young Asian woman shuffling her feet and leaning on her roller bag.

Where was Stefan? After more than a month of planning, he'd finally persuaded her to join him on the Thai bat study, then didn't show up. His human COVID surveillance with the Thai hospitals was ongoing for several weeks.

She decided to follow the monks' example and relax, jacket padding her seat on the hard surface. More than twenty-four hours of traveling was tough on a COVID-ravaged body, but the months lifting weights with Mark left her feeling stronger than she might have expected.

She pulled out the foundation's mobile. Thank God she had one which allowed personal use. New Mexico was thirteen hours earlier, so nine PM. She punched in Manolo's cell number, then just as quickly clicked it off. "Damn, what am I doing?" she said out loud, drawing a stern stare from the closest monk. The desire to reach out was still coded like a permanent file in her brain.

Stefan sauntered up, sleek with a shaved face, spiky short brown hair, and a traditional white Thai shirt over linen Bermuda shorts.

"Holy cow." She stood up to hug his waist. "Other than your height, you fit right in."

"Sorry to keep you waiting. A hospital banquet last night was rowdy and I overslept."

"The tan, plus everything you trimmed off—how did you manage all that?"

He rubbed his hand over his face. "COVID surveillance's a whirlwind and I need short 'me' breaks. I run every day, and lightened the hair load last week."

Pulling her roller bag, he headed out of the parking area, pointing to the white temple with its cascading series of sloped red tile roofs. "A nice touch for the masses who come here to the Wat Khao Chong Pran car park to see bats exit from the cave at dusk."

Maya wiped a tissue over her sweaty neck. "Maybe I should whack off my hair. I forgot about the deadly combination of heat and humidity."

"Could be worse—April's the hottest month. We'll get rid of your bag and find something to eat."

Within three blocks, he led her through an alley to a ground-floor two-bedroom suite. He directed her to the back bedroom with a thick mattress smaller than the wooden platform on which it rested. "You clean up while I review my data."

She showered, put on a white cotton dress, and yanked her ponytail high on the back of her head. "Do you think I'll blend in?" she asked with a pirouette.

"Exactly what the doctor ordered." His riposte was reinforced with a deep bow.

At the coffee shop around the corner, a yellow robot delivered croissants, black tea for Maya, and a caffè latte for Stefan marked by a bat face artfully poured with the milk. Maya snapped a photo of his drink before reclining on the navy blue cushions.

"I'm excited to have you here." Stefan said. "Especially after you turned me down flat in April."

Maya grabbed for the almond pastry. "You threatened to blackball me from any future work with the EU or WHO if I didn't come."

A sly grin creased his face. "You must admit, getting you out of New Mexico and all those memories was brilliant."

"With almost four million COVID deaths worldwide, I'm surprised I didn't run into travel restrictions."

"But we're at the lowest number of new cases since the peak last winter. Maybe the pandemic's dying out with herd immunity from infections and vaccinations. Anyways, when you're on official business for the government or a nongovernmental agency with clout, it's easier to get around."

He was right—she wasn't blocked from travel last September to Denmark for their mink work. But that ended up a disaster.

She wiped the moisture from her forehead with the napkin. Her turnaround in attitude toward this Thailand trip surprised even herself. The few weeks with Manolo as a married couple in her apartment had crowded out earlier months of living there alone, and she couldn't bear the silence any longer. Her physical and mental recovery was huge at the Pecos ranch, but that didn't block all the ghosts when trying to resume a normal life.

Shifting the neckline of her dress to allow more air, she asked, "What's on tap for today?"

"You're making such drastic changes and I recommend one more." He playfully tugged on her ponytail. "They can whack this off—get you comfortable for your new environment."

An hour later a few blocks away in the salon, she stared at the black strands littering the tile floor. For all of her twenty-eight years, her hair had been shoulder-length with a slight wave. Her parents might freak with any big change, but they were on the other side of the world.

Sideswept bangs of a pixie cut feathered her forehead. Her hand drifted to her neck—no hair, just a few wisps covering her ears to the level of her upper cheek. The stylist handed her a mirror and twirled the chair so she could see the back. She gasped.

"I don't recognize myself."

Stefan's smile was hidden by his mask but his laugh reinforced her impulsive choice. "You're a new person. New life, new adventures."

"A little color, yes?" The stylist showed her a photo.

"I don't know. We're here for bats, not beauty. Do we really have time, Stefan?"

He checked his mobile. "Of course, go all out."

Another hour later, two assistants finished heavenly foot massages for both of them. Tears pooled in Maya's eyes as she reveled in the streaks of red highlights brightening her face. Stefan passed over his handkerchief. "Happy or sad?"

"No regrets."

"Good. Let's see some bats. This is the major attraction here, and I haven't squeezed it in yet."

. . .

Buses unloaded tourists as the sun dipped behind the mountain to the southeast. Neon glow sticks lit up the tree branches and Maya grabbed a snack of shrimp chips from a small cart. Experienced with sunset bat exits from American buildings, bridges, and caves, she pointed out the dark calligraphy stroke in the sky.

Stefan jerked up his binoculars. "I've never seen so many bats. But something bigger is swooping at them." He slammed the binocs into her hands with excitement. "Can you make out what they are?"

The black bodies, white necks, and white feet matched the bird photo she'd seen. "Bat hawks out to catch their dinner."

They joined other tourists in recording the spectacle with cell phones. As the wide bat ribbon danced through the deepening red and orange stripes of sunset, they took advantage of the food stalls. A brief concern for food safety flitted across Maya's public health mind, then she admonished herself: *Be fuckin' adventurous.*

One woman in a broad-brimmed hat cut up vegetables for a salad. Next they ate small helpings of mango sticky rice and Gai Tod, chicken spiced with shallots and chili sauce. In Stefan's bowl of Malang Tod, Maya scrutinized the fried grasshoppers, beetles, crickets and worms. Grateful that they no longer wriggled or buzzed, she opened her lips to one bite that he dipped in soy sauce with his chopsticks. Crunchy, too much like salty sawdust. She gulped her tea to wash them down.

Plumes of meat-sizzling smoke lured them to a portable grill on the back of a motorcycle, where strings of sausages hung from a rack. Stefan ordered a skewer but Maya declined. Ice cream served in a coconut husk and topped with sweet corn soothed her mouth and throat.

Motorcycles backfired and bat enthusiasts exclaiming in multiple languages boarded idling buses as the car park emptied. Maya stumbled with Stefan's help the few blocks back to their rooms. Greasy sweat led her to another shower, then she fell blissfully asleep.

FORTY-FOUR

Photharam, Thailand—Wednesday, June 9, 2021

At the cave opening partway up the verdant mountainside, a temple monk stood like a gatekeeper, reassuring those waiting to enter. "These bats eat insects, so they are no threat to you." He smiled at the mix of Asians and visitors from all over the world.

Maya agreed with efforts to undemonize bats but bristled when disease risks were ignored. In the US, bat bites accounted for the majority of human rabies deaths. And bats were suspected as the origin species for coronavirus, the reason for her trip.

In a side cave, pilgrims prayed to statues of Buddha, pausing only to wipe away bat guano falling from the limestone cave roof onto their clothes. Maya and Stefan didn't linger long in the public areas and joined a local researcher at the sloping entrance of a cave tube.

"Welcome, Dr. Maguire. I am Dr. Chakrii. We are happy Dr. Duda persuaded you to travel here." He pointed to men who shouldered bags of guano as they ascended the boulder-strewn floor. "Not only do we have science and tours, but also a booming fertilizer industry."

"Thank you," Maya said. "I'm eager to learn about your efforts."

Lights mounted on the rock ceiling glowed on another collection of larger-than-life golden Buddhas perched in the lotus position along the wall.

"We have ten species of bats with an estimated three million individuals." Their host was middle-aged, close to Maya's height, and wearing a surgical mask like theirs. He shone a wide-beamed flashlight to the roof far above, illuminating the jostling bodies.

"This evening, we will apply nets to cave openings and capture bats for testing of multiple viruses—corona, lyssa, influenza, Nipah, and Ebola."

Maya hadn't realized the research program was so extensive. "Amazing effort—I'm proud to assist."

Dr. Chakrii turned to face Stefan. "Dr. Duda, I appreciate your valuable work investigating human cases. However, you have no experience handling bats and your presence may trigger scrutiny."

Maya hugged her arms. Stefan had promised they would not be a hindrance, but he responded with enthusiasm. "I am an experienced videographer and have equipment to help in documenting your efforts for education, like advising people not to eat bats or drink their blood."

"I'm surprised those warnings are still needed," Maya said.

Dr. Chakrii's eyes narrowed. "I hope you're not implying that our citizens are stupid."

Maya flushed, still not diplomatically proficient like Stefan. "Not at all, I'm sorry."

Their host continued. "Cultural beliefs are deep. Unfortunately, bat blood is considered by some as an aphrodisiac."

Scuffing her boot in the thick, acrid layer of bat feces, Maya wondered whether to venture another comment. "We're finding coronavirus in our wastewater. Have you thought of testing guano?"

She couldn't imagine the challenge, even worse than filtering thousands of gallons of water. But it could offer a virus signal that wouldn't require capturing and handling live animals.

"Good recommendation. I will talk with our laboratory."

"Thanks for the orientation," Stefan said. "What time should we meet you tonight?"

"Six PM. Dr. Maguire, you didn't arrive here until yesterday. With a confused body clock, are you prepared to work in challenging conditions for many hours?"

"Of course."

Stefan jumped in. "She can rest this afternoon while I assemble my photography equipment."

In response to Dr. Chakrii's concern, Maya tightened her lips under the mask. She'd make sure to represent her country's scientific acumen appropriately.

Back in the sunlight, Stefan guided her several blocks to their rooms. "Testing guano is a good idea for surveillance. Bats and all their products are so important to the economy, they even sell little guano bags at the gift shops."

"Why would people buy those as souvenirs?"

He shrugged. "I'm going to check in with the hospital on the antibody testing we set up for asymptomatic volunteers. Positive tests are tracking up and the government might restrict local flights, disrupting our plans."

"Okay, I'll take a nap—get myself ready for the bat work."

After he left, she showered again, anxious to breathe in clear mist to counteract the guano smell in her nostrils. Her head felt bald with so little hair to shampoo. When passing the mirror as she toweled dry, she startled herself. Who was that unrecognizable skinny sprite? The haircut made her weight loss and cheekbones more prominent.

Even with ceiling fans, the room baked like a sauna. She draped her body with a single sheet and tried to rest, sensations of a foreign world crowding out Manolo memories.

. . .

Covered head to toe in a white coverall, Maya took deep breaths through her N-95 respirator, resolved to keep going despite the oppressive heat. The team strung black mist nets over the smaller cave openings to capture the bats as they ventured out for their nighttime feeding. Stefan adjusted his additional light sources to document the bat handling on his video and still cameras.

Wings beating like rushing river water, the only true flying mammals sped out for dinner and struggled when caught in the thin mesh. Wearing vinyl gloves, a researcher carefully pried the bats loose, careful to avoid their teeth. Then the bats were deposited in cloth bags before they became too stressed.

On a portable table, one Thai assistant grasped a fruit bat while a second assistant spread its right wing and held off the vein to allow it to engorge. Maya said a quick prayer to the temple's Buddhas to protect her from bites and infection. She wiped the venipuncture site with a cleansing scrub and inserted the syringe needle with her right hand, applying gentle intermittent suction to avoid collapse of the vein.

For a smaller insectivorous bat, she used the needle without the syringe to penetrate the vein. Then she pressed a capillary tube to the hub and collected a small sample, avoiding any risk of taking too much blood and jeopardizing bat health. Before release, she pressed cotton gauze on the venipuncture site until bleeding stopped. She swabbed its mouth and rectum for samples, then painted the bat's toes purple with nail polish so they wouldn't bleed it a second time if recaptured.

By midnight, the teams had collected more than a hundred specimens and removed the nets. "You are fast, efficient, and gentle with the bats," Dr. Chakrii complimented Maya. "I wish there was more international support for this research. Will we see you tomorrow?"

Stefan uncharacteristically stumbled over his words as they shrugged off their gowns. "We need to review our plans . . . I'll let you know."

Dr. Chakrii led them to one of the smaller side entrances. "Poachers used to capture bats here for local restaurants."

As they exited the ridge, they startled two men wrestling a quivering net full of bats, and Dr. Chakrii addressed one of them by his name. Under the gaze of the scientist and Stefan snapping photos, the men released the bats and, with hunched bodies, disappeared through the thick forest down the mountainside.

"With my previous warnings, I thought they had stopped doing this, but they're counting on the restaurant income to feed their families. In recent years, they took enough bats to reduce the guano supply, which impacts their neighbors' income from fertilizer sales. We need more money for a game warden."

"Will you arrest them?" Stefan asked.

Dr. Chakrii shook his head. "Education is better. The community will appreciate the benefits to their economy and to the natural world if they earn money from keeping the bats alive for fertilizer and tourism."

They bowed at the waist and Stefan promised to get back to Dr. Chakrii about their plans.

. . .

In the small living room between their bedrooms after they cleaned up, Maya glanced at the time. One-thirty in the morning. Exhausted muscles begging for bedrest battled a growling empty stomach. She cornered Stefan on the couch while they finished pastries leftover from breakfast. "Why are you so mysterious about our next steps?"

He locked eyes with hers. "Remember in April when I said your being Asian would prove helpful on this trip?"

"I assumed you meant it would lead to greater acceptance, if others resented you as the big bad European telling them what to do."

He laughed. "Yes, that's somewhat the issue."

She got up to increase the fan speed. "Dr. Chakrii appreciated your video footage."

"I won't be able to do that on our next sampling."

She rejoined him on the couch. "Come on, Stefan, fess up."

His lips turned up in a slight smile and his eyes narrowed as if he were plotting something devious. "Comparing coronaviruses in people and bats here in Thailand is valuable, but we should do it closer to the potential source in China."

She brushed the crumbs from her shorts and frowned. "WHO scientists have not been allowed back in."

"I discovered a back door." He smirked, visibly proud of himself. "A Chinese wildlife specialist reached out to me when he learned of my studies over the past few months in Thailand. We've been strategizing how to get someone in to collect samples, then get them back out."

With a dawning apprehension, Maya gripped his hands tight. "Stefan, it sounds hazardous. Can't the Thai researchers help?"

"First of all, you'll blend in—you're Han Chinese. Second, your government may have more clout if you get in trouble."

She rubbed her bare arms as goosebumps broke out, and her tone was stern. "You're hardly making a convincing case, Stefan."

He tugged on her hands with childlike impatience, reminding her of Paula, his daughter. "Think of the contribution to science, Maya. Maybe you can address the huge question of whether the pandemic began with wildlife contact or the Wuhan lab."

"I'm as passionate as you about figuring that out. It makes me sick to think that someone in my birth country could be responsible for a deliberate or accidental lab leak."

He started to respond but she held up her hand and kept going. "I agree that cave bat collection is crucially important, but it might not provide a definitive answer." Panic started bubbling—she took a deep breath and ordered it down. "And it doesn't have to be me. This Chinese scientist can identify local allies for bat sampling."

"Don't decide now. He'll meet us in Hong Kong and you can talk it over. For the first time in your life, you're untethered to family, school or a job—a great time to make a giant leap for humankind."

"Your grand statements make me less likely to agree, but I'd love to see Hong Kong again. We traveled through there on a visit to my orphanage when I was twelve."

"All right, let's fly there tomorrow." He glanced at his mobile. "Well, it's already tomorrow. After some rest, I'll check on flights for early this afternoon."

Maya had mentally prepared for a few more days in Thailand. "What's the rush?"

"COVID cases have dropped but are going up again—the Chinese Government scheduled a travel ban starting August first. We can't afford to lose any time."

"I wish you'd proposed this sooner."

After heading to bed, she cursed Stefan sneaking the Sherlock Holmes adventure on her. If he'd been clear a month earlier, she would have refused the trip. But his excitement was contagious. There was nothing to lose by listening to the wildlife specialist.

FORTY-FIVE

After the ride up more than a thousand feet, Maya and Stefan hopped off the tram car at Victoria Peak. From the viewing deck, Maya willed away dizziness at the steep drop to the panorama of skyscrapers on Hong Kong Island, then Kowloon on the other side of the harbor.

"Stefan, your work trips are always a whirlwind, but this takes the cake." She was reeling from arriving in Southeast Asia only forty-eight hours earlier and the long night bent over a table sampling bats. "Now I'm on some wildlife skullduggery. I'm flat out fried. We don't all have your Olympic swimmer's stamina."

He flexed an arm muscle. "If you're telling me again I'm built like Michael Phelps, I accept the accolade." His eyes darted around as if he were a spy on a secret mission. "Thank goodness we came up before sunset when it gets crowded."

As other sightseers drew close, he tugged her a few feet back from the overlook. "Mu Jian will meet us here. As you probably know, in China they use both names with surname first, but his older American half-sister could call him Jian."

"Half-sister?" Her whisper seethed. "Are you talking about me? We've never met."

He looked affronted. "I'm easing you into this little drama and you can back out at any time. Your passport says you were born in China but are an American citizen, right?"

She pulled it out to show him. "Correct."

"Some Chinese men abandon their first wives for better economic opportunities overseas. We'll pretend that your Chinese father took you with him to America and adopted the name of Maguire. Then your poor mother stuck in China remarried and had Mu Jian. He told me he was born in 1997."

She couldn't believe her mind was engaging with his little masquerade. "So he's four years younger than me. You mentioned a wildlife biologist and I pictured someone more senior, like Dr. Chakrii."

"No, Mu Jian is relatively new to his profession and eager to make his mark, like you. Perhaps that's why he's willing to take chances."

Maya wasn't sure she was willing to do the same, but so far, there was no risk. She'd at least hear out their plan.

An energetic voice with heavily accented English came from behind them. "Dr. Duda?" As they turned, a young man just a bit shorter than her five foot six inches embraced Maya in a hug. "So nice to meet my honored jiějiě. You don't look as Dr. Duda described you."

She feathered a hand through her red-streaked locks, what was left of them. "That's Stefan's fault. He lured me into several radical decisions on this trip."

Jian linked his arm through hers and led them to a quiet grassy cove of Victoria Peak Garden with marble gazebos clustered in a protective alcove of deciduous forest. They found a shady bench and Jian gestured for Maya to sit.

He dressed like a casual tourist in a pale loose shirt and shorts to the knees, not dissimilar to Stefan. But his language was formal as he bowed deeply before her.

"Dr. Maguire, I was so sorry to hear about the loss of your husband and pregnancy from COVID. My own revered mother passed away at the beginning of the pandemic."

It was easier to accept sympathy eight months later. "Thank you, and my condolences to you. So many of us with our lives turned upside down."

He joined her on the bench. "That is why I am so dedicated to this mission. My work is to protect endangered river dolphins and alligators, but I am trained for multiple species. I want to help my country discover how COVID started."

"Except your government is stonewalling the required research," Stefan inserted.

Maya nodded. "Everyone's fighting over what launched the pandemic. If we can sort it out, we'll be more prepared next time."

"I am not so arrogant to think we can do this alone," Jian said. "But even small studies in our caves, like you did in Thailand, may provide some answers."

"I don't understand why we need to be relatives for me to help."

He smiled. "Duānwǔjié, our three-day Dragon Boat Festival, starts Saturday. Family members often reunite for holidays. Getting permission to enter China is challenging during the pandemic, especially for westerners, but I can bring home my long-lost sister."

"Even in a COVID lockdown? It's all over the TV."

"Cases are very low now and requirements vary by region, as you can see here. The extreme rules have worked; now everyone is excited about reuniting with family for this holiday."

Maya looked from Jian to Stefan, then back again. "Stefan hatched this plan and won't join us to carry it out."

Stefan grunted. "Sorry, Maya, I have no training in wildlife. I'd love to take human specimens, but there's no way I'll get in."

"So if something goes bonkers, it's all on my shoulders." Despite the heat, her skin prickled with a sudden chill. She couldn't believe she allowed them to continue the discussion. But answering such important questions might be one way to achieve justice for Manolo, her baby, and her grandmother.

"I'll be here in Hong Kong to collect your specimens," Stefan said, "then bring them back to Bangkok where they've agreed to do the testing. If you can't get across the border into Guangdong Province, we've failed; so be it. Nothing ventured, nothing gained."

Jian jumped in, his deeply tanned face animated. "We will split samples. There are some laboratories in China willing to do analysis, if the government officials do not find out. One way or the other, we may get some results."

"The foundation sponsoring our project, it supports this hare-brained scheme?" Shut up, Maya, she told herself. Stop asking questions as if you're entertaining their proposal.

Stefan flashed a wide, confident smile. "Only a few of their leaders know about our idea, but they need a success story for continued fundraising."

She focused back on Jian. "If this plan falls apart, is there any chance I could be imprisoned?"

He ducked his eyes, appearing to be deep in thought, then looked up and half-smiled. "They're really strict on drugs—you don't have anything, correct?"

"Of course not." The travel stress washed over her like a tsunami. "You two have been planning this for a while, and can't expect me to make an immediate decision. Let me have at least one full night's sleep."

They strolled back to the overlook railing, crowded with sightseers to view skyscrapers lit up in a multicolored splendor, matched by the sunset palette above the curve of mountains beyond Kowloon. With most visitors still ascending the Peak, they had seats to themselves on the descending tram.

Still leery of indoor dining with strangers, Maya agreed to another dinner of street food. Jian picked out a variety of treats for them to share. After slipping a curry fishball off a skewer, she choked on the strength of its sauce. Jian handed her a bite from his bag of roasted sweet potatoes and chestnuts to counteract the flavor. Stefan offered a morsel with his chopsticks. "Cheung fun—steamed rice noodles. This is bland and should settle down your system."

At her squeamish limits, she declined, then braved a brown cake of stinky tofu. If she'd been pregnant, the fermentation funk would have done her in but with a dab of chili sauce, she savored the crispy crunch and creamy center. Stefan waved two skewers in front of her eyes, offering a choice of deep-fried pig or cow intestines. Too many hours of disease dissection in pathology made it easy for her to turn him down once more.

Stefan prematurely celebrated the trip's success with two bottles of San Miguel Pale Pilsen, then they weaved their way down an alley until they located the gleaming hotel lobby. Remote key entry avoided contact with human attendants, and the pleasure of a full stomach dropped Maya into an immediate deep sleep.

FORTY-SIX

Shenzhen, People's Republic of China—Friday, June 11, 2021

Maya and Jian exited his car at the Shenzhen Wan Port for the customs queue to enter the People's Republic of China. Her wiser angels denounced her acquiescence to Stefan's plan, but the cooler, low humidity day encouraged an optimistic attitude.

Earlier that morning, they had visited the Hong Kong visa agency where Jian presented her passport, vaccination record, COVID test results, and their travel itinerary. Surely they would be stopped there, but the business was only interested in receiving its fee. At noon, when Stefan waved goodbye at the hotel front entrance with an encouraging grin plastered on his face, she should have panicked. But she didn't.

Now as Jian's arm around her waist guided her forward, a bitter taste of anxiety rose from her stomach to her throat. She feared getting caught in a lie about their relationship, but embraced a chance to visit the country of her birth.

To her surprise, her paperwork and their story held. Within another two hours, they were driving into Guangzhou. The last time she had been in the port city, previously called Canton, she was only a five-month-old infant. All adoptions had to be cleared by the local hospital and American embassy before families exited the PRC via Hong Kong. Her parents had described Guangzhou as massive and overwhelming. Twenty-eight years later, it was still true.

"Largest built-up area in the world." Jian maneuvered his vehicle through streets jammed with cars, trucks, bicycles, and the occasional human-pulled or bicycle rickshaw.

Maya wished she could let her parents know she was back in

China, but Stefan had advised against it. He didn't want the Chinese government to detect she wasn't Jian's half-sister. He insisted she leave the foundation phone with him, so she was totally reliant on Jian. It seemed unreal to be traveling in China with a young man she'd met only yesterday.

Stefan had assured Maya he'd thoroughly vetted Jian, who gave off no vibes of being a kidnapper. However, the PRC was short of wives because so many daughters had been tossed away like trash. The fact that she was one of them bothered her more now than on her previous visit at age twelve.

What if the playacting was more elaborate than she and Stefan knew? Jian could be the spoiled son of a Communist Party official who developed this scheme to procure an American wife. The possibility should have been considered earlier and did her no good in Guangzhou. Besides, if he wasn't a wildlife biologist, he sure faked it well.

"If we have time in Heifei, I'll introduce you to Dr. Peng, my supervisor. He was the last person to see the baiji dolphin in the Yangtze, in 2002. He also cared for a captive one that died the same year."

He continued nonstop for hours about the dolphin's description—31-36 teeth on each jaw, small eyes, gestation of 10-11 months—and folklore. A girl escaped from her kidnapper on a boat by diving into the river and transforming into an animal symbol of peace and prosperity. Maya prayed she wouldn't need an escape act of her own, but living as a dolphin wouldn't be a bad option.

. . .

Jian pulled into a car park under the Guangzhou hotel. "If you were really my sister, we'd spend the night doing tourist activities. Government monitors are everywhere, so we should play along."

She agreed, tired from the trip but eager to see the city.

"Public places may have people listening to us and rooms can be bugged. I will do most of the talking about China, all the wonderful things to see and do. We must say nothing about my job or yours, or your real family."

"How can we plan our wildlife sampling?"

"Here in the car or in an outdoor area away from people."

As a painfully shy child, Maya had avoided any reading out loud or playacting except for a few school assignments. Despite her frayed nerves, a surprising thrill energized her for the evening's agenda. She never imagined becoming Nancy Drew or Jane Bond, and short, mild-mannered Jian looked as far from an international spy as possible.

The air conditioning in Jian's red Riich minicompact was on the fritz, so once in her hotel room she leapt into a cold shower. Wearing her shortest dress, she twirled for Jian in the lobby, the gossamer white skirt floating around her thighs. "Appropriate for our plans, dear brother?"

"Yes, dear sister, we will have a lovely evening." They adjusted their surgical masks as a suffocating gray fog of humidity and air pollution closed around them on their walk to the Pearl River dock. The Las Vegas-style neon lights of a three-level boat beckoned, windows outlined in glowing red and the prow lit by a golden dragon. They started their tour at the boat's lower level maritime museum, grateful for the blasting air conditioning.

Back on top, palming cold sweet drinks, they caught a race in honor of the holiday. All three dragon boats were long enough for a dozen oarsmen in lifejackets of red, orange, or green to distinguish the crews, plus a monk in a golden cloak marked with a blue dragon. Another man perched near the front, rhythmically beating a vertical drum to set the pace, and each boat sported a waving flag and colorful imitation paper torches.

When the winner crossed an invisible finish line just ahead of their tour boat, firecrackers startled Maya away from the railing. Four years earlier, she'd seen a less-elaborate replica race in New York harbor while completing her master's degree.

She thought carefully before speaking, remembering the bones of their cover story. "Bàba will be pleased I got to see this. Perhaps I can persuade him to come home to China on my next trip."

All other words burbling around them were Chinese,

recognized from her high school class, but some weren't Mandarin. "Cantonese?" she asked.

He nodded. "Among other dialects."

On her visit to the Tongling orphanage at age twelve, she'd seen no foreigners. But in a massive port city like Guangzhou, she was surprised to find no Europeans or Americans on the boat. COVID travel restrictions had limited outsiders. Stefan was right, her being a Chinese relative, even a fake one, was the only way to get in.

"We celebrate this holiday to commemorate a Chinese poet and national hero."

"Yes, I remember Bàba telling me about it." Proud that she was falling so neatly into this imagined family, she smiled. Her parents celebrated the Chinese holidays in a limited way with a few others in the Flagstaff area. Once they moved to Denver, there was a larger Chinese community, but Maya focused on finishing high school early and was no longer interested in a home culture that made her stand out from other teenagers.

Manolo and I can come back together on another trip. She almost dropped to the floor, consumed with grief that she would never get the chance. Jian caught her and guided her to a table. "Are you hungry? Let's order dinner," he said.

From the Cantonese dim sum buffet with Jian's guidance, she selected the Char Siu Bao BBQ pork buns, Jian Dui sesame balls, and seafood dumplings. She finished her meal in silence, aching to share the wonder of new flavors with Manolo. Jian pointed out the Guangzhou Tower, colorful bands circling its six-hundred-meter height. Excitement of other passengers cocooned her from sadness.

On their stroll back to the hotel, Jian detoured through a Chinese wet market. "If you did not get enough to eat on the tour boat, how about yě wèi?"

"Which means?"

"Wild taste. But we won't really try anything, and keep your mask on." He leaned closer and lowered his voice. "I want you to see this since so many believe COVID started in a similar market in Wuhan."

Stray cats darted between their legs as he guided them through tables with live snakes and blackened dog heads sold under umbrellas at streetside. He directed Maya's attention to a twitching mesh bag, full of frogs, on the pavement. The vendor opened it to finger through, tossing dead ones behind him before holding the bag out to Jian, who waved his hand in refusal.

Under the high roof of the main market, they passed a bin of wriggling eels before pausing at a table slathered with pig intestines, no refrigeration. The vendor pinched the organs with bare hands and invited Jian to verify they were fresh. Maya was bumped aside by an older man on a scooter who raised the slimy intestines into the air to smell them. When he nodded his interest, the vendor licked his fingers before tying the plastic bag and counting the money.

On the other end, a cacophony of voices and motor bikes vied with tinny sounds of Chinese music. Chickens, ducks, geese, and vultures squawked from large wire cages on the dirt floor. Seated on the ground, an older woman wrung the neck and whacked off the head of a white stork, then rapidly stripped feathers into a red plastic bucket with water. She heated the flesh with a blow torch, then shoved the body in a plastic bag, long legs protruding, and handed it to a patron. Bird flu flashed through Maya's mind.

Jian stopped at a table where a vendor sold live rodents as snacks, then told Maya in a low voice, "All of these are for eating, dogs and cats too." Behind them, a three-legged dog licked up discarded animal waste as a man butchered a red fox. She fought back tears as they passed a pen with sprawling medium-sized dogs. A miniature version of Dave's black lab Bo panted and pawed at the wire. Nearby in another cage, a scrawnier twin of her grandmother's Persian meowed plaintively in chorus with other cats.

A woman shouted to get their attention, waving a thick stick penetrating a charred bat. "She brags of their marvelous flavor and health benefits," Jian said.

Maya tugged on his arm, begging for the fresher air of the street, and Jian agreed. "You see how viruses can spread between species, but I have one more stop." Inside a small alcove jammed with jars and boxes of powders, the double-horned snout of a rhino was mounted to a shelf. "Medicinal," he said.

"I can't take any more," Maya told him as they emerged into a quiet alley. Her entire body ached for a shower or bath, especially her nose. She imagined friendly waves of water washing over her head, scrubbing her clean from all the cares of the world.

"As a vet, the animal conditions make me want to vomit," she admitted. "I'd love to rush in and save them, but I understand cultural traditions around food."

"This is an affordable way to feed 1.4 billion people. Our elders value fresh food and never had modern supermarkets until recently."

She verified they were alone. "Jian, this reinforces why we need to figure out if bats are spreading the virus here before they're killed and cooked. Or perhaps it jumps to some other species. So much to be done."

"You only saw a fraction of the stalls. On other trips, I've seen crocodiles, hedgehogs, badgers, and marmots. There are some regulations to reduce the proportion of live animals. You can look for wounds from gunshots or traps, which implies illegal wildlife harvesting."

Maya was grateful Jian exposed her to the monstrous problem, but her senses were flooded. Reminded of the poverty and pollution she saw on her childhood return to China, she was once again grateful to grow up American, then ashamed at her judgments about the people of China, just trying to survive. She forced her mind back to its public health prevention track. "Some are insisting on a total ban of wildlife in markets, but clearly it's not happening yet."

Back at the hotel, Jian walked her to her door. "We should start early tomorrow. Our drive northwest to Guilin will take about six hours. Knock when you're ready to depart."

Within minutes, she immersed herself in the shower to erase the wet market imprint. She longed to open her mouth and fully drown in the slick sensations, but remembered that in China water quality was not guaranteed. Only a day's drive into the People's Republic, she was still close to the outside world. She could change her mind at any moment. Nothing illegal yet, no danger.

As she toweled dry and crawled between the covers, all those animal faces, dead and alive, crowded back in. Spillover. With her public health vision, she was the only one in the wet market besides Jian who saw viruses drifting in the air, creature to creature, and bacteria coating every surface, ready to infect with the next touch.

FORTY-SEVEN

Guilin, People's Republic of China—Saturday, June 12, 2021

With every mile in Jian's car, a bat net of dread draped Maya's pores. She squirmed in the car's passenger seat but couldn't break the illusion. The long trip offered plenty of time to fret about the possibly illegal cave work the next day.

"Why are we stopping in Guilin?" she asked. "Bats south and west of Wuhan are believed to be the SARS-CoV-2 source."

"Guilin's cave system is world-renowned as a tourist destination, so no one will question our reason for being there. And we'll be in the region where coronavirus might have originated."

"Stefan collects Thai human blood samples to match the bat genome. Do you have that worked out?"

"Friends and colleagues in Anhui Province where I live."

For Maya, drawing blood from people in an *E. coli* outbreak had been easier than doing it in animals. No fur to get in the way of feeling and seeing a vein. "I can help, but Anhui is east of your target area."

She didn't reveal her birth in the same province, concerned about oversharing with a stranger. Apparently Stefan hadn't mentioned she was an adoptee. Jian might assume her parents were immigrants who Americanized their last name to Maguire, like the cover story.

Maya had good reasons for her reluctance to discuss the adoption. When she visited China at age twelve, her family got pushback from Chinese people in denial about the abandonment of female infants. A huge loss of face, admitting that white people could take care of their girls. Local officials required disappearance of female babies. Unexamined were the details about dumping them in caves or rivers. The lucky ones were brought to overcrowded orphanages with possible placement around the world.

Her American parents weren't wealthy and didn't buy her like a China doll, even if Jian might think so. So she didn't share her origin story, regardless of Jian's nice-guy appearance. "If the baiji, the Yangtze dolphin, is extinct, how can you study it?"

"I get rare reports of sightings which require investigation. The baiji is viewed as our goddess of protection—its loss is a tragedy."

"Why do you think it disappeared?"

"Overfishing with electricity, boat propellers, and likely the Three Gorges Dam. Marine mammals downstream are heavily burdened with parasite infections."

Maya shook her head in disgust. "China has monstrous overpopulation but there's got to be accommodation for other species."

Jian's eyes darted in her direction. "We have special reserves with bans on fishing. Doesn't the US have similar issues with endangered animals?"

"I'm sorry—didn't intend to play Ugly American." She reached her hands behind to rub her aching back.

"Don't apologize, I shouldn't be impatient with you, my guest. Can you open my bag and take out the portable CD player? My mother used it on her lengthy travels between our home and her work at a Wuhan hospital."

Maya studied the compact disc with a bamboo flute on the cover, then hit **Play**. Soothing trills filled the car and her muscles automatically relaxed, tension over the long drive releasing. "You lost your mother at the beginning of the pandemic. With her job, was it COVID?"

"We don't know. She had typical respiratory symptoms and I brought her to a hospital. It was November, 2019, before recognition of the virus."

Maya flooded with empathy and sadness at their connection. "My grandmother had a heart attack in February, 2020. It appears she was infected from being close to our first Arizona case."

Jian glanced her way again. "You have more tragedy than most, with the loss of your husband and infant. Forgive me for bringing it up if the memories are still painful."

"They died eight months ago while I was on a ventilator—not awake to know. It's unreal, like it happened to someone else offstage. At least with my grandmother, I got to see her body and say goodbye."

With a tissue from her pack, she wiped her face, damp with the heat and Jian's sputtering air conditioning. Her prolonged healing represented profound emotional pain, but she wouldn't admit that much weakness to a stranger.

"I've always loved music. Manolo wanted our child to be bilingual so he held his phone up to my belly playing Ruth Fernández, a famous Puerto Rican singer." *Until I followed my ambition to Europe and brought back the COVID that killed him.*

She gulped from the plastic bottle on the seat. "The sound of the bamboo flutes is so sweet and mellow. Just what the doctor ordered for my nerves."

Giving herself over to the lilting notes, the final hours vanished into the fog enveloping the mountains. She tried to suppress a gasp whenever another vehicle emerged coming toward them around a curve. Once in Guilin, the chill air of the modern hotel was a blessing.

"I apologize for the sweating in my car," Jian said. "Temperature here today is in the mid-nineties, as you calculate it. Rest up and I will knock at six for dinner and a tour."

After a cold shower, the time alone promoted a lengthier obsession about their plans. She perched in the chair, making a pros and cons list for the next day's bat expedition. The top pro: *Help answer biggest COVID question—bats or lab leak.* Then she circled the top con: *The PRC probably doesn't want us doing this, especially me.* She studied the list for another half hour, then tore it into tiny pieces.

. . .

From the upper open deck of the cruise boat, much smaller than the one in Guangzhou, she snapped photos like the happy visitor she pretended to be. Not a difficult challenge in such spectacular scenery, no doubt one of her favorite places in China.

Mist hugged the Li River like a gray blanket, almost obscuring the conical limestone peaks dramatically pushing skyward from the river banks. Her parents would have loved this magical voyage. Before sneaking into the PRC under false pretenses, she'd emailed them that she was still working hard in Thailand.

The tour boat slowed as Jian and other passengers took photos of a classic Li River fishing raft of bamboo tubes lashed together. A single middle-aged man in black pants, black shirt, and a wide-brimmed hat stood in the middle and adjusted the boat's position with a long pole to the river bottom. As the sun set and the skies turned a deep navy blue, fishermen on multiple boats lit lanterns, creating an eerie mélange of small fires dotting the river's surface. "The light attracts fish close to the boats," Jian explained.

On a pole at the front of the closest boat, a sleek black cormorant flapped its wings. With the trigger of a chant, the bird dove underwater after the fish. When the cormorant resurfaced, the fisherman leaned over and grabbed the cormorant by the neck to haul it on board. At the man's soft whistles, the bird regurgitated its catch into a bucket.

Jian pointed out the string around its neck, preventing it from swallowing a whole fish. "Is that offensive to American eyes?"

Maya blanched at what appeared to be rough handling of the cormorants. Then the fisherman hacked off a small piece of fish and fed it to the bird. She told herself it was an ancient partnership, man and animal working together as a team, each benefitting from the care of the other.

Jian shouted down to a raft close to the tour boat. The man tossed him a carp and he showed it to Maya. "This hole in the flesh is where the cormorant killed it. Fish caught in this way are prized for their flavor because of the quick death."

He left to get the fish on ice. When he returned, he put his arm around Maya's shoulder. "We will have a special dinner tonight."

His mood was so light, only their ever-present masks reminded Maya that they were embarking on the most hazardous, and most important, part of their journey. But if anyone was scrutinizing the young Chinese woman who was clearly American by her posture and language, they would only see family members bonding after a lifetime of separation.

FORTY-EIGHT

Guilin, People's Republic of China—Sunday, June 13, 2021

Maya reached out her hand to caress a dewy stalagmite, its slime cooling her fingers. Massive stalactites suspended from the ceiling were lit by gaudy bands of blue and pink light reflected in the liquid pool, and the stalagmite jagged peaks glowed orange, red and green. The Reed Flute Cave doubled in size with an invisible line in the flat water between the real above and the reflection below. There was no denying the visual beauty, even if the colors were artificial.

Along the public tour route, it took no effort to play enthusiastic tourist. But the cloying humidity from the underground lake suffocated her breathing and amplified her countdown of the hours until she snuck in to capture bats.

After they exited, Jian continued the façade, pointing out the forest of green reeds in the lake which gave the cave its name. Or maybe he wasn't playacting; he seemed genuinely thrilled by the natural world. Maya relished the peaceful view one last time as they headed for his car. The next time they returned would be less relaxing, on a treasure hunt for the origins of a pandemic.

. . .

In Jian's car after a late afternoon dinner, as Maya quizzed him on their plan, tentacles of anxiety tied her down to the passenger seat like ropes. "If we pull this off tonight, where are we going tomorrow?"

"We will collect samples in Hubei Province south of Wuhan. It's not too far off the approved itinerary to my hometown, and we can claim I became too tired to make the entire drive in one day."

Maya failed to shake her unease as they embarked on the real reason for their trip. On the morning's tour, a man walking alone had stopped and stared when she spoke English to Jian. Was that someone following them, waiting for her to make a misstep? And if caught, would Jian dump all the responsibility on her, an aggressive American scientist?

Her rational brain couldn't conceive why anyone in the midst of a pandemic would be interested in a sole American tourist. Unless some bureaucrat ran foreigner names through the internet and discovered she used to be a CDC veterinary epidemiologist. The PRC government was so paranoid about outside investigations, they might get suspicious with that information.

She slapped away the unwelcome thought like the mosquito circling her head, a prophylactic move to prevent an insect bite and to amp up her courage for the work ahead.

Curious about her host, she finally decided to get more personal. "What city do you live in, by the way?"

"Heifei, capital of Anhui Province."

She jerked her head around to stare at him. Their life circles were closing in on each other. On her China tour when she was twelve, her family visited the orphanage in Tongling, the province mining hub hugging the Yangtze south bank. She'd recoiled from the nonstop pats and hugs from the staff who swore they remembered her. Spending the night in Heifei, fireworks burst over the city as they settled into their hotel room. Staring out the window, she told her parents the celebration was a signal from her biological family, saying they knew she was okay.

Jian continued. "Since Māma's death from COVID, I've spent more time with my grandparents at the family's ancestral home in Tongling. They need me and I may move in with them full-time."

Spooky—they pretended to be half-siblings and they came from the same hometown. A chance in a million, a billion, given the size of China.

She hesitated about revealing their surprising connection. Maybe just a little of it, without having to justify the complexities of adoption.

"My family also originated in Tongling. Have you heard the expression, it's a small world?"

"Ah, a good sign for our important scientific sleuthing. Confucius believed everything in life and death is determined by fate." He checked his mobile for a colleague's instructions down a rutted track to an empty parking area. "This will give us access to the noncommercial part of the cave system."

Setup took more effort with only two of them compared to the larger team in Thailand, but Maya's recent experience allowed them to expedite the process. Anxiety fueled adrenaline for the work.

"Can you imagine if these variants match human cases?" she asked Jian as she shouldered a pack with blood-drawing equipment. "A final answer on the COVID origin, unbelievable."

Jian carried a load of tarps to cover the ground for urine and guano samples. "A Nobel prize for medicine—we'll be the youngest ever."

She caught his sly smile and figured he was joking. As they entered the cave system, sunset dimmed the light outside and bats stirred on the ceilings for their nighttime exit. One swooped close to Maya's ear and she ducked, grateful for the rabies vaccinations recommended for veterinarians.

After stringing nets across the openings, Jian removed the first captured bat from the mesh using leather gloves and stretched its wing. "This is *Rhinolophus*, nicknamed horseshoe by the shape of the leafy structure on its nose, which helps in echolocation."

"Laos found viruses similar to SARS-CoV-2 in these bats," Maya said.

"In the 2003 SARS outbreak, human viral genomes were closer to those in this species than any others."

She completed a blood draw. "Are they in the wet markets?"

He shrugged. "It depends. Horseshoe bats don't have as much flesh as flying foxes, but some people use them for oil in medicinal treatments of baldness, paralysis, or mental illness."

Maya finished the throat and rectal swabs. "In Thailand we painted the toenails purple so we didn't bleed one twice."

He placed the bat gently on the ground and waited for it to fly away. "I'd rather not do anything to reveal we were here."

. . .

As some bats returned through other cave openings to rest after feeding, Jian's mobile rang with an alarm and he checked his notes. "I set this for eleven—five hours nonstop collecting specimens from forty-six bats. That is enough for one night."

Stepping outside for a damp breath of fresh air away from the acrid guano, Maya took off her protective mask and wiped her face. She'd always been proud of needing only limited sleep but bending over bats depleted her energy. Perhaps she wasn't fully recovered from long COVID.

Jian joined her for drinks from plastic water bottles. "Let's gather up the ground cloths with the guano and urine. Then we'll come back for our equipment and other specimens."

At the parking area with the first load, Maya noticed another vehicle, an older black sedan. Her public health brain had been pleased by the color of Jian's car because red ones stood out against the environment, reducing collisions with other vehicles. But now she wished it wasn't so visible.

She hesitated, a few hundred feet from the two vehicles. "Would it be safer to go back to the cave until this other one leaves?"

"Probably just a spelunker." Jian's fearful expression belied his reassuring words. He opened his trunk and they deposited their supplies.

As they turned back toward the cave opening, a masked man in nondescript green pants and shirt came out of the forest. His Chinese words were delivered to them with an authoritative heft. Jian pulled out a badge and the man studied it carefully before turning to Maya. When she couldn't understand him, Jian jumped in with a long explanation, then told her to hand over her passport and visa.

After the mystery man barked another order, he turned for his vehicle and sat in the front seat, pulling out his mobile. "What does he want?" Maya whispered.

"I'm not sure. At first, I stuck to the holiday story but that didn't explain our tarps, so I said I was on official research work for my agency."

"What about me?"

"As planned, you're my American sister visiting for the Dragon Boat Festival."

Anxiety triggered throat constrictions, and she swigged from her water bottle. "What authority does he have to order us around?"

Jian grabbed her arm and pivoted her further behind the car. For the first time, he came at her with a stern voice like the man detaining them. "Shut up. We heard what happens in your country with George Floyd. It's worse here."

Her panic disorder reared up like a dragon breaking out from her body. She wanted to scream. Years of treatment and therapy seemed to swoop out of her mind into the air with the few bat stragglers, leaving her bereft of coping mechanisms. Her eyes darted between the calm, cool forest and the tranquil blue of the nearby creek but she couldn't get far, not in a foreign country. Impossible thoughts of escape provided no real solace.

She hadn't spotted a weapon, so perhaps Jian could back out. She glanced down the road, then at their car. Jian jumped in with an angry whisper. "We will not try to drive away. Do you think my car can outrun his? Besides, he wrote down my license number."

When the man returned, he directed them to the back seat of his vehicle. On the short ride, Maya's legs shook harder when he bypassed their hotel and stopped in front of a rundown multistory building. From his trunk, he donned protective gear similar to their own—a white protective covering, booties, bonnet, and face shield. He guided them into a creaky elevator, the bump at each floor ratcheting up Maya's pulse. Outside adjoining rooms on the fifth floor, Jian peppered him with a burst of questions in Chinese.

"Don't worry, I'm right next door," he comforted before Maya was left alone in a room with peeling paint, a single metal bed, and a window too high above the street to escape from. She tried the door handle—locked in, no key. In the bathroom, there was no toilet seat, just a hole in the floor like her parents described for the pit toilets in Beijing airport on their adoption trip. The shower stall dripped a slow stream of rust-colored water.

She dropped to the bed, thin mattress barely protecting her body from the springs. No sound from televisions or cell phone chatter pierced the walls but a repetitious cough began on one side and a more prolonged one crept in from under the door. The rasping coughs continued, punctuated by horns honking outside.

A frightening realization filtered into her brain like the fog from last night's boat tour. She understood the man's full PPE—this was a COVID hotel. Although alone in the room, she pulled her mask from her pocket and slipped it back on. As she reclined with the single pillow protecting her back from the metal headboard, she knew she couldn't be comfortable wearing a mask for long with her rapid breaths from panic.

In the clammy heat, she discarded her coverall, then tugged at the thin coverlet for comfort, like a baby fondling its blankie. No suitcase, no daypack, no toothbrush. Nothing to do except lose her mind.

FORTY-NINE

Guilin, People's Republic of China—Monday, June 14, 2021

As dawn broke, Maya's stomach grumbled. Unused to a day with nothing to do, she paced and flinched with every cough filtering in from other rooms. After several hours, the door was unlocked by a stout masked woman carrying a tray with bowls of soup and white rice, no utensils.

"Nǐ hǎo," Maya said, grateful to see someone bearing sustenance. But she received no answer to her simple greeting of hello. A few Mandarin phrases from culture camp and high school beckoned, as if behind a fuzzy-paned window. She tried again. "Xièxiè." The woman didn't respond to her expression of thanks, either.

On the boat tour when Maya couldn't recognize a single word, Jian had mentioned the local dialect was influenced by Cantonese. The woman turned to leave and Maya's "Thank you so much for the food" still resulted in no response. Either the woman didn't learn English in school or she pretended not to understand.

Maya used her fingers for the rice and drank the soup straight from the bowl. Thirsty from the strong spices, she cranked her head under a faucet. In modern Chinese hotels, bottled water or hot water thermoses were available for a safe drinking supply. If COVID patients were forcibly quarantined here, why didn't they provide better sanitation to avoid a gastrointestinal outbreak on top of coronavirus?

Regulating the shower temperature was challenging, but in the claustrophobic room with no air conditioning and a window that only opened six inches, the cooler water was welcome. She brushed her teeth with her finger, then picked up her clothes. Guano smell still clung to everything, especially her protective gown and booties piled on the floor. To counteract the odor and room heat, she rinsed her underwear and tee-shirt under the sink before putting them back on wet.

For a while she half-crouched with her nose in the window's bottom open crack. Fresh, throat-soothing moisture from the Li river seeped in, unlike the industrial pollution or dust she remembered from her childhood trip to Beijing and Xian.

She knocked on the wall adjoining Jian's room and he knocked back, but she didn't know Morse code. She shouted his name out the window and someone in another room yelled in Chinese—she didn't try again.

An eternity later when the sun sank behind the buildings across the street, the door was unlocked and opened.

Weak from heat and stale air, hoping for more food, Maya wracked her brain for more Mandarin greetings. Maybe the woman would take pity and respond to a request for a toothbrush and tea.

A man in full PPE, more imperious than the one who found them, stepped in and gestured her over to Jian's room. Their captor's face was carved into canyons by wrinkles but his short hair was jet black, matching his harsh eyes above the surgical mask.

Jian's hunched body and red eyes conveyed fear and a lack of sleep. Maya joined him sitting on the edge of the bed.

Their minder spoke English. "Your travel should not have been approved without quarantine. A supervisor in Shenzhen reviewed your itinerary and alerted authorities in the cities along your planned route. Then we spotted your vehicle in an area not used by tourists."

"We loved the Reed Flute Cave and my brother wanted to show me another part of it." Maya lungs filled with a prayer that their holiday family reunion story still held.

The man's tone turned brutal. "We know you are unrelated and not on a vacation. So you can drop the mask, Dr. Maguire."

Did he mean for real or metaphorically? She raised her hand to her face, then stopped. Catching COVID again or getting arrested— either way she was fucked.

"The director of the Centers for Disease Control and Prevention denies your employment," the man continued, "and disavows your work here. We don't believe him. We think your government used our scientist Mu Jian with the intent to embarrass the People's Republic of China."

She leaned back against the wall, sick to her stomach. Overzealous work in the previous three years had generated reprimands only from her immediate supervisor. If she ever came to the attention of the CDC director, she'd hoped it would be for achievement, not a major blunder. Switching to the truth, an abridged version, might set her free. "I haven't been a CDC employee since last fall. I'm sorry, this trip was my idea, to get back in the game and contribute scientific understanding."

"A clever cover story but unlikely. You would not spend this much in personal funds if unemployed. You worked with Dr. Chakrii in Thailand, and we are looking at his funding sources."

That would eventually lead them to the foundation but she wouldn't bring it up. Clearly Jian hadn't named them yet, and she couldn't see how it would help their situation.

"We also talked to your university and the river agency, Mu Jian. They confirmed your work with other species, but bat collection is not a regular duty. They authorized only holiday time, not cave sampling. Your family members know nothing about a newly discovered American sister."

Jian started to stand up and respond in Chinese, but the man shoved him back down. Switching to English, Jian said, "This was spur-of-the-moment to make a big discovery for a promotion. It was an unapproved trip; one I deeply regret."

The man turned back to Maya. "You have been to China on two previous occasions. You lived in a Tongling orphanage after your February 14, 1993 birth, until your adoption that summer. You visited China and that orphanage again in 2005."

Jian was visibly shocked by the man's statement. Maya regretted hiding her adoption status, although it wouldn't have made a difference to their current predicament.

She wasn't sure how to get them released. "As you said, sir, I've always been curious about my home country, especially after my return as a child." Through her mask, she smiled and gushed with enthusiasm. "That trip with my adoptive parents was spectacular. The Great Wall, Terracotta soldiers, the Oriental Pearl Tower in Shanghai. You have such amazing landmarks."

Their captor's scarred hands relaxed and he shuffled his feet. Could he be convinced that the scientific sleuthing was something informal on the side of a homecoming trip?

"I couldn't wait to be in China again to create new memories. Mu Jian and I found each other through academic circles, and I proposed a holiday with cave exploration. It wasn't his fault—I talked him into it."

Their interrogator placed a call on his mobile, then turned for Jian's door. Maya burst into strategic tears. "What will happen next? I'm still weak from long COVID. You can't leave me here to catch it again. Why can't we stay in our hotel until this is straightened out?"

With his eyes lowered like a subordinate canine, Jian held her hand and questioned the man in Chinese. Their captor's staccato response didn't sound like good news.

"They have my car but he suspects we have collaborators. So nothing's changed and we have to remain here."

The man grabbed Maya by her upper arm and forced her back to her room. The electricity shut down again overnight. She was unable to sleep or distract herself, hunger gnawing from the single small midday meal.

During long hours with invisible neighbors hacking their lungs out, hope flashed on and off like fireflies. Her immunity from previous infection and vaccination would hold. But other Americans had suffered horrific lengthy sentences for mistakes or trumped-up charges. The PRC would realize she didn't come from wealth, so her parents might not go bankrupt in paying a bribe. But the State Department might have to trade her for a Chinese spy.

She thrashed in the bed, trying to drive away uncontrolled panic. Even without closing her eyes, the ghosts of her grandmother, tiny embryo, and Manolo floated in from every corner and vied for center stage, mocking her reckless decisions.

. . .

Guilin, People's Republic of China—Tuesday, June 15, 2021

The interrogator from yesterday directed a stumbling Maya to Jian's room again. Then the woman who delivered yesterday's food, still silent and with eyes to her feet, dropped their suitcases on the grimy tile floor before she spun on her heels and left, no food offered.

After a phone call, the man put his mobile in his pocket. His wrinkled forehead and drawn-together eyebrows transmitted his displeasure. "We have received payment of your fine, Dr. Maguire, and your government is sending someone from the embassy. Mu Jian, you are to proceed directly back to Anhui Province where you will undergo appropriate disciplinary retraining. We confiscated everything from your vehicle and teams have checked the cave for your illegal samples."

Genuine tears of relief ran from Maya's eyes like rivulets in a rainstorm. Her overnight glimmers of hope were coming true. Perhaps Stefan arranged the money transfer and her parents weren't on the hook. However, an embarrassed CDC might never allow the resumption of her training.

They hadn't mentioned Stefan, his WHO employment, and the research foundation. Hopefully she'd be safely out of this COVID hothouse before they connected all the dots. Maybe they wouldn't locate all the cave rooms and samples—she was certain Jian was thinking the same.

The man allowed them the briefest of hugs. "I'm so sorry about all of this," she whispered. That was true, even though he and Stefan dragged her into it, not the other way around.

Just get out and get home. The chromatic urn with Manolo's and her baby's cremains would greet her from the bedroom bookshelf, a reminder that she'd made no plans for a celebration of life. Dr. Grinwold had dangled a state position. Would the offer hold after this level of screwup? And there was still the matter of learning to adapt to life in Santa Fe with all the phantoms and should-have-beens.

. . .

Hong Kong—Tuesday, June 15, 2021

The American embassy staff dropped her at the same hotel she'd stayed at with Stefan. When he didn't answer a call from the front desk, she left a voicemail. "Hey, asshole. I'm finally safe but feeling like roadkill. Meet me in the restaurant at eight PM and give me back my phone."

She needed to sort out her feelings about the trip and learn who paid her fine. Her mind filled with ways to torture Stefan for the disastrous SARS-nCoV-2 investigation he induced her to join. After that, it would be a long time until she'd listen to her physician colleague again—that eager beaver, double-dealer, conniver, and snake in the grass.

First, she placed a call to her parents using her credit card and the hotel phone. As she reassured them she was safe, they initially held back from criticism and only focused on the joy of her release. But before hanging up, her mom asked, "Have you given any thought to a memorial service? Manolo's dad texted about it."

"I've had a few other things on my mind. We'll talk more when I'm home." How could she put into words the haunting visions during her thirty-six hour imprisonment?

She wanted to check on Jian but didn't know how to do it. Stefan had served as their intermediary and Maya didn't have Jian's number or email address. Her poor planning bit her in the butt again. He was still in China, and the phrase 'disciplinary retraining' was ominous. Hopefully when she had dinner with Stefan, they could jointly try to reach him.

The final call before facing off with Stefan was to Mark Zielinski. He was the only person she knew who was wealthy and connected enough to quickly transfer money for the fine, $10,000 according to embassy staff. But he didn't fess up.

"Maya, I'm at my Phoenix office this week if you have time to stop by after seeing your family."

"I'm at a loss for what to do. After recovery at your ranch, I thought the best option was to leap into work with someone I knew well like Stefan. But that was a huge lapse of judgment."

"I've always admired your work. Even if China was a bust, your help with the Thailand study may pay off."

She ran her fingers through her hair, what little there was left of it after the Thailand trim. What would Mark think of the new Maya when they saw each other? "You're right. Science doesn't advance through a single big discovery. It's the small incremental steps, performed multiple times for verification."

His deep voice rumbled with a chuckle. "I'll take your word for it. In the legal line of work, insight is pretty valuable. Ever hear of Seneca?"

"Some kind of Greek or Roman poet?"

"You're in the ballpark. Lucius Annaeus Seneca was a Roman philosopher. He had a lot of ideas that we can turn to today. Try this one on for size, and I hope to see you soon. 'Every new beginning comes from some other beginning's end.'"

FIFTY

Tongling, People's Republic of China—Tuesday, June 15, 2021

Seeing double after driving twelve hours nonstop from Guilin to Tongling, Jian embraced his grandparents and showered to eliminate the stench of bats and fear sweat.

On the edge of his ancient carved wooden bed, he thumbed WeChat on his mobile using an encrypted messaging service to connect with Stefan and avoid government surveillance.

[Jian] Stefan, is Maya in Hong Kong?

[Stefan] Right here, reaming me a new one.

[Jian] What are her plans?

[Stefan] Unsure, anywhere away from me.

[Jian] Hand her your mobile.

[Maya] Stefan shouldn't have talked us into this.

[Jian] I have 3 weeks indoctrination. You?

[Maya] Maybe more COVID work. One colleague found it in deer.

[Jian] Americans can no longer blame Chinese bats.

[Maya] Ha-ha. Too many infected animals, never get rid of it.

[Jian] Keep in touch, we're both Tongling natives. Surprised.

[Maya] Show me around there, someday?

[Jian] Yes, someday, "big sister."

[Maya] No siblings before, even a fake one.

[Jian] Me too. Take care.

In the musty bedroom, cooled only by river breezes spiraling in through the central courtyard, Jian turned off the phone. With any luck, his retraining and reassignment wouldn't restrict him from future wildlife work. And maybe he could locate a colleague to check the cave for any undetected samples.

He certainly didn't regret meeting Maya—they had so much in common. It might be possible at some point to collaborate again, making the world a healthier place for all species. But nature's balance was on a rapid road to chaos, with conundrums and excitement for both of them. Weirding microbes and weather would keep on weirding.

CODA

Coronavirus continues to spread through personal contact and the air, but at least there are no flying blood-seeking missiles for transmission. Mosquitoes are the most numerous disease vector and each year they invade new areas. As the climate warms with increased precipitation, breakbone fever from the dengue virus imperils more than half the planet.

[“Dengue: A Microbial Mystery” is available at https://books2read.com/dengue]

About the Author

MILLICENT EIDSON is the author of the alphabetical Maya Maguire microbial mysteries. The MayaVerse at https:// drmayamaguire.com/ includes references and links to prequel and side stories. Author awards include Best Play in *Synkroniciti* and Honorable Mention from the Arizona Mystery Writers.

Dr. Eidson's work as a public health veterinarian and epidemiologist began as an EIS Officer (like Maya Maguire) with the Centers for Disease Control and Prevention, and continued at the New Mexico and New York state health departments. She has authored over a hundred scientific papers, articles, and book chapters. Currently, she is a public health faculty member at the University at Albany and the University of Vermont, and teaches a UVM course on zoonoses and climate change in its Larner College of Medicine.

With formative years in the Southwest, Millie enjoys reconnecting with Arizona family, heritage trips to Norway, Ireland, and China, and wider travel worldwide. In retirement from full-time public health work, she has settled in Vermont with her husband Tom Henderson and daughter Lian Henderson, inspiration for Maya Maguire.

Other interests are photography (website and book cover photos are primarily the author's), painting, hiking, and bicycling along the beautiful Burlington, Vermont waterfront.

Social media links: www.linkedin.com/in/eidsonmillicent
Maya Maguire Media | Facebook
Millicent Eidson (@EidsonMillicent) / Twitter
Millie Eidson (@drmayamaguire) • Instagram photos and videos

Acknowledgments

COVID-19 has made epidemiology and public health more visible. However, animals and the environment are still under-recognized for their part in microbial life and disease transmission. Veterinarians play a key role in public health, agriculture, and environmental agencies, universities, and corporate and private practice. Our work is always in partnership with others having diverse backgrounds.

The MayaVerse would not be possible without my initial training in research design and statistics at Michigan State University and the University of Colorado. The recent 40th reunion of my Colorado State University veterinary class reminded me of the dedication forged during four years of challenging but supportive training.

Ultimately, the greatest inspiration for the MayaVerse comes from collaborative work at the Centers for Disease Control and Prevention and the New Mexico and New York state health departments. If these stories capture even a small part of their ceaseless devotion to excellence and duty, I'll be happy.

The MayaVerse benefits from my family team of Lian Henderson, inspiration for and feedback on the Maya Maguire character, and Tom Henderson, audio and visual media advisor for Maya Maguire Media.

"CORONA" has been critiqued in its entirety by Vermont author Liz Teuber. Writing groups providing feedback to individual chapters include The Burlington Writers Workshop (https://burlingtonwritersworkshop.com/), which I proudly serve as its Secretary. BWW reviews were contributed through its Fiction Novel workshop (Dick Matheson and Mike Magluilo, co-hosts) and its Romance workshop. The Green Mountain Writers Group led by

Stephen Kastner has been a key sounding board from the beginning (https://greenmountainwriters.com/). Finally, the MayaVerse has benefited from two Sisters in Crime (https://www.sistersincrime.org/) critique groups. Others providing key COVID information include Anya Wylder.

Additional organizations contributing education and support are the Sisters in Crime local chapters: Grand Canyon Writers (https://grandcanyonwriters.com/) and the Tucson Old Pueblo Chapter (https://www.tucsonsistersincrime.org/). I can't imagine being a successful publisher without membership in the Alliance of Independent Authors (https://www.allianceindependentauthors.org/).

My continued growth is fostered by academic affiliations as a language and creative writing student at Champlain College, emeritus epidemiology professor at the University at Albany, and instructor for a zoonoses class at the University of Vermont.

Provision of information by agency employees or workshop participants does not imply endorsement by those individuals or groups.

Scientific nomenclature, including when to italicize organism names, can be confusing. For more information, see:
https://wwwnc.cdc.gov/eid/page/scientific-nomenclature.

COVID is a huge topic and hundreds of nonfiction resources were consulted. A curated list for general education is provided at https://drmayamaguire.com/corona.

"Corona" *Discussion Questions*

Book groups interested in discussions with the author should email <u>drmayamaguire@gmail.com</u>.

"CORONA" crosses genres, with multiple themes in the framework of a zoonotic disease. The following questions may help in thinking about and discussing the novel.

1. The genre elements include mystery, women's fiction, and romantic suspense. How do each of these elements contribute to the overall arc and your enjoyment of the story?

2. The main character is a young Chinese American woman adopted as an infant by an Irish-heritage family living in the Southwest. What elements of the character's background enrich the story?

3. What are some biological, regional, cultural, and religious influences on our perceptions of 'the other'?

4. How does the 'me too' theme impact the story? How do you define sexual harassment? What do you think of the decisions the characters take in response to it?

5. Geographic locations are intended as characters in themselves. How do geography and history influence the story?

6. Maya's perceptions are enlarged by her work in other countries. In what ways do you think exposure to other cultures and ways of life impact us?

7. What do you think of Maya's challenges and choices for handling personal grief?

8. What are the roadblocks to achieving a work-life balance based on gender and economic status?

9. This story begins in late 2019 when the pandemic starts in China,

and extends to summer 2021 when some functions of daily life begin the transition back to pre-COVID days. Although the story is fiction, what elements of the story resonate with your own experience of the pandemic?

10. How should public health policy balance the needs of society versus those of individuals, especially in the face of different perspectives?

11. Zoonotic diseases are those in common between humans and non-human animals. How are transmission, investigation, prevention, and control more complex for zoonotic diseases than those infecting only humans?

12. What is the role of climate change in the story and for zoonotic diseases?

13. How can someone with a veterinary medical degree contribute to disease investigations?

14. For authenticity, writers often rely on personal experience, while protecting the privacy of those sharing life events with the author. Writers also use research and close consultation with others to create characters, plot events, and settings not their own. As a reader, do you have a preferred balance of work informed by an author's imagination, research, and representation of their background?